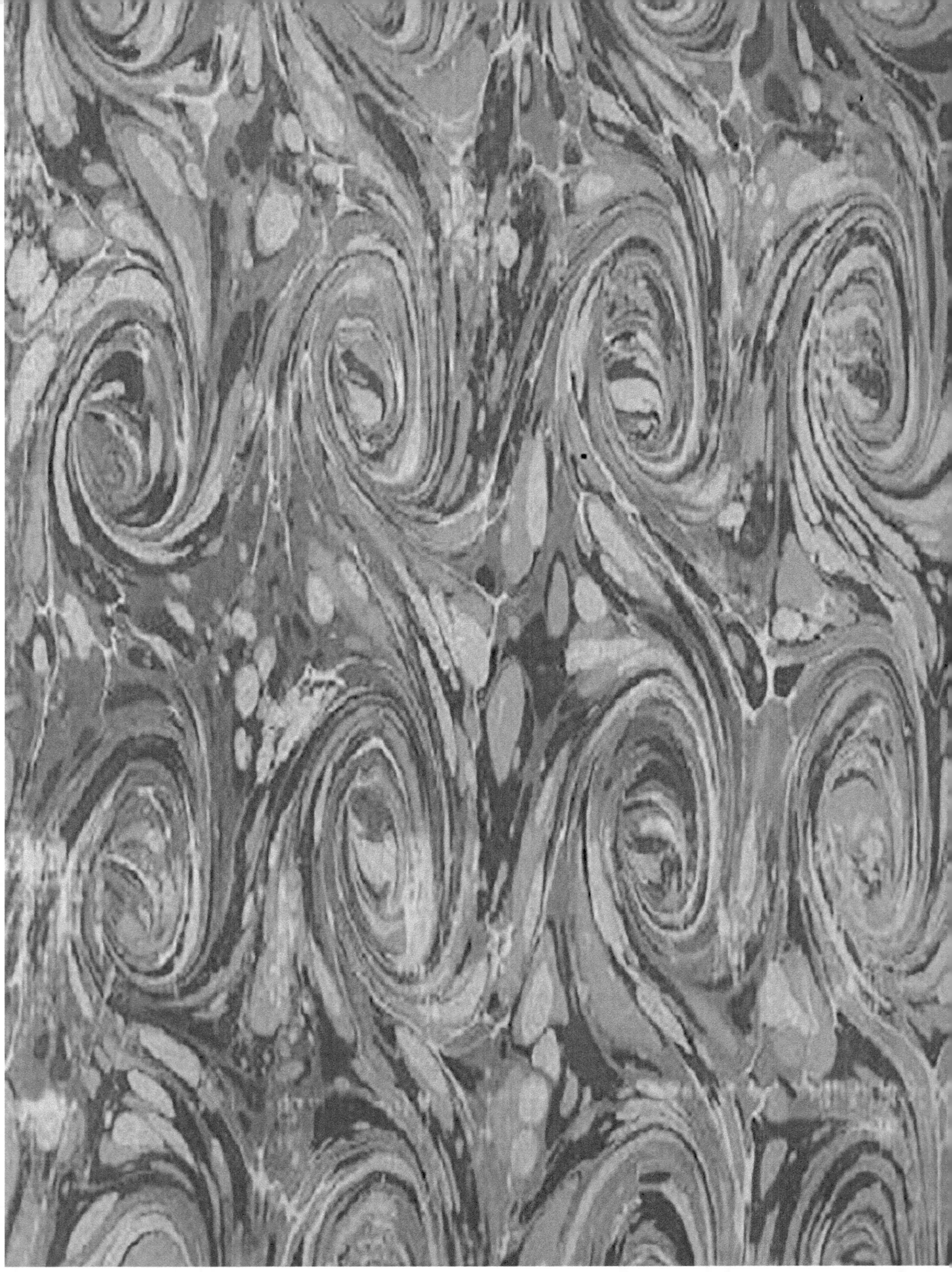

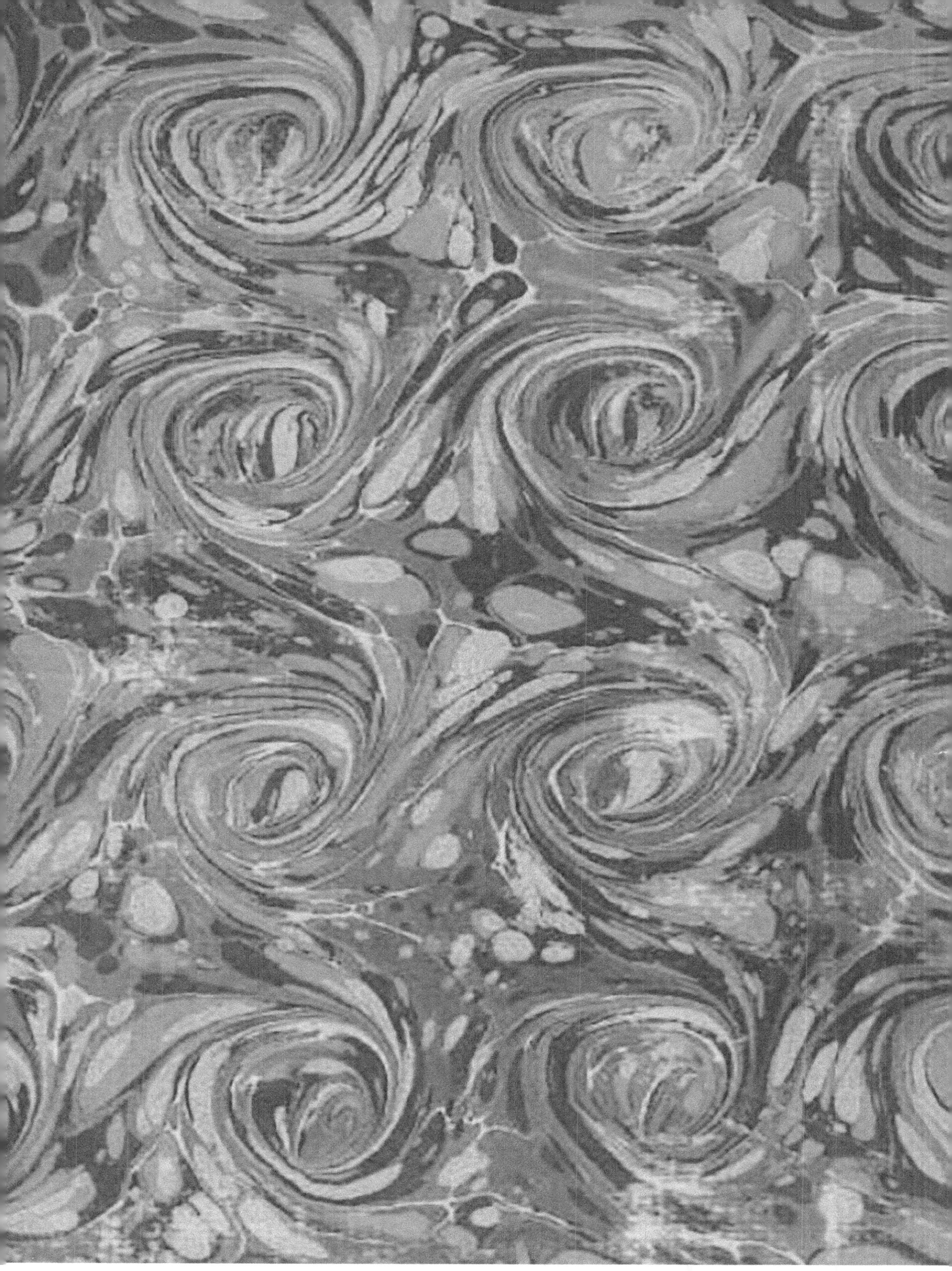

An Officer of the Crown

Printed in the United States in 2015

Perrioe Publishing

ISBN: 978-0-9969980-0-0

E-book version ISBN 978-0-9969980-1-7

Fonts used: Century for modern American and Covington for British English, Wingdings, Vijaya, Vinner Hand ITC and MV Boli.

An Officer of the Crown

The Middlecombe Expedition to the Aral Sea in Turcomania and the Khanates of Independent Tartary, 1837-1838

========

Volume I

========

Reminiscences of an English Ensign's Journey to the East in 1836

Illustrated

Being a complete narrative of its inception, formation, travels, discoveries and adventures by
D. A. Driscol, Ensign
Bombay Artillery

Wayne S Rutledge

Editor's Preface

It is common with this genre of book for the editor to explain how the work came into being. That being the custom, I shall follow it. On September 9, 1999, I had the good fortune to marry Anne O'Driscoll. She and I had met on the first day of orientation for new teachers at a college we both would be teaching at in Dubai. From her I inherited a rich and varied number of European relatives and one in particular is germane to this story. For without her, the full story of the Middlecombe Expedition would not have come into the light and would have remained lost amongst a few footnotes in obscure 19th century history tomes and the archives of the East India Company. The expedition was forgotten under the glare of the Siege of Herat and the even greater flare up of the First Anglo–Afghan War, all of which led to the beginning of the Great Game, the political, economic and military conflict between Russia and Britain over the control of Central Asia and the passes that lead to India. The expedition came into the light in the following serendipitous manner. It began with my not knowing the definition for an obscure word, which I came across in my work to develop a computer game concept, based on the 19th century Northwest frontier of India. The word was 'mumpsimus'. I mentioned it to my English wife in passing before undertaking to look it up on the ubiquitous internet but I was astounded when she was able to provide the definition without reference to the internet or a book. For an English teacher to know an obscure word is not in any way extraordinary but the nature of the word itself and why she knew it made me curious.

That it meant, 'an unreasonable or stubborn man who wouldn't change his ways', prompted a query from me as to how she knew its meaning. Her reply would open up a new world for me and bring to light a mislaid man of the Victorian era.

My wife had an Aunt who held a large amount of materials from one of her ancestors who had been an officer and explorer, and who my wife believed was her great, great, great grandfather. It was in this ancestor's journals that she had read the word as a child. The Aunt in question was an extraordinary Irish woman in her 100's, Katherine Mae O'Driscoll, who had had the foresight to keep almost everything her mother had given her in the 1930's.

[Editor's note: see Appendix I-I: Genealogy of the Driscol siblings and the link between David Driscol and Anne O'Driscoll]

In 2008, we traveled to Ireland expressly to meet Katherine. We took the train from Dublin to County Cork, the heartland of the O'Driscoll's. There I met the grand old lady and was presented with tea, excellent scones and two cardboard boxes full of books, stained and yellowing papers, tin boxes that rattled mysteriously and a few photographs, maps, drawings, packets of letters, and old magazines turning to dust. In it were the varied notebooks, dairies, secret books and journals of a man whom I was to become intimately involved with, David Alexander Driscol. On top of it all was a letter to Katherine from her mother noting how she had come into possession of two, strong, well-made, iron-clamped boxes, lined with tin and sealed with lead and wax. At some point, the Victorian boxes had disappeared to be replaced by the more pedestrian cardboard. The dear Aunt also presented me with shoes boxes which held letters written by Driscol to his mother and other siblings, plus a few they had written to him — in all, a historical researchers' treasure trove.

In the first book I picked up I found the name 'David Alexander Driscol' written in a surprisingly sloppy hand for a Victorian writer. Inside the cover he had noted the date the notebook had been started and stated his location and title at that time while he also annotated which notebook it followed. Then, in a different ink and obviously at a later date, he had noted which volume would follow this one. His name was not as I had expected; it being 'Driscol' instead of O'Driscoll. My first question, obviously, was: if the family name was O'Driscoll, why was his Driscol? But Katherine, having returned to the room with the tea, was not able to answer. This would be the first of many mysteries I would discover about Mr Driscol.

Katherine was very adamant that I take his materials. I agreed and, having promised to take these rare gifts in care and produce a book from them, this following manuscript is the result. It is a great sadness that Katherine passed in 2013 at the grand age of 106 and never saw the final draft of her ancestor's work.

The work was delayed by many circumstances but the most daunting obstacles were Driscol's outrageously bad handwriting, his habit of writing his entries in whatever foreign language he was learning at the time and his use of codes and icons which are still unknown to me at present. He also knew and used Taylor's shorthand which he modified to his own use, learning to mix it with Persian and later Arabic words and script. There are over one hundred and twelve books and manuscripts from those cardboard boxes, and these following four volumes use parts of seven of them plus several other books, papers, letters and newspaper clippings that will be described later.

These papers consists of his private journal for this period where he kept track of his expenses, made observations about the world, the women he met and his own failings plus anything which interested him. He also had a task book which he used to record his daily duties. Finally, there were the two books in which the actions, discoveries and findings of the expedition were recorded. These journals begin in English, slowly change to Persian then become dominated by Persian halfway through. The first book has certain parts written in Arabic, Greek, Latin, Danish or French, or even in code. These linguistic challenges were overcome with some difficulty and much outside assistance, and all Driscol's writings, combined from his various books, you find here.

At some point, a hand different from Driscol's edited the journals that I have so far read. They inked out a number of items, mainly dealing with women, politics and the anthropological discoveries that Driscol made in Asia. In some places they made necessary emendations. In a few key places, pages were cut away. Who this person was is not known to me but I do have suspects. When they remove or add something, I will note this by using the term 'Unknown editor'. Additionally, some of the journals suffered gravely from the attention of termites and other insects; heat, moisture and physical damage from Driscol's time; and later generations of children with crayons. Where the journals are unreadable or missing, I will use the symbol {...} to show a break caused by physical loss.

One of my intentions is to avoid something I have observed and disliked from others who publish materials from diaries and journals of past protagonists. In their initial words, they give out the substance and conclusion of the story before it is told. I do not intend to do so. To find out about the birth and fate of the expedition, the reader must read these volumes.

Those who wish to read the book without knowing too much about how it ends should read the preface and heed the headline 'Spoiler alert,' then skip over the sections recommended. Driscol's efforts to write a book have come down to me as 103 pages of a rough outline with only a few areas written out in detail but neither the printers nor the public ever saw the document. You may wish to skip ahead to page 1. Alternatively, if you don't like surprises, you can read the preface, both his and mine, which gives some hints as to what occurred but not in any detail.

Acknowledgments

My greatest help came from three of my former students and friends from Iran and Syria, one of whom has asked that I not mention his full name. Bowing to his wishes, I'll use only his internet user name. Imran, only your ability to read Driscol's initially bad Persian allowed this book to be written. Many thanks. A special acknowledgment to my other student Saman Einabadi whose knowledge of nineteenth century Farsi was unsurpassed, whose wisdom was most helpful, and without whose assistance the Persian parts of this series could not have been written.

Mary Alia Haddad, another former student who helped immeasurably with Arabic translations especially with Driscol's occasionally cryptic comments written in bad Arabic my fullest appreciation is given. Special thanks also to Dr. Jihad Al-Ghamdi who helped me understand Shi'ite and Sunni myths, Hadith and the way the Qu'ran was viewed by the faithful in the 19th century. I would also like to thank Stephen Bull, the Curator of Military History and Archaeology for Lancashire County, United Kingdom, who answered many questions of historic importance and was knowledgeable in the specific details of the 19th century.

Also, many thanks for technical assistance from Dr. Pamela Yei Sung and Jamie Reynolds, experts in palimpsest multispectral imaging from the Rochester Institute of Technology, by whose efforts the faded words of Driscol were brought to the light of day.

My endless gratitude to the much-beleaguered librarians at the India Office Records, who tirelessly answered long lists of emailed questions, and especially Sally Turtle, who was kind enough to guide me thorough the nightmare that is their records.

Thanks to my many editors; my wife Anne, who helped in editing this work, a published author Edward Joesting, who added many good suggestions with this unique editorial style (emails starting with "what does this crap mean" where frequent and always useful). Zoe Atlas who showed me that someone very much from the 21st century might be interested in the 19th. Special thanks to Clayton Koskey, freelance editor, an aspiring fiction writer and graduate of Southern Oregon University's Creative Writing Program who made sense of the nonsense, asked all the right questions, and provided the editing knowledge and ability to take a collection of words and shape it into a coherent narrative. Two editors David Nolte and Greg Hines passed away while editing this volume and they are remembered for their efforts.

A special acknowledgment is given to Emmy, my grumpy Arab cat who did her best to delay the writing of this book by swatting at my left hand whenever it reached for the 'a' key. She seemed to believe its movement was an attempt to annoy her august presence and our contest has left my left hand singularly scared.

Proem

This book covers the inception, development and notable occurrences of the Middlecombe Expedition, with particular interest in the men who aided (or hindered) its planning and formation, and inaugurated its objectives and accomplishments. A full discussion of its discoveries and the aftermath of its actions will be covered in a future volume V. In addition, I will cover the impact of the expedition on its members.

I was not the first member of the Driscol extended family to attempt to publish David Alexander Driscol's works, there had been two previous attempts.

The first was by Sedgwick, the grandson of one of Driscol's brothers and whose work was left to me. From his notes, it seems he had decided to learn both Arabic and Persian to allow himself to translate the material with greater ease. His work was disrupted by the outbreak of the Great War, however, and he was soon in service with the cavalry. He was later transferred to the Royal Flying Corps as an artillery observer and, in April 1917, he was killed in the line of duty when Richthofen's Flying Circus shot down his Be-2c.

The next attempt was by Father Thomas Brennan RN, Driscol's great nephew, who began his researches just before the outbreak of World War II. Unfortunately, he took some of the material with him to war and it was lost. We however must grant him kudos for finding and securing letters that Driscol wrote to his mother, friends and other relatives. He also found a number of official reports taken from the archives of the East Indian Company. He also sketched out a rough time line of Driscol's life. On 29 June 1944, he was aboard the S/S Nellore on her way to Sydney, Australia when she was attacked by the Japanese submarine I-8. She was torpedoed and then shelled until she sank and some 100 people aboard were killed, including the good Father. With him went a number of Driscol's materials to the bottom of the Indian sea. Our Driscol had entered India some one hundred and eight years earlier before his ancestor left the port on its ill-fated journey

The book you are about to read was assembled from many sources. The majority of the information comes from Driscol's unpublished journals that came to me in the way described in the preface. I have followed the general outline of the book that Driscol had laid out but never had published. Some materials came from other books, from letters preserved by various personages, and parts of the story were later published in magazines like Blackwood's and Country Life, and in letters to the Times as rebuttals to articles on other issues dealing with Persian and Central Asian natural science and politics.

I also have excerpts from the expedition report that Driscol and the Secretary of the Expedition dutifully wrote. Two copies of the report were made; one was sent to the headquarters of Honorable East India Company (HEICS) and another to the President of the Geographical Society of London (GSL). One copy of the report seemed to have found its way to Russia soon after sent to London. The copy to George Greenough of the GSL was lost when that organization moved from its location in Whitehall Place to new quarters on Savile Row. The copy to the HEICS is alleged to have been lost at sea but perhaps, like Burton's Zanzibar manuscript, it too will show up at some unexpected time. Despite an extensive search by earlier researchers and myself, no sign of this report was ever found in the archives of that company.

There are also the letters and pamphlets on the expedition and personalities involved created by Alan Horne, Gregory Hynes, Dafydd von Nolta and Eduard Vickery, whose valuable comments shine a light on a number of issues that were left out or shrouded in mystery by Driscol.

I have mentioned his 112 journals, but not the 9 Qu'rans, one was untouched and different from the rest and the other eight much worn and every inch of them covered by the infinitesimal writing. He had written in them in Persian, Arabic, Latin, Danish, Greek and English written in the Persian or Arabic script.

In the Qu'rans, Driscol kept his observations. At that time, foreigners were not trusted in Central Asia and Russian spies had made the normally suspicious Central Asians even more paranoid. Obviously, carrying a journal and writing in English would have been dangerous so he used the Qu'rans to hide his writings. Some of my modern Muslim translators were offended by Driscol's writing in a Holy Qu'ran, which is considered a sin to do so now days but not so much so at that time. Furthermore, he wrote what he observed, not in Persian – which would also be suspicious and readable, but in Arabic and often used the script to disguise the use of Latin, Greek, French, English and occasionally Danish. This would have prevented a Central Asian or even a Russian spy from reading it but it also makes translating it troublesome.

Generally, 1 out of 5 words cannot be read while others are completely clear. I apologize in advance if I have used any Americanism or words that were not in common use in Driscol's time, being American and not an expert on the language used during that time. I hope well-educated readers will not hold these faults against me, as I must at times glean from the context at what Driscol might have meant.

I have placed into the volumes his journey out to India for it is interesting and gives much of the 'back story', to the expedition. A purely scientific rendition of the expedition would make dull reading.

I have followed a method I believe will make it easier for the reader to understand what Driscol wrote. I have inserted superscripts linked to each chapter and consolidated them as endnotes at the end of each volume. I hope that this will be less distracting than the footnotes that Driscol originally intended to use. Where I can, I explain an unusual word or description in a few words within { } and written in italics. I did this to reduce the number of endnotes. I recommend that readers take the time to read the endnotes as they greatly enhance the understanding of what was occurring in the greater world around

Driscol. Where ( ) appear these are in the original and have replaced Driscol's occasional use of hyphens or dashes some of which I have retained.

Driscol also recorded in his journals conversations by noting the person speaking by using their initials placing a = then paraphrasing what was said; so one ended up with:

DD=You find those actions objectionable Sir. DP=I do, I do indeed. etc. I have reconstructed those into a more modern conversational style by using 'he said', 'I replied', and other conventions.

I do on occasion make editorial comments to clarify something I believe needs immediate explanation or to explain why I have redacted or abridged a section. I have done so to delete sections on matters that would be tedious to modern readers. Driscol could be quite detailed in his research. One of the items I have left out was twenty pages on the difference between British liquid measurements and the systems used in Central Asia. Where I have abridged, I will offer a summary and an explanation of why the abridgement has occurred. These will be noted in the manner below.

When I wish to interject a comment, I will do so using an Editor's note, as shown below:

[Editor's note: Brilliant comment on x, y, and z]

In reading material from nearly two hundred years ago some of the references, names and associations are now lost to us. At a few points in his journal, Driscol will note a person, place, or occurrence but never mention the who, what, why, how and where behind the comment. I will note these and in most cases offer an opinion on what he might have meant. When he uses Greek, Latin, French and other European and oriental languages, I will not present it as written, but in Roman script followed by a translation. Where large blocks of non-English text are used, the original text will be curtailed and the translation provided. Common phrases in French will not be translated. Names for cities and places will use the spelling that was used at that time, with the current name in parenthesis if the identification might be unclear. For some cities, I will continue to use the original spelling, such as Bombay instead of the modern Mumbai, Djedda instead of Jeddah.

Enjoy.

Dedication

To the many, people who made my journey into the life and times of David Alexander Driscol possible and so interesting with special appreciation to my wife Anne, and her family who helped me find him.

David Alexander Driscol

As Driscol put few details about his life in the outline of his book, I have gone through his diaries and other writings and produced a short description of his life up to the time of going on the expedition. One critical part of his life is missing; his first six months in service of the King lost with the death of Father Brennan in WWII.

On September 20 1817, an Englishman was born in Eccles, Lancashire on the outskirts of Manchester to an Anglo-Irish father and Danish mother. He was quite an astounding arrival to this middle-aged couple. His mother would give him the cognomen of ' *Vidunder'* Danish for "miracle," for he was born when she was past the conventional age of carrying a child, being near 50 at the time. His Danish grandmother called him Lune for his green-blue eyes, which turned hazel as he aged, the name coming from the Chinese porcelain that had a pale, grayish-blue glaze applied to it and was one of the items traded by his mother's family. In his family, he would be referred to as Hans Lune, Hans being liked by his Danish relatives more than the given English name of David.

He was christened David, after his paternal uncle who had died during the Napoleonic Wars at the battle of Maida and his middle name, Alexander, was that of the great conqueror of the Persian Empire, which would prove to be a somewhat exalted prophecy in retrospect. David always favored his mother so we shall speak of her first. She was born Maren (Mary) Margaret Christensen on the 7th of November 1768 at the family home atop a shipping office in Vyborg, Denmark, the daughter of Frederick and Catharina Christensen, nee Rosenthal. David's maternal grandfather was a Danish merchant with contacts in Russia and Germany, as was his father before him. His grandmother is lesser known but according to family legend was descended from a Russian based Prussian mercantile family that had settled in Denmark during the early 18th century, perhaps during the time of Catherine the Great since it was a family conviction that Catharina had been named after her.

The family was a well-off middle-class family having extensive mercantile contacts in Russia and Germany and a carpentry business that was celebrated for having directed the building of Vyborg's many wooden structures and the rebuilding of its cathedral a number of times after a series of fires in mid-century. Their family was involved in some scandal in the early 18th century. It was rumored that the name Christensen hid a recent pagan past or that the Rosenthal name was from/descendant of a Jewish bloodline. Nonetheless, the family appears to have fallen on hard times or was looking to expand its reach and was on its way to Frederiksoerne, the Danish colony on the Nicobar Islands of the Indian Ocean, when the Christensen and Driscol family would encounter one another.

Driscol's father had a more colorful and less wealthy background. His name was Angus Brennan Driscol born on 23 November 1766 in Bantry, County Cork Ireland. To a Scots-Irish-Anglo family devoted to the sea and from which came a long line of seamen and masters for the Royal Navy. His family manned the Newfoundland and Greenlander whale fishery in times of peace and crewed Royal warships in times of conflict. His grandparents are only dimly remembered in the family history, having both died in their twenties one at sea in a war with the French and the other in childbirth. Angus Brennan had the fate of being the last born to John Driscol and his wife Eleanor Brennan, who unlike his paternal sea-faring family she had no 'salt water' in her veins and consequentially her son was chronically seasick. Having failed to establish himself as a man of the sea, he joined the 52nd Oxfordshire Light infantry Regiment at the age of 15 (known then as the 52nd (Oxfordshire) Regiment of Foot) where he was later shipped to India. This transfer involving 6 months at sea is remembered as a long bout of seasickness, a part of his life he called the 'dark passage'. He fought in India, the Peninsula campaign and finally at Waterloo. He would end his career as the 1st Battalion's Sergeant Major but spent most of his career as a Colour Sergeant in its first company. He was twice granted a battlefield commission the last time at the Battle of Waterloo, he later sold this ensignship and returned to the non-commissioned ranks before retiring with thirty-seven years of honorable service. He spent a number of years building up a thriving farm and industries in Swinton, he had moved here because of land won in a card game over the spoils garnered after the battle of Vitoria and in nearby Eccles he built a three-story house for his wife and family. By tradition the fireplace and lintels came from the Hoghton Tower; a derelict manor house from nearby Hoghton, Lancashire. The Driscol house is known today as the Old Institute House.

The World Driscol Lived In

In 1836, when Driscol jumped from his family into the role of a military officer, he did so at a time when England was at the head of the world. Having led all of Europe into the industrial revolution, she was the greatest manufacturing power of the time. He saw that revolution as a child growing up with the textile mills of Manchester that provided the world with clothing and covered the city in dense clouds of coal smoke. Steam and waterpower had been added to human and horsepower as aids to humankind's efforts, and this changed everything. He grew up in a world where the Protestant work ethic was a state of life. Education had come to the middle class and was making its way into the masses of working people where literacy was seen as a way to a better life.

Science had become fashionable and had produced practical results to make life longer and more pleasant. Farms could now produce cheaper food supplies. England was master of the world; her European competitors had fallen from the race. Commerce was alive and much of it was shipped around the world in British ships, protected by the unconquerable Royal Navy. France, still rising from the ashes of the Napoleonic wars, had lost much of its colonial empire but remained a power on land. The Germans and Italians remained fragmented, not even states yet. Spain was decadent, her empire melting away from her and, when Driscol was a teenager, had been striven by the first of the Carlist civil wars. The Dutch and Portuguese empires were old and not expanding. They would rest on their laurels until the 20th century when their empires dissolved. The Austrians and Russians would free the Balkans of Ottoman domination but the Hapsburg Empire was already beginning to show the signs of its future devolvement into Austro-Hungary and later dissolution. Russia, however, was on the move, having conquered the vast areas of Siberia and taken a part of the North American continent; she was now on the move in Central Asia, but she was shackled by an outdated social organization and a weak economy plus a mass of poorly educated people and grasping nobility.

The non-European powers, except the United States that had its eyes solely on its own manifest destiny, were of little account, behind in military technology, science, sanitation, organization and economically unable to face the British or weaker European states. The Ottomans moved from crisis to crisis, the Persians had no heart; the Moghul Empire had melted away due to a lack of interest. The Chinese, immense and arrogant, couldn't deal with the foreign powers they had encountered, instead of being the middle kingdom, they found themselves to be insignificant on the world stage. The many new states in the Americas had little power. The states of South America involved themselves in European style military and political squabbles and took out huge loans, they couldn't repay. The kingdoms of Africa had either dissolved or become implicit in the slave trade but at this time were protected by biology, for Africa was still the White man grave, except in the south where the Boer was pushing north against the Bantu tribes pushing south. Thus was the world. Johnson in his book 'The Birth of the Modern: World Society 1815-1830', stated it well, in the years 1815 to 1830 (*Johnson, P. (1992). The birth of the modern: World society 1815-1830. Harper, Perennial*),

'during which the matrix of the modern world was formed'

It was into this dynamically changing situation and an era that became known, as the Victorian age, that Driscol and his expedition would be a part.

The ritualistic British military had nearly one hundred thousand men divided into thirty-two active regiments made up of cavalry, infantry, artillery and guards plus a small corps of necessary engineers. More than half of this was overseas at any one time. The officers bought their commissions, advanced by purchasing the next rank and were mainly from the upper class with a few middle-classes thrown into the mix or more rarely risen from the ranks. The soldiers came from the lower classes and signed up for 21 years of duty.

Yet there was another army. This one had a quarter of a million men and nearly a hundred regiments of all arms, cavalry, infantry artillery and engineers or sappers. Here the officers could not buy a commission and most were middle-class and were advanced by seniority and occasionally on merit. This was the Indian Army, the private army of the Honorable East India Company, and used to protect and expand its investments in India.

The British system of money was quite unlike anything that exists today. In this book I have used the system the Empire had in place at the time of Driscol's travels and in a few specific places I've added equivalent values to United States dollars of 2015 value for comparative reasons.

The pound is shown with the symbol £ and is the main unit of British money its value at that time was supposed to equal to one pound of sterling silver or, more accurately, 240 silver pennies, giving its other name the pound sterling.

£1 consisted of 20 shillings that is shown as an s standing for the Latin Solidus the old term for a Roman coin, each shilling is made up of 12 pence shown as d standing for the Roman term denarius, thus a pound is made up of 240 pence.

Sums were written as £1 11s 6d would stand for one pound sterling eleven shillings and 6 pence.

Other coins were also in place, these were the crown; worth 5 shillings, the farthing; worth ¼ of a pence, the ½ sovereign which equaled 10 shillings and finally the Guinea which was valued at 21 shilling, or 1£ 1s.

Each country had their own currency and were often used in conjunction with one another making money changing a necessary occupation. At one point in his travels, Driscol was carrying gold and silver coins from 17 different nations.

A Marriage Made By A Quirk Of Fate

David Driscol's mother and father; Angus and Mary met by great happenstance in Africa. As an eighteen-year-old private soldier in a transport on his way to Madras, India he had the misfortune to be struck down by a virulent fever complicated by his seasickness – and so depleted was he that he was left to die in the care of the reverend of The Dutch Reformed Church in Cape Town. While he invalided here, the ship carrying the Christensen family had arrived from Denmark and decided that this was a place to stay instead of pushing on. The three-month voyage under sail from Denmark had tested the mettle of the Christensens, making their torturous way to India.

While recovering from his illness, Angus made the acquaintance of the Christensen family. Having been left to die, he had also been left with no money, orders or instructions on how to rejoin the Regiment. As family legend has it, he played a bit of 'hookem-snivey'[1], to remain at Cape Town until he had won permission to marry his Danish bride to whom he couldn't initially speak. Additionally his Church of England upbringing didn't appeal to this Danish Methodist family. Angus bowed to the pressure and became a Methodist, a faith that he didn't follow very religiously. With these obstacles overcome, they were married December 7, 1784, Angus being 18 and Mary 16. Angus knew he would need employment and had written to the authorities and in January of that year he found himself in Madras, India with his regiment which had stricken him from the lists as dead. Private soldiers with White wives were frowned upon in India at that time but Angus would win the day by the simple explanation given to him to use by his company commander when he faced the ire of the Battalion commander, a stickler for the rules. He told the story that at the time he married the Regiment had deemed him dead and had sent a sum of money to that effect to his relatives in Ireland. Being dead he had no reason to follow Regimental rules. Why the regiment hadn't communicated with Cape Town is unknown perhaps a bit of the earlier referred to 'hookem-snivey'. He was reprieved and shortly afterwards granted the position of orderly room clerk. Mary and he lived apart for nearly two years, with infrequent visits with her living with relatives in Tranquebar[2].

Angus and Mary would remain in India until 1798, during which time he was in constant campaigns with his wife accompanying the Regiment on many of their expeditions. Here she had been revered as a nurse, a teacher of English and methods of cooking to Indian wives and *bibis* (native concubines). In 1785, Angus volunteered to lead a party to storm the breech in the walls of Cannanore. They did so under the command of Sir Martin Hunter and he made the rank of Corporal due more to loss of men from sickness and battle than his own skills, or so he claimed.

The third Mysore war involved the couple in a series of notable battles at Seringapatam and Bangalore, and in 1792, Corporal Driscol was given the rank of Sergeant after being cited for bravery during the crossing of the Kaveri River.

He was part of the force that besieged Trincomalee and took Ceylon from the Dutch. In 1798 the Regiment returned to England. A second battalion was formed and Driscol was transferred to it against his will, although he seemed to have moved between the two battalions at times during the following years.

In 1803 the regiment was designated to become a light infantry regiment and spent months training to act in the manner of light infantry at Shorncliffe camp in England.

He was part of several forays against the Spanish and French at Quiberon Bay, Cadiz and Ferrol. He went in 1806-1807 to Sicily, with Mary unable to go, and later to Sweden where his knowledge of Danish, learned from his wife, was useful.

In 1808 his battalion landed in Portugal and later was forced to retreat to Corunna in Spain, defeated the French army pursuing it and left Spain to land again in Portugal, in this battle it gained more honor as a reliable and solid regiment. He was wounded but gained the rank of Colour Sergeant. At the battles of the Torres Vedras lines Angus was wounded yet again and in April 1811 worked for some time with Captain George Scovell who was Wellington's intelligence officer and who would break Napoleon's codes.

He later rejoined the regiment at the siege of Ciudad Rodrigo and again volunteered to join an assault force called a forelorn hope, a very dangerous assignment. He lead the attack and was the first man into the breech yet somehow survived the enemy fire and was promoted to Sergeant Major for his courageousness, which brought the attack to a success.

The French were in retreat from Spain when the 1/52nd caught up with them at the Battle of Vitoria. Angus looted a great deal of money from the baggage of the French. He continued to fight with the Battalion as it entered France. He earned an officer's commission, which he accepted but soon sold and reverted to his senior non-commissioned officers rank, finding the trappings and actions of an officer were certainly not his cup of tea, and he found it difficult to 'not blot his copy book'.

After the peace, the Regiment quartered in England and Mary obtained her first house but the regiment was soon called back. Napoleon's army at Waterloo was the reason for his departure from domestic bliss. During that long battle the Regiment formed squares and was under vicious French artillery fire when he was wounded yet again but he fought on. The battle ended successfully by the efforts of the regiment in no small part by Angus; keeping the unit orderly, his sergeants keen and his officers well prepared for their duties. Again, he obtained an officer's commission, accepted and sold it within a few days.

He and Mary then lived in-garrison in Paris until 1818, with Mary returning to England to give birth to David. The regiment returned to the Midlands. After completing a tour of duties in Dublin, Angus retired instead of taking his family to Newfoundland in 1823. He retired after nearly 37 years of service.

O'Driscoll Or Driscol?

One of the first questions that comes to my mind is why was the family name Driscol? Why not Driscoll or O'Driscoll? The name originated in County Cork and was derived from the Gaelic '*Eidirsceol*' meaning "intermediary." The first hint of why the name became Driscol from the commonly used O'Driscoll was due to the family splitting over the question of whether to follow the Catholic Stuart King or the Protestant sovereign.

In 1739 the family split into three, permanently, following the fortunes of three brothers. One migrated to the colony of Carolina in America and became a staunch member of the Church of England but retaining the surname O'Driscoll. A second brother stayed Catholic and remained in Cork while also retaining the ancestral name. The third brother moved to the Plantation of Ulster becoming a member of the Church of England and changing the name to Driscol (some sources show the name with two l's) and marrying into the Scots who came to colonized the area. Driscol's father's first name of 'Angus' showed that the Scots element had left its mark. The family would have 11 children with only one who would die in infancy, unusually auspicious for the time, while another, one of Driscol's older brothers, was disowned and removed from the family tree. His tale will be told later.

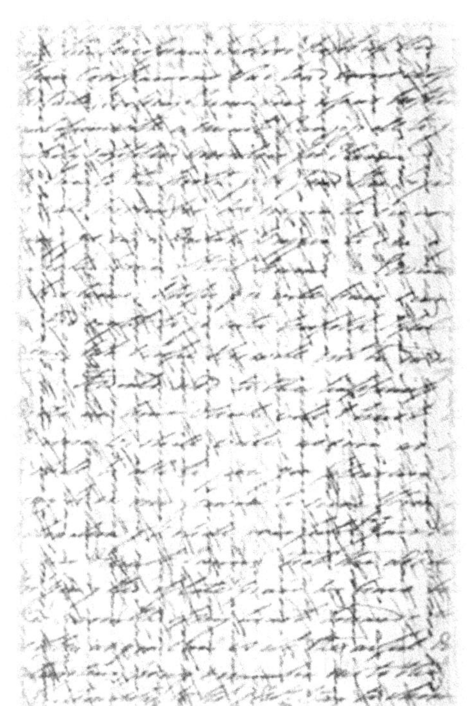

An example of Driscol's journal, page 49 from Volume I showing the quality of writing, the effect of bleed through by the ink on the other side of the page and general deterioration of the paper. Preface I-A

Additional examples of Driscol's writing are these pages from a letter he wrote and does not suffer from bleed through as the early journals did, and one can see a more graphic example of his handwriting. Preface I-B

فلا عبثًا وا لُنخلق لم يُخلقوا سُدىً ــ وإن لم تكن انعالهم بالسديدة

An example of Driscol's writing in Arabic script, which he used extensively in his journals. Preface I-C

Education

David received an excellent education. Being educated at home and later at the school run by his Irish twin brothers, older siblings Arron and Stephen, he received what at the time would have been a standard education. He learned to read Greek and Latin, English composition, French, Church of England dogma, somewhat adapted to Methodist beliefs, mathematics and history. He was not noted for his devotion to study but read voraciously everything he could find to include a reader's paradise that existed where he lived. He was make known to the Chetham's Library in Manchester by his brother Mark, where he found his Latin was of use, allowing him to read the catalog of books printed only in that dead language. His favorite books as a youth were Daniel Defoe's *Robinson Crusoe*, Antoine Galland's *One Thousand and One Nights* and Swift's *Gulliver Travels*. His preferred book of all was Caesar's *Commentaries* and he would always carry this with him if he could.

Driscol was a dabbler in natural philosophy and had an interest in the science of the day, and showed a partial interest in geology, archaeology and the practical sciences.

For years, he was a member of the Manchester Literary and Philosophical Society. From this and other associations, he received a strong background in the natural sciences. He met a number of luminaries of the time and was much pleased to have received a copy of *Confessions of an English Opium-Eater* from the author himself, Thomas De Quincey, who included the details of a murder that occurred near Driscol in 1827. He mentioned this in a short essay entitled 'On Murder Considered as One of the Fine Arts'. Driscol had a signed copy of this in his collection.

When he set out to join the 52nd Oxfordshire Light infantry in April 1836, he was a young man with a commendably conservative middle class view of the world but in a number of areas, he would be at odds with the Victorian age that he would soon find himself in.

His father and mother had disagreed over his future; his father had wanted him to become a naval officer for he had shown that useful ancestral Driscol trait, of not being disturbed by the sea and being immune to seasickness. However, his mother would not agree, nor does it appear that his father had any success in obtaining a position for him in either the Royal Navy or the maritime trade. He would obtain some sea experience during the summer of his 13th year by going to sea with a Danish relative. There he learned the Danish language, the basics of seamanship and saw how their business ran. He had sailed around the Baltic Sea and learned some of the Russian language.

He would always regret that his mother wouldn't allow him to go to sea at 13 but from her he learned a great deal about pottery and other antiquarian things, the former from her family, which imported and exported pottery and later from her owning an antiquarian shop in town when he was older.

When he was fifteen, Driscol spent a season with the Green-men (Greenlander whalers, British whalers who hunted Baffin Bay, the Norwegian and Greenland Sea and the Arctic Sea near Greenland) as a supernumerary seaman[6]. At sixteen, he had gone with his brother Stephen and visited Europe in a truncated Grand Tour of Western Europe. Visiting France, Switzerland, Netherlands and the areas of Europe that would later be known as Germany, Austria and Italy.

Symbols

Driscol used symbols in his writing and I have, for clarity, left out the majority of these, however, I will at the start and end of each volume include them for demonstration purposes. Driscol used a wild variety of symbols and what they may have meant has been left to us to decipher. A few I was able to ascertain by his mentioning what they were. These were:

▤ A small rectangular box with some lines in it, which he noted down when he had received mail and usually the initials of the person it was from, however, he did not always do this.

▤• The same rectangular box with a dot to one side. This meant he had sent out a letter. Again, it was usually associated with a person's initials.

The following symbols were used regularly and as to what they meant has been a matter of much debate between myself, the editors and other learned folks. These are shown below:

˜ ¬ Ø ∫ + ± These are taken from MV Boli font as they are the closest within the fonts to what he scribbled, which changed over time but retained the same general shape. Now, what did they mean? They are listed in the order of their commonality; the first was used several hundred times, the last one just six, and fourteen other variants or completely different symbols were used from once to three times. I would theorize that these symbols stood for his; having cleaned his rifle, groomed his horse, gone for a ride, went for a walk, or had an original thought. It is also possible that they are a marking to note that he had remembered someone special, had a bowel movement, a notable luncheon, masturbated, experienced an erotic thought or noted that he had sinned, or meant he had deferred writing in his journal and that the entry put down is a delayed one.

On some days, he noted none of these while on other days he put down a number of symbols. The most for any one day of a different type were on 23 December 1836 where he wrote;

Friday 23 December ˜ + ± ¬ Ø ∫ and added two others seen only once, I will leave it to the reader to associate these to what occurred that day and the day before. The only once seen symbols were Ç and ¤.

Welcome to the occasionally preposterous world of David Alexander Driscol.

===

Spoiler Alert!

Go to page 1 if you wish to avoid any specific details of what the book contains

If one does not wish to know any details about the actual course of action in the following four volumes, you may wish to skip over the following sections. As I warned you earlier, you may wish to come into the book without knowing some of its secrets or 'how it turns out'.

However, I do realize that some souls will not read a book unless they have an idea of what is going to occur so this presented as a concession to them.

Driscol had intended his book to be written as one volume but the amount of material he left has made it more expedient to make it into four, covering his preparations in England for his voyage to the East, the organization of the expedition, the search for personnel, material and permissions needed. In India, the expedition will be officially and ceremoniously constituted, and finally the expedition will move off into Central Asia, or Independent Tartary as Driscol called it, and there it will all but disappear from history.

In Volume I he will bid farewell to his family and friends, journey to London, outfit himself to survive the hardships of the east and take passage on a steamer to Gibraltar. He will met another officer going to the east who is tasked to form an expedition to enter Central Asia and finding Driscol eager and qualified he becomes its first member.

After some seagoing adventures he arrives in Gibraltar and makes his way to Suez to find the East India Company steam ship that will take him to Bombay. On the way there he has as an incident with 'pirates' and an encounter with the Royal Navy in Malta. Becoming going to Suez he lingers in Cairo and assists a fellow traveler to scrutinize the slave market.

Volume II he sails down the Red Sea and is involved in altercations in Jeddah, and elsewhere, gains some credit for his knowledge and engages in a number of spirited actions and is wounded twice. A third and fourth member of the expedition will be also be found.

Volume III He arrives in Bombay and begins his regimental life while planning and preparations for the expedition continue. A number of incidents occur, several more members of the expedition are found, and obstacles overcome. In Chapter XI, from Bombay to Bushire there is an overview of the situation in Southern Asia during the first part of the

19th century. The chapter then looks at how and why the expedition came about, its backstory with the political ramifications of its creation. With some difficulty, the expedition leaves Bombay for Persia, but not before Driscol has a number of fascinating encounters with the east and its people.

Volume IV the expedition heads from Persia into Central Asia disguised as Caucasian mercenaries looking for horses and makes a number of discoveries but is swept up in the native's fear an approaching Russian army and are forced to do the bidding of the ruler of Khiva. In the desert, the expedition is attacked and after a desperate struggle is dispersed and destroyed. Driscol is separated from the other survivors and is captured by another group with a very unusual background and in time he goes from prisoner to leader within that group. However, in many ways he is still a prisoner and he plots to escapes them, does so and is found near death and returns to India to find out the facts dealing with the fates of his fellow expeditionaries, which will be explored in detail in Volume V. In that I hope to illuminate some aspects of why the expedition was 'forgotten' to history.

Editor's Note

Driscol left us only an outline, a great deal of notes, and a few fully written out episodes for this volume. He also provided names for the chapters and a few sub-chapters. To fulfill his vision, I have taken his outline and entered into it his daily journal entries and information from other sources. I suspect that he did not plan to do this but intended to cover briefly, in forty or so pages, his movement to the east, highlighting a few specific incidents that related directly to the expedition or influenced later decisions concerning its direction. As he did not provide sufficient material to do that, you will now be witness to all the incidents of his life during this time, as outlined in his journal.

Had he intended that his personal journal entries be published? Absolutely not. And if he were alive today, I'm sure he would sue to stop me from doing so or shown up and shot me or his relatives for having authorized this.

His outline of the book would have been:

Volumes I & II = Chapter One

Volume III = Chapter Two

Volume IV = Chapters Three to Seven then a large supplement with a copy of the report to Geographic Society

Original Preface, Dedication And Introduction To Driscol's Unfinished Manuscript

Written by David Alexander Driscol

This preface is written by me to those whom I either; do not owe money, or who owe me money and in this manner I suggest to them a way to earn their keep by writing a book, as I am, or repay me with a favour, or I them. To those who I owe a debt of honour and there are many of you that I do, both living and dead. To those I have the heavy weight of responsibility to remember you and memorialise those events that occurred some years past, and to whom I love best above all.

I thank the latter for your close attention in these matters that so deeply inspired me to inscribe and put down these words. To the former I will give my thanks for your help when as a young man amongst a group of the finest fellows possible, we rode out of Persia and into the wilds and uncertainties of Independent Tartary. While there, we shared a grand adventure and all the delights of foreign exploration and did our service to our nation and our duty for our passed King.

It was for these men who had been like my brothers that I was moved into action. I came upon a man from that time, who had been with us on the expedition and so great was our mutual joy in meeting by chance once again that after a fine supper at the Oriental Club with a full afternoon of reminiscing over those event and incidents so long ago I found myself greatly inspired.

I was determined to plunge into those cases into which my papers, journals and notes had been thrown many years ago. Regrettably, from that day they had lain not purveyed or assayed for their value, by anyone or me.

The texts I had prepared with great care so many years ago I found in good order, diminished somewhat in their constituents by age, water or insect. When written, these facts, and the feelings, scents and emotions, were strong to me and they still vibrate in my being. To that which they relate is still warm and alive within me as it was then and now as I recall them. I can rightly say that the nonsense I will write, the scents I smelt, the anecdotes I relate, the myths I tell, and the accounts I do write down here, do actually belong to this world and are not the cheap collection of other people's stories taken up and reprinted as my own. Hitherto, I had vowed never to publish these researches until word came out of Asia that I had been vindicated, my claims found whole and truthful, and until that time I intended to keep my secrets. Sadly, that has not happened as I had hoped.

As I gazed on the mass of material, my foreboding began again but instead of falling victim to it, I decided to use bibliomancy to bolster my resolve. I then searched my room for a book worthy of such a great effort. For this book would be centre stage in the arcane ritual to follow, in following the style of Eastern style bibliomancy one has to place a great book on it spine and to allow it to fall open and then with eyes closed to pick a sentence at random. This, I exclaimed to the empty room, would put pay to my vacillation! Saying this, I plucked from the bookshelf a Qu'ran, given me years ago by greatly favoured Hayathem, and I noted with regret that it had been inadvertently stored under profane books of science, a sin to the pious Mohammedan. Having secured the book, I shut my eyes. I balanced the book on its spine and let if fall open. I then counted, with eyes stilled closed, seven pages back, using as my guide the *Bismillah al-Rahman al-Rahim* (In the name of God, most Gracious, most Compassionate), which has exactly 7-8-6 letters in Arabic and to which the virtuous follower of the Prophet Mohammed finds of these three numbers would be in our words 'luck'. I then opened my eyes counted down eight lines and read the first six words and continued to take in the entire line due to my curiosity. It was the 71ˢᵗ line of Surah An-Nisa:

> *'O you who believe! Take your precautions, and either go forth (on an expedition) in parties, or go forth all together'*

My delight was excessive and my belief that random occurrences could be used to build motivation repaid. I set to work to create from this raw material the book you see before you but before you read I must give ample warning that I am not a historian, so I ask that my simplifications of the complications that is the history of the expedition, Persia and Tartary be understood in that light. I was not a tourist, so the story of the expedition is not a tome to take with you on an excursion to these places. I am not a writer either and I offer up my apology in advance, for what you must suffer from in reading these primitive and unworthy prose.

I am most certain that what we learned wherein should be enough to terrify equally a senior officer of the Army, a Captain of the Cavalry, or a Babu *{Indian bureaucrat}* at his work desk. It will cause disquiet to a politician concerned with the safety of the three Presidencies by the advance of the sons of Rus *{Russians}*. Enough it will be if they will speak out about it and it shall be notably frightening to a shareholder of the Honourable East India Company. The neophyte explorer will find it disturbing for he might fear what happened to me will happen to them. Finally, it may cause stark apoplexy in classical historians. Yet it might also delight the antiquarian, armchair traveller and engineer.

With my faithful thanks for your attention to this matter

D A Driscol

David Alexander Driscol

[Editor's note: Driscol never completed the manuscript he started and left us only the outline the draft of his book being lost]

Original Dedication

To Sir FritzWilliams from whom all things began

Introduction

It was the east that had always lured my soul, causing me to reply in earnest to a circular directed to the regiments in England by General Rowland Hill, I[st] Lord Hill, Commander-in-Chief. At this time, there was a shortage of officers in the junior officer ranks within the Indian Army. At that time, I was newly commissioned as an Ensign in the bulges[7] *{52[nd] Oxfordshire Light Infantry}*. I held my position as a First Class Volunteer and aide to my *patron {Brigadier Sir William 'Red Jack' FritzWilliam}* by whose intercession I was both granted a commission and a position with the august regiment above, the regiment of my father due to my father saving the general's life or more correctly his foot many years before. This was the official reason for my acceptance but I found also that my prior preparations in learning a great deal about military matters and practice was greatly prized by the officers of said regiment.

[Editor's note: See Appendix Supplement in volume III; What constitutes a Gentleman: for an account of how Driscol obtained his commission, from Blackwood's Magazine, Volume CXIII, January - June 1873]

Officers who were interested in going east could do so for four years, without relinquishing their regular army commissions and would obtain the greater pay afforded to Indian Army officers. My regiment and family sadly acknowledged my acceptance of this offer. I was eager to get to the east, having grown up with my father's stories of India and as I was desirous to become an explorer. I could see this as my chance to meet and shake the pagoda tree *{to make a fortune in the east}* and to aid in the triumph of Christian civilization over the barbarous and un-enlighten peoples of the Orient. This volume is about my journey to the east and the expedition in which I was a part.

End

Spoiler Alert

==

Brigadier Sir William 'Red Jack' FritzWilliam

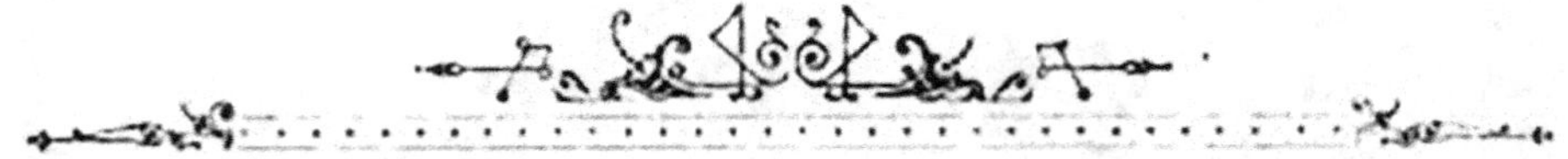

An Officer of the Crown

The Middlecombe Expedition to the Aral Sea in Turcomania and the Khanates of Independent Tartary, 1837-1838

Reminiscences of an English Ensign's Journey East In 1836

The Middlecombe Expedition to the Aral Sea in Turcomania and the Khanates of Independent Tartary, 1837-1838

Being a complete narrative of its inception, formation, travels, discoveries and adventures by
D. A. Driscol, Ensign
Bombay Artillery

========

From his personal journals and containing excerpts from the expedition's report to the Geographical Society of London

========

In four volumes:

Volume I: Reminiscences Of An English Ensign's Journey East In 1836

Volume II: A Narration Of The Actions Leading To The Formation Of The Middlecombe Expedition And The Life Of An Ensign In The Bombay Artillery 1836-1837

Volume III: Chronicle Of The Middlecombe Expedition In 1837; With A Full Report And Narrative On The Expedition's Departure From Bombay, Travels Though Persia And Turcomania, And To The Cities Of Independent Tartary

Volume IV: The Final Volume Of The Middlecombe Expedition To Central Tartary 1837-1838 With A Partial Recollection Of What They Found There, A Recounting Of The Engagement At The Sullen Tower Of Saleh Khan, And The Fate Of The Expedition With Illustrations, Maps, Observations, And Associated Papers By An Officer Present At Its Final Moments

========

With remarks and comments by
Colour Sergeant G. B. Hynes, Grenadier Regiment of Bombay Native Infantry, Indian Army
and S. P. Michaelson Assistant Surgeon in His Majesty's Indian Navy, Herr Dr. Dafydd zum Nolta,
MA, MD(P) and E. K. K. L. Vickery, Esquire, Secretary of the Expedition

========

Illustrated

Written by: David Alexander Driscol, Ensign

London

Sampson Low, Son & Co, 188 Fleet Street (the proposed publisher)

CONTENTS

In four volumes

========

Volume I

Reminiscences of an English Ensign's Journey to the East in 1836

========

========

Editor's Preface

Chapter V

Alexandria to Suez

========

Chapter notes

========

Appendixes

========

Plates

========

Maps or diagrams

=======

Illustrations, artworks, photographs & drawings

Preface

Chapter I

Chapter II

Chapter III

Bibliography

The consolidated bibliographies for volumes I-III are located with Volume IV

The Middlecombe Expedition to the Aral Sea in Turcomania and the Khanates of Independent Tartary, 1837-1838

========

Volume One

========

Reminiscences of an English Ensign's Journey to the East in 1836

========

Chapter I

Preparation for a Journey to the East

Onward My First Steps Towards The East - The Persian Professor - I Speak With Perkins - Donald Pleasanton Perkins - Travelling Home - Eccles - Muu's Thymed Rice - The Chests - The Emperor's Chambermaids - A Contest Of Tales - Foxhunting With The Light Dragoons - London - The Oriental Club - Preparations In London - Ascalon - The Honourable East India Company - Supper With An Assortment Of Devils - The Merciless Attack - Farewell To My Regiment, Family And England

========

[Journals entries by Driscol will be used now. He fortunately started a new journal in the manner noted in the preface to celebrate his new adventure. The previous journal covered his time in the 52ⁿᵈ Oxfordshire Light Infantry but, as noted earlier, was lost in WW II. Sadly, his journals from his early life are also lost. To add to the challenge of unraveling his writing, after the first month he began his preparations to go east and started learning Hindustani, Arabic and Persian from those officers in the regiment who were familiar with these languages. In his new journal, we are happy to state that he kept it in English but in his horrible handwriting.]

Onward, My First Steps Towards The East

Monday Sept 5 ‡ ¬ Ø 🗎• PR,

I received by messenger this day full acceptance of my application for secondment to the Honourable East India Company on temporary duties of not less than four years. As I had been led to believe this would soon occur by our all-knowing Adjutant, a man to whom error was an uncommon occurrence, I had prepared accordingly. I was fully ready to depart and had said my farewells to my batman *{servant}* Alyson. He will be missed and despite my daily attempts to persuade him to join me in my undertaking, he declined under the excuse of having lost two brothers to the climate of India and understandable reason but showing a lack of dash in the man. Chastened by my loss of this important man, I collected my due debts from *Dauber {An Ensign of his regiment}*, spoke to my collection of sergeants and lastly saw to my horse, Pedasos, who, although not an immortal horse, served well and never once attempt to throw me[1]. I sadly sold him to Staffer *{a Lieutenant in his regiment}* who, despite his limitations as an officer, is good to his horses and he paid me a fine sum for the animal. I had spoken my leave-taking to the depot company at the Church Parade on the Sunday past, being as I was determined to depart if not on secondment then on leave to my parents this day. Finally, I wrote to a number of the officers, thanking them all for their kind words, help and especially to Captain Rollingston-Smythe by whose efforts I was commissioned and the fatherly help I received from Captain Webb and his teaching me the rudiments of Hindustani, the Adjutant and, of course, Colonel Raddick. The Regimental Colonel *{General FritzWilliam shown in the front piece}* who had been so accommodating was at his estate and I had to write him a departure word as all were disappointed in his not attending our mess party on the 10th due to his ill health.

Not caring for such words and times, and knowing that I would not see this post for over four years, sadden me greatly. I rode out on a carriage with a man detailed to do so from my company. I was saddened also by the lack of a parade in my honour or at least a throng of the officers to say their leave at the gate. I was not to be so honoured in that manner but took as a consolation that the Sergeant Major was, at the time of my leaving, inspecting the gate guards and his salute made up for any lacking formal tradition of departure. I remind myself, again, that I was merely an Ensign and one with less than six months of seniority. In the greater scheme of things, my pride outweighed my true value to the Regiment. After we had travelled a pace or so in the carriage, I looked back at the gate and by the time, I did so I could only make out the green and white sentry box but no one was in view except the lone sentry in red.

At the main road, I met with the man who arranged passages on the post coach that evening, leaving him my baggage and other items I would take with me to the family in Eccles. I had decided to take the post coach to Liverpool, planning to leave it early when it neared Manchester. Prior to that I intended to make a diversion, for I had an appointment elsewhere this day. Having made my arrangements and the time at which I must return that evening to board the coach, I set off again.

The man from my company was a young Irishman both taciturn in appearance and manner. We had pleasant ride. We travelled together in silence, his thoughts in Gaelic harbour visions of Old Hats *{harlots, because they are frequently 'felt}* and beer, and mine on the east and what I might say to the man I was about to meet. It was afternoon when we made the East India Company College[2] within the esteemed town of Hertford Heath, Hertfordshire. I made arrangement for the keeping of the carriage and care of Private Daniel Brennan or, as his mother would have known him, Dainéal O'Brennan. I too had noted that we shared relatives somewhere back around the time of Adam. What a dullard of a young man was he! Besides his name, I had only been able to determine he was of Galway, his English was hidden deeply under his brogue and he had not a thought in his head for his future besides his preoccupation with how much sleep he could obtain once he had delivered me and stood by to await my departure. Yet he was a good driver and knew the horses well and I left him at the stable with a stock of food to keep him in good company.

Visiting professor's house of the East India Company College, Haileybury, Hertford Heath where Driscol found the Persian Professor. I-I-1

The Persian Professor

The man I was to meet lived in the village near the college. I found his dwelling easily enough as it was old Rye House and it had the crest of the college on his front fence with his name, title and what he taught. The crest read:

Fear God, Honour the King and in Latin *Sursum Corda {Lift up your hearts}*
Mirza Ibrahim
Professor
Lecturer on Persian

I had come to meet with said Professor Ibrahim[3]. He had, in the past, kindly answered my letters to him on the subject of learning Persian and was the first Persian I was to meet. A modest man, he had acted as his own butler, greeting me at the door. After I had stumbled through a modest welcome in Persian, to which he smiled regardless of my horrid pronunciation, he honored me greatly by asking me to afternoon tea. Despite my loathing for that warm drink, I, of course, accepted.

Will I ever be free of this despicable drink?

His house was small but well-appointed and completely in English character. My timing had been good and I entered the room where four people sat; his Dutch wife, Mrs. Ibrahim, who somewhat forwardly announced herself as Sterre. The other three men were the Principal of the college, a Mr Charles Le Bar, another colleague of the Professor whose name now escapes me for he said nothing substantial during my time there and a young man introduced to me as Mr Perkins, a fellow traveller. I found Mr Bar most interesting as he was a mathematician and minister and well informed on all subjects. The centre of attention was, of course, the Professor who began, after a service of walnut cake and some abominably bad tea which I left un-finished, to discuss the matter at hand. It was Persian we were here to discuss and its learning by Englishmen. This was the *raison d'etre* and a passion of the Professor. I sat with his wife on my left and Perkins on my right with the Professor at the head of the table and the two other members of the college across from us. He also granted my request that I take notes of our discussion a request that Perkins also asked to be allowed to do.

In part he said; 'I am honoured that two young men would wish to learn Persian with such desire that they would visit me. Most of my student clerks heartily loath the language yet you two have sought it out and I must first ask why.'

He looked at me and I explained that I was an officer of the 52nd seconded to the East Indian army just that day and in the process of learning the languages of the area. From discussions with men who had been there, Persian, as the language of diplomacy, command and commerce in India, was one of the languages I wished to master.

I was most delighted to hear Perkins then describe his reasoning, for he too was student of the language but much more advanced than I in its study. He had been in India for four years having previously studied at The Calcutta *{modern Kolkata}* Madrasa set up by the Administration of the HEIC to promote language study and was presently on leave in England.

To these lines of scholarship, the Professor was most happy to assist in any way possible.

A meal was then served, which was a surprise as a hearty meal was usually not the course for an afternoon tea but the Professor explained, saying to the Principal that he knew he would not do well to serve a superficial meal to young men who had travelled far and hard to reach him. As a bachelor I always appreciated a free meal; a clear oyster soup, larded lamb braised and glazed in its own juices and presented as a fricandeau of lamb, and a disappointing breaded fish of little taste. I was both astounded at the fricandeau as I was by the Professors' effortless use of the term 'superficial' for it was a word rarely heard and pronounced perfectly by a foreigner. I was more use to foreigners speaking abominably bad English often demonstrated to me by my mother's own relatives. She herself had never lost her accent and had certain odd turns of phrasing still.

Few foreigners ever master the idiom and accent of English but with the Professor, I felt I was speaking with an Englishman who had graduated from 'Oxbridge'[4]. Despite his foreign look, if one closed one's eyes, one would think him - almost - a highborn Briton.

The other man noted that he was most pleased with the food which although good, was not as good as that produced by his cook at home, a Frenchman with forty years' experience before the oven and well known in the vicinity of the college for his skill in the arena of cuisine. The Professor who was less enthralled with this man's expertise stated, 'he may have been forty years before the oven but he appears to still be somewhat raw yet. He could not produce an eatable Javaher Polow[5] to save his life'.

I, too, was displeased with the food, not that it was not good but that it dashed my hopes I had had for some examples of Persian food, but perhaps with a Dutch wife and in England such food was not procurable. Having spent several minutes in silence constructing a sentence in Persian, I asked the Professor this. I could see the phrasing had not been good and my tense incorrect but that he understood the question at all pleased me greatly. I also noted that Perkins was un-able to ascertain what I had said. The Professor in answer produced from a drawer his notebook, jotted down my question, and promised to send me a recipe as soon as he could. He assured me that once in India, a good *bobachee* or *bawarchi {Indian cook}* would be able to produce it with alacrity.

The Professor spoke again about his *rationale* after we had finished the meal and the general discussion of the events of the day. He began, thusly, and I paraphrase:

You see my friends, at the beginning of the 17th century as you English view matters of time the learning of *Farsi* (Persian) has been at odds with the administration of the English in India. The matter is this; two sides debated and conversed on this subject for many years, one side are my true friends, the orientalists and my own people, they see the teaching of the Persian language as something that is part of the greater culture, to understand one you must undertake the knowing of both. Yet in the officialdom of the company and he nodded his head to the Principal Le Bar, the Anglicists treat Persian as a kind of pragmatic language with no soul, a poor cart to send messages from the rulers to the ruled. To be used to express their requests, queries, and thoughts and through which the myriad of details that is the bureaucracy of India is done. To use Persian in this way does not require highly specialised forms of knowledge, just memorization of a language that is similar in structure to English.

For our part, Persians and Persianphile scholars wish to teach both the cultural values and their techniques of rule, order, ethics and thought to new British officials and military officers but we are losing this battle as Asian born teachers are gradually losing out against Persian speaking Britons, and he pointed at Perkins, for control over the Persian teaching institutions.

The Professor continued after a long drink that came from a decanter. The decanter contained a yellowish red mixture that I had passed on, finding the smell close to that of gin.

Have you read the infamous Minute on Education by the Honourable T. B. Macaulay, which he put out last year?

He asked this to all but none responded and there was an awkward pause, I took this time to scribble down my notes.

You should because in time it will end the reign of the orientalists and begin the triumph of the Anglicists[6].

At the end of the Professor's declaration, it was the Principal who restarted the conversation by declaring, Mirza the decanter has been halted in front of you too long. Pass the bottle, Mirza what do you call in Persian the man who stops passing the decanter and keeps it from his fellows? What is this thief of thirst called amongst the imbibers of Persia?

The Professor replied that we call him Mohammed, peace be upon him!

To which the Principal replied smartly, yet you do not follow this teaching?

I do, for you see the prophet spoke out on this prohibition as given him by Jibril *{the angel Gabriel}*. The Holy Qu'ran speaks of drinks made from grapes and dates - because these are specifically mentioned they are not permitted. The professor held that other forms of drink are, in his opinion and that of others, permitted or halal and not haram, forbidden. He concluded that as long as one is not intoxicated when in prayer he is within the right. Our lovely decanter contains a Dutch drink known as *jenever oude* or *bessen* which is aromatic and mellow due to it malt content and flavoured with juniper berries and red currants, this fine deliverer of 'Dutch courage' was provided to me by my beloved, he then spoke Dutch to his wife, and she smiled.

We Persians like our drinking, debauched nights in the courts of Caliphates were enshrined in the *khamriyaat*, or odes to wine, by Abu Nuwas, an eighth-century poet.

I recorded an interesting exchange between Perkins and Professor which while paraphrase went something like this

"Was he not an Arab poet?" asked Perkins.

And the professor replied, "He was but he had the sense to write much in Persian."

Perkins agreed with the Professor and announced how he would love to devote his life to the understanding and writing of Persian poetry in the manner of Sa'di or Hafiz. The Professor asked why a British military man would wish to do this.

"To woo women, of course," was Perkins response.

To which the Professor wittily replied, "Ah, but you must first teach them Persian so they will Understand you!"

"Why is this prohibition then held over all drinks?" said the Principal to return to the subject he had broached.

{Driscol ended his reconstruction of the conversation here}

Ah well you see the mullahs and I have a difference of opinions over this and their estimation of me is that I fall short of orthodoxy while I hold there estimation of life is what falls short.

A messenger arrived at this point, hammering on the door. One would have thought the enemy was at the gate but it was a trifling administrative concern that took away the Principal and his associate. The Professor had to interrupt our conversation to confer with them in private before they departed. They excused themselves with ample apologies and the Professor's wife directed Perkins and I to the garden. She left us there to attend to her servants.

Mirza Ibrahim; the Persian professor is shown in his formal court robes. The image is undated but may come from a time after his return to Persia. I-I-2

I Speak With Perkins

We introduced ourselves again and he complimented me on my Persian. It was excellent, he declared, for a light infantry Ensign and a neophyte to eastern languages. He also observed that, despite my claim to be an Ensign in our army, I did not look at all English but that I must be English as I did speak with a pronounced and slightly un-usual Manc accent[7].

Perkins also stated in the garden that he was not a Mister as the Professor initially introduced him to me. Instead, he was a Lieutenant. Until that time I had thought him a civilian member of the HEIC. He stated he was instead in another department but did not state what it was.

In reply to his query, I stated that my mother was Danish and my father an Englishman from Ireland and of Scots descent.

He thought this was splendid and I informed him that I could also speak some Russian and German, and Danish thoroughly. He showed great interest in my ability to speak Russian and I understated my ability to do so, and explained my mother's family interests in the trade in the Baltic. He then asked a bold question, which I repeat in its entirety, for I shall remember it always.

Let me be intrepid here Ensign. When do you head to the east and, if it is soon, what do you hope to do there? He did not pause for my answer but instead thought for some time, holding his hand up to quell my attempt to speak, and then added, that he had a matter which may of be of interest to me but pray may I tell him in earnest why I was going east?

I answered with some enthusiasm that my father had served there and my brothers were now in the region and I had heard many tales of the places and people. I hoped to be an explorer as I had found soldiering in England to be somewhat tame, like chasing a three-legged fox. I would rather I was a Christie, Grant or Pottinger[8], if I could arrange such an opportunity, and added that I had orders to a ship yet not named that is to leave from the East India Docks on or about the 20th of September.

Perkins smiled broadly and I found that he too was scheduled to take ship at the same time and that it was probable that we would be shipmates. I expressed my delight at his idea, we then spoke of the excellent possibility we would have to study our Persian together if we were on the same ship as it might take eight months for us to reach India, and perhaps we could indulge in Arabic and Hindustani too.

He smiled and shook my hand and said that he and I would talk once 'the shores of England slipped beneath the waves'.

We talked of things that are more common and soon found a shared interest in the military doings about the world. We spoke of the battles leading to Mexican independence and their more current battles against the Jonathan[9] interlopers in Texas. The great Boer treks and their continual strife against the Bantu savages and the French campaign in Algiers - that last issue we discussed in French, to which Perkins remarked rather acidly that he not often heard French pronounced with a distinct Danish accent spiced by Mancunian before. Most disagreeable old chap!

The return of the Professor interrupted our discussion of French and returned to the one about Persia, Persians and its language resumed. It ended some hours later with my need to continue my journey. The good Professor loaded me up with grammars, dictionaries, exercises and other language learning apparatus and his wife with cakes and other good things to eat. I also left with that thing that was more precious, a stern warning to write him in Persian and to keep him up to date on my undertakings in the east. To have the patronage of such an important man of Persia I found most encouraging.

I had also met Lieutenant Perkins to whom I have taken a liking to immediately, to have a man I know and share an interest in languages on board during the eight-month voyage to India will be a great boon.

[Editor's note: I have gone forward thru his journals and done additional research to give a clearer picture of this man Perkins, as noted below]

A image thought to be of Driscol's writing apparatus with the a box inscribed
in Arabic which reads; 'Arabic Dictionary'. I-I-3

==

Donald Pleasanton Perkins
Lieutenant, Royal Engineers
Great Trigonometric Survey *{of India}*

Perkins was born on May 8th, 1808 as the first son of Dr. Julian Perkins, Bishop of Westchester, and his mother, Elsie Marie Bonesteade of a long respected family from Devonshire and with an ecclesiastical ancestry. Donald was well grounded by private tutors and his father's un-relenting attention to classical and Biblical learning yet he nevertheless confounded his father in declining tradition and his father's strong wishes to enter the church. Instead, he entered Queen's College, Cambridge taking up Oriental languages and graduating with a first. He was famous for his assiduity to his interests. Perkins learnt in his time at Cambridge five oriental vernaculars. Originally a Francophile, he developed a deep interest in all aspects of the east. Donald again tried his parent's temperament by declining firmly to enter seminary and using his language skills to create Bibles in those tongues or leading missions to those people. Instead, he took what was considered a thoroughly barbarous step for a Cambridge graduate; he entered Addiscombe[10] by special permission and obtained in short order a commission in the East Indian Army and then attended Woolwich to become a Royal Engineer. He then served one year in the Madras Sappers where his ability to learn Tamil in less than two months earned him the notice of the Governor-General and the awarding to him by his soldiers of a greater reward; the epithet of *Thambi {younger brother}*, something not before granted a British officer. He was able to enter the great survey by his being well known by this incident, his passing out of Woolwich as the top graduate and being aided by his great social skills. In the survey, he focused his efforts on the areas presently beyond the boundaries of British India of that time.

His contemporaries had the highest praise for his keenness, noting he was one of the best British polyglot's in India at the time, often compared favourably to the later Richard Burton and Christopher Rigby *{the first and second best}*. His presence in India also provided a clue as to why he had avoided life as a man of God. He was deemed the most relentless of poodle fakers[11], a lothario of the first order and often taken to be a complete rake by the more moral. He was described as the most handsome man in India with his appearance being commented on by many, mostly women, in their memoirs. He was 5', 11" in height, 13 stone, broad shoulders, thin in hip and leg, an exquisite rider, dancer extraordinaire and blessed with a complexion of peaches and cream that any woman would envy. This was improved by a set of perfect teeth, brown wavy hair and the 'dark brown eyes of a Greek god', as noted by the wife of Lord Guildford. He was granted a lieutenancy in the Royal Engineers in 1835 well before his peers and like Jeremy Taylor was noted for his golden voice and angelic aspects. One senior officer described him thusly, 'He was the flame that ignited all who knew him to accomplish that which was impossible', and he did so with rarely a reproof to anyone but solely by the look of eye, a kind comment or a well-worded query. He was revered and beloved by contemporaries, senior officers, junior officers, non-commissioned officers and men. At one time, it was held by many that he had been challenged to over twenty duels concerning matters concerning his actions and words towards women. This dual nature of his being a peerless leader and insatiable libertine led to some difficult times. It was rumoured that he was put up for the leadership of an expedition to get him away from India for a year or two.

==

Travelling Home

I arrived back at the post station with no time to spare. The Post coach thundered up out of darkness, a postbag exchanged, my luggage secured and I climbed aboard unable to see anyone else in the coach as I did. I anticipated my father un-braiding me on the extravagance of travelling by a post coach. I therefore had marshaled my reasons for it and had been practicing what I would say. It was faster than the stagecoaches, although somewhat dearer in price, and it travelled at night avoiding for the most part the slower transport wagons, flocks and other interfering itinerants. This one started out in late afternoon near sunset with six passengers in its black and scarlet livery, with an enormous guard armed with a blunderbuss standing at the rear. We had a good run for when morning came we had made half the distance, nearly 90 miles, despite having to stop six times to change horses. Their method of delivering post being to throw the mail bag at the postal clerk while snatching the new one while *en passant {in passing, a reference to the taking of a pawn in chess}.*

I had come armed with my pistol and carried my stirrup hilted regimental sabre like a walking stick. The damn thing has cost me nearly five Pounds and I would not risk it in my luggage atop the coach. I had some concern about highwaymen and loaded my pistol with three balls. On my departure from the Regiment I had been given a fine gift and as had been explained to me the gift was a practical one was in appreciation of my demonstrated skills, that I could not hit a horse with a pistol if I was riding it but admittedly I was a fair, if only fair, rifle shot. They had presented me with a fine silver chased Westley Richards made cap lock musketoon, with the regiment's bulge horn badge and '52' set into the stock and base. After the presentation, I was told with some seriousness that such a weapon would be of great utility in India for hunting fowl, dealing with resurgent and un-repentant Pindaris, un-discovered thugs, lazy dhobi and pestiferous dogs and snakes[12].

I gave out a hearty good evening but was met with a darken coach and a few mumbled replies. I was fortunate to have gained a seat next to Captain Lumbridge who, in the darkness, guided my path with a firm arm. He is the superintendent of stores at Portsmouth but a dull old cadger was he when relating his present duties. He told a number of stories regarding Copenhagen *{a naval battle in 1801}* where he had fought in the H.M.S. Agamemnon and told of their attempts to float the ship after her grounding during that battle. Mostly we remained silent and tried to sleep un-comfortably or tried too as the coach rattled along all night. My not being sure of who or where the other passengers were in the darkness made the ride rather ghastly although I had heard at least one woman's sweet voice then a second. As dawn broke, I made the acquaintance of the Roach family and spoke for some time with their daughter, Marguerite, to whom, despite sitting across from me the entire evening in the coach, had not said a word to me.

I was wearing my new dark grey frock coat with a hat said to be a D'orsay but more to my mind a regency style. As I was so eloquently dressed, my confidence was high and I was bold enough to discuss the Pickwick paper subscriptions and the first Shakespeare jubilee at Stratford-on-Avon that presented itself in the spring. Her father was the senior engineer of the new Garnkirk and Glasgow Railway. Marguerite was shy with brunette hair but she set with her lips quenched tight and her long head cocked slightly to the left when she spoke. We stopped and dined that mid-morning at Grey Bank's Hotel where the food was potted ham, sheep's tongue with olives and a fine scalloped cod and sundry other vegetable dishes. While eating I saw that her teeth were un-even which may have explained her reluctance to smile. After her father determined that I was an officer in a fine regiment and not some jobless swain, the family spoke long into the morning with me. It was my first conversation with people outside the regiment for many months. I was able to bide them good morning just at noon and gained some much needed and un-interrupted sleep with some happiness in my heart from speaking so long with Marguerite.

Tuesday 6 September

A busy day. The company was off in good time in the evening and the quiet coach of yesterday which had only I and the Captain speaking was this evening full of good conversation on a wide selection of subjects. I spoke at length with Marguerite's father on the future of railroads and astounded her mother by not only knowing why Poland was restive but also the price of crockery, a relic of knowledge from my Mother's family business. The good Captain told a story or two of what one might find in a cask of salted meat after it had lain in the wet hold of a ship for two years off the Gold coast *{off West Africa}*. The journey had now become tiresome and I regret not retaining my horse Pedasos to ride up and to leave him with my parents but in spite of my paying for him he was a 'regiment' horse whom I had inherited from the man whose position I had taken. It would have not been cricket to take the horse from the regiment as he was trained well to the bugle calls of the light infantry. Marguerite and I had taken to smiling at one another and I felt she was being lusciously coy.

At midnight, we passed through Cheadle. The coach stopped to change horses and the passengers disembarked to tend to their needs. I was able to gain a refund for the rest of my fare and found where I might hire a horse of suspect quality so that I might ride on to Manchester. As the men returned to the coach I was able to approach Mr Roach alone and asked if I might have permission to correspond with his daughter while I was on active service in India. I had been told in the officer's mess that this was the method and words to use in this situation and like a siege-one, my approach to the goal were with measured steps. He was most happy to grant this and mentioned that his wife had hoped just for such an approach by me. I explained that my need to move up to Manchester in more haste meant I must leave them. He and the family understood and I was most pleased to be able to say goodbye to the young lady without her younger brother sitting next to her. I wished her God speed and good health, and having secured her father's and mother's permission to correspond she granted hers with a most warming smile.

1848 Ordnance Survey Map showing Eccles, Lancashire
Location of the Driscol house and main farm buildings. 1.5 inches (3.8 cm) to
the quarter mile (.40 kilometers). I-I-4

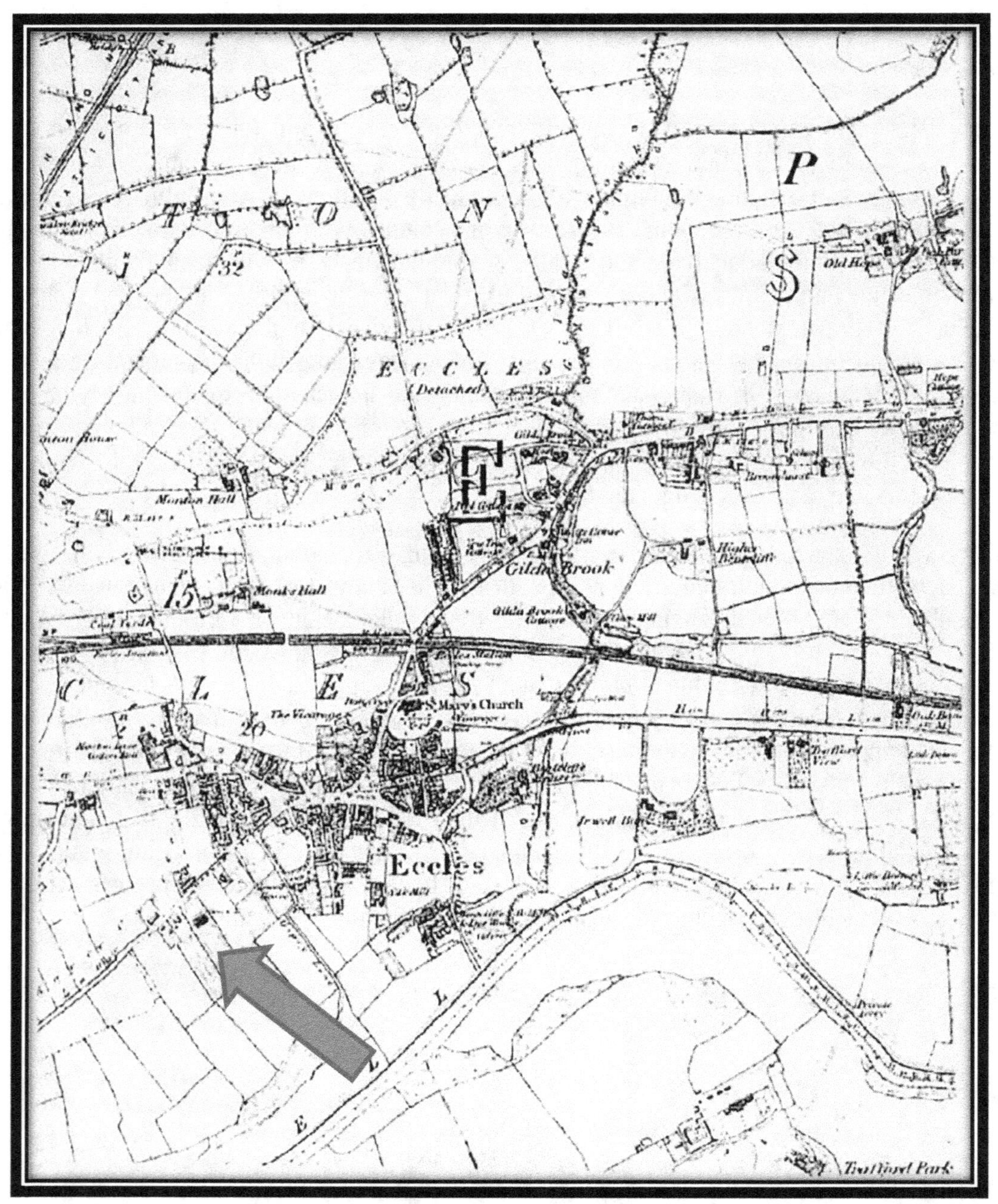

Eccles

Much buoyed by such a dalliance, I made for Manchester having obtained a horse a rather suspect one as I had noted earlier for a trifling sum for use that morning. I was able to do so as I knew the stationmaster, who was in the Militia with my elder brothers. In the early morning chill, I rode and walked at intervals with no haste in my pace but only in my heart. The road I found was in the same horrid state it had been when I had passed here six months ago. I was fortunate to not break my horses and my own neck riding down it in the dark of dawn, avoiding three-foot deep ruts, some filled with fetid water. I went by two broken down carts, their wheels shattered by the stones, which had been laid down, perhaps as a failed attempt to fill said ruts but had instead formed an obstacle to wheeled traffic. In all it was a deplorable journey to take when going home and added execrable delay to my arrival. I prevailed however and rode on until I arrived at our family properties in the darkest stage of the morning. I could see in the distance the lights of the textile mills reflecting from the low coal smoke clouds that hung over Manchester - a mockery of more delightful moonlight. I ate little on the ride as I was saving myself for my mother's cookery. I had dreamed quite often of her *pundkage {pound cake}*, *helstegt svinekam {roast pork loin}* and her well-braised English lamb shanks with copious amounts of her Danish style spiced rice. As it was in the quiet of the early morning and sun was still below the horizon, I came into our courtyard as quietly as I could.

Old Paunch, our dog, did not bark as I rode in but, as was his way, he came and sat near the horse in exactly the place one would dismount to. He had always done that and I was glad to see him continued in his way. He was quite happy to see me once I reached ground awkwardly to avoid stepping on him, something I had done since I had begun to ride. He was a very old dog now but still gave a romp around me in his happiness but without the slightest sound he knew well the penalty of barking at this early hour with no evident threat to the household. I made my way to the barn where the cows and geese made a small commotion for they too knew me still or so it amused me to think it so. The family horses remember me also. One in particular Gallant was gallant, and she was she was always slow to waken but this morning she was tugging at her harness to get near me as soon as I entered. I used her supply of water to clean myself up and put on my uniform. Since that day when I had walked from the house to enlist in the 52nd I had not been home and was desirous, to see my mother and father's reaction to my officer's uniform. I knew I need not wait long for the household to awake and as the false dawn broke and I chewed on a straw, out strode my elder brother Gary who, like my father, could never sleep if the sun was threatening to rise. We had a glorious greeting for even in my uniform he knew my outline in the dark and called me out before I could speak.

In a swirl of action after his greeting soon everyone was up and clustering around me, with my mother last to come. She, of course, made the most of the uniform by her words and expressions, lapsing at times into Danish in her delight. My father I could see was conflicted and I knew well from my mother's letters that he had not approved of my actions in taking the commission but he ended the stalemate by snapping to and giving a rather stylish light infantry salute[13]. It was too bad that he was not the first to do so and I could not give him a Guinea *{It was a custom for a newly commissioned officer to give a gold Guinea to the first man to salute him}*.

Within an hour, all my brothers and sisters still at home had come in to greet and meet me. Gary *{Gideon}*, who had acted as a second father to me when I was younger, had greeted me first, of course. He took on the task to update me on our various family ventures, my father's hands were now off the tiller and he had taken on the guise of a paternal overseer as Gary now ran most of industries and farms. My other bother Stephen, formerly my stern taskmaster and teacher in my youth. I spoke too with my favourite, red-haired sister Zoe who is quite the beauty now and my shy 'youngest', sister Lauren[14].

As the morning grew old, I was able to pull away from my family and went to see friends. Few of the boys, now men my age, still lived in the area for they were either at school, involved in the management of the textile factories or with the Navy in the West Indies, India, Africa or South Seas. I knew that Karen[15] would be about at this hour and, as she was my best friend and confidant, an hour with her would be a catharsis of the finest quality for my soul.

I began my walk to see my old childhood grounds. Places where I had tested the patience of the three great authorities of this rural area; the squire, his crony the parson and my own brother Stephen the School Master.

I passed the Jolly Carter Inn where Mr Blears was landlord and I remembered the bloody details of the murders there and how, as a child, I would lay afraid in my bed that the murderers would come to my house for I had never wished to play the part of the boy in that story.

[Editor's note: Driscol later wrote about this and the dreams he had. See his entry for March 30, 1837 in Volume II]

I walked past the butcher shop of Thomas Turtle whose daughter Sally I had kissed once as a lad and gained a great deal of trouble over it as my mother could never again go there to obtain meat when our own farm had none and instead she had gone to Thorley's whose wife she detested for she was Unitarian. I walked by and stood some time outside the practice of Sorby, our Surgeon, who it was said saved my life when I was down for tonsillitis and who, in some way, prevented my succumbing to rheumatic fever. Next was the house and shop of poor Mr Race. I stopped here too and he was outside but did not recognise me which was not un-expected as I knew his daughter better and missed her ever since she had died when I was thirteen one day she had not come to school, the next she was buried. Then his son, my sworn enemy, had died the day after, followed by his wife. He was a cheerless man after that. I came to the un-happy house from which my good friend Michael Haehnlin, son of a Hanoverian officer of the King's German Legion, had lived. His family had come here after the dissolution of electorate of Hanover *{in 1803 after the Convention of Elbe}*. There on a warm summer's evening in July 1833, he had fallen from a scaffold while rebuilding a chimney shattered by lightning and died soon after in the parlor of Sorby's house. Such had been the losses during my childhood.

I paused for a time too next to Pearson's blacksmith, and Mr Hunter's establishment where he made nankeen *{a cotton cloth}* in his manufactury. I saw two men I knew to be part of the Watch and Ward *{an informal rural village police - before real police}* who were on some duty or another over a missing cow; they were Mr Greenwood and Hampson, who acted like I had last seen them just a day ago instead of six months and now wearing a uniform. They were after said cow and the few pence they would receive for these duties.

[Editor's note: At some point, undated but in a different color of ink Driscol added the following in the margin, in pencil]

'Watch and Ward, They had no sense, They stand a' night for eighteen pence.'

I remember, as a twelve year old a run away from my chores and studies that a bold pack of us boys had been making a lot of noise at dusk's arrival, as boys will, when we were told to go home for supper and to stop our insolence. One of the boys, perhaps Turner's son Thomas, never officially identified, was very coarse in language and one of the Watch and Warders, possibly it was Mr Worth the Linen draper had taken offence and run after us. We had gone down from Shelmerdine square and jumped one of the over-filled sewage gutters but our pursuer either had not seen it or lacked the legs to do what we had done and submerged himself in the slime, sludge and muck. It was quite the adventure indeed!

I lingered for a time at Our Lady's Well which we boys had called the Old Lady's Well and where we planned our complex military campaigns to gain fruit from places not owned by our parents. It was here, too, in the meadow next to it, that we had met often and violently with wooden sword and makeshift armour. I broke my right forefinger twice in honourable strife here.

I walked past the Parish church, being aware of the conflict between its present Vicar and my family and a source of much grief. However, it was here that the famous Eccles Wake's were held each year and those festivals were always a favourite of mine. Those four days in September held two or so weeks before my birthday lay brightly on my memory. Especially the foot race on the 1st, which I am proud to say I usually won amongst the boys of my own age, and at sixteen all comers. Also well remembered were the jackass and wheelbarrow races. The distemper of those who tried the smoking contests. I remember, too, the time the local Baron's son, Sir Humphrey de Trafford, just then retired from the Dragoons, joined our festivities and let us ride his richly decked out charger.

My final stop before reaching Karen's house was the Birch's shop on Church Street where I purchased five Eccles cakes *{a local pastry made with currants, raisins, candied orange and lemon peel and a touch of nutmeg}*, ate one there and took the rest with me.

I came to the Wainwright's house, spent some time in idle chatter with her parents, and then took Karen for a walk as we shared the cakes, for she and I had known one another since we could talk.

I was, at the end of our talk, ready and willing to go to the east, for twenty years if not four. I spoke of Marguerite and she of three boys, now grown to men, all whom I knew that she had an interested in. I did warn her that one was a complete rotter but that the other two might be true friends or more to her. I did promise her fabulous gifts on my return; silks, rare books and a brooch or necklace set with a ruby the size of a pigeon's egg the smallest of what would be in my private collection I told her. I received in return a promise from her to write and to delay any marriage until I returned for on that day we made a pact that should we both reach the age of five and twenty without gathering up a spouse she would save me from bachelorhood and I her from becoming spinsterish. Although, I said I would be reluctant to marry such an older woman *{she was less than a month older}*, which she made a face on. This was all in good jest as we had found earlier in life that exchanges of kisses came not with delight but distaste and ill ease, more on her part than mine, and marriage between us was not something either of us would desire because of this.

Father and I finally spoke towards the end of the day manoeuvered together in fine style by Muu[16]. His concerns were that I not become indebted to those whose actions had gained me my commission. He felt strongly that I must not be tied to them by debts of money or honour. To ease this I promised my father to repay my benefactor the cost of my commission despite how long something like this might take. In truth, I had no hope to do unless I would gain a fortune, if not I would be making payments on the price of the commission for the next several decades. He was dubious as always of my reasons to go east. Since I was a young man, I had been discouraged from my youthful desire to be an explorer, to seek out the dark corners of the world, and to fill in the blank spots on the world's map. I therefore made no mention of it and painted my movement east as that of a young officer wishing to see the east, find his fortune and the price of his next promotion, like my father and mother before me and my older brothers at this time. This he seemed to accept and for a time we discussed at length the few men he still knew in the regiment and the chance of war with France or Russia or some native prince in the east.

He then gave me advice, as he always did. It was the same given by fathers to their sons since Roman times and probably by Biblical fathers to their begats, the same given to my older brothers; to be careful of money, avoid shiftless friends, degraded women, investments, and devote myself to the study of my craft, and fulfill the calls of my duty. This was all worthwhile advice but I thought overly tarnished with tradition. I remember as a child hearing nearly the same speech given to my two brother's John and Mark prior to their departure to the east.

Muu served a gargantuan meal on our finest china. We had two soups; sod soup and gule aerter - the latter at the start and the former at the end of the meal - a fine roast beef, carrots, leeks and cucumbers in various guises, and, my favourite of all; her Danish rice. How I had missed it while on duty with the regiment where rice was never served except in a pudding. I had watched her make it and recorded the procedure for at my meeting with the Persian Professor I had become aware that I could take a recipe with me and have it made by Indian servants. Thusly disposed, I recorded her recipe as best I could based on observation and helped by the hints of my two sisters.

Muu's thymed rice

(Also known as Danish Rice[17])

Take $\frac{1}{4}$ pound of good melted creamery butter and a half-pound of the finest West Indian rice that is mixed and browned until the butter is gone. This is placed aside and a large pot is filled with fresh water and brought to a rapid boil, into which goes a large sliced Spanish (yellow) onion, a half ounce of thyme, parsley, garlic, an ounce of good Indian pepper, the carcass of a chicken, or other parts to give it flavour and a small pinch of salt. Bring back to a boil for some 5 minutes then pour this onto the rice, and put a lid on the pot and put it in the oven at medium heat for half an hour. After it is cook remove from the pot, taste and add more thyme and salt as necessary

The meal was a great occasion with everyone in good spirits. Mr Gweniston the banker came by and gave his regards, as did a number of others. I even was able to stay away from Brother Stephen's wife, a woman I had always found irritating in her Welsh ways and again thought how much I would have preferred her to have stayed on the other side of Offa's Dyke. *{an 8ᵗʰ century earthen wall separating Wales from England}*

I felt very much an adult at this supper, for I was the guest of honour. While with the regiment my horizons had expanded, for the officer's mess had had subscriptions to many newspapers and periodicals, and these I had read in solitude while my messmates made mad noises in their drunken revelries. I found for the first time in my life that I was knowledgeable of the world outside of books, history and science, I knew of politician names, of actions in the parliament, of the death of foreign kings and intrigues and revolution everywhere and many scientific and natural discoveries in foreign lands. All of this was cheerfully discussed at the table and I was able to fully participate.

A view of Driscol house in the 1840's where it is now painted white instead of the plain brick of Driscol's youth. Driscol live in the second floor room whose window shows in the left of this print (third floor for Americans).
1-I-5

The Chests

My family had put together a small medical chest for me. This I expected, for we had spoken of it and my brothers who had departed this house had also been gifted with such. In it were a goodly amount of items to include several pounds of Pears' transparent soap which is a favourite of our family and one traded by my maternal side thorough out the Baltic; eleven bottle of Warsburg's tincture[18], a medicine for fevers, especially tropical fevers; Mothersil's seasick remedy, something I was not bothered by but perhaps they had overlooked this for it could also dampen upsets of the digestive tract; a bottle of Smythe-Brotherington mixture (vinegar and brandy) for tooth health, which I reviled;

[Editor's note: Driscol later amended his journal in pencil noting he had disposed of the foul tasting mixture]

a jar of Coulard's lotion, which prevents eye illness; Opodeldoc lotion, for the prevention and healing of sprains; Cockles anti-bilious pills; a bag containing a dried mixture to make Abernethy's Bread-and-Water Poultice; and Citronella oil, which, I was told by my father, would protect against insect attacks. There were also other vials, enough to heal an entire tribe of the downtrodden and sicken heathens, glass phials of ginger essence, Calomel, Tannin, Easton's syrup, Dovers' powder and a useful iron & arsenic compound. The reddish leather covered cedar wood chest also included syringes and other instruments to include a partial veterinary medicine kit.

Much to my delight, a second present was presented by my brothers; it was a Dutch made natural history philosopher's laboratory and, more importantly, contained also a partial suite of Cooke & Sons scientific instruments to include a finely made French Fortin mercury barometer, an incomplete set of well used Troughton & Simms survey instruments too. A James Adie made Sympiesometer was also given - it was a lovely item.

This made me very happy as they were supplying me with the tools to be an explorer. I was much taken by the barometer which was a very fine instrument, if somewhat battered by its previous use. The mercury cistern had a glass portion through which the mercury was open to the atmosphere and an ivory needle made just to touch its mirror image in the mercury before the reading could be taken. I expressed my admiration for such a fine gift.

My father had also provided a saddle; a French Parisian style courier's saddle, with broad stirrups coated with cork and leather, making dismounting easier. A thickly padded saddle - cloth and a bridle, reinforced with chain mail, to keep this important piece of horse furniture from being easily severed by an enemy blade. My mother, who knew well the power of the eastern sun, gave me an umbrella of double silk and in a dark green shade, suitable for protection against rain, yes, but made to keep the murderous rays of the Indian sun off one's soft British head. Brother Stephen provided a straw hat of admirable style with a jaunty red ribbon worked into wide rim - also to keep the sun off one's head and neck. A tin basin, sealable water flask, a tablecloth, a foldable campstool that my father had secured made of teak so it would not rot and it was four inches higher than most so my tall frame would not be discomforted. Zoe provided a fine white towel suitable more to a woman than an army officer but I appreciated it deeply as she had sewn my name into it. I received a number of other useful and some equally ridiculous gifts. Overall, they made up an interesting assortment of items. I thought I had enough but my sisters provided me a very fine book, Samuel Taylor's '*An essay intended to establish à standard for an universal system of Stenography, or Short-hand writing';* a way to write faster this I found made me want to withdraw off and read it immediately. They knew of my interest in just that subject.

The after supper conversations went on long into the night until I retired to my bed; the last time I would see my room where I had spent my entire life, now a lonely room once filled with four of my brothers. Now I was the last. I was lugubrious I was to have a new life. My old cat made his appearance and, as if old times, took up his sleeping position nestled on my chest.

Map of Lancashire from Driscol's Gray's New Book of Roads, published in 1824. In Driscol's copy, he wrote in the margin the word 'home' in Greek and had penciled in an arrow that pointed to Manchester. He took this guide to India and placed on its maps where the people he met were from. I-I-6

On The Road To London

Wednesday 7 September

I awoke early for I was in a hurry. Last night my father had informed me that he had arranged a horse and carriage for me but that I must manage it myself. I would take it to London and he provided the name of the stable in which I would deliver it. By doing so I would complete some transaction that my brother Gary and father had forged with a merchant near Islington, London.

I had decided to leave behind with a heavy heart my beloved German made air rifle. Its seals were failing and I could not bear to think its stock would be eaten by the white ants *{termites}* of the orient. I would have no use of it there anyway but it saddened me to be parted from it. It was a good friend. I left also my gifted 52nd musketoon for the same reasons.

I had received an advance of pay for the month of September and my parents and elder brothers had given me many additional funds. I had a quite formidable sum. I secured for travel a few items from my own and the family library, reference books and some non-military clothing and items I thought might be necessary in India and on the voyage there.

I had planned to leave the house with thirty pounds of books but left instead with forty pounds of books and two chests, weighing in at one hundred and ten pounds. So much for being a light infantryman!

Muu had another gift for me; a warm bath, something I had not partaken of in some months. I did so and by the time I had emerged in my civilian clothes, most of the family had drifted away, leaving me to make my final farewells to my parents. I gave them a warm farewell, Muu crying but father stony faced, as was his tenor. He was now nearing seventy years of age and, although hale and hearty, you could see that he had aged noticeably in the months I'd been away. Dear Muu seem frail too. I wondered silently if I would return to their graves or a great welcome?

I held and said another good bye to my two preferred cats from the small tribe that lived around our farm, of the same colouring but differing greatly by temperament and size. I petted and held Littlerer and Bigger, two fine white and brown spotted cats; one smart, the other rather dim witted but both fine companions. It had been Littlerer who had joined me last night, as he had during my entire childhood as far back as I could remember. Like many other things, I wondered if they would be here when I returned. I petted Old Paunch for I knew he was older than I was and I did not expect to see him again. Pauch was a good acquaintance while my cats were good friends.

As I drove out, brothers Stephen and Gary did show up to speak to me, as did my sisters. I had hoped to see Karen but our separation had begun since last night and I realised I must prepare for four years without her presence and guidance.

As I drove on, I did as I had at the regiment for I stopped and turned around to look back at my home. My mother and my two sisters stood still and waved. Of my father and brothers, there was no sign.

I had with me Gray's to guide me

[Editor's notes: He is referring to the Gray's new book of roads, a guidebook that has not survived yet his first translator, Sedgewick who noted its existence and Driscol's labelling Eccles on the map of Lancashire with the Greek words for 'home' as noted above]

My carriage appeared to be in excellent repair but the horse was a three-year-old mare of indifferent quality and unused to the harness. I made a quick inventory for I had two chest, two bags and a full satchel. I made sure my weapons were loaded and I resolved to make London as soon as I could. I knew the road well now, having traversed it several times, and made plans in my head as to where to stop for the night.

After a long and rather trying day of travel which led me to a poor night's rest, for I had travelled too far and the place I had intended to stop was full of guests, I made to move on to stop at a place less reputable. The horse and carriage had a better night than I for not only was I forced to move all my luggage up to the second floor but the meal was inferior leaden dumplings in a thin sauce served with a clumpy pea soup. The bed appeared un-clean and lousy to my eye so I slept on the floor, using the provided blankets, which seemed cleaner and less used. I had to pay in advance and at higher rate than expected for what I received.

Thursday 8 September

I was relieved to find the horse well fed and watered, and the carriage ready to go. I also found the stable to be under an appreciatively better management than the inn. I left there with a curt comment to the foul proprietor about my displeasure but also left him a more enduring reminder of my displeasure. During the night, as I was un-able to sleep, notwithstanding my weariness, I had taken a candle and written with its smoke onto the ceiling, 'Damn bad quarters by an officer of the King's forces'. I found as I rode on that recalling of this past night's action was most rewarding and it helped to keep the chill out on the road. I half expected the owner to rush after me and demand payment for damages but I had determined that they probably rarely ever visited their own premises. I vowed then and there to not accept such poor lodging again.

I faced another day on the road with my horse doing well but the carriage's back wheels had begun to squeak and in the afternoon to shriek. I found a wheelwright in a village past Birmingham and he set to his task while I lounged in the trees nearby and, having been 'on parade' with regiment for months and under an even tighter inspection while at home, it was good to idle my time away with no immediate cares, and I did nothing in fine style. A squadron of cavalry came up moving smartly in dust covered red uniforms. They were light cavalry but I did not know which regiment. As they stopped to water their horses, I made myself known to a young cornet who quickly summoned the other officers. They were a good lot all. Men of the 14th, returning from Royal escort duty[19]. We quickly found an acquaintance in common, and I was invited to be a guest for supper at the location of their temporary camp that by luck was in the direction of my travel and I agreed happily to do so. I found that this smartly turned out regiment was recently returned to Glasgow, Scotland from duties in Ireland and that two squadron's had escorted John Campbell, 2nd Marquess of Breadalbane, to London and were awaiting his call to escort him home again to Balmoral, hopefully before an inspection in October. Another squadron was at the city of Hamilton taking on similar duties

I made their encampment by late afternoon and found it to be on one of the estates of their absent regimental colonel, Sir Kerrison[20]. They were grandly set up and I was most welcomed. The old hall of Straithedean House was a large two-storey Tedifice set in modest grounds but was rather chilly, hardly equipoise by a large fire that was blazing in a field stone fireplace taller than myself. I was introduced to the officers on duty at the time and given comfortable quarters and a bed which I looked at with anticipation considering my shallow rest of the night before. I was very soon called for to attend to supper at the officer's mess. I was back in uniform and the Red of my coat standing out well from the uniforms of the cavalry that was much commented on by all as they were a shade of scarlet with blue facings. I could thank Lieutenant Mumpsimus for this as I had taken over his uniforms after a tailor had adapted them for me *{see Volume III, Appendix Supplement, for an explanation of the Lieutenant's part in the story}.* As a guest, I sat at the head of the table with an aristocratic looking Captain named Hamilton Charleswitt-Stapleton. He turned out to be a country gentleman of the old school and my companion to my left was the cornet I had just met earlier by the name of R. H. Gall, a thoroughly wild young man and the embodiment of the romantic cavalier.

Unlike my own Regiment's mess, my declining of a drink was not an issue and I found myself supplied with water in a bottle, from the Cachat Source in Savoy, by the *Société des Eaux Minérales.* I found the water delicious and naturally carbonated. I had heard of such things and had tasted such on my two trips to Europe. They gave me several bottles for my use when Charleswitt observed my pleasure in the drink[21]. He stated that no one came to the Regiment's table and went away thirsty!

The supper began with much good-natured shouting and the talk was of horses, the road, horses, beautiful and bewitching women sighted, horse tack and types of girth's seen, and those that rode them well, and horses yet again.

I made one un-intentional blunder; for in my mess, finger bowls were not placed on the table until after the soup course but here they were already on the table. We had stood to drink the Royal toast to the long life of the Crown when R. H. Gall saw that my hand and glass were poised over the finger bowl. This he commented on loudly and the entire proceedings became an uproar of laughter, mock challenges and questions about my Jacobite ancestry. I was quickly told of how holding one's King toast over a finger bowl was considered to be 'drinking to the king over the water', something that would have cost a man his head in days gone by when the Stuart pretender was a challenger to the then sovereign's ancestors, and then residing overseas, 'over the water'. I adjusted my poise and the toast continued. I then had to explain to Mr Vice when he held me to task about this and the method my regiment's table was set. My regiment's table had no finger bowl which was brought out with the first course.

They thought it quite barbarous but suitable for a light infantry regiment. Another Lieutenant interjected that my Regiment had probably done that to avoid just such a misstep *{It had}.* Another toast was made to regimental missteps, to my being from Manchester and a number of other trivial toasts; the most amusing being one rather risqué. A rather large headed, and balding cavalry Captain loudly toasted, 'Hoping that no gentleman, or light infantryman, who fancied dabbing it up with a naughty bobtail in a quiet Cheapside hotel would ever make the mistake to put such a query to a polite woman, or if he did that, she would not understand what he had suggested or, better yet, that she would understand and agree to such a wicked suggestion, proving she was not polite at all'. This was greeted with a thunderous pounding on the table, cries of disgrace and much good cheer.

A contest was then proposed, that the representative of the 52nd to tell three stories and the 14th to respond in kind.

Straithedean House; the estates of regimental colonel, Sir Kerrison of the Emperor's Chambermaids. I-I-7

A Contest Of Tales

Mr Vice called upon me to tell three stories; one about of my regiment in battle, one of honour and one of dishonour. I told first the one of honour. A very recent tale of two officers in the regiment who, in Spain during the Peninsula campaign, had come to blows over the attentions of a fair dark eyed senorita. Ensign Mann and Lieutenant Fleet challenged one another to meet at dawn that very next morning and exchange three shots over her love. A wiser Captain, knowing that passions were high, did not report the duel that would have been against the standing orders prohibiting such. Young officers were to lose their blood only to the French and not one another, and those not following this edict would face the loss of their commissions and return to England in disgrace. As the dawn came quickly in Spain, the Captain had placed himself in an officiating position as the second of the Lieutenant. Both men arrived and, as was the custom, the men met before the exchange of fire to see if an accommodation could be reached. Neither would agree to any such arrangement and the Captain said,

'Gentlemen, this contest is un-equal for the sides are not matched in force, even if both are the same in honour and courage.'

Both the Ensign and Lieutenant were puzzled by this statement and both, despite the enormity of what they were about to do, both neither commented nor understood the remark. Although assailed by guilt and foreboding about what was to soon occur, they felt bound by honour to continue. The Captain un-deterred also continued to try and prevent the occurrence of a misfortune.

'Gentlemen, I say again that this meeting, while well founded in love for a woman, is irregular, un-fair and un-gentlemanly. I pray you reconsider this rash act.'

Both duelers cried, 'What do you mean, sir? We are evenly matched, both lusty and hale and steady with the aim of a pistol and 'tis not a rash act but for the love of woman.'

'Nay, gentleman, you are not, for how can a single Mann of War hope to engage a whole Fleet?' With this the duelist and the seconds fell into a laughter that could not be extinguished for some time. The fate of the lady was decided not by leaden ball but by cutting of cards and their being drawn two equal cards with the value of the suite being discarded both men forswore the Spanish vixen and re-affirmed their friendship and camaraderie.

This story received gentle approval and I received a few moments of mostly faint praise.

I turned to R. H. Gall who rose to defend the honour of the 14th and as I had begun with an affair of honour, he continued on this subject.

A Gentleman of the regiment came some years ago into conflict with a not so gallant man commissioned, they say, in the Royal Marines over comments allegedly made by our regiment's man. A note was sent to him by the bastardly Marine stating:

The Message

Sir, I am sad to relate to you that it has come to me that you did, on such a day and time at the place I believe you will recall you did, rudely and in public announce that my Lady was of doubtful character. I write to you to obtain an explanation of it and if not provided a full apology, must challenge you to account for your disreputable actions. If it comes about that you are not a Gentleman, I will meet you next morning with sword or pistol, as you choose. My man will await your answer.

The Answer

Sir, I do not remember using such an expression referring to your beloved. Nor do I think it likely that I would have done so for I know of no other female in our circle of acquaintances in whose character there can be less doubt.

This brought up a small call of approval and denunciation of all Marines, which is as it should be.

Moreover, it was again my turn I told the next story by standing on my chair:

It was early on the morning of 18th June 1815. It was very early on this day of Waterloo. Our commander, Lieutenant-Colonel Sir John Colborne was placing his soldiers in the dark and forming square behind Major-General Cooke's 1st Division when he encountered other officers doing the same, as there was a battery moving in nearby, he presume them to be artillerymen. At that moment, out of the darkness and down the road came a squadron of cavalry at a canter, scattering everyone from their path. Our commander could hear the artillerymen cursing the equestrians and he replied that he too thought little of this cavalry haughtiness. A cultured voice in the darkness asked what he thought of the cavalry generally.

He replied that he thought the heavy horse to be overweigh louts with more arrogance than courage, the Guards cavalry he knew to be theatrical bounders with weak pretentions to manhood, lancers as catamites with sticks, dragoons as little more than mounted infantry with long knives and short on honour, and all others an affront to nature as the dumber animal is riding EXCEPT the light dragoons who are men never bested on battlefield, bedroom or betting table.

As I told this story the room had gone quite but when I came to dragoons it erupted in a standing ovation when I came to the end. Wisely, I had changed the story for in the real one the light Dragoons were characterised as light on courage, intelligence and the greatest insult of all, horsemanship. At the battle of Waterloo a fight that came to be known as the 'early morning skirmish of June 18th' was fought by words in the dark between the light infantry and the offended officers of the light dragoons, fortunately not the 14th I knew the story as my father had heard the exchange.

Gall had clapped me on the shoulder, pushing me down on the chair as he rose up too and stood on a chair to also emphasis his story.

July 22nd 1812 was a hot day in Spain and it would get hotter still. For Major Brother it was another day to fight the French, twice wounded in previous encounters with French cavalry in the days before he received another wound on his bridle hand, so much so that he had difficulty in handling his horse and worse he had tasted French steel through his body. Despite this he reported for duty but was immediately ordered to rest as he looked like he had risen from the grave. Nonetheless, he joined another regiment, fought bravely which ended only after a horse was shot out from under him and while making his way back, blooded and thrice wounded that day and burdened still with his two previous wounds he was asked by the regimental surgeon, who stood amazed that the man in front of him was not only alive, but that he could still stand but seem desirous of returning to the fray. As Brother stood dripping blood from his wounds he replied to his surgeon question on whether he intended to fight more that day, his resolve left him and he said, "I feel very un-equal to further exertion, as my uniform seems to have a few too many holes in it and it would be indecorous to go about the battlefield improperly dressed'[22].

For my third story, I was about to begin but Charleswitt chided me, 'The last two were excellent but I charge you to come up with something VERY dishonourable.'

I replied, 'Sir, I am sure you are an expert on the dishonourable,' which earned a groan from all. 'I will tell a story I heard from a man with many years' experience in India' - deliberately leaving out that he was a Corporal at the time and my father.

An officer went with a Lady to the governor's ball and all was well until a more senior man began to make advances to his Lady, asking her to dance out of turn and monopolizing the conversation. The Lady, instead of doing what society required, to dismiss this suitor in favour of the man who had brought her, instead began to philander to the newcomer and, with high insolence, dispatched her outraged and jilted original escort to get drinks for the Lady and her new suitor. He did as bided, obtained the drinks and, while beginning to return to his Lady and his competitor, he saw them openly sharing a quick kiss. He detoured quickly behind a stair case and spit into each drink in open view of many other guests who were aghast, for they had observed the taking of his Lady and expected violence or, at best, a loud scene something that just must not happen at a Governor's ball. Silence descended on the ball room, brought about by the whispers passed by those at the party who had observed rejected escorts actions with the drinks.

In the time it took him to walk over to his former Lady and her new interest, everyone in the hall, from the native waiters to the governor himself, had fallen silent and were watching the approaching encounter. He approached the pair who were so lost in one another that they were not aware of what had occurred. He gave them their drinks and stood to one side. All the others in the party watched in silent anticipation. She and her paramour made a toast to one another and drank deeply for it was a hot night in India. The party gasped and then dissolved into an insidious tittering. The two, sensing that the party had stopped and that something was amiss, soon realised to their joint horror that they were the focus of the joke and, promoted too by a not to be un-recalled look from the Governor's wife, departed in some haste. The original escort and diluter of drinks was censored sternly by his colonel for his public action but afterwards was told he had the support of every man in the garrison, from the governor to the lowest private soldier.

This story met with some polite approval but some questioned whether it was dishonourable enough. To which I replied that I had heard two versions of the story: one version for the

Infantry, that I had not told, and another for milksops and cavalrymen; for in one he spits and in another he did something far less wholesome with his privates. This brought about howls of laughter, the denouncement of un-faithful women, praise for the first man and a round of riotous drinking. Gall was about to begin his third story but instead others took up the mantle and insisted on a toast for their guest and a lovely oversized silver cup was brought out. I accepted a small amount of champagne and drank to my own health. This completed, Gall began his last story, which lasted nearly half an hour with plethora of names, regimental details, places, instances, intrigues, reports and finally to the climax and quintessence point of the story. I provide a much-truncated version here as I cannot recall it all now as I sit in bed and write this.

The story begins right after the victorious battle of Vitorio in 1813. The defeated French forces, burdened with the spoils of having looted Spain for several years, attempted to retreat but regiments of British cavalry rode them down. It was the good fortune of the 14th to chase down and capture King Joseph's carriage; a present given him by his Imperial brother Napoleon. One of the items of booty was a linen covered chamber-pot, given the appellation of 'The Emperor' and still held by the regiment who use it now to grant good fortune to their guests by having them drink from it. I realised that this was the 'cup' before me. I was most appreciative of the honour given me perhaps Napoleon himself had handled this pot. I was quite surprised by this as my father had been at the battle and, in all the tales, he told he never once mentioned it. I felt this was good omen.

The meal came and it was something I would expect to be served in Paris for I enjoyed a truly elite meal of creme bresilienne and saumon du rhin bouilli with sauce mousseline. While the rest of the 14th light dragoons drank, I ate and ate very well indeed. By midnight most of the regiment was very drunk. I had been invited previously to join the officers on a foxhunt next morning. Despite my wishing to get on to London, I had yet to ever go on a foxhunt and agreed.

A sketch of Driscol I believe made by an officer of the 14th Light Dragoon and sent to him in India. It probably shows him in his attempt at foxhunting. I-I-8

Foxhunting With The Light Dragoons

With some keenness, I was up early, before dawn but, finding no one around, I made my way to the mess where I found the officers sprawled over the carpets, under tables and across chairs. As I stood there in my travelling clothes, as I had no traditional hunting garb, I was wondering if the hunt was off when the squadron's sergeant major came in with a detachment of men. He greeted me heartily and surveyed the scene with hands on hips. Finding the commander of his regiment prostrate by the embers of the fire he marched over to him, snapped to attention and shouted a loud, 'Sir, GOOD MORNING SIR, WILL THE OFFICERS RIDE THIS MORNING?'

To my astonishment, the lieutenant colonel did not shout a rebuke. Instead, without stirring, he opened his eyes and in a loud clear voice, 'Good morning, Sergeant Major. Please gather up the officers and prepare them to ride out in twenty minutes.'

The Sergeant saluted, then turned with great gravity and grace to motioned to his bevy of corporals and Batmen who spread amongst the un-conscious officers overturning some, lifting heads to peer into un-focussed eyes until they found the ones they maintained. Within twenty minutes, all were mounted. A somewhat clearer head being provided them by the method of dunking their heads repeatedly in ice-cold water, their dress uniforms replaced with riding gear or an odd mix of the two. I viewed Gall strapped to his saddle and seemingly asleep. Charleswitt's servant brought me out a fine little light grey horse that I mounted and found it a good seat, and I was provided 'tea'. I enjoyed the hot water with sugar, having convinced my assigned Batman that I liked to steep my own tea which of course I did not, setting those shredded tea leaves free to kill weeds.

With another ten minutes, the cavalryman in each smashed and drunken man had come to his senses and taken hold, the regiment recovered from a self-imposed drunken rout and was ready to charge forth. Even Gall recovered nicely, even after slipping from his saddle twice to hang off the side of his horse in his straps.

The regimental commander came up to me perfectly dressed and shaved, and he complimented me on my retaining my faculties after a night of drinking he had not realised I had not drunk but a drop. I did not correct his mistake, for I had partaken of a sip of bubbly water from the Emperor's cup and nothing more. We were soon off on the hunt for a fox

As most of the regiment was on escort duty, we had but a dozen or so officers to do the deed. A short discussion occurred with the whipper-in *{the man handling the dogs}*, debating with the Colonel whether they should do some cub hunting as it was September but the Colonel held it was too early and that they would search for their prey in the gorse and blackthorn over the ridge, away from the rising sun. Like a good commander, the colonel arranged that, should no prey be found before noon, a *drag {a bag with fox or other blood to attract the hounds is dragged on the ground}* be obtained and held in readiness. For the morning was wet and I knew the signs from hunting more eatable animals, there was dew in abundance and cobwebs on the grass and the hounds were rolling in the wet and eating the grass and the scent of a fox might be a thing hard to find in these conditions. A bugler was called and equipped with a hunting horn and 'moving off' sounded, and a half a pack of dogs were released and we were off to the ridgeline. Several likely places were checked and found wanting. Even an osier bed *{a streambed full of brush}* was found to be occupied by hares only. A moment was lost to call back in a few of the younger dogs who began to 'run riot', chasing these lesser animals. Then the hounds went into dense brush and part of the party followed them but Gall went around and I followed him with a greater share of the party.

We came at speed towards a hedge intermixed with trees. The line of dragoon riders took to the hedgerow with some joy riding abreast one another. Jumping the fence on line, the first five made it. Those nearer the trees did less well. The first man losing his hat to a tree goblin. Charleswitt struck a sturdier branch which swept up into his face, sending him to one side. His horse being thrown off balance, sank to her knees on the landing, sending the man tumbling ahead. Gall did far worse, for he was knocked off his horse nearly entirely and dragged a short distance with his lower body caught in the straps placed there earlier to keep him in the saddle when we first saddled up, and he was un-conscious from drink. Thusly forewarned, I made the jump with great deliberation but well away from the tree and quickly caught up with Gall's horse after a short gallop through the yellow stubble of the field. Charleswitt's mount had stopped on its own volition and I gather her up too. As I trotted back with their horses, both men had climbed to their feet or released themselves from their restraints Gall covered in dirt and debris down his side and back while Charleswitt was altogether cleaner but sporting some bloody scratches to his face and neck. They said as I came up that I was to never tell the regiment that they had been out jumped by an Ensign of the light Bob's *{the nickname of Driscol's regiment}*. I swore to do so if they would hold as secret my inability to keep up with their companions.

I told Charleswitt that if we were in India, he could blame his wounds on a tiger. He ruefully agreed that it might sound better than losing blood to a swipe from a vengeful larch. Gall took a minute to recover his breath and sense. We mounted up in the chill of the morning and the wind picking up at that moment brought to us the delightfully raucous sound of a foxhunt in the distance. At that exact moment, we all heard the hunting horn sounding 'gone away'. A fox had been found!

We could hear the hunting horn blaring out its call and the faint yelping of the half pack they were in pursuit of their quarry. We were soon on the trail, going with some speed down a declivous patch of grasslands when, nearly a half mile away, we saw the dogs emerge from a small copse, followed a few moments later by the majority of the regiment's officers. They were in chase of a prey we could not see. They were passing to our right and we angled to catch them up when, a quarter of mile away, the dogs turned directly towards us and, in what seemed a moment later, a blur of reddish colouring tore between our horses headed back the way we had come.

I knew enough of cavalry tactics not to try and turn in front of approaching riders and instead we passed through the oncoming horsemen then turned to join them with cries of tally ho! I made an excellent turn, for I was mad with the hunt myself and the horse was trained to it also, and she knew what to do even if the rider was unseasoned.

The fox, it seemed, was not in a hunting frame of mind and had entered a dense thicket near where R. H. Gall and Charleswitt had been bested by the tree. Other men had gone to circle it while the dogs could be heard barking away within the darkness of the *Prunus spinosa* and we dallied a moment taking to feasting on the berries which having been seasoned by frost and had lost the hard bitterness that make them un-eatable except in the fall after it freezes. Suddenly, the sound of 'doubling the horn' could be heard someone had sighted that troublesome fox again. We were away again. In some confusion, my horse crossed Gall's, delaying us both, and it took a minute to catch Charleswitt who was off like a swallow through the sea of stunted grass.

We came up to him and were moving towards the sound when, coming up, from a draw we were shocked to see coming at us that which is most frighten; not a French lancer regiment charging down on us but across our front a solid line of dark clouds coming quickly in our direction. A chilly wind caught us at sea we would call it a squall. As we were atop a small rise, we could see nearly a quarter of mile ahead of us the rest of the party. They too had stopped at this sign from nature that perhaps this fox really did not wish to be part of a hunt. We waited and a moment later came the sound, the sad notes of 'going home'.

The fox would have its revenge, for a rain of Biblical proportions fell on us well before we returned; nothing being sadder than wet cavalry men denied their hunt except hounds denied it too.

As we returned in this downpour, the squadron commander, lieutenant colonel whose-name-I-do-not-recall, came to speak to me. The gist of his words was that the regimental officers would be pleased if I came into the regiment. I seemed more a light cavalryman than a pedestrian infantryman. I thanked him greatly, for I had to admit that one night with these men had been more pleasant that the stifling atmosphere of the 52nd. I did ask what the market was at this time, and the price he stated for a cornet's rank *{the same rank as an infantry ensign}* was nearly four times as much and the cost of keeping one's expenses up would be nearly six times higher. The cost for fox hunting alone being nearly 500 pounds per annum. In all, it was a financial impossibility for one such as myself. I told the *{lieutenant}* colonel such, saying that my 'estate' would not permit such a pleasure and that was one reason behind my going east. I could see then that the Major had meant the invitation as a compliment and perhaps was taken aback that I considered it a serious offer. Nonetheless, he said that I was to consider myself an honorary member of the regiment and their mess was my mess for all time. To this, I agreed, for what else could one say?

We returned in low spirits and as soon as we arrived, we had some Irish luck and the rain began to lessen and between my changing clothes and coming outside again the rain had stopped but the clouds seemed to promise more moisture.

The 14th had returned to its duties and I made my way to the gate in my carriage, thanking those officers I could find. Seeing no way to graciously remain, I headed out, leaving a note thanking all and particularly R. H. Gall, Charleswitt, the lieutenant colonel and, of course, the absent commander whose estate I had enjoyed.

I was dressed rather grandly in my best clothes, as my other set was completed wetted, I could not officially travel in my uniforms, as I was on leave. I determined to make London, as I had tired of the road and the weather was threatening. I knew too well the impossibility of moving along these roads if they became sodden, for the mud here was known to swallow wagon's whole.

Friday 9 September

After the foxhunting noted above, I declined to fritter away my time and made a fast pace towards London. I had to arrive, find where the carriage and horse could be returned then make my way to my quarters. I had never been to London in my life, my father having avoided the place, which he considered un-pleasant and dangerous. He had mentioned several 'rookeries' or places I should avoid and emphasised that I should stay away from the locality of St. Giles *{poor section of London, tenements, den of thieves}*. The country continued to be extremely agreeable. There was no continuation of the rain, which was fortunate as the soil here was chalk and makes for a mud that hinders one's travel. The road, in time, came to be completely straight and carried on so for many miles, it being the site of a Roman military way. The road filled with traffic of all kinds. No threat of brigandage here if they had ventured on to the road, their chances of being run down by its volume would be high.

It was late afternoon when I arrived on the outskirts of London. My excitement grew, for I was a young man entering a city I knew little about except from books. The skyline was enticing. I did know that I would live like a 'True Gentleman' for a few days or so, and that I was looking forward too. From a map drawn by my brother Gary who had been to London many times, I found without difficulty the premises of the concern my father had arranged my carriage. I turned over horse and carriage and they provided a four-wheeled growler wagon and I took a fine ride into the north of London. Being no longer concerned with bringing my own carriage safely in and figuring directions, I enjoyed the views. Many walls, I saw, were plastered with signs and emblems of places and things I did not fully understand but here and there I saw names I had seen in the Manchester Weekly Journal.

I enjoyed the sight of Palace of Westminster that still showed signs of the fire, which had destroyed it. I saw many fine sights until I came to my destination.

London in a fanciful depiction. I-I-9

Driscol enters London. I-I-10

The Oriental Club

Our resourceful Adjutant had made good use of the virtuous reputation the 52nd had with the club. Our regiment had served in India with great success for many years. As my Commander had made clear to me in my instructions before I had departed our barracks that to not stop at the club when in London was both a mistake and a tragedy. I named the club and its location to my coachman, who replied in a horrid manner of speech that he knew it well. The substance of his reply was that Gentleman could find good lodging and the fiery cookery of the east but that it is populated with faded, cripple and jaundiced men living out the rest of their lives on health-earned pensions; having traded with the devil for gold, they had the gold but not good health. Armed with his editorial opinion on matters of no concern to him, I issued a rebuke for his insolence and told him to drive on without further ado. That he was a retired sergeant was evident by his sharp salute and knowing grin, for he gained his amusement by tweaking a junior officer; always a sport of much delight to all good non-commissioned officers.

I arrived at the stately three-storey building and rolled up. The driver whistled and I was buried instantly under a flurry of black livered men who pounced on me as if my luggage were plumb birds and they hungry cats. I gave the man his fare and a generous tip and he saluted again, told me his regiment, The Saucy Greens *{36th (Herefordshire) Regiment of Foot}* for he had served thirty years, and told me to be sure when I arrived in India *'To put Nebuchadnezzar out to grass'.* The phrase I did not understand but, given the quality of his regiment, it was probably foul and un-mentionable.

[Editor's note: Driscol came back and penciled in its meaning in October learned as he noted, from Perkins. It meant to conduct sexual intercourse with wild abandon]

I was soon in the finest room I had ever seen. I was congratulating myself on my good fortune when a smartly set up servant appeared to inform me that supper would be served shortly and asked if I needed assistance in dressing for supper. I did, as I had no civilian dinner jacket but he informed me that my uniform would do nicely and he took it away with my boots. In what seemed only a few moments he returned them in immaculate condition and with the boots shining in such a way as to make a guardsman envious. He certainly did finer work than my old Batman Alyson had done in the past. Supper would be at 7 o'clock and would cost 12s; a large sum if I thought I might have to pay for it myself but our beloved Adjutant had also fixed that these meals would be at regiment expense using up the last of my September mess dues - and greatly to my advantage.

Well-dressed and feeling less anxious having completed my journey, I admired the many portraits of Indian administrators and battle heroes that graced the halls of the establishment. I made my entrance with minutes to spare. There were twenty or so elderly Gentlemen at the tables and they paid no mind to me at all, although some appeared feeble. I could not help but notice that some had bright ginger, brown and black hair. It would seem the East had agreed with them. The table was nicely set and I was provided with bread, potatoes, a selection of cheese, a substance I presume was beer and a cruet filled with vinegar. I amused myself until the rice and curry arrived. It came in fine time for it was a Turnham green pigeon done in a reddish curry sauce - much unalike my own mother's yellow curry. The waiter most kindly informed me that it was a Masala or Bengali curry and I found its burning substance objectionable but eatable. It was served with a white celery soup seasoned with Cheshire cheese that I used to cool my mouth between bites of fiery food. The desert was something I could not recognise but it seemed eastern in origin and smelled of roses that I did not find palatable. From the table about me I heard much talk that glorified our rule in India while censuring the current crop of politicians for neglecting what the victory at Plassey and against the French had granted us. There was talk of Hindostaun, of hideous massacres, of adventures in Poona, tiger hunting, hunting boar with spear on horseback - overall a good way to get one's blood to boil with zeal. I do believe I heard reference to Calcutta, Madras and Bombay continuously.

I did ask the steward about one condiment that came with the curry, something called Major Grey's Chutney. I had not heard of it before. Instead of answering, he begged my pardon, went off to another patron, and brought that man back to me. He introduced me to a Lieutenant Colonel Grey, the son of the Major in question, recently retired from India after being in the service of the Nizam of Hydrabad's 3rd Regiment of Infantry. I was most pleased to meet him. He explained that his father has spent three and thirty years in India and had loved their food immensely. When he returned to England he set about to produced his own chutney to replace that which he could no longer find. It had in it lime, mango, onion, raisins, spices, sugar, tamarind and white vinegar. He had just retired, having been born in India. He wished me well in my duties and he had the steward bring me three free bottles to take with me. I had not the heart to tell him I found the stuff revolting and when I could I returned them to the kitchen as I suspected taking chutney to India would be like taking coals to Newcastle or mud to the Netherlands.

After the meal, I went to the common lavatory and noticed that the hairbrushes were discoloured and dirty, and mentioned this to the boy in charge. The lad replied, 'Please sire, that is not dirt, it is dye off the Gentlemen's heads'. I found that droll and returned to my room with the desire to read and rest, for I had London to explore before Monday came and I could report in to the offices of the East India Company. I had asked the staff how I might bathe, for bathing on a transport is either not at all or under a stream of seawater from a pump in full view of the deck. I decided to indulge my cleanliness needs while in London. I was told that with some two and thirty guests and only two tubs it would either have to be very early or very late. I selected very early for my ablutions.

I asked the servant what the dues were for the club. The admission money to the Oriental Club is twenty pounds; the annual subscription is eight pounds. So, for me the cost would equal a third of my salary for one year, and that is without the cost of the food and lodging being extra of course all well beyond my feeble reach at this time.

To arise early to obtain a bath was no difficulty, for my father had never slept more than four hours in his life while my mother never slept less than nine and I was fortunate to need only six unless I was greatly tired. Rest eluded me and I was soon up and dressed again, and wandered the halls stopping in the club's library. I secured a volume by Lieutenant John Shipp[23] a Lieutenant in the 87th Infantry, which I read with much interest, then induced sleep by taking up Taylor's book that I had received as a gift, taking notes with an eye to the future.

The Oriental Club where Driscol stayed during his time in London, this photograph is from 1901. I-I-11

Preparations In London

Saturday 10 September

I bathed in the large copper tubs and found the bath an experience I could not fault in any way, so much so that I vowed to do so each day as the cost was minimal and I thought it might even be covered by the mess bill.

Having dressed in my recently sponged and brushed clothes, I set off in the early morning to walk about London and do a great deal of legal pillage and looting. I skipped breakfast, hoping to be very hungry for a much thought of dinner at one of the famous eateries of London.

I made my way through the streets, often stopping to consult the best map I had, which was at best incorrect, and at worse misleading. However, I did find the street I sought and after some delay arrived at Truefitt's, a Gentleman's barber shop at 40 Old Bond Street but they were too busy to take me, there being some minor MP *{members of Parliament}* in need of shaving (or, if my father was here, to have a needed cutting of the throat). I found my way by asking passersby, buying a few trifles in the various shops that I required on 314½ Oxford Street, until I arrived at the Mekkah *{Mecca}*. It was James Purdey & Sons Limited where I was warmly greeted, for they saw me immediately for what I was; a young Gentleman on his way to the east, and in need of armament.

They most kindly took on board my declaration of limited funds and produced a number of possibilities. One of their boys went to another dealer and soon appeared with what I had requested; a combination shotgun rifle, fired by percussion and in the general style and manner of the Danish designer Valentine Marr, similar to a weapon my maternal grandfather had had. This was also Danish made but by a designer, I did not know. I soon held in my hands a fine weapon; not an ornament but a working weapon, not new but in excellent condition. The stock was of traditional oiled walnut with a strip of paler wood atop the shoulder stock, a butt plate of buffalo horn with a forestock displaying a slight checkering pattern. It is un-deniably a fine-weapon indeed, with a muzzle loading, 10 bore lower smooth barrel and atop it, a rifled barrel of double that bore. Two triggers, fore-and-aft, within a robust trigger guard. I bought it immediately and obtained one hundred rounds for each barrel, seven hundred grain *{1.6 ounces}* for the lower and much less for the upper, which was .60 calibres, a cleaning kit and sealed tins of percussion caps. I was much determined to use percussion despite the opinions of many in the light infantry that the test at Woolwich in 1834 *{where the British army has tested percussion versus flintlock for muskets}* was flawed. I firmly followed Reverend Forsyth observation that birds *{and by extension - men}* had learned to avoid shot by taking wing on sighting the initial puff of smoke from a flintlock powder pan. The percussion caps corrected this by giving a shorter interval between pulling the trigger and the shot leaving the muzzle.

I had the gun tooled for a heavy pull for the shotgun and a lighter for the rifle. I was then able to go out the back and fire a few rounds. The discharge from the lower barrel was substantial but I considered that when making up the paper cartridges used in the weapon I would lessen the powder by a fifth. The rifle I was more pleased with finding I needed no adjustment to my way of shooting, hitting the target after only one miss slightly to the left. The gun clerk assured me in all seriousness that the upper barrel would induce a tiger to charge and the lower to deliver his death. The sights were the common iron ones.

Driscol's drawings of his new weapon's sight and the image obtained. The first editor Sedgwick had added the word 'Lyman' but that technology wasn't used in Driscol's time and the true Lyman sight was not created until 1879. The writing in the drawings below is by Sedgwick. A man named Leeman made a similar sight in Driscol's time and this may be what we are seeing. I-I-12

I asked about pin-fire pistols but received a rather stony reply that they did not deal in such items.

They showed me how to make up the paper cartridges, to oil them and how to insert the percussion caps, I had ten cartridges made up and sealed in a waterproof packet. I had the establishment secure the gun for transport overseas and then sent by messenger to the club.

I thanked them all, for they had treated me as royalty and I could see why everyone I had met had recommended their institution. I was glad to have visited here based on the advice of those had come before and granted them all a small gratuity which was well received. Somewhat lessened in wealth, I continued my ransacking campaign, heading for the legendary culinary stop of the Blue Posts. On my way, I came across a shop at 15 St. Johns Square. A Mr Ross was most helpful and I secured for my use a pair of used japanned *{black lacquered painted}* brass Galilean style glasses *{binoculars}* of French merchant navy make of x 6 power plus a new leather case and sold as *Jumelles {opera glasses}*. The case was new and made up for them and, notwithstanding my having a telescope; I thought these would be more serviceable in the field.

French maritime binoculars similar to what Driscol purchased. I-I-13

I had brought down with me from Eccles the telescope given me on my 15th birthday of four powers, set in wood and made by Harris, Thos. & Son, London but, by discussion with veterans of India, I had been informed that telescopes were considered old-fashioned and they were more suited to observations of the heavens than any military work.

I found without difficulty the tavern on Bennet Street. The two famed 'Blue Posts', two cerulean painted poles, stood proudly in the forecourt adorned with a fading advertisement for a fleet of sedan chairs which used to ply for hire but were sadly no more having been replaced by carriages some years back.

I had a disappointing luncheon at the eatery. The fare was good; a goodly portion of baked goose with plum sauce, but what made it less thought-provoking and therefore disappointing was that the establishment NOT being filled with presentable Ladies, a fact sworn to be the case just a few days ago in my regiment's mess. Somewhat defeated by no visions of fashionable beauties, I consumed a fine dish of stewed apples with cinnamon to drown my sorrow. After the meal I detoured from my tour to view the hastily repaired but still incomplete Houses of Parliament which had burned down two years prior. This made me sad to see.

I returned to weapon hunting, finding what I needed in the store window of a shop selling Dutch goods. In it was what I sought; a *Zakrevolver Lefaucheux {Lefaucheux style pocket revolver}* made by S. de Jager. These fired a conical lead bullet from a copper base and cardboard powder cartridge, the weapon taking five cartridges of .51 calibres. The pistol was all of metal with ebony handgrips but much lighter than the horse pistols I had used before. They un-fortunately had no holster, as its designer made it a pocket pistol but the weapon had a ring set in the bottom of the grip to which I intended to secure with a lanyard. I purchased one forthwith, along with a box of two hundred pin-fire water proofed cartridges while being warned by the shopkeeper that such cartridges might be difficult to secure in India. Having left the shop, I returned after a few minutes reconsideration and bought a second cylinder, which could be quickly changed instead of the reloading the cartridges in an empty cylinder, something that struck me as both slow and dangerous if in battle. I had considered trying to do that on horseback and thought twice about it. With cartridges, additional cylinder and pistol secured, I continued my wanderings, planning to have the necessary lanyard made by the artisans of India.

I went to Burton Street and viewed the Museum of the Zoological Society, and that of the East India house which merits some attention, if only for the eastern manuscripts it had. Some of which I could make some understanding of if only to spell out the words.

It was now late in the afternoon and I had wandered long and far but found myself near Covent Garden. I went to see Drury-lane and whatever it might contain, and gifted myself to see at the park theatre the play, *Cataract of the Ganges*. I found the plot hard to follow but the scenery was spectacular. The heroine, Zamine, rode her horse to safety by leaping over the artificial waterfall. It was a spectacle indeed! It was a succession of splendid and gorgeous scenes, with almost magical effects, with beautiful horses; arrayed in all the trappings of eastern magnificence, gold chariots pulled by fine steeds dripping in purple and gold. The play's actors and actresses paraded about in glittering princely apparel and making heroic speeches. All this passed before me in a dazzling parade. While sitting there, a cold chill ran down my back when I realised that I had left a cartridge in the newly purchased pistol. I secretly checked to make sure the hammer was not cocked. It was, of course, not but the incident ruined the mood of my delight.

Two streets that Driscol walked down during his time in London. 1-1-14 & 15

Ascalon

Having walked ten English miles that day, I made it back to the Club, happy in the fact that I could find it and still more when I found that all my purchases were sitting on the floor by my bedstead. I was quite happy to find them safely there. They came ready for travel but, nevertheless, I opened the packages and was admiring the weapons when one of the elderly servants came to enquire about my supper plans. He said it was a most handsome weapon, and it was. I named it Ascalon; the spear that Saint George had used to kill his dragon. I was resolved to give it a correct classical god's name but could think of none at the time except Hades' <u>Bident</u>, but it did not seem the right name for such a fine firearm. I was sorry that the Greek Gods had not had firearms. I thought a thing that had cost a month and a half of pay should be so grandly named.

I found that the servant was a most clever man, for by checking with me, he received the tip for having secured the packages in my room. I was, however, embarrassed that I had no small coins but he took a larger coin and returned in time with the correct change all beautifully shined. I asked how that was and he said it was a tradition of the club to shine all coins with a leather buff before returning it to a guest. I thought this an agreeable, if somewhat wasteful, ritual.

Supper was mulligatawny; a pepper-water soup that I found poisonous in its seduction while it tortured and burned my mouth, throat and stomach but I could not help sampling it until it was gone. I followed this with something more sedate; a Melton Mowbray pork pie, the waiter having offered up two styles; the traditional that I partook and a club special spiced to perdition, I suspected, with India aromatic herbs and molten lead. During the meal I was kindly addressed by two old company (HEIC) veterans at the next table who gave me their good wishes but, as they had been 'fighters of paper battles', the conversation languished at times, for my knowledge of India bureaucracy being most fortunately limited.

One told an interesting story, which I asked permission to write down, and they retold it so I could record it so. They spoke of how I was now doing the opposite of the Doolally tap, for I was, in fact, bouncing my leg up and down under the table a nervous trait my mother use to confront me on often at the dinner table. They said that in India they had a name for that 'tap', it being the before mentioned Doolally tap which was done by those who were waiting for a ship to leave India. This waiting was done at the main hospital at Deolali, for to die of fever while waiting to leave was deemed unsavory by the administration and the solution was to have men wait out there time at the hospital during times of peace. There the many hopeful, anticipating to return home to England waited and waited. All had to pause, from the richest to the poorest. *{Because in the time of sail driven transport, no schedule could be kept}* The men who waited had been discharged for many reasons; illness, lunacy, honourable retirement; and they consisted of civilians and soldiers all who waited and waited. It all sounded rather melancholy.

They also spoke of companions, list of names lost to illness, madness. They also advise me to,

'Beware the sun my boy beware the *sun* or *sooraj*, native guile, eastern religions, native women and drink, mighty killing drink'.

It was only at the end that I found out who these men were, for their names meant nothing to me. When we did our introductions it was my kindly waiter who added title and history for the two long-term residents who had had the much sought-after covenant status[24]. They had not just shaken the Pagoda tree, they had brought back a branch each.

So it was the London version of the Doolally tap that I did as I, too, waited for a ship.

That night my extremities were stiff and I read and finished Shipp's book. I had asked about him at the club and one man had happily known him. I was sad to hear that he had passed just a few years ago at the age of only fifty. The man who had known him said, 'For a man to have won his commission from the ranks is always a rare achievement but to do so TWICE before the age of thirty makes it an extraordinary accomplishment despite his acting in ways not always considered to being on the path of a true Gentleman.' Considering my father had done the same, too *{twice been awarded a commission on the battlefield}* I was filled with admiration for him for he had never told me how un-usual it was for it to have occurred.

Sunday 11 September

I rouse and had another satisfying bath and then entered into the less satisfying Sabbath day but there was no stultifying regimental church parade to neither attend or avoid by taking on odious military duties, nor even my mother's Methodist upbringing to make the day one of boredom. I remember fondly playing with a wooden Noah's ark until I was old enough to follow my brother's suggestions of escaping outside and into the surrounding countryside. This strict adherence to Sabbath keeping had disappeared when I was thirteen. The family had begun to stop going to either Methodist or the Church's *{of England}* services. Now, on my own, I could do as I pleased. As food would not be easy to obtain, I breakfasted at the club in high style. I had come into the dining room set on an English breakfast but was persuaded to sample the eastern variety. I had a lentil omelette, which I found rather flavoursome but passed on an early morning potato curry. I was still suspicious of potatoes in general and took instead some good cold English veal tongue, a small amount of a rissole with a probable occult background and a large plate of deviled bones, deviled eggs and even a deviled mutton chop, in honour of the Sabbath. Having spent an hour just eating, I knew nothing un-mindful could be done today. I queried the always-helpful tablemates and waiters. I soon found that I was very mistaken. The Sabbath did not shut down the city like towns around Manchester. This was London and London was no quaint provincial town.

A list of suitable opportunities was given out and I selected an evening of dancing at the Vauxhall Gardens. Not that I liked dancing, for I loathed it. However, I thought it might have some ladies to examine. I found, too, that the bookstores would be open around Piccadilly and nearby streets. Despite the full breakfast, I headed out as soon as I could into a grey forbidding day. I took with me my new revolver finding a feeling of security in having it along. I soon found that its weight made carrying it in my pocket difficult and I secured it in my waist, checking often to make sure that it was un-cocked, and finally stopping in a park and removing one cartridge so that it could not possibly fire.

I made my way through the cold day to Piccadilly. I passed by the famous Fortnum & Mason store which my mother had often mentioned. I had not thought to visit it but, viewing what it had in its windows, I decided to give it my custom as soon as I could. Next door at 187 Piccadilly was Hatchards', a famous book store, but I could see no discernible sign that it was open and was about to leave when a man with a heavy iron key appeared from behind me and asked if I was going east and did I wish to purchase some books? I had to agree that I was and planned to do so.

Again, they knew me as a man going overseas to the east! I wondered if my forehead was marked with a Hindoo trident? Was there some easterly mark of Cain on me?

I then enjoyed what was probably the best few hours of my young life; books, books and more books; floors of books and all that I could purchase and buy, not just borrow and read! So intent was I that the day passed only interrupted by helpful clerks who, I must say, where the liveliest, the kindest, the civililest and the patientest of men I had met in the great city, observing my searches, made many useful suggestions and having trained them early on NOT to offer me tea, I continued my hunt for readable books.

I secured some books and arranged to have them 'India proofed' sealed in tin containers with molten lead and wax. I also selected six and twenty for reading on the ship. The shop owner also made a point to give me his particulars vowing to send me any book I might need by ship. He proudly said that he could get a book to India within six months now with some regularity. His prices were outrageous but I could not fault neither the supply nor its organisation, which was by subject AND author, the books being duplicated for a hunters ease.

[Editor's note: Driscol has listed the books he bought, which I have placed in the Chapter notes but part of the inventory is lost, torn across the bottom. See the list[25]]

Taking one book and a pamphlet with me, the pamphlet being the *Cryptographia or the Art of Deciphering by David Arnold Conradus, List of the interpreted cipher words of a French cipher Description*, and although not signed I am sure it was penned by Major Scovell whom my father knew and had worked with during the Peninsula War. The other book being a hard to find Latin classic I had heard much about but never read, Vegetius' *De Re Militari* coupled with a partial English translation of the work by Lieutenant John Clarke. Delight!

I found also a shop that would have delighted the angler Izaak Walton. They had a full selection of fishing tackle and fripperies but I had in this area all that I needed and had brought down from home my twelve foot three-sectioned bamboo pole and a brass bait casting reel made in Scotland, a gift given to me on my 16th birthday. I also had a wide selection of the best cast iron and brass hooks and all other matters related to fishing. Therefore, I did not need to linger in this shop overlong.

Vauxhall Gardens. I-I-16

I made my way to Vauxhall Gardens in the late afternoon to listen to the music said to be there and perhaps to see the types of people who might come to such a place. I toured it grounds and enjoyed the Grand South Walk with Handel's Statue and the Chinese temple. I stayed until it opened and listened to the music, enjoying a song I later learned was the *Lass of Richmond Hill* and the *Dashing White Sergeant*. I sampled some ham that was, somehow, sliced so thin, one could see through it, and surprisingly good custard. The dancing had started by now and I was of a mind to escape, for I hate to dance.

If I should ever start my own church, its first rule will to forbid men to dance and to make it a sin for women to not. Instead, they must dance, alone and in the view of appreciating men. Such were the lesser of my sinful thoughts this night.

I was standing out of the way, enjoying the music and swirling women when two red-haired women, twins in look and dress, came up with Lieutenant Richard Gall of the 14th Light Dragoons to greet me and grasp my hand. He was down in London and whom did he spy? He introduced me to his cousins, Patricia and Philomena Barton. How can a man refuse two ladies of such beauty? They were both comely and I did my best to dance with them, enjoying their company but disliking the pirouetting. The hours passed and I was completely befuddled as to which was which but by luck I noted that Patricia had the smallest imperfection on the cuff of her left limb. For it was she that seemed most interesting and as my interest in her grew, coldness came over Philomena. Their father was a well-to-do surgeon and they were un-abashedly looking for husbands, for at the elder age of 19 they were eager, it seemed, to leave their family home. They were even thinking of joining the 'fishing fleet'[26] in the autumn of this year. Being that I was un-married and would be in India at that time, I secured their interest and, as Mr Gall had fortunately disappeared in the limbs of a Cornish woman some time ago, I took to escort them home, they sadly declining my several offers to dine. Patricia dismissed her now sullen sister as we stood on the steps of her two-storey house located on the edge of the fields of White City. We agreed to remain in touch and I was thinking madly of taking her hand when her mother appeared, introductions made, and I was politely chased off the premises.

Ascalon a Danish made combination rifled musket and smoothbore shotgun, in an 'over and under' configuration, 60. Caliber rifle, 10-bore shotgun. I-I-17

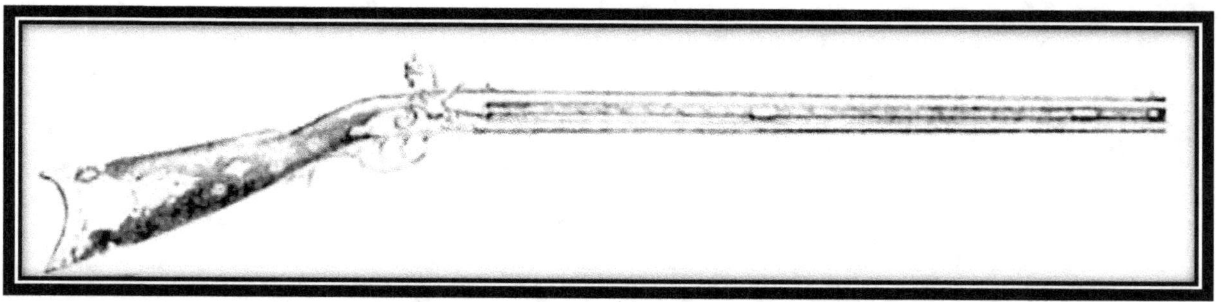

A later model of the French Lefaucheux type pin-fire revolver bought by Driscol, he never noted which model he obtained. I-I-18

The Honourable East India Company

Went to the East India Company main offices. I got up early this morning and put on my uniform, gathered up my associated paperwork and I presented myself at the East India House on Leadenhall Street. The building's facade consists of a portico of six fluted Ionic columns but otherwise it was plain and all right angles. To me, the massive construction reflected the strength and fortitude of the great company. I had come too early, of course, *{Driscol always came unfashionably early}* and was told to come back in thirty minutes. I took this time to explore the building, for few were the doors that were locked or even guarded a very different attitude prevails here versus other public buildings in London. The interior is fitted up in a fashion that associates sophistication with convenience and several of the rooms are very spacious. The rooms are rich with Oriental curiosities; in the museum are numerous trophies and reminders of British victories in India. I found and viewed the great oval ceiling painting called *The East Offering Its Riches To Britannia* in the Revenue Committee Room. I thought the painting yet another good omen of my future success.

I returned to the same clerk who had dismissed me before but this time he had me take a seat in one of the mooghal *{Mughal}* style teak chairs in the hall and I waited. As time went by, I found that I, an Ensign, was joined by two Colonels, a Naval Captain, three cavalry Captains and a desolate looking Royal Marine artillery Major. Summoned first, but I was curtly stopped at the desk by a functionary, and in my stead one of the Colonels was allowed to proceed before me, and another hour was lost. I was then called in, and presented myself to a grey man in dark grey clothes who took no notice of my splendid uniform or my smiling face.

Driscol came to East India House to arrange his passage to the east and obtain his orders. 1-1-19

He looked at my papers, shuffled them around in his own and found a match of some sort. He wrote out a few notes on another piece of paper and with no sound a young man came forward and took up the papers, motioned me to follow him and I did so, telling myself at one point not to march in step with him. So was my first meeting with my future employer, the Honourable East India Company. The next man stood to greet me; he shook my hand and made me most welcome. For once, I was not annoyed by his offer of tea, which I declined as graciously as I could. He did his business then handed me a number of sheets of papers, covered with wax seals, India-ink stamps and signatures galore.

'One for this office, these two for that office and then come back here', he said slowly as if I were some dunce. I did as he directed with willing alacrity, receiving at the first office my official orders making me a supernumerary to the East Indian Army for four years and it ordered me to report to a Mr William Ransacke in the East India Company offices in Bombay *{Mumbai}* for my appointments. I received two months' pay in advanced, all in gold sovereigns, at the second office, which I much appreciated and I took a moment or two to transfer these to a money belt that a club member had suggested as a means of securing ones wealth. The good man had also provided it *gratis*, the clerks took no notice of a light infantry officer removing his blouse and strapping on a belt laden - in my mind - with un-told golden riches. At this moment, I was richer than I had ever been in my life or could have hoped to be. I then received a billet for a cabin on a ship called *William Fawcett* of the Peninsular Steam Navigation Company to transport me to Gibraltar where I was to present a bill of travel to the HEIC resident for my future method of travel. They gave me their address, and directed me to make arrangements or adjustments as suited me.

I was somewhat put off by leaving England in a commercial ship and not one of his Majesties transports or, better yet, an East Indiaman. However, the weight of my gold-filled money belt overrode any annoyance. I then completed my tasks and reported to the pleasant man. He seemed the happiest man in the world to receive my completed paperwork. He reviewed my recent collection of signatures, nodded his head and sent me, after another deftly applied stamp, back to the un-pleasant man who was still un-pleasant but he took this last piece of paper up acting like he had never seen the like of it before and that it might attack him at any moment. He studied it for some time, making three notes in two different ledgers, then he turned his head up and actually wished me good luck and bon voyage with the slightest of upturned eyes. I asked him if he knew if a Lieutenant Perkins was on the list to travel in the same ship. He gave me a look of offended officialdom, when asked to give out information only they were privy too, but he could not think of a reason NOT to tell me that, so yes a Lieutenant Perkins was so listed.

I went immediately to No.122 Leadenhall Street and found without difficulty the offices of the steamship company. They took my papers and informed me it was for a second-class passage that was worth 9£ 10s and for a mere 3£ 2s more I could have first class. I had with me an envelope given by my adjutant containing just that sum. The 52nd took such care of its officers. I did so, as the cabin would not be that much better but I would be allowed 2 cwt of luggage *{224 pounds or 101 kilograms}* and as I had close to that amount I thought it was a good idea. The voyage on average took eight to ten days and depending on local conditions the ship might berth, or not, at Vigo, Oporto, Lisbon, Cadiz and certainly Gibraltar. It was there *{Gibraltar}* that the balance of my regiment had recently been garrisoned but I knew from the papers that a substantial number of them were now in Portugal supporting the government of Maria II against the instability caused by the rebellion *{An aftermath of the Liberal War 1828-1834}* and the current civil war in Spain *{First Carlist War}*.

Since I felt quite rich, I took a carriage to a sight I wished dearly to see. The Artillery grounds and house where the oldest regiment in England had once been accommodated I had seen an image of Artillery House and thought it would be masonry but found it was brick. In uniform, I gained entrance and was treated as royalty. Had family tradition and finances not been as they were I would have enjoyed attending Woolwich and the becoming an artillery officer.

Artillery House. I-I-20

My next stop was to Coutts and Co. where I exchanged half of my gold for one of their popular circular notes, which I hoped to leave unused until I could exchange it into a bank in Bombay. I had the note prepared in the eastern way and I was allowed to watch. The parchment, after being dated, signed, stamped and embossed, was placed between two plates of clear class, the edges sealed with wax and the plates placed in a wooden case the size of a book and stitched into an oiled leather bag, which itself was well coated with wax again - water proofing of the finest kind.

I returned to the Club somewhat apprehensive because of one months' worth of gold I carried along with the circular note worth another months pay, and me without a weapon on any kind for showing up armed at the offices of the HEIC was frowned on. I arrived without difficulty and changed into my best clothes again, having supped un-usually well on some tender but well spiced beef covered in rosemary, basil, and savoury. I was in high spirits. I realised now that nothing less than a full-blown European war would stop my going to India. I did so hope that the bear, vulture and frog *{Russia, Prussia and France}* would remain calm for a few days more.

That afternoon I gifted myself with a visit to two contrasting sights. The first was a visit to Moorfields to view the edifice put up by government for the comfort and care of the insane. My father had often railed against such an expense and officers of the Light Dragoon's had spoken of the delightful tour one could have of the inmates of Bethlem *{Bedlam insane asylum}*. One of the senior officers had been related to James Lewis, the architect of the construction, and had recommended an excursion. The driver of my conveyance was full of stories about which lunatics and women to visit, and what they did to justify their incarnation in that place.

Despite my misgiving that arose in me by the remarks of the driver. I did make it to the structure and found it a large fine building. I paid the entrance fee and made a short tour. One man I found chained to his bed and he lay screaming that demons were on and about him. I hurriedly completed the tour and I must express my distaste for such an entertainment of what else I saw I will not put to paper. I rejoined the same hackney whom had brought me out and who was quite vocal about wanting to know why I had not liked the site or its amusements. I mollified him by asking him to take me to my next stop and I suggested I would pay him more for the trip if he made no ill comments he complied post-haste.

We arrived in the vicinity of the four-storey Astley's Amphitheatre in London. I exited the hackney well short of it. I did so, so I could see view the neighborhood. I walked up to it by Lambeth road and found the cream coloured circus establishment on Westminster Bridge Road which stood in a charming stand of woods although the roads leading to the site were in sad condition. I had decided on this expedition some months before when I had seen and read in the papers the short story by Charles Dickens, Sketches by Boz where it mentioned Ashley. I was disappointed to find that Pablo Fanque[27] would not be performing, as he was still up north. I secured a place in a third floor box and settled down to watch the coming and goings of the customers. I was more charmed and entertained by the odd characters in the audience than with the display of the circus. I found the comic performers less than witty, the clowns too outlandish and the tragedians more wretched than moving. The orchestra was fine and I devoted my time to observing the actions of a maiden to my right. The horsemanship and display was, I had to admit, of the best quality but I was happy when the long show ended.

I was waiting in the box for the rush of people to clear the stairs when I was spoken to from behind my back, not in English but Danish. I soon found myself speaking with a well-dressed man, whom I found was Henry Williams-Wynn, MP and the British Ambassador to Denmark, now in England on the business of the Crown. He had thought I was a Dane and had come over to speak to me. I secured an invitation to his house in Kensington, on Sloane Street for supper the next night. What luck to gain an invite to an actual ambassador's residence?

Having exchanged cards with the gentleman, I then accepted his invitation to ride with his wife and he to the club. As we passed through the crowds, I saw some distressing scenes of the sort I had seen more often than I cared to in London. The lower class of actors were seen on public stage demonstrating the ugliness of public drunkenness and distress; these dirty swells attempted at one point to block the passage of the better-born but were dispersed by a showing of a raised walking stick by a large man whom I took to be a naval officer by his stride. This bit of additional theatre having been dispersed with, I had a pleasant ride back to the club with Mrs. William-Wynn and her husband who had lived many years in Denmark and who professed to know of my mother's relatives whom I took as polite diplomacy and not fact. I was disappointed to no end to learn that the couple had no marriage-aged daughters and only limber sons, serving the Crown in the standard trio[28]. My un-happiness with this line of male only progeny was heighted by the fact that the 'Mrs.' had been a striking beauty in her day.

I arrived at the club in early evening the first time I had seen it at night by the light of the gas lamps, which I found wonderful in the light rain that was coming down at the time. After I had entered, I conflicted with another odd Oriental Club ritual. It would seem they had a tradition of dislike for copper coinage and would not have it in the house when I wished to purchase some biscuits. In honour of my stay in such comfortable lodgings, I had another sufficient dinner at the club, consuming two different curries I had not asked the names of. One was fiery, one of tender chicken and the other all of vegetables. Agreeable in taste, less so to my bowels which during the night signaled their manifest distress.

Tuesday 13 September

I had been London for four nights now and, having received word at the club that my ship was available for boarding, with some rush and trepidation, I arranged my departure from the Oriental Club. I packed up with some sadness, for this was a fine place and it is always pleasant to be a member of such a club. It certainly excludes an air of Gentlemanly snobbiness to have packages delivered to one club or to mention that you are living at the 'club'. I had seen how the Ambassador had taken to my living at the club. I was certain that my mentioning I was staying there had led to the supper invitation for how could I not be important if I was staying there? I added another vow to my long list of things to accomplish that of being a member of a club such as this.

List of my goals in life formulated while awaiting my carriage outside the Oriental Club on Tuesday September 13, 1836

1. To go east

2. To see the highest mountain

3. To fish in the great rivers of the world and all its oceans

4. To see the splendors of magnificent Egypt and ancient Greece

5. Explore Asia, Africa, Oceania and the Americas

6. Command troops in battle

7. Take a degree and learn ten languages

8. Become rich, have an estate with a vast library, and belong to a club

9.   Write a celebrated book   10.   Marry an incomparable woman

[Editor's note: Driscol made multiple changes to this list and what you see above is what he settled on some weeks later during his voyage to India]

I was quite pleased with this list I had dashed off in a few moments with a pencil on the back of one of the more trivial of the HEIC orders I had received. The ever-resourceful club arranged for a carriage to take my small baggage train and me to the ship. At just the right moment, the carriage came and again swarmed with helpers, I soon found my way off. Given a lusty good bye and good voyage notwithstanding my knowing I must return that evening to settle the account and to pay out another round of paltry remunerations to the staff but I was resolved to do so in copper only, being irksome in the face of petty traditions being one of my personal divertissements.

I took this conveyance down to the East India dock basin.

I had not seen this part of London before and what stretched out before me was the immensity of British maritime commerce. I marveled at the size of the East India docks and counted nearly two hundred ships berthed at the stone quays. The well-laid toll road was a gentle ride and often without the offences to the nose and eyes, one had deeper in London. The road was paved in the centre and macadamised on the outsides and I had my copious luggage taken out and deposited on the steps of Palm Cottage at No. 153.

After I had stepped out, I was surveying the route to the ship when I spied in the muck by the road a silver three pence. To me it seemed a miraculous stroke of good luck, another omen of the first class; I felt the Greek Gods had spoken directly to me my first silver gained on my trip to India. It was a newly minted coin with obverse inscription reads '*GULIELMUS IIII D G BRITANNIAR REX F D*'. I thought it might have been Royal Maundy money[29] and placed this sign of good fortune in my watch pocket. What had been ones travellers ill luck had been my good

I reflected on my father's often stated observation on superstition, 'It was un-lucky to not be superstitious' which I found amusing at that point. There was a rail line where burly men and unhappy looking Welsh cob ponies pushed or pulled carts from this area to the ships. I approached men willing to take my baggage on such a contrivance. They said I could ride atop and, although in the mufti[30] of a common traveller and not an officer, I thought it might be demeaning to do so. I walked alongside keeping a wary eye out for thieves, or what I had been specifically warned about at the club; a Sneeze Lurker[31]. As we moved down the line, for one line went up and the other down, we arrived at the quays themselves and I began to look for the ship amongst a forest of masts and black hulls. My pusher had the scent, without evening looking up he stopped before one ship, and began to un-load. I was confused for a moment but then saw a small wooden sign that proclaimed here to be the ship I sought, the *William Fawcett*, a 206-ton paddle steamer of the Peninsular Steam Navigation Company. She seemed a fine looking ship with a brigantine rig, the *de rigueur* black hull with a cream coloured port line. A curved bow and strong bow spirit made her a lively looking ship and the second steam ship I had travelled in. A faint whiff of smoke came from her single funnel, which was painted bright red with a black top. She could carry only a few passengers and seemed a small ship to cross to Gibraltar.

Written in Gothic style letters across her stern and paddle wheel housings was her name. At the time I saw her, she was loading and her copper sheathing was showing. I spoke to the mate directing the men loading all manners of cargo into her and was pleased to see he had with him - if un-read - the 1835 regulations or Lloyd's Rule[32], a subject much discussed in great anger by
my Danish maritime relatives who thought any regulation of a merchant's method of trade a dagger to the heart.

[Editor's note: Driscol travelled in a Danish trading ship to Denmark when he was thirteen, around the Baltic, in a similar ship and later, at sixteen took, a ship to and from Calais when he and his brother Stephen had travelled around Europe, not to mention a summer season of whaling in the Arctic. Based on his earlier comments he travelled to Europe a second time but I have found no information on this journey]

I soon gained the attention of a pursuer who took up my documents and signaled for some seamen to gather up the luggage. The pursuer asked which side I would prefer. I asked his

advice on this and he suggested the port side as that would be landward during much of the trip to Gibraltar, which I took. I asked if he knew what ship the passengers would transfer too

Drawing of the East India Docks. I-I-21

but on this subject, he was mute. I was given a small pamphlet outlying the rules, meal times, use of the head, washing of clothes and persons and an invitation to the Captain's *soiree* the first night out.

The ship was obviously rather old by steamship standard but was freshly restored, indicated by the scent of paint and sawn wood, all mixed up with intoxicating perfume of tar, wax and a hint

of bilge as we went up the gangway and onto the weather deck. We approached the main hatchway that led into a building style staircase, which led to the 'rear' of the ship. I was nonplussed by not having to climb up and down ladders as had been the case in my earlier adventures on ships. Pursuer Little, for he had introduced himself as such, turned and accessed my height and said he had a cabin that by the curve of the hull had a bit larger berth. The ship had two passenger areas; one before and the other ahead of the space taken up by the Paddle wheels and boilers. There was a central table transected by the mainmast and around it in cream and gold paint the cabin doors.

My cabin was on the main deck near the stern of the ship. I had steeled myself for a small dank closet but found I had a sidescuttle *{port hole}* and a room I could nearly stand up in. In it was a hammock fixed to the left side with safety ropes to keep it from swaying too much, shelves above that and a mirror and shaving stand to the right with a tin chamber pot. There were some pegs on the left 'wall' (the name for a partition in a ship eluding me now). There was also a copper spermaceti ships lamp. To my dissatisfaction, the walls were solid and not knocked down partitions to allow cannon to be used in time of war. The ship, built for peacetime use, carried only one very shiny Spanish brass 3 pounder for signaling. I found this disappointing for I had been prepared to share my cabin with a 12-pounder carronade or the like. He gave me a ponderous latchkey. Some of my larger items of luggage would not fit under the hammock so I made a false floor in the 2 feet or so of space I had, making a second decking. I would need to bend over to make my sleeping spot but I felt it was the best solution and the luggage would not be tossed about as it was fitted together well on the floor and was sturdy enough to take my weight without damage..

I next wandered around, finding, after a time, the engine room. From Karen's father I had learned all the aspects of steam engines. This ship had a sturdy looking one and I recognised it as a direct acting side lever type built by Fawcett and Preston. I had seen some of his earlier and smaller engines in use at Liverpool on land and sea. An engineer appeared and, being a young man, we soon fell into a vigorous discussion of his beloved engine. It had 140 indicated horsepower and the young man claimed she could do eight knots in a mild sea. With this I was impressed as the ship could almost make ten miles an hour using her engine and with sails and an appeasing sea she might make twelve perhaps thirteen miles per hour. She had been built in Liverpool just seven years ago and I had probably seen her before, on the stocks. Quite the wonder at the time but she was, now, shockingly out dated as steamer ships now were three times her size with engines the same magnitude larger. They had been making the London to Dublin run for a year and before that had made numerous trips to Iberia. This was their first trip south after being refurbished. In an attempt to gain, the admiralties mail packet contract. I also found the galley and was both delighted and perplexed by its equipment. Despite stories in the newspaper about the use of steam heat to cook meals, this ship's ovens and stoves ran with wood and coal *{charcoal, sea coal was the name of actual coal}*. It was crewed by a villainous looking group; to include a lead cook who was a Tyke[33], two dark skinned and renegade Frogs of un-sure parentage, one Dutchman and another Frenchman who, by his accent, was from La Rochelle. A Portuguese blackguard with a put out eye, and of more interest two Goans[33] who, were the cleanest of the lot. The two stewards were more presentable, being of some indeterminable Mediterranean parentage. Overall; what one expected. All, however, were well dressed, and the galley immaculate, even if they were not.

I found the ship well founded and nearly deserted. I checked that I locked my cabin and found I had earlier missed the number, cabin 49. To this I was beside myself, for as a child I had taken as my lucky number not a pedestrian lucky 7 but 7 x 7; 49, and now I was to go to the east in cabin 49. Again, I was impressed and emboldened by the many signs of good providence in my arrangements. I did note that there were no cabins number 1-34 but I could find no answer to this oddity. I found the Pursuer Little and determined the times I could board and leave the vessel. He was of a mind that they would do the main loading of passengers tomorrow and leave the morning next all depending on the weight of traffic in the yards and as he told it, the whim of the Captain, God and the wind - stated in that order of importance.

I made the weary trip back to the club again, making sure all the financial arrangements completed, necessary chits signed and notations and all things made in good order. There was for me a letter, addressed to me at the club, and in a hand I did not know. I took this and was about to depart when one member, to whom I had spoken days earlier, invited me to join him for luncheon. I did, despite having left the club but by now the waiters knew me well enough and dismissed my weak observations that I was no longer a guest there by pointing out that I was a guest of a senior member. They presented me with a large plate of curried pork, lentils, onion and that lamentable root vegetable potatoes, and I ate all that I could. Finding the pork not of the best quality but well covered by an un-surpassed curried sauce that did not feel like a heated musket ball in my mouth, I enjoyed the meal greatly and took in another dose of stories about the east. These in particular being tales one would not write in a journal such as this, or let one's mothers or any female have any hint of. I received detailed information on obtaining a bibi, a native 'temporary' wife or servant courtesan. Exactly what my father had warned me against in his final guidance. I, of course, asked leave to take notes on a separate sheet and did so.

[Editor's note: Sadly, these notes have not yet shown up in his collection of papers]

I had to wait until my fountain of information on indelicate subjects had finished his dining and then had excused himself to go off and sleep away the afternoon. Once he was gone, I could open the letter. It was from Marguerite. I felt a great distress, as I had not yet worked up the courage to write her. I purchased a quill from the club and some fine paper with its watermark for some slight sum and wrote a small note thanking her for wishing me a well on my venture. Her note was but three lines so I felt constrained to writing no more than six. As I was there and no one in the club seemed to be in a brother about my occupying a chair and desk, I stayed there that afternoon writing everyone I knew. I sent letters to my parents, all my brothers and sisters, a long letter about my adventures to Karen and a tentative note to Patricia, and later I add a shorter note to Philomena. I also sent a more formal letter to the Adjutant and officers of the 52nd, thanking them again for all their attentions and advice. I composed but decided not to send a letter to the officers of the 14th Light Dragoons, thinking they might take me as being presumptuous. After a few moments of indecision, I asked an elderly man, a veteran of many years in India and a retired Lieutenant Colonel of the native Infantry, what I should do about the situation. He asked a series of precise questions on the matter and pronounced the solution without a moment's hesitation: write them from India when I was in my new position and not before. With such a firm declaration, I could no more than submit to its correctness. I redirected this letter to Lieutenant Gall and I thanked him greatly for introducing me to his twin cousins.

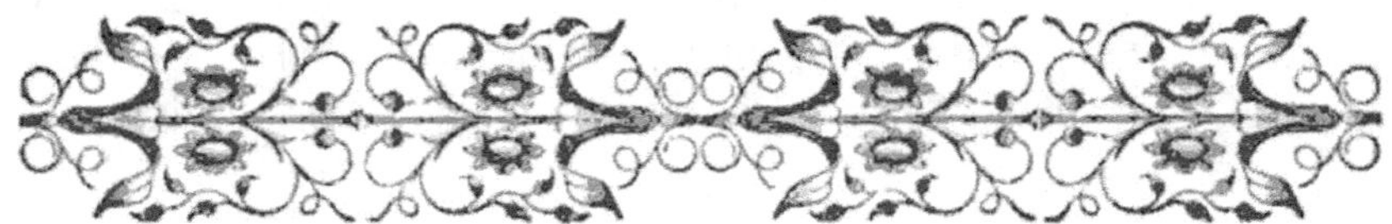

The front of the British Ambassador to Denmark's home. I-I-22

I arrived at the ambassador's residence in dress uniform somewhat early but found much to do

in what I thought at first glance was a modest home but it continued back some great distance. I secured some Cherry Heering; a Danish drink I liked as it has a good cherry flavour, and with it in hand, no one would feel the necessity to press drinks on me that I did not want. I listened awhile to various conversations as I knew no one but the hosts and they were too busy to spend much time introducing a very young Ensign to very important people. I listened for some time about a discussion of the Texas War *{The Province of Texas rebelling against Mexican government}* and a rather heated discussion about the Deccan prise-money case of Narroba *{a complex court case}*. However, it was the women at the party chatting endlessly about French fashion, the latest scandal, who had married or who had broken an engagement, while the men talked of horses and sport involving horses. The other subject of great interest was doings of the Royal family and the higher nobility whose actions were discussed rather indelicately in my opinion. This mingling seemed to go on forever and my stomach was beginning to rumble rather distressingly. I was considering making my way to the necessary but I was defeated in my manoeuvre by the approach of the butler who chimed the bells announcing dinner.

Supper With The Devil For Dessert

We were called into supper and I was pressed into service by the lovely hostess to offer my arm to a Lady I had not met during the interminable mingling. Un-fortunately, she was elderly and her steps un-certain. She walked like she was in leg irons. I completed my gentlemanly task slowly and found my place card well towards the end of table, well after everyone else was seated. I found this with some happiness as I had felt I would have had little to say to those who populated the upper table. As was the practice, I was sitting across from the older woman I had escorted in and to my left and right were two middle-aged married women. In something less than a good position for a young bachelor, I decided to concentrate on the meal. The woman to my right told me she was Lady Boredom (or so I named her) who gave me an un-solicited comment that she had a son my age. Across from me at an angle was a Naval Officer whose accent betrayed him as a Glaswegian Caledonian. As a good maritime Scot, he was drinking freely which drove the obvious displeasure of the elderly Lady across from me.

The collection of forks and spoons were confusing but thanks to my officer's mess training and a bit of hurried study, I figure out the uses for the eight spoons and forks. Of more use was a heavy sterling saltcellar in the baroque style, a nut dish filled with those disliked hazelnuts, and a menu. The menu showed the varied parade of food that was to come. I then took up the idea, one I felt was the best course, to ignore as much as possible the socializing going on around me and eat. Caviar, lemon and toast were served and were excellent, followed by a mushroom soup that tasted of soap and basil. Some Spanish olives that seemed to have been left in brine from the Peninsula War some five and twenty years ago, finally from platters well handled by the footmen came some good food and they provided a good piece of broiled sole heavily peppered and to my taste.

My stomach and bowels at this moment began to rumble and groan a sound I thought must be heard across the entire table but no, no one noticed and Mrs. Boredom continue to chat on about nothing in particular.

It was here the Scotsman's drink began to take him over and with the arrival of a large and perfectly cooked piece of English beefsteak, he launched on his course of collision. It was somewhat tough, the fault of the cow and not the cook, but eatable. It was at this point the Gaelic Naval officer decided to say in the loudest possible voice to the elder woman next to him that the beef he was trying to eat was not up to his naval standards. He did so by stating, "Madam, this beast is tougher than gaining a harlot's love for free". Her elderly husband took offence to this. A great deal of whispering and comments were made, and the supper disrupted around the officer. I continued to eat, using the chewing of large pieces of beef to silence the uproar about me. After some time the Naval officer made his pardons and left the table. I barely noticed his departure for the footmen brought in a pheasant breast with artichokes, the latter I scraped off and found the pheasant the best thing yet in the meal. All this time the woman on my right, Lady Boredom, had been droning on about her nephews, taxes, long-winded vicars and the lack of good servants. This one-way conversation suddenly ended when I found after bringing a large slice of succulent pheasant to my mouth that she had stopped speaking and was looking intently at me. I begged her pardon and she repeated her question, 'What was the greatest moment of your life', she repeated.

I replied in all seriousness and, having had to swallow my pheasant all but whole I spoke, 'Well Madame, I would have to say that having this conversation with such a lovely women as yourself would be tied with the other greatest moment of my young life', she was greatly charmed by these sweet words, and asked what the other great moment was, to which I replied in all seriousness again, 'When I was fourteen and won the cup for fattest sheep at the fair'.

She seemed taken aback by that, and I was saved from being challenged to a duel by her ancient husband by the arrival of a delicious creamed sweet and, for the first time in three quarters of an hour, I could eat in peace. Conversely, another devil sprang on me as the women on the left, seeing I was no longer speaking with the woman on my right, began to engage me. Observing I was about to be outflanked, I tried a desperate measure. I caught the eye of a distinguished man to my left front, the man to left of the elderly woman, and made to him the movement of eye and head that signals the need to answer nature's needs. This secret motion of the head and the coded message in my movement used between men to say that a visit to the necessary was, well, necessary. With a mumbled apology, I stuffed a large spoon full of rather tasty clotted cream in my mouth and headed away from the table. A liveried man noting my haste pointed to the necessary *{lavatory}*. I lingered there some time, counting to myself as I had failed to note the time on my watch, so I did not know when the dinner would be completed. I had hoped to wait out the meal, for I was very full and had no need for fruit or cheese and my stomach felt like I had when as a child I had bolted down a two pound round of Havarti cheese.

I wandered about the large house and I became somewhat lost finding my way to the kitchen where a servant directed me back to the dining room. As I came down a corridor, I could hear that the dinner party had broken up and instead of the ladies and gentlemen dividing into two groups as tradition demanded. They had come back out into the central hall where more of the accursed mingling was occurring.

The evil demon man in Driscol's stomach who wished to escape to the open air. This picture was found in his writings and labelled 'The evil man of wind'. I-I-23

The Merciless Attack

As soon as I had left the necessary, I had begun to feel a certain need to return and do what was actually now a necessary. I thought the fullness that I felt was the results of the food I had eaten. I was about to turn about when I was sighted by the host who gathered me up and introduced me to a number of elderly and possibly important Danish and English men. I remember not one name, for now I was tortured by what seemed a devil, I was sure, the extent and shape of a thirty pound parsnip who was trying to impale me from inside by ramming into my stomach and guts with great violence. I went through some great anguish until I saw an opportunity and made for the door. To my great horror and embarrassment, I did not make it. The chamber we were in after several hours had turned airless, warm and the atmosphere was laden with a potent mixture of tobacco smoke for the ambassador was one who smoked inside[34], opulent perfumes and powders and the scents of those who live outside of England. My Indian dinner had been treating my inside rather shabbily for the last twenty minutes and an un-relenting case of wind released itself. Had I been tortured for the secrets of the Crown in this manner I would have talked. I could not make the door and I girded myself to do what was obligatory, hopefully as silently as possible - nay what must happen - or I felt I would die just then. I simply could not retain it any longer, damn the consequences, it fled from me like a lamb from wolf.

What I would later hear from others about the incident was that it was described as a 'silent deep stench from infernal places un-known' that it came into the atmosphere silently while I maintained the most proper attitude and pleasant chit chat with those about me while trying slowly to make it to the doorway. This un-pleasant slayer unfortunately reflected the rather advanced age and spicing of the food I had un-fortunately eaten earlier that day. The resulting stench being bad enough to gag an archbishop and make a MP's wife swoon. Most unfortunately, the Scottish officer, already in an un-steady state by the gallon of spirits he had ingested, was upset and he let loose with a foul geyser of epic proportions - but of this, I heard later for at that moment I was walking as stiffly and as fast as I could to my much-needed objective. I learned that even the staid people in the chamber could not act as if nothing had happened. As I fled the room with a number of others, and in a small gift of God to me, I found the necessary just in time, barely.

I rejoined the host and hostess, after having relieved myself of a great deal of personal belongings. They fortunately blamed the drunken Scot for both the offensive smell and ending their supper party with a social disaster. I tsk, tsked the rudeness of the sailor man and made my compliments to the pair for having invited me. The hostess was sorry that no younger women had been present and the host handed me three letters, one a letter of introduction to the governor of the Danish colony in India and two letters to important friends of his in the east. He asked that I deliver them in person, or if not to post them, once I made the sub-continent. For these, I was most grateful and nearly confessed my great sin but decided that this would be a poor idea, as I knew I would laugh if I did, and that would be socially un-acceptable. I made my good nights and, in what seemed a long trip, made my way to back to the *William Fawcett*. I found the hammock unique but much less comfortable than the quilted bed of the club. I became intimately acquainted with the crude and exposed sanitary arrangements on shipboard during the long night.

Visited Fortnum & Mason's store and secured some rations; some of the new tinned foods I had seen in Manchester but never sampled. The food was cheap so I purchased a number of tins from Grosse and Blackwell and other makers. I obtained in the end a tin each of Scotch broth, preserved milk, minced steak, beef tongue, and two items of American made Underwood's devilled ham, one in glass the other in tinned iron. I also took up some doubtful looking peas, a large tin of corned beef and some preserved peaches. I could not pass by Hatchards', as it was next door, and I visited them again. I purchased six more books; *The Heart of Midlothian* by Walter Scott, and *The naval history of Great Britain from the declaration of war by France in February 1793 to the accession of George IV* printed in January 1820 by *{William}* James in five volumes. Although I had read the family copy as a boy, the original was now with my brother Mark in Singapore and I wished to read it again for I had deeply enjoyed it.

I then went to the Tower *{of London}* to view its many wonders. To only see the weaponry and the lions would have been enough but I saw much more. I had not seen a lion before. Once in Paris, at the Ménagerie du Jardin des Plantes, I had seen these large cats from a distance but it had been rainy and they, as all cats, had hidden themselves away. While at the tower, I could see them feeding on a good side of beef. I vowed then to hunt one of the monsters in the future for I felt that Ascalon could serve well to master this king of the beasts. I viewed the display of ornate Hindoo cannons and firearms there.

I was not hungry until mid-afternoon having taken nothing since the supper the night before. I therefor made my way to Simpson's on the Strand. I had heard much of this place and it did not let me down in any aspect. Several chess games were in evidence when I entered and I ordered a portion of very rare roast beef rib. It came out to me in minutes on a silver-domed trolley, and a man with a large knife asked most politely how much and from where on the joint of beef I would like to dine. I selected a goodly part and ate well on it, aided by horseradish sauce. I added in some sprouts in au jus and further helped myself to some savoury puff pastries later. Afterwards, I watched for some time chess matches between who I was told was Howard Staunton[35] and a befuddled opponent, and another game which had a Captain Evans and a Frenchman playing. I quickly found that my own level of chess was nothing compared to these men. I was glad none challenged me for challenges and games were ending and starting all around me. I took interest, too, in the chess pieces used by Staunton. They were of a different design and I admired them greatly. I resolved to have a set of ivory ones made for me in India, perhaps from an elephant I would hunt myself.

I took the rest of the afternoon to walk back to the ship, stopping at one point to purchase a large supply of writing materials for I had realised that I would, in future, be writing a great deal of correspondence. I purchased some two hundred sheets of Wedgwood's 'carbonated paper' *{carbon paper}* which I had seen used and thought would be useful in managing my correspondence

[Editor's note: the unknown editor penciled in 'carbon paper' for carbonated paper, for that is what it was and is known to modern audiences although now, in the computer age, rarely ever used]

I made the *William Fawcett* again which was preparing for 'boarding day' tomorrow when most of the passengers would embark. The rigging festooned with flags, tassels and rugs covered much of the weather deck. The seamen were polishing everything that could be polished, and two mates were discussing in loud terms just how taunt said rope should be. I read for several hours, having had some difficulty in determining what I would now read. I finally decided on Washington Irving - Voyages and Discoveries of the Companions of Columbus and found it enthralling. I did note a grievous error in his work, however among several questionable points. For in the book, Irving seemed to think that Columbus and the Spanish court were under the idea that the world was flat. I thought the Spanish society of learned men would have read the classics and would have known that the world was indeed round - it was the diameter that Columbus contested and on that matter, he was wrong. For the first time I noted the slow creaking of the ship and found it comforting.

Some of the activity in the East India Docks from where Driscol left for India. I-I-24

Farewell To My Regiment, Family And England

Thursday 15 September

I came up on deck earlier where the Pursuer, now known to me as Jackson Little, suggested that the boarding ritual would soon begin and that I might dress for the occasion. I took up his suggestion and appeared in full uniform just in time to see the first of the passengers arriving. I was not at all surprised that the first man at the gangplank was, of course, Lieutenant Perkins, RE of the Great Trigonometric Survey. He had with him a copy of a map which he had obtained in Paris and, as he had promised before at the Persian's door to show me and tell all once the British shore was behind us and then and only then would we 'talk shop' as he called it. I was eager to hear of his planned expedition and to see the map. He had not seen me in uniform before and he too was in his official accoutrements. He had on a rather good quality uniform for a Royal engineer, his red coat not, however, being as deep a shade as mine, the poor beggar.

I spoke with Mr Little and with his small notebook out I secured for Perkins cabin 47 next to mine. It was actually slightly larger both of ours being 'first class' which meant only that we slept alone and not in berths within a common room, which he joked was his due as Lieutenant. We set in his luggage, which was tenth the volume of my own, and he looked me in the eye and said he had actions to take and with that, he departed back to London town after securing the map case. Saddened, I went back to my place on the side of the ship to wait and see who would be joining us on this passage. They soon began to appear and I was happy to see that it was mainly families and not single men; married men and older men with daughters being the majority, I would say. They streamed in over the next few hours and I made my time watching them and using my French binoculars to spy on the shipping around me. After a time I grew restless, went down to my deck, and remembered that I needed to finish Taylor's book which I took the afternoon to do, making many notes. As I finished the book, I noted in my book list journal that this was the 600th book I had read.

[Editor's note: Driscol journal in which he lists the books he had read has not been found, however, this number would mean he read over 2 books a week which seems a very large number indeed]

When I returned to the deck, Mr Little at this time introduced me to the ship's officers; Captain Acornish, a large man who seemed more like a prizefighter than a Captain, with a great grey beard. I made the resolution not to cross this man for he looked like the type to nail you to the main mast or throw you overboard if you spit on HIS deck.

The Pursuer made an interesting observation that only around fifteen hundred people went east each year and he asked if I would like to venture on how many came back the same way. I said I did not know and he hauntingly celebrated that only twelve hundred or so came back. Getting no response from that weighty comment, he said that this month the fishing fleet season would begin and he would enjoy those trips greatly, with the ships filled with marriageable women going east to seek husbands. To that, I did respond, congratulating him on an employment that came with such benefits. I thought if Patricia and her dark sister would come on this ship perhaps?

Over the next hours, I spent the time on deck viewing those who would be making the journey with us. I had found out that our cruise would be a slow one with stops at to Vigo, Oporto, Lisbon and Cádiz, and it was from this last port that we would make our way to our destination, Gibraltar. Perkins appeared again making me feel more comfortable by bringing a large sea chest aboard but he was soon off again, in passing he applauded my present mission and tasked me to look out for 'eastern looking men from whom we might indulge in a bit of linguistic piracy with' good advice I thought.

I had brought my journal up and I will list those who would make up the passengers that I met that afternoon.

Darby Georgian, a kindly Cornish man on his way to Malta with his fat wife and African servant to take up a position on the Governor's staff, and he turned out to be a man learned both in survey and hydrology and the drilling of wells.

The next party aboard was Captain William Dalrymple, late of the Royal Navy on his way with a manservant and aide to take up staff duty in Naples with the fleet of the Kingdom of the Two Sicilies. To me he seemed a man all crumpled, grey and angry at something.

Mr John Barrow, architect and engineer long widowed and to whom melancholy hung over with great gravity. He was the man in charge of the docks at Gibraltar. He brightened up a bit upon meeting me and finding someone actually interested in the earlier work he had done with the dockage in Bombay.

After meeting that wretched man, I sighted another man, well dressed in the best London tradition, approaching middle age and definitely from the east. He was kind enough to greet me most welcomely. He was indeed from the east and a most interesting man indeed. His father had been a sailing master on an east Indiaman and, during the French wars, had taken out of a French flagged prize ship a servant girl of an Omani Princess on their passage to Zanzibar. She herself had been half Lascar and Arab from the Trucial coast. As she was a slave, he claimed her and with Christian charity freed her but finding that she had no desire to return to her home, for they had cast her out as child and sold her into slavery, he married her. He himself was born on ship at anchor off Kochi and he was very glad to make my acquaintance. He was Warren Salem Beer - his middle pronounced *Saleem*, in the Arabic manner - he proudly said. He was the private secretary to a magistrate in Bombay and most assuredly yes he spoke three languages Bengali, Persian, Arabic and of course English with a curious accent, and again yes he would gladly undertake to teach young gentlemen languages as he had done so before - but he added for a small fee. The amount he suggested was a mere nothing and I committed Perkins and I to him to learn Arabic and Persian a language I was most interested in mastering.

He then introduced me to his employer, the Honourable Gordon Germann-Debly, judge of the Bombay judiciary on his way back east after two years leave in England and most appropriately taking his family back with him. He had the face of a man who drank heavily but was clear of the influence at the moment, but I could see he would soon not be sober in the future. I had seen his type before in the regiment. His wife was a revelation; a woman who looked half his age and who spoke with an accent I could not place. Later that day I learned Mrs. Germann[36] was a Hungarian, the daughter of a professor at a Bavarian University where Germann had studied Europe's trade law, and she was but a year younger than her husband. It was his other family members that I was more interested in; three lovely daughters seventeen, nineteen and twenty; the classically named Danae, the French named Millicent and English named Prudence. The youngest was Danae, a freckled light brunette in curls who was stout, buxom and had a quick wit about her but somewhat boyish in her movements and comments. Prudence, the eldest, had dark brunette hair, brown eyes and gorgeous skin. Her eyes flashed with intelligence but it was the middle girl who attracted my immediate attention, for the others were 5'2" or 5'3" but she was a stately 5'9"; willowy, with a long, thin and fair face surrounded with ringlets of light blonde hair, her eyes were green with hints of brown and spoke of cleverness, grace and charm.

I was most taken with her from the moment I saw her. She was taller than her father was, and I think my own 5" above her she found of interest. They had to settle so I aided them in obtaining their cabins, which were about as far from me as possible, they being in the fore part of the ship.

After that, I met more people. Many men travelling by themselves and associated with the sherry trade or dried fish and other commercial concerns in Spain or Portugal.

The Penn sisters; two middle-aged women, one married, one a widow, going out to Gibraltar to be with the daughter of the married one who was soon to be with child. I could not see why the one sister was still a spinster, for she was had a striking lovely face in a petite form. Still, she had been a widow for ten years. I wondered if she might be a Shakespearean shrew under all her outwardly niceness.

Another family, probably lower middle-class, with two daughters of possible interest but one had teeth like a beaver and the other was marked badly by acne vulgaris. The man walked with a limp, and he had a hard eye and line, and I avoided him on general principles.

Two sets of earnest missionaries; Marcus Keith and new wife, going out east under the auspices of the Church Missionary Society and fated to go to Mauritius, Madagascar or the Seychelles.

Another missionary couple I found abrupt, from some church group I do not remember the name of but I fancy the name was the 'courageous church of plucky soul hunters'. Their first address to me was to ask if I had prayed that day and whether I knew that if I had, I had done it wrong and that I was destined to inhabit the nether regions for eternity. I escaped them by speaking to the crowd as if someone had called for my attention.

Mr and Mrs. Maynard, who I recognised at having been at the supper party with the ambassador. They did not recall me at all but did make mention of the drunken Scot. They had been un-happy with the new way of serving food and the 'opening of a sewer into the house after supper'. I, with some difficulty stifled my conspiratory laugh, asked her what her husband did, as he was busy with the Pursuer over some matter. She said with all weightiness, "'Do? Sadly, my husband has not done much for these last 25 years.'" Are you retired, I asked? "'Oh, no, dear. He works for the government; he deals with budgets and lists of figures and all that.'"

Ashton Vadeboncoeur, a flamboyantly dressed American writer & artist, on his way to gain inspiration, commissions and fame from the Iberian Peninsula. He seemed an interesting man despite his, as the American's say, foppish ways.

Next on was a Maltese Jew, Emmanuel Catania; a middle-aged man who introduced himself to me and to, my amazement, spoke to me in passable Swedish. He was a traveller and businessman of many years' experience all over Europe and it would seem he spoke nearly every European language, if only a few phrases or words. He had thought I was a Norwegian *{Norway was governed by Sweden during Driscol's time}*. I corrected him as I had found that many considered me a northern European and not an Englishman. He now lived in Malta, trading in supplies of resin, ship's wood and cordage for the use of the Royal navies of England, France, Spain, Portugal and Egypt. I asked him, of course, about languages. Beside European ones he could write Hebrew *{Yiddish?}*, of course, and knew Arabic well but no Persian. He felt he could only offer up some instruction in his national tongue *{Driscol seemed to think his native tongue was Arabic while it was Maltese, however he also spoke Arabic}* and in Turkish. He was a descendent of those who had escaped the Pope's inquisition in Spain, had made their way to Istanbul, and had family connections all over the Baltic, Dutch colonies and the Mediterranean. To gain some respect in his eyes I used the only Hebrew phrase I knew. I had learned it by rote as a boy in Copenhagen, from the only other Jew I had ever met. I remember that he had said to use this to gain the friendship of any Jew I might later meet. It was a short jest, which translates roughly as;

Moses once broke all the commandments at once and God let him live only for a while. I, on the other hand, strive to break them only one at time and at a decent interval and therefore will live forever.

Catania, I could see struggled, with my pronunciation but then to my complete satisfaction burst into laughter once he comprehended what I had said. 'Your Yiddish is terrible, Mr Driscol', he said, 'but we can work on that.' We parted after deciding on a small fee, knowing we would soon meet again on such a small ship.

So the afternoon went. Two more men boarded, Portuguese or Spanish, but by then my interest in others diminished. I found the bustle of the ships loading to be bothersome and went on a walk along the quays, studying the ships and people.

I came back aboard somewhat late for the evening meal and the Captain's soiree. I hurriedly dressed and, as the door of my cabin opened into the main dining hall, I had to pass through it to put on my uniform, for I had worn civilian dress to walk about the ships. I was soon relieved to find that no one had noted my protraction in regards to my walk.

Perkins was there too and I was able to sit next to him. We exchanged news of the day. He had arrived just a few minutes before so I was able to introduce him to a number of the people sitting closest to us. The meal was un-remarkable and I spent it in tension. Trying to eat and not steal glances at Miss Germann. We made our way through some untidily cooked fish and vegetables and went up on deck. Perkins and I were going over the options in regards to languages as we watched the sunset darken the busy shipyard around us; it grew quieter as the darkness closed around us. He was most complimentary in my having found Warren and the Jew.

Mr Little came up to us as we loitered on the upper deck in evening air. He was a jolly fellow and we found that he was Pursuer only temporarily as he intended to take the navigation tests to gain his certificate as a mate. He went on about his need to practice his navigation maths. Perkins offered to assist as he was naturally mathematical in his thinking and an acknowledged expert in the techniques of survey. We made an ally, for it is always good to know one of the ship's officers, even a lowly Pursuer. We stayed up until the moon set near ten in the evening. We had talked of the ship, the food, London, and the possibilities of which route we would take to the east.

During that pleasant evening, two French Admirals made themselves known to me, Monsieur Willaumez and Duperré[37]. These were the ship's cats who, like all cats, favoured me above all others. Not for the first time I wondered at what attracted cats to me and not men with wealth who wished to grant me large sums, powerful men who wished to offer me influential positions or beautiful women their grace and attention. The last item seemingly had been struck down in the last few days. They were attentive cats, one all black and the other all white. Perkins thought I was mad to pay attention to the cats, he having nothing to do with the 'contemptible rat eaters', as he named them. He liked dogs; large ones that barked a lot and occasionally would eat a neighbour's child.

I went to my hammock enthralled, excited and happy for I was going east. I was an Ensign in the light infantry. I had three beautiful women to think about, there was the intrigue of not knowing fully what Perkins might divulge tomorrow, and two cats found me a good and desirable companion. Would I become the explorer I had hoped to become? The implications left me un-sure of myself to the extent I began to doubt my wisdom for going to the east. I remembered well the words from Julius Caesar's *Commentarii, {Commentaries}* the first adult book I read in Latin.

As a rule, men worry more about what they cannot see than about what they can.

[Editor's note: One mystery about this first chapter is that Driscol begins his journey near Oxford, yet the 52nd was stationed at that time in Gibraltar. It is also known that her depot, for recruiting and training, was established at Carlisle in Cumbria, 120 miles NORTH of Eccles. he was assigned to that depot for reasons unknown. The only sense I can of this contradiction is that he was relating his departure from Carlisle, left out some days to visit Oxford then went back up north to Manchester then down again to London. This would not be only time that Driscol's entries will cause confusion!]

Driscol's steamship the William Fawcett. I-I-25

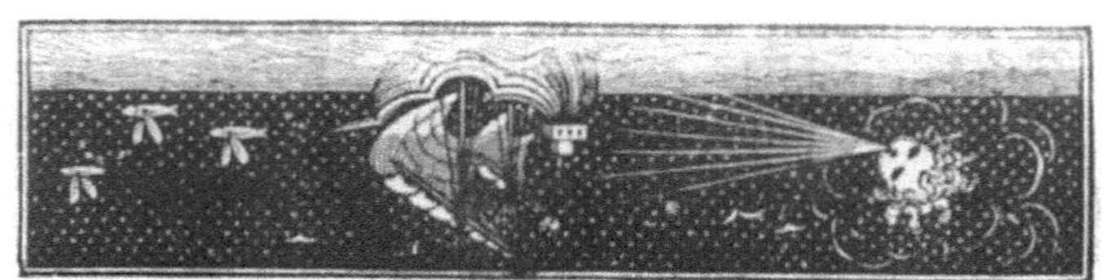

Chapter II

To Gibraltar and the East

The William Fawcett Sets Sail - A Prussian Defeat Comes Near To Ending My Journey - Blusterous Redux - A Well Drubbed Spar - A Pleasant Function - Acornish's Dissolution - Cristenos Corunna - Extraordinary Mathematical Fortunateness - An Un-visited Funeral - A Surprise Announcement - The Port Of Oporto - The Portuguese Coast And The Wages Of Sin

========

The William Fawcett Sets Sail

Friday 16 September

I awoke early as the sound of the crew on deck; made a clear alarm to me that the ship was about to undock for I had heard the routine many times before when at sea. I hurriedly dressed and went up on deck. It was early morning and knowing as I did the mundane actions of the merchant ships and whalers I had earlier been on I took a position near the bowsprit. The funnel was belching smoke. The two masts festooned with flags and limp sails for morning lapse was in effect. The first officer, a Mr Shimmins, a small man with a cast in his eye, or *strabismus,* which gave him a somewhat comic appearance at a distance, bade me a good morning and I asked him if the conditions to sail had been met. He replied that they had and we would back out and into the Thames and from there down to the sea to meet with the ebb tide off the coast. He spoke with an un-usual accent and I asked from where he was from. He proudly stated he was a Manxman and that half the crew was of that ancient and noble breed. He even bestowed a few lines upon me of Manx, which sounded like Gaelic and were completely un-intelligible.

The rumbling sounds of the engine grew in magnitude and with the ropes cast off we began to move at a child's pace for a smaller steam tug had come up and would tow the Fawcett out of the constricted space of the basin. I spent the time writing in my journal and viewing the other ships with my binoculars. I sighted a number of interesting ships; from Dutch Indiamen to French coastal traders with their decks stacked high with casks of brandy. How such overloaded ships, with their hulls ballasted with lead, did not upturn was beyond my understanding. We soon made the Thames and released from the tow, and our own engines started to drive more strongly. The river was full of shipping but most if not all was not moving and the docks as we left them were miles of prominent quays and ranges of warehouses where the hundreds of ships formed a forest of gaunt, leafless trees. We passed a grand factory that made varnish and its odour disturbed the serenity of our passage. I had no map of the Thames estuary and did not know what lay ahead.

As time passed by more people came on deck, Danae and Millicent came up in black silk dresses and offered me a melodious good morning. I pointed out some sights but they soon left me to join their parents and others in the stern of the ship. I preferred the bow as the action *{the movement of the ship's bow up and down when at sea}* of the ship was greater and I liked the sound from the bow working through the river's water to the inconsequential conversations I knew to be going on behind me.

Scullings, gigs, whiffs and punts scattered before us. Although ours was a small ship, we were the only steam ship moving out to sea in the early morning and all others stayed out of our path. Perkins then arrived, his eyes heavy with sleep. He looked around and was manifestly un-impressed and went below. Breakfast was served prior to our arriving at Gravesend. Having seen the galley crew, I was suspicious of the food but the two stewards were now well dressed and their hands spotless and the meal set out in the style of *a la Franciase* with small cards to state the name of the dish and its main ingredient - a most welcome addition to have them labelled. The meal was an orgy of eggs and I found one dish of Portuguese origin that was eggs, garlic and anchovy and another of duck eggs, salt cod and potatoes; the potatoes; I picked out and discarded. The French admirals were underfoot at all times being comfortable among the un-caring passengers. I was surprised that no one tripped over them or elicited their outrage by stepping on one of their tails. I ate with the Germann family who invited Perkins, who had not slept well, and me, and we were trapped into a long conversation with the parents while Millicent sat quietly between them and Danae sat to one side with me and always lucky Perkins speaking separately with the lovely Prudence.

I could tell by the movement of the ship and the looks on the faces of some of the passengers that we had entered the estuary. After some time Pursuer Little informed me we were off Sheerness and would be taking the Queen's Channel out to sea to avoid the large number of ships inbound from Margate roads. The day was now turning grey and the wind had picked up. The number of ships around us was immense; at least three hundred sail and a dozen steamers could be seen. We passed one large Indiaman by less than a hundred yards away. She was at least fifteen hundred tons and named the *Nizam*. I felt I was in a rowing boat compared to that massive ship with her row of cannon ports and three masts.

By early afternoon, a luncheon was served and, as I had eaten well at breakfast, I took up some fruit pudding only and bit of a rasher. Perkins joined me on deck for he had slept some more and now seemed in full control of his senses. His first words were amusing. 'Avoid that Germann girl.' And I soon found he meant Prudence for he added, 'She is smarter than any man I have met.' Perkins did not like clever women, it would seem, but I did agree that in some manner she was certainly frightening.

We could still see the south estuary shore but Perkins laid out his plan.

[Editor's note: Driscol wrote his first coded entry at this point but the unknown editor had added the translation and, in addition, showed it was a simple substitution cypher and all further 'coded' messages will be translated without identification. This code was simple but not so the entries into his private journal which at the time of this writing still remain unread]

His first words were like a thunder stroke to me and I will always remember them. He said:

'It is a hope of mine that once we reach India that I shall lead an expedition into Turcomania by way of Persia. Are you with me, my good man?'

I was, of course! We retired to his cabin where he opened up a map and it was the securing of this map that had occupied him since we had parted company at the Persian professor's. The map was a wonder. It showed the country ranging between Kashgar and the Caspian Sea drawn from the knowledge of eastern geographers and historians, and penned by the Jesuit d'Anville. A direct copy of the original its name in French was *Carte la plus Générale et qui comprend la Chine, la Tartarie Chinoise et le Tibet* and had been printed in Paris in 1737.

He then explained that he had more details to tell but wished to wait some time until he had the minutiae firmly in his mind and if I could mind the wait. I said to him that I would do what I must and so of course do so. He hinted that he hoped to find at Gibraltar a communication that would give him the necessary papers and final permissions to proceed. However, he assured me that those in London in certain positions had been favorable to my inclusion on the proviso that I learn Persian. I was cautioned to the secrecy of our plans and by the time we arrived on deck the weather had grown cold and windy in the mid afternoon. I knew from my sailing relatives that one should always assume the Channel will be rough and if it is not, it is your good luck and the gift of providence.

As the sea swell had begun some hours ago, many of the passengers were seasick. I was quite happy to be immune to this habit of Poseidon to ill-treat new comers. I called on the Germann's and found the father in his cups, and the mother and two daughters' were quite ill. Danae seemed unaffected and was acting as a nurse. I found the central cabin spaces empty of all but Captain Dalrymple of the Royal Navy,

[Editor's note: I will refer in to this man in the future as Dalrymple to avoid confusion between him and the ship's Captain Acornish]

and his aide who seemed in the worst of moods but, seeing that I was not casting accounts *{sea-sickness}*, they asked if I was a sea-bred man.

I replied that I had been to sea in the mercantile trade of the Baltic as a boy and had spent one season in the Arctic as a Greenlander, and that my father's line had for many generations been Greenlanders. This gained their appreciation and he asked my opinion of the Captain's decision to go to sea. I was puzzled for a moment but then I recalled the wisdom of my father and mother's relatives who were seamen and knew what he referred to. The Naval Captain was beside himself that the Fawcett had moved out to sea on a Friday that explained the few other ships we had seen making to sea. I had disremembered that piece of advice that Friday was *'dies infaustus' {unlucky day}*, and all sea going men considered it as ill-omened. The aide whose French sounding name I never could remember added that the barometer had been falling since we had left our berth. It was the considered opinion of the Captain, a man who had been years on the blockade ships off Ushant in the rank of Midshipmen and Lieutenant, that we were in for a bit of a Bay of Biscay sea *pique-nique {storm}*. He added that as we were now only in the Channel it was just an early sign of worse weather ahead.

He asked and I expanded on my sea going experience. I explained in brief that as a boy I had taken a summer's cruise across the North Sea to my mother's homeland of Denmark. I had visited Vyborg and Copenhagen, taken a small craft across to Goteborg, Sweden, and helped to crew my relations trading ketch-galiot, the green painted *Sofugl*, to the Island of Gotland then to the port of Lubeck, of the old Hanseatic League. Then we had sailed on to the great cities of

Stockholm and Saint Petersburg. He said that I should have come to the sea but I offered the excuse that my mother would not let her favourite go to sea at thirteen. I did not tell him that that had been partially because of my fear of heights for climbing a mast at sea was a task I had rather never do again.

We spoke of my time as a boy-servant-crewmember of a whaler in the seas off Spitsbergen and the east coast of Greenland and the hunt for *Cetacea {whales}*.

I mentioned also my time aboard the Russian man-o-war, the 36 gun Kreyser, a year or so prior to her being broken up at Kronshtadt *{Kronstadt}* guided by Rear Admiral Istomin, a compatriot of the now famous Lazarev[1] whom my relatives knew well. The Captain then decided to retire after explaining to me his own interesting life at sea.

During the night I made several journeys up to the deck in my oilskins for it was raining hard now and a bone chilling wind from the northwest was driving the sea. The ship had a green light on her starboard side, a red one to port and a very bright lantern at the foremast. The moon was low on the horizon but I could see several lights of other ships in the Channel and they would fade in and out, as the storm grew in intensity. Perkins was dismissive of the rain, noting that this would be but a small Scotch mist versus the true Indian Monsoon, even as he was becoming more and more ill. He gave me a mild cursing when I told him that I was immune to the illness weakening his inner workings.

I determined that the chance that the ship would plunge to the bottom while I was asleep was less fearsome than staying awake the entire night either wet on the deck or alone in the salon. I went to bed gingerly and found my hammock swinging wildly at times. I slept in my clothes with just my boots off.

Saturday 17 September

I awoke early to a moderate rocking of the ship. It was still dark out and I was afraid that something had occurred. I had not noted the time when I had retired and could not see it now as there was no light in my cabin to read my watch. Nothing but darkness was outside my porthole, or more properly a port-sashes or a sidescuttle, showed nothing but some colour from the side light.

I went up on deck again and found the First officer Shimmins in a good mood for the weather was abating, or, as he called it a *blout,* a northern term for the sudden breaking-up of a storm. He warned that he expected a wicked *glog* to follow which he explained was the Manx term, describing the swell or rolling of the sea after a storm. He too asked me about my sea experience and was appreciative of my time as a whaling man - more so than I, for I remember those days as frigid, adventurous and overcome with the stench of whale blubber being rendered. He asked me some questions about the rigging and soon found that I was not telling tales.

I found that it was nearly seven in the morning and decided that I was done with sleep to prepare for breakfast, or at least I hoped for some, for I had had little the night before due to my piggishness over the ample breakfast the day before.

Several other passengers were on deck, all sickened by the rolling of the steam ship. I spoke with Mr Georgian who had much to tell me of his years in postings about the Empire. He was a surveyor by training and by experience a man with a familiarity at finding, digging down to and piping water to where it was wanted. Of no formal education, he was very much an engineer's engineer and I soon introduced him to Perkins who came up on deck to die, I believe. I watched as they outlined how a capped well could be used to move water hither and yond at the whim of a good engineer.

Perkins was being a good soldier but his stomach was a rank coward and would have been drummed out of service, or shot, for it betrayed him again and I had to take him back to his cabin.

I enjoyed not being sea-sick. It gave me a great sense of importance to be able-bodied when others were not, although in a storm off Trinity Island *{Jan Mayen}* in 1832, the waves were so violent that not only were the ships masts badly sprung *{cracked}* but I felt un-well and the thought of food was not one I could hold in my mind at that time.

[Editor's note: The next half page was wetted and attacked by a mold, it is unreadable]

Dear Karen was always enamoured of Lord Byron's poetry and she had learned his Childe Harold's Pilgrimage, XIV by heart and from it a line on the Bay of Biscay, which she had reminded me of when we said our good byes.

On, on the vessel flies, the land is gone, and winds are rude in Biscay's sleepless bay.

Sleepless indeed! Although at this time, we were still within the English Channel.

The galley was not in operation, the heavy swell suspending all such endeavours. The ships 'doctor', an assistant surgeon of limited skill in my eyes, made the rounds of the cabins and the crew came around to clean up the many mistakes and purges that had occurred during the rough night.

Besides myself who had found a way to wedge myself in-between a fixed chair in the salon and the main table, I rode out the swell reading as best I could Irving's book. The Naval Captain and his two men, the Portuguese who turned out to speak French and was a navy man himself who had quickly recovered his sea legs, joined me. Much to my happiness, Danae was also about and we all greeted Miss Germann with pleasure. I raided the galley and found a small keg of butter and day old bread, a nice sea stand that held marmalade and made a breakfast of sorts. I was the complete Gentleman and offered the best parts of the bread to Danae who accepted them with pleasure.

Sometime after my provision incursion, the stewards appeared and more fare that was more substantial provided to those who could stomach it. I found, however, that my stomach began to sour when the smell of coffee filled the salon. I beat a hasty retreat but soon recovered. Danae found it hard to believe that anyone was put off by the smell of coffee, but I was proof that she was wrong. To tease her I made mention of the fact that the freckles on her left cheek were in the pattern of the stars in the constellation Canis Major. She found that un-settling but I found it fascinating that they would be there in that order, for by God's grace they were.

I mentioned this to Perkins who was un-impressed and who asked me, 'Which nation produces the most marriages?' I could not immediately reply and after a time said China, it being the most populous, but it was instead - 'fasci<u>nation</u>' he said - annoying but clever, I thought.

The rest of the day I stayed in my hammock beside fearful trips to the head. Duperré demanded entrance to my domicile and I allowed him to enter on my acceptance. He was doing well with the rolling of the ship and after studying the situation launched his attack. He sprang on to the small stand and then took a flying leap landing lightly on my legs in the swinging hammock. His prize was pieces of my kipper I had plundered from the ship's pantry along with more bread and a large supply of limewater liberally sweetened with sugar. After a meal from my hand he fell asleep on my extremities. I was bothered only a few times by the ship's Captain, first officer Shimmins, Pursuer Little, the useless surgeon, the stewards, the Naval Captain and lastly Perkins who was white as a piece of boiled cod. The smell of the kippers drove him away after a short dialogue. I would have preferred visits from certain other passengers more.

Danae and I found that propriety allowed her to stand at my door with it wedged open and speak to me as I swung in my hammock. Millicent was completely disabled by her sea condition. I spoke with Danae about the fantastical fictional worlds, of Plato's and Bacon's Atlantis, which, she thought, might exist, somewhere where I held it was but a fanciful construction of the author.

At one point, the weather cleared while I was on deck during the evening and the ship's officer has declared that the lights seen were those of the town of Portsmouth and later the Isle of Wright. Those few flicking lights would be my last view of England for many years.

Sunday 18 September

With the Sabbath came a lessening of the wind but the good weather was punctuated with sharp squalls and slowly the storm began to build up again. I spent the day with walks on the deck then recovering from the wet and chill in my hammock. Many of the passengers were still green around the gills and the stewards were supplying food on demand. I demanded and obtained several excellent chops with a bottle of Brand & Co's condiment for fish, meat and fowl[2]. I had never tasted it before and it rose immediately to first place as the best sauce I had ever had, especially one out of a commercial bottle. I was glad the steward had suggested it and gave him a small sum of money to pass over the bottle and a few of its friends to my perpetual care.

I obtained some dry toast and brought it to the Germann family. Prudence was better but Millicent was still in the deepest straights of discomfort. Mrs. Germann thought my gesture most courteous and commented several times that my mother would be so proud. For some reason I found mentions of my mother while around Millicent disturbing. I remembered well her reaction when meeting my brother's future wives for the first time.

The missionaries were remonstrating amongst themselves about tracts which I was amused at since their matter of grave contention was that these holy materials contradicted one another. Yet still they ran about setting up prayerful meetings and 'unions for the consolidation of faith', something I dared not ask about. I collected two of the tracts to send to Karen, who has an interest in spiritual matters well beyond my own. One was called *Metaphysical Healing* and seemed filled with nonsense and the other was called the *Science of Man*, which seemed to hold that sickness was not real but just a fable and all could be cured or healed, to include small pox and a broken leg, by faith - I had to wonder why these believers ever died? I ended up with several copies, kept a pair for her, and consigned the rest to the sea, not out of spite, but to test the rate of our ship's speed, which I found was nine knots.

I have noted with interest that Lieutenant Perkins is always perfectly presentable. Rarely is a hair out of place. He always appears freshly shaven and no speck of dust, smudge or un-slightly drop of food ever despoils his appearance. I find this miraculous even on coming down from the deck where the wind and salt spray can do one serious sartorial damage yet he always seems to come down un-affected. I found him once using a small pair of French scissors to trim the hair on his hands. He was taking the time to ensure that the hair on the - and I realise now that I do not know the name of this part of the hand - the flat area beyond and below the little finger, perhaps it is called the 'side'? The hair there he was trimming to insure it lined up properly. I simply marvel at this demonstration of excess ardor on this specific point of one's toilet.

The first officer in one of my sojourns on deck had said that he thought we were in what he described as a feeding-gale. He explained it was a type of storm that is on the increase, getting worse with each succeeding squall. The first bad weather had actually been in the English Channel and we had only now come into the actual Bay of Biscay noted for its angry weather.

Pummeled we well were by the fierce westerlies the rest of the day. We were under double-reefed topsails and, to my discouragement; we did not see the twin towers of the Lizard light that are often the traditional last sight of England.

There was scattered social intercourse during the stormy day but most of the others were too under the lash of the demanding commandant *mal de mer {seasickness}* to converse much. I saw the usual un-daunted ones and had a pleasant talk with Danae, and Perkins; who, for a time, seemed to have recovered but as the wind and sea rose, so did his bile.

[Editor's note: A map showing Driscol's route to the east can be found on page 289, Appendix I-V with spoilers!]

A Prussian Defeat Comes Near To Ending My Journey

Monday 19 September

The officers were able to get a sighting done in the early morning and I watched the procedure. I had seen it before and had worked out the mathematics of it some years previously. Our position being fixed at 48 degrees 05 minutes and 7 seconds N and 7 degrees 8 minutes and 48 seconds W, or due west of Brittany. The wind had fallen and was but a small breath on the cheek, and all around us were patches of dense fog. The ship was moving slowly one to two knots, and every minute the blast of the steam horn shattered the day. On occasion of entering a fog bank the forward 3 pounder was fired with a ¼ blank charge. The problem with a steam ship is that it is noisy all the time, un-alike the natural sounds of a wind driven ship. There is a great deal of rattle about in a steam ship so one cannot hear clearly the sounds of another *{sailing}* ship's manually operated foghorn or bells.

It was just after nine in the morning. I knew the time because Perkins had come up and was looking much better now (he was perfectly dressed and shaven but his face was still white) and had asked the time. As we spoke, the *William Fawcett* emerged from the fog bank. We had been in for the last ten minutes and were once again had clear seas ahead. The ship's Captain was about to restart an earlier story, which he had interrupted when we had entered the fog as he had to act as if he was listening for signals from other ships, when I felt a presence behind me. For all of us, the Captain, Master, First Lieutenant, the helmsman, Perkins and I, were behind the wheel in the stern and looking forward. I turned and was startled to silence as a great black shape appeared out of the fog behind us. Rushing towards us was an immense bowsprit that seemed by itself larger than our entire ship. I was bereft of speech, but forced myself to act, thumping the shoulder of Mr Shimmins, who turned annoyed at my touch as I gripped his shoulder. He was not mute, his shout all but shattered my eardrums. HARD A PORT, FULL AHEAD!

Behind us a gun had gone off and we could hear the rush of the sea as the black ship came on and mercifully began to swing ever so slowly to starboard. it seemed that nothing would prevent us from being run down by the ship that by now had half emerged. It seemed to me that our limp spanker survived by inches a heavy blow from the bowsprit of the behemoth that had moved up behind us and ever so slowly was now pivoting away. Our little ship was moving slowly too and she was a huge three-decker warship, which must outweigh us by five and twenty times. We heard some shouts in French and several seamen on our ships returned comments as earnest and crude as were given. Our steam whistle had also gone off not a single bleat but a shill screaming that did not stop. The initial shouts had brought up our resident Naval Captain who arrived to see the disaster just missed with our little steamer turning away nimbly from the huge lumbering Frenchman.

For that was what she was. It was Dalrymple who identified her on sight. 'Damn, if it is not the Jena, by Jove, with 112 guns of hate'. At that time she was a half pistol shot away and had I had a pistol I might have fired at her. Our gob smacked group was thrown to one side as following the Frog ship was a wind, a squall that was driving her at great speed for she had her full suite of sails up. The wind obliterated the fog and as we were caught up in our turn to port the strong wind hit our limp sails, filling them out with a sharp crack and we keeled over nearly to beams end. Perkins and I gripped the railing out of self-preservation where we had both been thrown by the movement of the ship, and stayed to keep out of the way of the seamen and crew who were a demonstration of haste and violent motion and word. By their earnest actions, they brought the ship back under control. Dalrymple did his part in giving voice to a most violent stream of abuse of all things French and Naval - and in excellent French, I might add but the Jena was now too far away to hear us, I would suspect. With that squall of wind the fog had now fully dissolved and showed to us a full French Naval Squadron, their masts straining and in fair order running before the power of the wind. We counted five ships-of-the-line; two 80's and three 74's. The Naval aide identified them but I could not catch the names as the steam whistle had become stuck, as we later learned. The engine was at full capacity and the wind was shrieking like baby banshees. I remember Perkins cursing and throwing to me a comment. 'Damn the sea, I was so hoping to have some good fare'.

He went below deck but I waited to see the ship brought back under control and on course. In all, I found that my watch was still in my hand and that much less than a minute of time had passed. My heart was beating like I had run a mile and my mouth tasted of fear and blood for I had bitten my cheek somewhat. Chastened by my perception of the cowardice of my reaction, I was about to go below when the Captain sent his thanks for my timely warning. He had noted that my action might have saved the ship from a collision or even being run down and sunk. The two Captains were indignant that the French were in violations of the rules of the sea - professional seamen in a crowded sea-lane simply did not run at full sail through fog. Well sane ones and those that were not French.

The wind began to pick up even more and Dalrymple remarked that as a fourteen-year-old midshipman on the H.M.S. Prince George he had experienced the famous Christian's Gales. That great storm of 1795-6, with its blasts of savage winds that had desolated the fleet proceeding to attack the French West Indian Islands under Admiral Christian and had driven a half dozen ships on shore.

The missionary's came and gave a prayer that they wrote down and gave to each one of us as part of a tract. Pasted:

[Editor's note: Driscol appears to have torn out the prayer and pasted it in the journal. It came loose at one point during the next 180 years but I did find a torn sheet in an envelope containing a number of odds-and-ends and the missing piece of paper found and it is reproduced below]

THOU, O Lord, we beseech thee to stillest the raging of the sea, hear us, and save us.

O blessed Saviour, that didst save thy disciples ready to perish in a storm, hear us, and save us, we entreat and plead with thee.

 Lord, have mercy upon us.
 Christ, have mercy upon us.
 Lord, have mercy upon us.
 O Lord, hear us.
 O Christ, hear us.

God the Father, God the Son, God the Holy Ghost, have mercy upon us, save us now and evermore. Amen.

[Editor's note: The odd title of this section was from Driscol himself and for those not aware of the history of the Napoleonic wars, this French ship, the Iena or Jena, is named for a famous French victory over the Prussians, the Battle of Jena; a Prussian defeat]

A three-decker similar but somewhat smaller than the French 112 gun Jena, which nearly ran down Driscol's ship in the Bay of Biscay. I-II-1

Blusterous Redux

Therefore, it began again I met about half the passengers clustered around the stairs. Overhead, the crew was 'battening' down the hatches again and the movement of the ship needed no explanation. The screaming of the steam whistle finally died gargling away. I gave an abbreviated version of the events on deck, greatly downplaying the danger. Danae and Millicent who were up from their seasickness both wished to see the French ships but I persuaded them that this was not a good time. As I spoke, the sun was covered by dark clouds and the stewards ran about the main salon to light the spermaceti *{whale oil}* lamps. After repeating my story of the events a score of times, I made my way to my cabin. I observed Perkins in his hammock with chamber pot at the ready but as he had not eaten much of anything for two days I wonder what he had in his 'hold' to share with the chamber pot?

I took this as an excellent opportunity to continue my reading as attempting to romance a seasick girl is a ruinous waste of time. Having secured some biscuit, cold corned beef, a small onion, and a lemon or three for rations, I went to my hammock, doing as I had before; reading for two or three hours then making my way up to the deck. This became my routine. I was nonplused that the French Admirals did not come to call. In the afternoon, I played a game of chess with Danae, to whom I gave a longer and more heroic rendition of the events of the morning. The motions of the ship, however, had become more un-steady and I began to regret that corned beef and onion I had consumed for it seemed it wished to come out. Danae opportunely was falling ill also for she had beaten me badly in the first game and I was holding out, but barely, against her un-failing attack. Did she not know that it was un-lady like to beat men at games of intelligence? I hastened her departure by mentioning some Danish delicacies, which I was thinking of. I won by default but barely made my cabin, bashing my head against the side of the door in my haste to enter. Again, the small group of those un-affected visited me. I had tired of this and feigned sleep when they next came around, having left my cabin door open and well wedged, to prevent my having to answer the knock. I suspected the cord holding the door would break soon and at six in the evening, it did but my cobbled together wedges held.

I went on deck again and found the wind still howling its rage, and the only one small sail still set and the WF's *{the ship William Fawcett}* engines stopped with the wheels rotating freely. It was nearly impossible to hear a man speak so after becoming chilled to the bone and four rotations around the deck, I headed back to my fortress of solitude. I was tired of reading now and changed books taking up Edward Bulwer-Lytton's novel, Paul Clifford, published just this year, and it began:

"It was a dark and stormy night; the rain fell in torrents-except at occasional intervals, when it was checked by a violent gust of wind which swept up the streets (for it is in London that our scene lies), rattling along the housetops, and fiercely agitating the scanty flame of the lamps that struggled against the darkness."

I found this opening line preyed on my mind and I could no longer read but instead wrote as best I could on a number of subjects.

A Well Drubbed Spar

A tremendous crash awakened me from my fitful sleep. I had been wakening on the hour listening to the crash of the waves, the creak of the ship and, earlier, the engine restarting. Now I could hear a torturous scream of metal and the steady rhythm of the engine stopped unnaturally, to my ears. I could hear shouts and running about. I made my way up to the deck, figuring that either a man was overboard or part of the rigging had come down, or a fault in the engine had occurred.

The wind was less and no shower of rain was coming down as before, just a dreary trickle. A shadowy group of men with shielded lights bunched over near the port paddle wheel.

Heavy weather in Biscay Bay, I-II-2

From the shouts and calls, I soon understood the distress of the ship: a tree or similar piece of lumber, some four and twenty feet in length, had, like a harpoon, been thrust into the paddle wheel. The wheel was now thoroughly jammed and had broken its shaft's seal and the ship was taking water through the shaft hole. Out of the darkness, orders came. I attached myself to the group headed to the engine room to deal with the water there. Perkins gripped my arm and we followed the Portuguese naval officer, who had appeared, and was brightly clad in a crimson and white nightshirt. On our way there, we were joined by two crew and Warren Beer who appeared clad only in an open shirt showing a muscular body not suiting my previous opinion of him as a clerk, he had been rarely seen so far this trip a victim of the seas restlessness and his own stomach's revolt at this treatment.

Mr Shimmins was in charge of the effort in the engine space. More light was brought and we then saw that we were gravely mistaken. The seal was indeed leaking badly but we had a far worse difficulty: the timber had acted like a harpoon. In actuality, the errant spar had penetrated the hull beneath the waterline and, with the action of ship and waves, was slowly tearing the hull planking apart.

Perkins, with his engineering skills, was most useful and in a number of shouted orders we secured canvas and wooden blocks, and quickly shored up the leaking seal. The spar was another matter- it needed either to be extracted from its hole or sawn off on the inside. As the ship's carpenter, a ratty little Portsmouth man, said the former was the only possible solution, we set to work. The crew left, needed on deck to fashion a sea anchor to keep the ship steady and work the two manual pumps as the steam one was un-able to keep up with the inflow of frigid Cantrabarian[3] water from the outside. The engine restarted but disengaged from the wheels, its power applied to the pumps only. The offending piece of wood was as thick as a fat man's thigh and protruded four and half feet into our ship. It was difficult to see as water was cascading past it, alternating which place it poured in from depending on the action of the boat and movement of the spar. The carpenter, named as always in a ship 'Chips', Shimmins and Perkins soon arrived at a plan to secure topside the spar to the ship to lessen its movement then we would saw off the protrusion here with a sawyers blade as a broad axe could not be swung with effect in this confined space. Chips took up the blade along with Warren Beer, who seemed the strongest of us. The spar continued to wiggle madly as before, splintering the wood around it. The four-inch planking was weakening as we watched in horror as more and more water made its way into the ship and the thump, thump, thump, thump of the manual and steam pumps reminded us of our plight.

It took some minutes for the team above to use a chain to snare the murderous pole to the ship's side. Even then, the harpoon still moved and the saw would not purchase. I made my contribution by pushing forward and placing both hands on the saw, holding it in place so the blade must bite the wood. I could barely hold my place with the water coming in and the boats movements beneath me but firm, desperate hands seeing my purpose grabbed my lower body and held me firm. With a struggle, the two other saw men got the blade going. It took some cursing and several tries but the strength of my hold on the blade and the efforts of the two men became like a dance. Soon they were lustily sawing back and forth and I could move back in the dancing lights of the swinging lanterns to help others to fashion a canvas and wood tingle *{patch}* to press over the hole once the cutting had been done. With a shout, the spar head broke away, leaving a tongue of wood that Chips took after with his knife and he cleaned it as best he could. A member of the crew, the carpenter's *Carfindo {assistant}*, had directed us in building the tingle - or, as I would call, it a 'batten'. The wooden patch was about two feet on each side and backed by an eight-inch block of wood. When the carpenter demanded it, we rammed it home over the cut off spar and the carpenter and the Carfindo took to driving in one foot long copper boat nails into the patch while we nailed the supporting angling timber to the deck. With that, the rush of water became much less although gallons were coming from around the patch. The Carfindo became, as if by magic, a caulker and I, knowing this trade from my youth on a ship, assisted him. It was difficult to force the caulking in against the pressure of the water and my eyes stung from my own sweat and the salt of the sea. I was somewhat indelicate in my work but I soon remembered my training and in but a few minutes the water had become a steady cascade instead of spurting torrent.

Mr Shimmins was well pleased and let every man know it, and he went on deck to tell the Captain that our crew had 'well drubbed' the spar. A shout from above announced to us that something had occurred but we noted no difference in the amount of water coming in and were soon told that the spar had been pulled out and was now gone from the paddle wheel.

The carpenter and some of the crew continued to reinforce the tingle while Mr Shimmins made it known to the passengers that our help would be required elsewhere for the boat was full of water and our presence was essential to help the bucket brigade. It was then I noted, despite being better and more warmly dressed than the others, I was soaked through and shivering. We made our way to the main stairway and found a place in the line with the crew and some of the other passengers. I found that Mr Catania had been behind me the entire time and it was he who had steadied me when I had held the saw blade to the spar. I thanked him most profusely for his aid. His reply was a nod and to pass me a bucket full of sea water which I passed in turn to Perkins and he to Warren Beer, who was a hero in my eyes as he was clad in only an open night shirt but seemed indifferent to the wet and cold. As his blood was half that of an eastern man and thinner and less capable of resisting the cold as us northerners, his resistance was notable.

The stewards had been on deck and now appeared, drenched and shivering but bringing with them boiling tea. I hate tea but drank it down and found, to my disgust, not only was it of that hateful infusion but it had been strengthened by a liberal amount of foul spirits. Perkins shouted to bring more of that rum un-spoiled by tea. Therefore, for two long hours or more, we helped to bail the ship out. My one arm braced myself against a part of the stairway, with my feet on two steps and the other arm passing heavy pails of water up. My shivering had become manifest to the others when Millicent appeared with a heavy coat. Perkins helped stripped off my wetted outer clothes and down to the waist leaving only my money belt. Millicent assisted me in putting the warm coat on. Someone else must have given it up as it was luxuriously warm and, notwithstanding my frozen legs and feet, I was much emboldened. The other men in the line were also partially stripped and re-clothed. I gained another long hot drink of boiling water treated with lemon and cinnamon. Now I had a painful need to return water to the sea in my own way. Nevertheless, I worked on for I was inspired not to quit by the presence of Millicent. Perkins had departed and to my shock Danae, with her skirts tied up in a resemblance of trousers had taken his place.

The Captain came by and began after another twenty minutes of torture to pull each of the passengers out of the line, replacing them with the crew and to my great relief my place was taken by one of the Goan galley men. Millicent, Prudence and her mother appeared and assisted me to my cabin, for I could barely walk as my extremities seemed to have become stiff from usage and cold. The so-called surgeon did some work on my hands, which were bloody, torn and raw. I suffered more pain from my need to answer the calls of nature than from my hand but finally I made my cabin, thanking the two Germann sisters and their mother who had aided me while they were stricken with seasickness, and I was able to make copious use of my chamber pot.

Perkins came by to see to my condition, as he seemed in better shape than I did. Before he left, he told of an incident on deck he had observed as he had gone about the ship looking for men, tools and wood. He said,

'Despite the un-couth weather which was so violent no two-legged man could stand on deck, never-the-less, our noble passenger sailor[4], Dalrymple, cocked-hat on his head, swaggered about above deck in his attempt to aid the ship in its distress. His aide-de-camp, however, found he had duties below with us. The good Captain continued so until an un-pitying sea wave deposited him into the main salon and carried away his gay hat, for which he loudly began to call for. 'Is my hat on deck', 'Do you have it sir', 'Good Captain Acornish, could you send me a man to find my hat'. A veteran seaman answered him while the man fought with his brothers to stretch and secure a tarpaulin over the main stairwell into the ship for the storm hatches had been torn off by the same wave which had swept the good Captain off his feet and sent his hat to the far winds. His remark was instructive, 'Your good hat, sir? It has set sail without your orders, I do believe, and I shall not be surprised if it makes Gibraltar before us'.

I found this tale most droll.

I stripped off my wetted clothes, removed the foreign coat and put on my second suit of civilian clothes, and, mindful of my exhaustion and pain, passed into sleep. Before I fell asleep, I was thinking not of the inrush of water, the chill, the fear or the burning pain of my muscles but of the thrill of Millicent's touch as she had help to un-dress and dress me.

A Pleasant Function

I was dreaming one of my torturous dreams from my youth when I awoke with a start. The movement of the ship was regular and, to my awe and delight, sunlight was coming into the cabin along with a variety of delicious scents. From beyond my door a babble of conversation was occurring.

I found that a pot of warm water was on my stand and I used it to shave and clean myself up. I found my right shoulder, arm and hand very stiff and sore. Having made myself presentable, I walked out and found half the passengers up and about, well dressed and smiling, and a full luncheon laid out in fabulous detail. I could tell that we were in good weather now but I acknowledged a number of greetings curtly and went up on deck to find we were indeed in fine schooner weather. The paddle wheel housing was still badly broken up but the paddle wheel itself was turning and we had all sails set, all damage to the masts having been made good. I found it was 10:30 in the morning and a quick tour of the ship and a few words with Mr Shimmins found that all was in order now. He thanked me most kindly for my valiant efforts in the night. He made some feeble joke about me being a whaler and having had my ship harpooned.

I did feel a bit like a hero, I must admit. I found the food and sat with Mr Catania and Mr Beer and we discussed the events of the early morning with some gusto. I partook of a generous amount of a pork shoulder in a white sauce and other delights. I spied the Germann sisters and gave them my best greeting, and even Prudence smiled at me. I soon found that the coat was that of their father who, much to his daughter's dismay had not given help other than his coat. This I returned, nonetheless, with thanks. Emboldened, I asked if I might walk out that evening with Millicent, which she and her mother consented to. I was speaking of our night's activities with my attention directed at Millicent when Perkins came up and said to me in Persian that most damning of expressions, the military adage about marriage suitability for officers by the tier of their rank. I did not understand fully what he had said until I used the Persian dictionary provided by the professor.

> *Ensigns will not marry, Lieutenants should not marry, Captains may marry, Majors can marry, Lieutenant Colonels will marry and Colonels are married.*

In return, I scowled at him and returned to him the one Persian curse I knew. Which stated how and why it was that a Persian named *Ghorom Saagh {pimp}* was involved in a most practical manner with his conception? He smiled and corrected my word order and tense, the scoundrel.

Danae accused Perkins of being discourteous as she considered it very rude for him to speak in a foreign tongue in front of young Ladies. Perkins and I were taken aback by this strong rebuke but halted in our explanations and apologies when Danae and Millicent's tittering made us realise that we were being tormented.

Perkins replied that we had spoken Persian concerning a military matter, but they would not believe it.

In a few hours, our cruise to the east was back in order. Warren, Catania, Perkins and I spent the afternoon discussing languages and I was in awe of the other three's travels and range of languages.

Mr Gregorian joined us and spoke with us for a while about the quaint method used by the Persians, Arabs and others in moving water, the *qanat* system; he even spoke for a time about how the Incans had moved water too. Speaking of water, our wetted and dirtied clothes were gathered up, tagged, washed and hung up to dry by the crew. The Captain also announced a celebration for that night, a thanksgiving for our deliverance, and to honour the many stalwarts among the passengers who had leant their support and labour in the ship's hour of need.

At one point, Perkins and I found ourselves alone and he said in a low voice that we must be on guard of spies! I thought it a supercilious remark but returned a knowing eye and wink.

The Portuguese and Spanish naval officers began a drinking contest amongst themselves over an argument they were having. This, it was explained to me by Catania who could speak both Spanish and Portuguese, was disagreement over whether the recently named Rennell's[5] current off Cape Finisterre really existed and what affect it may have had on historic naval engagements off that celebrated cape.

We met at tea and I had some excellent Orgeat Sirup[6] mixed with water as we discussed the possibilities ahead of us. With Catania's help, we outlined our possible ways to proceed once we had arrived in Gibraltar. In our discussion, I found from what Perkins excluded from our talk that he considered Catania to be a possible spy as he came up with details of our future plans in India and Persia that had nothing to do what we actually were going to do. Our future, as given to Catania, was that we were learning Persian to aid the British military mission now in Persia and training their army to help it resist the inroads of the Czar's Cossacks. His false comments seemed polished and believable. I took up these falsehoods as my own.

Our possibilities at Gibraltar would be that we could gain passage on a sailing ship, probably an East Indiamen on the traditional journey around Africa, the one my father had done. This would allow us a great deal of time to work on our languages. A second way would be for us to take a commercial steamer to Alexandria, then cross Egypt to Suweis *{the city of Suez}* and from there take up one of the east India steamers that were now plying the Red Sea. We also thought we could do a Syrian crossing. To land at one of the Levantine ports......*{Driscol never finished this thought leaving a blank line then repeated it on the next page}*, perhaps Beirut or Aleppo then to proceed overland to the Euphrates, take a boat on that Biblical river down to the Persian Gulf and then onto Bushire, the British/Persian port on that hot Gulf. From the Gulf, we would take a dispatch boat to Bombay. For our learning languages, the African route was longer and would give us more time but the ships rarely stopped except at St. Helena or, even more rarely these days, Cape Town. To go either way would give us opportunities to see the exotic lands and people. I shall hope for the overland route through the Syrian Desert to the great twin rivers and the Persian Gulf.

We debated these various routes but it was Perkins who observed that no matter which one we might favour, it was it would be the HEIC who would decide the matter. Their decision would be based on what available billets and ships were at Gibraltar when we arrived.

The entertainment was truly grand. There was a plentiful supper with a mix of Iberian and British foods served up for our pleasure. I found a rice dish called Lisbon Rice *{Arroz com figado de vitela a Lisboeta}* most un-worthy of its praise by the two Dago officers who were still rather un-steady since their wine drinking contest and argument in the afternoon but were quite personable otherwise. I found neither Officer's French understandable, nor did they mine.

I remembered then that it had been my birthday today. Perkins was surprised at my age as he thought I was three years or so older. As a matter of fact, of the half dozen people who knew it was my birthday, all thought me older than I was.

Catania mentioned that today was Yom Kippur. I only had a vague idea what that meant and resolved to become more knowledgeable about other religions.

Our Captain mightily praised the passengers who had assisted the crew for their courage and strong backs. Perkins was singled out for his engineering knowledge and Mr Beer was given special thanks for his part in sawing off the end of the spar. I was somewhat aggravated by no special mention of my part but the Germann sister and others made up for this by their attention. Dalrymple remained currish during the gala event and mentioned several times the fact of the ship's Captain having left London on a Friday and it was upon this that he blamed our misfortunes - and the loss of his hat.

Catania and Dalrymple had a fascinating discussion on where such a large spar could have come from and to my utter wonderment, they determined that it was off a French warship for only a ship of three thousand tons or larger would have carried such a large spar. Moreover, Dalrymple observed that the French naval mark had been on the end of the spar we had cut off while Catania noted that along with the French naval mark there had been a burnt in mark of the company that had supplied it. With his knowledge of naval stores, he stated authoritatively the company's name, its owners and the location in France were the offending tree might have been cut. I vowed at that moment to never know that much about European naval stores.

Millicent and I went later for our walk on deck and I lost count of the number of turns we made on that small deck. I would think it was more than a three hundred. We talked of everything of current interest in England. I can say that walking with a Lady on a moving deck at sea is most enjoyable for the movement of the ship constantly requires gallant attempts to prevent her from upsetting, which is done by keeping her close. It was a battle against the sea I for once did enjoy. My only point of sadness was that I had to share the deck with a score of people, including Perkins, who stayed behind me with Prudence on our circular deck pageant. It was a good birthday.

[Editor's note: Driscol was nineteen that day]

Wednesday 21 September

I found the day glorious and in the later afternoon, the ship's officer allowed the crew to fish. Several others and I joined them. Knowing the size of ocean fishes, I did not un-pack my sectioned bamboo rod but made use of a sturdy stud of wood and line provided to me by Mr Chips who had been most agreeable towards me since the morning of the spar.

We were using salt pork as bait and I was reminded of the Book of Job 41:1; *Canst thou draw out leviathan with a hook?* Not a nibble or bite and certainly no fish were taken and once Perkins was up (for he was a late riser that day) we got to our studies. During our luncheon, Perkins and I assisted Mr Little in his navigation. I found the theory easy but struggled with the maths, despite having once known it. We drilled away the afternoon in Persian and Arabic with diversions to Latin, Danish and Yiddish.

Later in the afternoon I had a short walk with Millicent on deck but as we neared the bow, a larger wave than normal erupted over the ship, drenching all on deck and doing some minor damage to the sails. Millicent was quite upset by the salt water soaking and seemed un-nerved by her wetted hair and she burst into silent tears. This mystified me until I was told by Danae that she had worked on her hair for much of the morning. I felt the cad for not noticing her actions or complimenting her hair as she was additionally upset for a voluminous hat she had been wearing had been washed away too, that was for the good as it was a hideous thing.

Shimmins' took the dosing of the passengers poorly and harangued the lookout and mate at the wheel soundly for their dereliction of duty. It seemed a harsh and un-founded charge but the seasoned naval officers I asked said that was one of their duties - but acknowledged a wave could come up at any time and the trouncing the men had taken was probably more for the passenger's ears than any real punishment. As Millicent had disappeared into her cabin and did not emerge again that day, I concentrated on my studies.

Thursday 22 September

An extraordinary occurrence. This has left me puzzled but divinely pleased, but disturbed in soul and mind.

[Editor's note: Driscol referred to his private journal which on this date, instead of a single word or a number of odd 'icons', has a long encoded paragraph and at the top of the page (he had started his private journal on the same day as his daily) he had but four short entries until this last one. He explains that he is using a book code but does not say which book it was. So what the matter was is left to our conjecture]

I skipped breakfast and returned to fishing as I was up before any of my fellow students. Again, the sea gods did not smile on me so I changed my bait from salt pork to a strip of yellow ribbon I had been playing earlier with, with Duperre. I also changed the fishhook for one of the crew brought out a smaller brass treble hook. We, a group of eight fishing advocates, were at our business when suddenly my wood and line were nearly snatched from my grasp. I had to brace my knee to retain a hold and soon found myself struggling with a fish. About me, all the others too were besieged and soon a group of passengers had gathered behind us as we wound in our hand lines. Two crew-members brought up fine white fish of about 8 pounds each.

The previously useless surgeon quickly identified them as blue jack mackerel, *Trachurus picturatus;* a species only recently described by Bowdich a dozen or so years before but caught for centuries in the bay. I had some difficulty trying to draw in my fish as I was trying not to break the scabs on my hands but belatedly I got him aboard. All the fish caught were the same magnitude and, with some enthusiasm, we threw our hooks out again. Scarcely had they hit the water that they were taken again. This time I ignored the torn flesh of my hand and hauled away. I was encouraged to do so by the shouts and speculations of the passengers who had gathered behind us. As soon as we could get the fish up and the hook thrown back we brought up another. My hand began to bleed and the surgeon who tried to be stern while he administered to my hand but I laughed at his pretense.

However, I handed my line to another when Millicent admonished me and I found that Danae had taken it and she and a dozen men brought up fish at a rapid rate. Her sister Prudence was beside herself in condemnation of Danae's un-ladylike actions and her sharp whispers were hard not to smile at. Danae continued and brought up two flapping fishes before handing the line back to me with a smile, and, as I was beginning to feel the pain, handed it to Perkins, who had finally come up but he was to have no luck. The fish had departed as suddenly as they had appeared or we, in our passage to the southwest, had outrun them.

Chips and one of the Stewards had gathered up the fish, smacking them down on the deck to stun them and, in a demonstration of good knife work, had them gutted and headed to the galley in a few minutes. A few minutes more and the deck was cleaned of all scale and blood. I found the sight of this blood grew no disquiet from my mind except for some distaste to my senses.

The rest of the day, we took up in the study of Persian with me trying un-successfully to describe the joys of fishing to Perkins in Persian but I lacked the vocabulary to do so. The dinner consisted of our prey from earlier in the morning and beautifully done with butter, winter savoury and onion.

[Editor's note: Driscol writes the next lines in Taylor's shorthand, noting how some of the marks are similar to Persian {Arabic} letters from now on his journal will be written in a mixture of English, Taylor's shorthand, Persian and Arabic. I will not note this unless it is necessary for clarification. The next line he wrote in Persian]

To God belongs the east and the west, wheresoever you look is the face of God

Friday 23 September

A week at sea. More study and my Persian is getting better. More time with Millicent and her family. Prudence seems to be hostile to both Perkins and I. Later that night at supper, I sat next to the American Mr Vadeboncoeur, who at one point in a conversation about the great artists of Europe, dislocated the flow of convivial conversation by saying that the Italian and French artists in pourtraicts[7] outdid their British rivals by showing more TALENT.

This caused a number of men to denounce his statement, not for the slur against British artists but for the use of the word '*talent*'. For no one on the ship had heard it before and some of the men thought it un-gentlemanly to use such a word before Ladies. I thought it might mean value and had come from the use of the term 'talent', a classical term for a weight of gold or silver. The assaulted man was perplexed and said it was a word in common use in America and meant simply their abilities. He failed to apologise for its use and the high point of conversation was not regained and soon everyone drifted back to their cabins after some music by a number of the passengers who had some TALENT in that direction. I, for one, found the word useful, if daring.

I noted it down for use in the Officer's mess in India where it would raise the antagonism of the conservative members to an occlusion *{seizure or in this sense outrage}*.

Saturday 24 September

I awaken to a tragedy; one of the crew has fallen from the masthead during the night. He lived but a few hours greatly un-manned by the pain of his many broken bones. A simple ceremony was performed by the Captain early in the morning and M. Keith *{one of the missionaries}* gave an eloquent eulogy about an ordinary seaman few knew and talked instead of a young man who had gone down to the sea and would not return. He was an Englishman from Dover. This brought a pall over the ship and once more Dalrymple blamed the un-wise departure from London on a Friday for this loss of life, and the loss of his beloved hat.

More study and another evening walk with Millicent on deck but as I write this my mind is alight from having been with Millicent and I cannot remember a single element we discussed.

Mr Emmanuel Yehoshua Catania. I-II-3

Acornish's Dissolution

Sunday 25 September

Shimmins' remarks that we are nearing Cape Finisterre and the wind is rising, and our first port call will be at Vigo, Spain. He believes we shall make it before sunset. We studied this day and only went on deck to see that the barometer is once again dropping at the same time the sea and wind are rising. The *William Fawcett* began to roll up to 45 degrees in a strong dry gale from the southwest.

Dalrymple and his aide approached our Captain with the Spanish and Portuguese officers in tow and soon a most animated discussion took place. It is the opinion of these experienced officers that the steamship is too close to the Cape Finisterre headland. First, they argue about whether the Cape is actually a headland or a foreland but Captain Acornish, supported by Mr Shimmins, will not change his course if he is to make Vigo before dark he must skirt the headlands of northwest Spain. The arguments are made that the Rennell currents are driving the ship closer to the coast than he thinks. This went on for some time but Captain Acornish would not allow passengers to adjust his course. He was firm on this matter and as I noted a head taller than the four men confronting him. He thanked them for their contribution and wished them a good afternoon, and turned his back on them. This discourse leaves a feeling of grave concern in my heart.

A Portuguese dispatch boat, lateen-rigged, or a Caravela, was seen but she ignored the William's flags to close her as the Captains think she has come out of Vigo. She sailed on and did not respond. The Portuguese officer was brought on deck but he, after a long study of the ship through a glass said, in French, that she is an Azorean fisherman, probably home ported in Sao Miguel and were of a people not noted for helping others, especially foreigners.

It was late afternoon and I had just come down to the salon after a turn on deck. The sea was grey green and heaving. The wind had shifted and was now coming in strongly from the south, the wind whistling a somber tune in our rigging as our small ship was trying to beat into it, trying to make our first port of call. Seasickness had stricken the passengers again but Perkins seemed to be doing all right and we focused on writing out Persian terms to retain them. We heard a commotion on deck, which carried to us despite the howl of the wind followed by a heavy shock to our starboard side and the ship skewing off course and losing way. We were thrown to the deck and our books and papers strewn all over us. In my disorder, I watched a pencil roll away and neatly pass beneath Perkin's cabin door.

Dalrymple was up in a moment cursing violently that we were aground. A moment later the ship shivered and violently seemed to turn each way at once throwing all in the salon to the deck again with the added distraction of women screaming, men shouting and the tearing of wood and metal. I could hear the call for all hands and soon men were running in every direction. It took some time to ascertain what the disaster had been. Dalrymple corrected himself within a few moments saying that we were not aground but had hit bottom or a rock but then had come off and he prayed the hull was sound.

There was nothing for us to do, no heroic action to employ. The word came down to us that we had struck a reef, and, as stated by Dalrymple, we had come off it a moment later. They thought we were about seven miles off Cape Finisterre[8], and it was exactly at four that afternoon that the ship had been taken off the reef. The previously un-damaged paddle wheel was shorn off cleanly and several gashes had been placed into the hull amidships. The funnel had fallen and the forward mast was badly sprung. The women were greatly concerned and I saw tears in a number of the older women's eyes for they felt tragedy more. The other naval officers went up on deck and I avoided the confrontation, which I could hear seated in the salon. After a stern verbal battle, the ship was put before the wind and headed towards the Spanish port of Corunna, the safety of the ship and passengers being more important than making Vigo.

As it got dark, I went on deck and saw the full damage. Not only was the entire starboard paddle wheel missing but the foremast had taken damage. But more striking was the funnel which was simply missing and only the great bolts which had held it to the iron plate on the deck remained. I toured the ship and found the steam pump working but there were only a few pounds of coal left to fire the boiler. It soon stopped and the manual pumps were manned but Mr Chips convinced me that the leakage was minor but that without the engines and with a damaged mast, the ship could not make her way into Vigo against the rising wind storm.

So we ran towards Corunna and the two missionary families held religious rituals of some sort but I would not attend such mummery. I could see that Mr Gregorian and wife were in each other's firm clutches.

I reported what I knew to the Germann's and several others. I did note that all the men with maritime knowledge seemed un-complaining of our fate while those others without knowledge of the sea seemed to fear the loss of the ship. Prudence and Millicent's eyes welled with tears but Danae had a fierce determination in hers. M. Keith and the other missionaries began to sing songs of praise and long-winded beseeching's. I readied myself for a long swim if necessary while thinking how I might keep Millicent afloat too.

Providence and the wind was with us and we reached the outer road early and dropped the best bower and two other anchors to secure our anchorage until we could enter the port at dawn. Several times the anchors began to drag but each time the crew was able to remedy it.

It was early morning before I could sleep.

Monday 26 September

We rode out the storm without difficulty near Corunna, or Groyne, as the British officers referred to it, and made our way into the port at first light and found we were in the Ria De Betanzos, the place that, centuries before, the Armada had sailed from to attack England. A small pinance from the shipping company led the ship to our berth near the town itself. We were boarded and the ship inspected by the company then the Spanish. We were at 43 degree 23 minutes north and 30 degrees 20 minutes west.

The Spanish officer went aboard a two-decked hulk in the harbour having the name *Guadamedina* and it had once been a 74. She sent a boat in reply to a signal he had set in the rigging without the crew's assistance or permission. The old Spanish warship looked as if she might have last been to sea during the Seven Years War. When the wind shifted we could smell her; bilge and garlic, it seemed to me. The Portuguese officer went off too but I missed how he did so. No one seemed to be aware of how the little man had departed our ship.

While we waited, Perkins annoyed me greatly by his bringing up a query about Millicent's middle names, Magdalena and Maximiliane. He asked if I had not considered the contradiction in these names I had not and he explained that while the former was the mother of our Lord and therefore as saintly as one might wish the second had a less savoury reputation, being he said a cognomen of a shameless profligate whose harlotry was notable even in sinful Rome. He seemed to be saying that Caligula wife's name Messalina was in some way related to the German Maximiliane. We debated that for some time and later I found that that name was that of her maternal grandmother. Prudence over heard this discussion which we un-wisely conducted in English. She attempted to berate him for his name but I for one could not think of anyone named Donald who had done anything remarkably wicked. All in all his argument was bereft of classical support and Prudence all but ripped out his eyes for having even suggested the idea. Defaming her Grandmother and sister - it was then that Perkins gave her the sobriquet of Clytemnestra. I disagreed with Perkins' suggestion about her *{Millicent's}* middle names and I thought her Prudence's words were noble like Artemisia I {of Caria} actions. I suggested at the end that perhaps she was Circe and as Perkins had touched her he had turned him into a hog.

[Editor's note: This passage from Driscol is heavy in classical history and mythology; Messalina was certainly a bad person or so later historians say, Maximiliane has no known connection to Messalina, as it is the feminine form of Maximilian, which means greatest. Clytemnestra was the wife of Agamemnon and she killed him for sacrificing her daughter and bringing home a Trojan concubine. Artemisia was a Greek who sided with the Persians against the free Greek states. Circe was a goddess who turned men into hogs.]

Cristenos Corunna

Tuesday 27 September

Now on land, the families are resident in the few hotels in town while bachelors are consigned to outskirts of the town. We are beyond the city wall that cuts across the peninsula in what had been the quarters of a Spanish cavalry regiment *{Dragones de la Reina}* located near a large country home called San Pedro de Visma. This was on the hill where Fraser's Division had stood during the battle of Corunna in January 1809, however, I was un-certain where father had been with the 52nd I knew he had been on flank guard and I suspect it was further to the west. The barracks had not been clean so we had spent the day in directing the crew in sorting out that muddle. I was pleased not to be drowned and in my first foreign land of my journey east. The ground consisted of whitish rock with green grass between them with few trees to be seen. My previous day had been most un-pleasant, many of the passengers being of foul mood and mouth to the crew and Captain. However, the British Consul was active, if very short: Mr Benito Santo, who dressed well but had some difficulty with English; Mr Little, assisted by Catania; and some less useful Spanish and company functionaries had found lodgings for all and had the luggage delivered.

We all received an extempore, or temporary passport, and we were allowed to bring in our luggage un-searched but had to pay the *Advaneros {custom-house officers}* for the privilege of bringing in our weapons and also had to pay an irksome levy on articles of drinking and eating, the *comestibles de boca* duty. We were also warned to not do anything suspicious to include, and not limited to, firing a weapon, making drawings or writing notes, taking plans or mapping the country. One should also avoid any interest in fortresses, barracks and arsenals, and should not ask the people about such things. The last piece of advice the English Consul gave us was to remember that the first thing the Spaniard of the lower classes wants is money. Their worship of the Virgin is often secondary to their adoration of Mammon. As for the higher classes, they want more money but will be somewhat more gentile in asking for it. The Consul also explained that the Spaniards were on edge as the Carlist Civil War[9] was underway and many families had split over whom to support.

In the harbour were two score of ships from many nations and a six-ship squadron of the Spanish navy but with yards down and no appearance of being active despite the country being at war with itself in its political fracas of the Carlist War. We also have a temporary laissez-passer from the presiding governor of this port but are restricted to the environs of Corunna who knows what a malevolent group of English passengers might do to this peaceful countryside. The Cristinos were polite as they were well aware of British political and un-official military support to them in the civil war, but were still wary of Carlist agents in our midst.

The repairs to the ship have begun. The crew is showing their strong backs, assisted by a large party of Spanish seamen paid for by the company. They have removed every item on the ship and she is in the process of being careened[10] in doing so, showing that along half of the starboard side the copper sheathing had been stripped off and in two places rocks still impaled the hull. We were blessed that the rocks had not fallen out for they were a foot or more in radius and had they been lost the ship may have foundered. Mr Little says that Shimmins agreed with the advice of the passenger officers but could do nothing more than support his commander in the disagreement over our being too close to shore. The passenger's had, of course, been right.

Catania with his command of Spanish soon found us a local woman who would cook us a meal and in a short time we had polenta and a robust Galician style stew. As one we then fell asleep in our chairs underneath the sparse trees outside our temporary home. I was awakened by what I perceived to be Duperre but it turned out to be a local cat, a pretty little brown feline who made my acquaintance.

Thinking perhaps I was a rodent was Perkins remark at this friendly approach. Catania spent the night in town and Perkins, Beer, the American, a few others and I spent the night in study of language.

Later that night we were called to a passenger's meeting and offered the following possibilities by Mr Little;

> Refund of our un-used passage money and we to make our way as we wished

> To await another ship to make it to the other ports but there was no information on when that might occur or what shipping might be available

> Wait for the Fawcett to be repaired

> Agree to travel by land to our destination.

> Perkins and I were quite happy to wait for the Fawcett as our billet orders were tied to that ship, and to change our itinerary was asking for a lengthy exchange of pointless letters and memorandum with clerks in London who were, as all officers knew, complete boneheads. We also agreed that we could well spend the time in our studies, explore the area and, of course for me, Millicent was here and the Germann's were intended on waiting for the Fawcett too. A number of the passengers led by Dalrymple were most vocal in their condemnation of the ship's officers at the meeting.

Wednesday 28 September

Catania and Beer joined us at our new bachelor quarters plus the other un-attached men. One of the missionary wives developed a tooth pain and Catania used his command of the language to find her a man to ease her of this concern as our own surgeon was I had stated before - useless. I went with him into the town and found the place no better nor worse than Manchester in the matter of cleanliness but the scent of sour wine, garlic and more pleasant odors assaulted one at every turn. I stopped by to speak with Millicent and found Perkins on her doorstep speaking amiably with Prudence, who, as usual, soured when I approached.

As Perkins was there we made a plan to hire a carriage and take the Ladies, *{Prudence insisted that Danae go with us also}* to see the *Farum Brigantium*, or as Catania described it; the *Torre de Hércules*, the next day.

I found Perkins to be a good chap; droll and knowledgeable but his forwardness towards women and his appreciation and association with the local demi-monde of the town annoyed me, but I must say he never said much of anything forward to Millicent or Danae, or at least in my presence. I guess with his good fortune in regards to his looks he had left me two lesser breeds from the herd. I appreciated his kindness in this. Despite his forwardness, he was held off by Prudence Germann with a stern eye; a stern eye she continued to display towards me also for reasons I shall not ponder on.

In our discussion of such matters, Perkins put it down to her envy of my attentions to Millicent and Danae, and I protested that I paid no attention to Danae but he only shook his head and smiled like an impish child at me! The rogue.

After we had left the Ladies, Perkins offered to escort me to a Spanish brothel, one called *Complejo la fuente Maria Magdalena Vázquez Lareo,* he had discovered. I decline as politely as I could but it left me somewhat shaken that he was so brazen in his un-clean acts.

I returned to our quarters and found Beer there and I asked him why he had no duties to perform for magistrate Germann. He scoffed and replied that the man was either getting drunk, drunk or recovering from being drunk, so he rarely had time to task him with any work. To all this he smiled and this made sense when joined with what Danae and Millicent had said in regards to their father's imbibing of liquor. My not drinking impresses Millicent and it had certainly been the first time this trait had been anything but a source of annoyance.

A committee came up to us at the bachelor's quarters with a petition directed at the shipping line about the service and a severe condemnation of the ships officers. It was poorly written and it complained about trifles such as the quality of wine. (I abhor that drink so could not comment) They also complained about the quality of the sack[11] and port, saying it was not up to standard nor were the poultry fat enough. The food supplied to the passengers was plentiful to redundancy but the cooking indifferent and too many dishes of Portuguese or Spanish origins were allowed. This seemed like prattle but the next paragraph was serious, charging the Captain with endangering the ship by failing to heed the advice of the 'maritime expertise' that had been on board.

I declined to sign it, stating that a ship's Captain at sea is solely responsible for the ship, crew and passengers and that parliamentary majorities did not have sway over him. Dalrymple went red in the face. I again declined to sign after more discussion but Beer and the American did sign. Perkins arrived, looking quite pleased with himself and to my surprise supported my decision on the petition but he did think I should have spoken more forcibly against the idea of a petition altogether.

Mr Vadeboncoeur, the American, invited us to supper and cards. The Spanish woman who was doing our cooking delivered a fine piece of roast lamb with beetroot and, of course, garlic, to us. I suspect she was making a fortune as Catania noted we were all paying her a rate that he had arranged for ALL of us, but it was trifle so we let our error stand as it was. We observed that we were ship-wrecked on a foreign shore and there was no need to antagonise the natives.

Beer made a fine joke by pointing at the lamb and wondering if the natives were cannibals. While dining, our American friend spoke about the superiority of the 'American system' and the inherent depravity of human nature. He passed from that observation to the need to bring a republican system to our Monarchist island but to also introduce African labour into our army and agriculture. It was pointed out to him that there was no need of wide-scale African slavery in England, an argument he dismissed with the idea that African enslavement was the path to civilization. He proposed depopulating Africa and Christianizing its inhabitants while they worked in the Americas, Europe and even Asia. He thought especially that given the lack of labour in India, Africans could be imported to work there too. He quoted a few passages of the Old Testament to support his view. When told that there was no labour shortage in India or anywhere in the east, he protested that he knew better, as he knew that there were no slaves in India, therefore, who did the labour? We found this Jonathan talk bewildering and off setting.

Extraordinary Mathematical Fortunateness

The card game began afterwards as it was a chilly afternoon for Spain and we had a fire burning merrily, and a number of lamps 'borrowed' from the ship. We could not play Whist *{a card game of Driscol's time a precursor to Bridge}* as there were seven of us so the American suggested we play a game he had learned on the riverboats of the Mississippi. That sounded intriguing.

[Editor's note: The players were Driscol, Perkins, Vadeboncoeur, Beer, Catania and Little but the other player is unknown. I have removed a page of instruction on how to play the game, which in all aspects is like the modern 5 card draw poker and played with a 52 card English deck no jokers]

I found the game the most interesting I had played; certainly one of chance but delightful in its possibilities he called it draw poker.

We were using as counters a bag full of copper coins; I *reales de vellón* and I *maravedies* to place our bets. The game was wonderful and the conversation even better. I regret that I did not take notes but some of the highlights were; during a discussion on the confusion that is woman's thought (for this was no Officer's mess where the discussion of women is forbidden) and how tiresome it is to deal with their irrelevancies. Perkins looked at me and remarked that we might get tired of one other company, 'for,' he says, 'you have a great flaw Driscol' and at that I bristled; until he explained his remark, 'you were not born a beautiful woman.' He said that and caused great merriment by it.

The game went on during the night, Little and Vadeboncoeur doing badly, Beer and Perkins doing well, and I was middling. I had a piece of paper with the percentage chances of certain card combinations occurring something that was passed around a great deal amongst the new players. We had all returned from a visit to nature when Vadeboncoeur dealt another hand. I was beside myself with wonder over the cards I had obtained and checked again the list. The betting had been at most a few coppers but a few times more money had ended up being in the 'pot'. Based on my cards, I put out a bet of 5 coins. This drew a collaborative in-drawing of breath from the other six players. For in the last round I had beaten them all with a bluff, which had most annoyed them. It was Perkins who declared I was nearing insolence for attempting to bluff again and he met my bet, as did every other member of the table. As the American was to my left all the others had to ask for cards, most taking three and Perkins but two. When it came to me I declared in a soft voice that I would take none. Little thumped the table, pointed at me, and mouthed without saying, 'bluff'. Another round of betting occurred ending with 3 coins coming to me which I saw and raised 8. Consternation! The betting continued. Each time I raised again. It so happened that both Little and Vadeboncoeur ran out of ready funds. By the rules he himself had explained that he must either drop his cards or find more resources. Declining offers of loans at ruinous rates of interest, he went to his luggage, came back with a box, and opened it, displaying a fine pair of pistols of a type I did not recognise and which he announced were American made Colt cap and ball revolvers of .28 calibres, with buffalo horn handles and black maple stock. This was worth 20 x more than all the money on the table but his blood was up and, having determined the value, I agreed to the bet. Little and Beer dropped out, as did Catania but Perkins was bold and matched it. The game was called, and the American laid down a straight flush, which was met with a cry of exclamation and victory by all. Perkins stood and slapped down his cards. Also, to our amazement, a straight flush, a discussion began over which suite had priority when I quietly laid down my cards. It was Catania who saw what I had, and brought it to the attention to all. Silence fell, for I had been dealt a Royal flush in spades; the odds of that were some 650,000 to one. I thought for a moment that the American would become angry but he was just stunned for he had had the second highest hand and Perkins the fourth in the game of poker. He recovered himself and slapped me on the back, and gave out with a string of curses that were said with the best intentions Perkins, too, was quite gobsmacked, but came up a good loser. I offered to return the winnings, as they were excessive but all declined. I had thought the American no Gentleman but he proved me wrong. I had won the equivalent of two weeks' pay in that one hand plus the pistols and the amenability of the night was an even better bonus!

[Editor's note: Driscol would later claim that he introduced the game to India and there may be some truth to his assertion]

Thursday 29 September

After our late night, Perkins and I rose even later, and having hired a carriage in town, and at the appointed hour, made our way to the Germann's hotel. The Ladies were lovely and her mother was to come with us as chaperone, a matter we had overlooked since we would be going outside the city walls. We made our way a mile or so out on the peninsula with Prudence for once treating me better than a mongrel dog. As a matter of fact, she was full of sweetness towards me. I suspected it was due to the presence of her mother. Perkins and I tried to tell the story of the game last night but its uniqueness seemed to be lost on mother and daughters. We found that Mr Germann had signed the petition with Prudence agreeing with him while her mother and the other two daughters, had not signed. We made the impressive tower, which was much more commanding than I would have thought. I impressed Millicent as best I could by relating the tale of Hercules defeating Geryon[12] and burying him there. No one was at the location so we explored as we saw fit. We found the original Latin inscription, *Marti aug.sacr c.sevivs lupus archtectus aeminiensis lvsitanvs.ex.vo*, - Architect Gaius Sevius Lupus, from Aeminium[13]. The five storey Roman light house was in excellent condition and we decided it had been 'improved' during the centuries by the Spanish. The square building has an inner staircase which for a small fee paid to the lighthouse keeper one can trudge up, which we of course did. I remain as far from the edge as I could and I believe none could sense my fear while atop it for there was no balcony.

We had a good picnic on the edge of the white cliff overlooking the sea and, while walking about the site, Perkins had the luck to find a stone arrowhead that I pronounced a Carthaginian one which he presented to Prudence who gave it to Danae who enjoyed the piece of history with much delight. Of course, I suspected that it was not Carthaginian but said nothing of it.

Their mother questioned both of us on our families condition and prospect, and in such a way that we did not feel we were face to face with a somewhat hostile tribunal. We were being sized up, Perkins being the much better catch but I could see no interest in Prudence for such a match or so I imagined.

As we ended our meal we were amazed to see Mr Barrows drive up with the Penn sisters. This was, of course, grist to the mill of female gossip and I found that I had been oblivious to what was then presented to me. That Mr Barrow had made the acquaintance of the un-married Penn sister. I had not noted this occurrence at all while aboard the *William Fawcett*. Perkins, by his remarks, had, and spoke in conspiratorial tones with the Ladies about it.

As we drove back, Beer met us at the hotel entrance and gave us poor news. Our worthy commander, Captain Henry Cabot Acornish, had departed his life on shore at the house of harbour quarantine official *{medical officer}* late this morning. The crew had been mustered and informed, and Mr Shimmins had taken temporary command pending approval by the Company. He will be buried on the morrow and his steward will proceed with his effects back to his family. We asked what the cause of his death was. Beer said the surgeon had announced it apoplexy of the heart but Perkins and I felt it was his dishonoured at being petitioned against by the other passengers for what he was blameless for. Catania thought he might have taken poison in a fit of despondency and become a suicide but I considered that to be eastern thinking.

This was most melancholy news, but we made our way back to our abandoned barracks and as we approached we saw that our guard - for being in Spain and isolated as we were we had agreed amongst ourselves that one of us would always safeguard our valuables with us rotating the position each day; a rotation we had come to by playing cards was not at his post. It was the American's turn and we entered our hall with some trepidation to find him rummaging in my luggage. He explained that he had found my luggage disordered after returning from nature's errand and was but checking if anything was missing. It was my medical chest that had been opened, but I found nothing amiss. For a while we argued with the man over his actions. He blamed the Jew but the matter was turned aside with the arrival of another bedmate with a tale to tell.

An Un-visited Funeral

Mr Little arrived at dusk to inform us that there would be no funeral on land tomorrow. For his directions on his burial *{the late Captain Acornish}* were found among his papers and, in accordance with this request, Shimmins' had taken a small French *Lugger {a type of small craft with two masts and quadrilateral sails}* under hire and had buried the valiant Captain at sea without ceremony, as he wished.

[Editor's note: Driscol, using a pencil, put a heavy black edged box around the above announcement]

The mood was somber that evening and each man did his own entertainment. I dug out another book and began to read.

Friday 30 September

Michaelmas, the feast of Saint Michael the Archangel, is today. This is the first celebration of it that I have missed. For the first time, I am homesick and miss the goose my mother would cook with apples that was the traditional meal of my family for this day.

Good news; Mr Little proclaimed that the repaired Fawcett would set sail tomorrow under sail for the other scheduled ports. As an aside, he noted that the ship could have sailed today but Shimmins wished to avoid a repeat of the 'Friday' curse on the superstitious passengers. After a morning of language work and rather poor dinner, Perkins and I withdrew to a rocky point over-looking the sea and took some shots with our new pistols. I fired five rounds from the French revolver, as did my friend. It was not accurate beyond thirty feet. My new American pistols were more accurate and he and I each fired one for five shots, he being the better shot than I. I attempted to give him one of the pistols but he declined - though, as we were walking back for supper, he asked if he might borrow it until we reached India. That was agreeable. The box contained only five and forty rounds after we had fired the ten. We both remarked that all twenty rounds had fired with no misfires and Perkins admitted that, while he was still skeptical of percussion caps, he took this demonstration as a factor in the mechanism's favour. While walking back we passed by a group of mounted men headed in the general direction of where we had been. Perhaps they were going to investigate the shots. It was only then that we recalled the Consul's reproach to NOT discharge firearms in the area. Oh well. The perpetrators ourselves, walked away un-hindered from the scene of the crime.

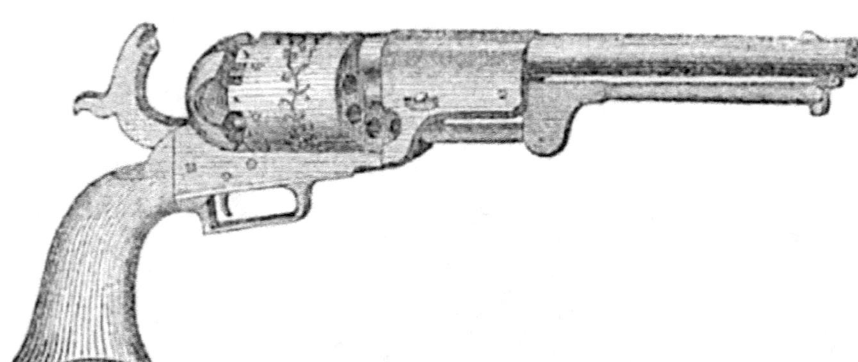

The Colt revolvers won in the card game by Driscol. I-II-4

We next walked the hills where the battle of Corunna had been fought. As we walked, the weather turned windy and wet, and greatly reduced our enjoyment of the stroll and our task. We ambled across where we believed the British line might have lain, between the village of Elvina and the sea. We found where the French had attacked and taken Elvina, and the spot, marked by a cairn, where Sir John Moore had lead the counter-attack until struck in the shoulder by a cannon's round shot.

Resting place of Sir John Moore, at Corunna I-II-5

A few days earlier we had visited his grave in Corunna and found it to our liking. I did not recall enough knowledge of the battle other than the 52nd had been in Paget's division and I had no book with me that covered the subject so I was unable to remember nor locate where my father's battalion had stood during the fight[14].

Farther from here, to the southeast, was Sahagun *{a town in Northwest Spain}* where my father had removed a French cavalryman's sabre *{French I[st] Provisional Chasseurs}* from the foot of the man who would later be instrumental in my obtaining my commission. I was sorry to not be able to see it. I vowed to someday return to Spain and trace my father's travels and battles.

[Editor's note: see Volume III, page 1019, Appendix Supplement, 'What Constitutes a Gentleman' a reprint of the January-June, 1873 issue of Blackwood's Magazine, volume CXIII for why Sahagun was important to Driscol]

That night we had another retched, garlic intensive Spanish repast of some stew and played cards - this time I lost heavily but as they were just copper coins, I lost nothing but a tiny percentage of what I had won before. The American, whom I had begun to distrust, was the big winner but his constant stories about how famous he was were beginning to grow tiresome.

Saturday 1 October

The dawn that came to us was wet with dew, and we took to move our luggage down to the port again. Here we found the Fawcett riding quietly at anchor off the quay and were un-ceremoniously transported to her by barge. The ship was transformed, her rigging fixed, repainted and the other paddle wheel and housing dismantled. The paddle wheel's shaft still stuck out, but she was now just a sailing ship, her tall majestic funnel of red and black had not been replaced but a temporary one of half the height and painted rose red up through the same hole now timbered=in to prevent the sea gaining access.

I escorted Millicent aboard but now at least a quarter of the passengers were gone and the ship had a somber disposition. She spent the time with me in an animated discussion of some wearisome epistolary novel she was reading. As she spoke, I spent the time seeing just how far her bosom would expand when she breathed in and out.

The Spanish port Captain was a gadfly with a mission of delay and only with the diplomacy and language skills of Catania, Little, and an ineffectual company agent did Shimmins finally weigh anchor in early afternoon. I could not say I would miss Corunna but did know my father would rejoice in my having trodden ground he had been over in battle when serving with the first Battalion of the regiment. I found the place redolent and tawdry. In addition, the civil war had drained away the men and the port seemed dead to civil and moral entertainments.

Mr Little and the Stewards had laid out a splendid meal for afternoon tea, and, after the two previous days of un-fortunate food, we dined well and long. As the passengers separated by necessity, there were many adventures to be found out and discussed but the timbre of the conversation was muted and restrained by the loss of the Captain, and our earlier misfortunes.

We found that the ship would circumvent Vigo as those passengers for it had departed to that port by land. Our next port of call would be Oporto but, as I tired quickly of the prattle and tattle, I took the leisure time to begin reading again and to avoid the return of seasickness and its awkward effect on the passengers. I could tell that the grasping fingers of the sea gods were twisting in the guts of the passengers once more. I could tell this by the many scurrilous invectives I heard directed at the ship, her crew and the moving unstable nature of seawater. I ignored the seaward passage of the ship out into the Atlantic and instead began to read Bulwer-Lytton's, The Last Days of Pompeii as I was in an ill temper after Millicent's baffling interest in such a poor piece of literature as she was now wasting her time on. At the very least, she could read the original in German, a language she knows well, but instead reads it in English. What raggle-taggle is *The Sorrows of Young Werthe*.

[Editor's note: Driscol wrote in his journal the initials 'TSoYW' which, I surmise, might be the book above, but it is only an educated guess]

Sunday 2 October

I awoke at dawn to find that Duperre had forced open my door in that way cats can do with their heads. I was glad that he had not taken French leave *{deserted}* of the ship while in port. I went up on deck and found the wind was coming in fresh from the west, occasionally in heavy blows and beginning to raise a considerable swell in which the Fawcett was pitching up and down. I felt sorry for the passengers as they as a whole seemed so susceptible to seasickness. I reflected on the style of the book I was reading. Its style was free and perspicuous, the language seemed well selected and the narrative often full of interesting tales but the book did not seem to be able to hold my interest.

I reflected on many things that morning. Having chilled myself sufficiently to rid myself of dark thoughts I made my way back to my cabin and began yet again to learn the meaning of words in Persian. I could hear the ship's officer discussing how the small vessel was acting as a pile-driver; a name given a ship that pitches badly in a seaway. This due to the departure of her paddle wheels which had given her 'balance', for my lack of the proper nautical term.

Breakfast was a mean thing; Flemish style rasher and some god-awful omelette made, I believe, with wool and tree bark. The table was set but I noticed that few passengers came to partake, however, Mr Barrow and Miss Penn did so. They sat so near one another and were so engrossed with each other that they paid no attention to me, the food, the pitching ship, or a Spanish rat that ran across the main salon with the two cats in pursuit. When I related this story to Perkins at our study secessions, he queried how I knew it was a Spanish rat instead of a good English one. I replied that it was simple; the cats were French and only a Spaniard, not an Englishman, would run from them. He thought it a splendid jest and we took some time to convert it into Persian - with the help of Beer. It came out translated with the original chased animal being a hound, the chaser a love stricken Afghanistauni, the role of the Spanish rat being taken by a *Mahratti {Hindu warrior}* and the English rat - well we made that up - by a British bull dog. However, it did not seem as apropos and rather confusing.

The two sets of missionaries having fallen out - again - over the true meaning of the Gospel of John held separate services. Perkins and I hid in his cabin and worked on verb endings. Again, as they had on past Sundays, they attempted to impose their view of Sabbath on us. To defeat this, we simply declared that we were discussing religion and not working. They could say nothing to dispute us as our discussion was in Persian and Arabic, broken here and there by queries between us in French, as Perkins had declared he would improve my pronunciation of French or throw me overboard, but rarely did we speak in the English tongue.

A Surprise Announcement

By noon, the sea had miraculously smoothed and the wind had moderated to a steady breeze, and we had the finest sailing since the day on the Biscay when we had caught the fish. The passengers were now veterans, and own skirmish with seasickness seemed over, and all came for dinner. Except for Mr Germann, who I suppose was drunk again. As we were enjoying a celery and leek soup, Mr Barrow stood up and spoke elegantly; first thanking all and, seeing that he had no family in the vicinity, he would like to announce his engagement to the now-no-longer-to-be-a-widow Miss Penn, whose first name I learned was Cerridwyn; a delightful Welsh name I had not heard before. This announcement dispelled the previous gloom and everyone wished the new couple the best. Acting Captain Shimmins asked when they might marry and it would seem that this point had not been decided, and after a whispered conference between the two, they announced as soon as possible. The Manx man offered his office and ability to perform the service, for where better to be married than at sea on a beautiful Sunday morning off the coast of Portugal? We were in line for another surprise for a man who had not spoken a word of any consequence during the entire trip offered up a suggestion. He was a Port[15] exporter named Mr Bearsley who lived in Oporto and that they had a fine church there built in 1817, and, although not yet consecrated in its name, Saint James, would serve well for a marriage.

As Miss Penn seemed to favour this direction, it was agreed that when we should drop anchor, the wedding plans would proceed forthwith once permission had been gained from the local British contingent - and if the Portuguese authorities did not interfere, as authorities are often compelled to do from a sense of boredom, petty tyranny or general stupidity.

We made the lights of Oporto in the early evening and, as the current from the Douro River made finding a berth difficult, the ship put down her anchors and we hove-to for the night. We had a pork and red cabbage meal with Spanish vegetables in a mildly spiced sauce. The crew was in good spirits and they broke out the hornpipes and tolerated the passengers to view their complicated steps to its tunes. I had seen Baltic seamen do a similar prancing but this was more spirited and lively, although nothing to compare with the drunken dancing of Greenland whalers after a 'fish' had been rendered down.

An impromptu entertainment took place. Catania astonished all by producing an exquisite violin and a mastery of its sound and technique that brought loud applause. Beer came forth with an exceedingly odd song in Arabic, accompanied on a drum of sorts, notable for its difference if not so for its melody. The Germann sisters sang what must have been a French child's song. There was a skit by one set of the missionaries and many others added seasoning to the communal stew. I, having no gifts of this nature, remained as an appreciative audience. Perkins displayed his powerful voice in singing a folksong. After this, the evening grew chill with a wind off the Atlantic and the passengers went below deck.

The four of us *{Perkins, Driscol, Beer and Catania}* continued at our languages until early in the morning. I noted, too, that the temperature was better and that for the first time in weeks my hands were not cold despite the initial chilly wind.

Oporto as Driscol would have seen it. I-II-6

The Port of Oporto

We will call for a wedding feast

And wedded they shall be

And he shall rule my lands so fair

And wedded they were

While I shall keep him safe from the sea

And wedded they remain

[Editor's notes: The poem above added in pencil by the unknown editor. It is not accredited except to note the name of Henry Scott Vince]

Monday 3 October

We came to anchor before I was awake and I found the sight of Oporto inspiring, and was eager to get to land. I was also inspired by the tradition of English churches, or at least the one I had attended, that kisses might be exchanged with ones companion after a wedding - the 'kiss of blessing', I believe Muu had called it. I intended to make full use of that fine northern custom that day. I met the Port dealer, Mr Bearsley, on deck and had my first conversation with him. He not only dealt in the drink but in a tin mine some sixty miles from the town. He seemed a deeply quiet man, very religious and completely contemptuous of the Portuguese officials while announcing with some pleasure that he had a Portuguese wife. I had not talked previously to the man as, at a distance, he seemed to me to be a far-reaching saphead but, up close, he turned out to be just a particularly dull simpleton. He apologised for having been so un-social during the voyage but when he was away from his family and Portugal he became lugubrious. He left his land of birth to return to England only every two years to tend to necessary family business but remained an Englishman at heart.

From him I found out more about the siege of the town just four years ago by the absolutist militia intent on forcing the local constitutional party to resign. The absolutists, lacking sufficient and appropriate artillery, had been defeated and the city granted the name *Cidade invicta' {unvanquished city}* with the departure of the then Miguel I, who was sent into exile with the loss of his kingdom. What little damage done was repaired or hidden to my eyes. From where we docked, I could see the river wall and the city rising above it in white walls and orange tiled roofs, rows of buildings rising high up. It seemed a pleasant place; a place of people un-alike un-happy ~~Oporto~~ (Corunna).

[Editor's note: The unknown editor had struck out Oporto and corrected Driscol with 'Corunna']

The Portuguese official who dealt with the arrival of new shipping made his presence known and, accompanied by the British Consul, a Mr Edwin J Johnson, our certificate of non-quarantine was soon arrived at and the Consul came aboard. He had words with our acting

Captain, for he was looking for a man named Custard wanted by the authorities but his description matched no man on the ship.

The Consul, informed of our hopes for a wedding, which he gladly assisted in arranging once he had gained an invitation. He helped us by sending his lackluster looking assistant, a Mr De Silva, a most un-promising looking young man, to find the British consular chaplain who resided in town by the name of Reverend Edward Whiteley, of Swansea.

Perkins was eager to leave the ship and we soon found our way ashore, the Ladies declining our invitations to explore the city so they could do some tasks related to the wedding. Before we left, we found that the church ashore was amenable to our plan and had set the hour at 3 Post Meridian. The Port merchant, Mr Bearsley was busy with influential looking locals so we took ashore a small boat passing through a flock of British schooners loading large wooden barrels called *'gallegos'* from barges called *'barcos rabelos'*; it was on these that the spirit was moved to England[16]. As we neared an entrance embrasure, I was pleased to see palm trees lining the far road. I was truly getting to the southern lands.

With our military eyes, we had seen a tower atop one of many hills in the town and decided to surmount it to gain an appreciation of the ground. It was a hard walk for, while Rome may have seven hills, Oporto can boast fifty at least. We navigated the steep streets, finding first where *Rua dos Inglezes {Street of the English}* was and the wedding would be, finding the church to be surrounded by lofty walls - to keep the Portuguese free from the pollution of our true religion, I dare say.

By chance, we also found a house with a placard on it declaring in Portuguese and English that this indeed was the authentic 12th century house where Henry the navigator had been born. This seemed fitting for him to have been born on English street as his investigations of Africa led to the finding of the sea path to India - which the British had followed to erect the world's greatest and most beneficial empire. Perkins and I were both greatly pleased by this. The many black-eyed peasant girls who were bold in their walk and glances also pleased us. They were also free with their pearly white smiles set so well in their darker faces. Well, it was to Perkins they glanced at, and not to me but it was nice to see their smiles directed in my general direction. We made our way to the tower and found it to be the steeple of a Romanish Church but my Latin charmed the man in charge to grant us the right to climb the Clerigos church tower. The bird's eye view was tremendous. Fair to the east we could see snow-capped mountains, and we could see the byzantine warren of roads that ran up and down the many streets. We sought out some interesting points but, being completely ignorant of what the buildings were, we could not determine where exactly they might lay.

The Clerigos church tower in Oporto where Perkins and Driscol spied out the lay of the land. I-II-7

We left the tower and found the *Ferros Velhos {old pieces of iron}*; a type of market marred by an infestation of dogs that seemed to be in endless contests over the ownership of some furiously smelly offal. We passed shops that made delicate filigree which we both considered as presents for the Ladies but considered this to be too forward as we had no formal understanding with them. As a rule, the Portuguese seemed to be taking snuff, from the youngest to the oldest and of both genders while in England that craze had begun to abate, replaced in turn by the smoking of cigars and *papelates {cigarettes}*. The Portuguese seemed to me to be an indolent race and their language harsher to the ear than Spanish with much hissing and severe tones. The tradesmen seemed, as a whole, un-familiar with their tasks, seemingly both awkward and un-skilled with their hands.

We ended our mornings' tour by finding the British Factory House where they were decorating the vestibule and the ballroom for the wedding reception. Frenzied strokes and dashing women were all about us as it would seem the British residences of Oporto were much given to celebrating a wedding since the siege the English speaking population had been somewhat muted and un-celebratory. Which I could understand fully as they lacked, among other things, the ability to conduct fox hunting due to the indifference of the natives to the practice, a decent cricket pitch and a library. We found here the Germann's and pretty much the entire set of passengers.

There had been in the meantime a series of passing showers which the local inhabitants had responded to by wearing cloaks made of straw.

After we had departed, Mr Barrow, who, it seemed, had deep pockets and, being so pleased by the welcoming of the British Oporteans, had invited all to a pre-wedding luncheon. We decided to have the feast prior to the wedding in all contradiction of tradition but someone said it was a tradition of the Welsh family from which the Penn sisters had come from.

A Portuguese man wearing a straw cloak called a *Palhoca*. I-II-8

We certainly did not object and soon were consuming the Portuguese fare, having to stop at times to listen to speeches, toasts and songs of celebration. The soon-to-be Mrs. Barrow was beaming like a Greek goddess watching heroes fight for her honour and she kissed on the cheek every man present, and thanked them for helping to arrange in such short notice her wedding. As I had done nothing, I felt guilty for my laxness. I decided that I would eat far too much to punish myself for taking off to explore the town instead of assisting. I did so with great aplomb too. Perkins, driven also by guilt did so too. I did note that Mr Catania was not present but no one knew where he might be. The un-charitable said it was because he would not enter a Christian church. Perkins remarked that many here felt he would burst into flames if he entered a Christian church. We had a long private laugh over that observation.

The wedding ceremony was mercifully short as Reverend Whiteley did not appear to have any interest in a long ceremony as there had been no time to practice anything elaborate and the couple soon found themselves married with Mr Barrow released from the melancholy of his widowhood and the former Miss Penn of her spinsterhood.

[Editor's note: Driscol seems to have forgotten that the bride was a widow and not a spinster]

Captain Shimmins had given them the Captain's cabin for their honeymoon and they were soon off by carriage, after taking a tour of the town - I did hope they would avoid the dogs near the market.

I noted that everyone at the party was shimmering with sweat for it was a warm afternoon in Portugal and the atmosphere of the rooms enclosed. Yet I saw that, of them all, Perkins seemed un-fazed, perfectly coiffed as if he had hidden somewhere an efficient French *friseur {hairdresser}* and his uniform not soaked through with sweat. I imagined that he had made a dark pact with the demon of sweat to bother him not. What he had offered in return I dare not speculate on. I asked him why he did not sweat and he gave me a look that one's dog does when you catch him behind the barn with one of your mothers laying hens in his jaws, *moi?*

Millicent cried a great deal for reasons I did not fully understand but, based on my previous resolve, I made mention of the 'northern tradition of kissing' and she agreed with wide but wet eyes. A few moments later, we met behind a pillar in the vestibule, whose formation of pillars made for good concealment while still being in a public place. The kiss was hurried but, un-alike the one I had shared with Karen many years ago, fired my blood. Millicent then kissed me back and we parted to merge once again with the party, our waywardness un-detected. I found that for some minutes I could not understand anything said to me due to the pounding of blood in my ears. Perkins thought I was drunk and the scoundrel, laughing, called into question my alleged vow of abstinence.

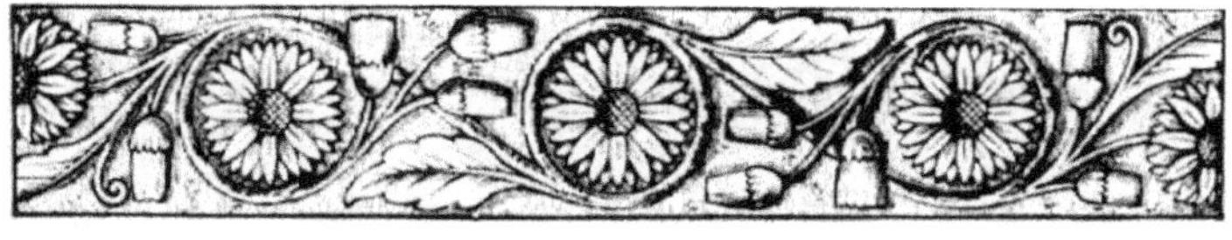

The Portuguese Coast And The Wages Of Sin

[Editor's note: Driscol wrote a full page in code on this date. It is surmised that the kiss from Millicent had inspired him]

Tuesday 4 October

Hamilton is in for it.

[Editor's note: This is a puzzling entry for there is no previous mention of this 'Hamilton' a possible explanation of the term will come later in the volumes]

Wednesday 5 October

The crew says we shall make Lisbon today and where we would probably take on new passengers.

Mrs. Germann has forgiven me my trespass but I have made definite enemies in Prudence, not that we were at anything but a place of conflict before and, of course, Danae, who is acting like she is Penthesilea, except that I am the one who killed her sister. *{An allusion to the Amazon in the Iliad who killed her sister and was slain by Achilles}.*

I suspect it was Danae who had seen us in the vestibule. With some diplomacy from Perkins, I found that the parents were upset over the matter because there was no understanding between us *{Millicent and I}* and that I was too young to marry, and lacking in PRESENT prospects, however, they granted what I believe was a temporary understanding. Such proceeding were so distasteful to me that I would have rather stood naked on top the walls off a snow covered fort and have arrows dosed in burning poison fired at me than deal with this. Perkins and Beer found it all very amusing. I suspect that had the Germann's had a son of age and not a drunkard for a father, I would have been challenged to a duel for my past forwardness. Millicent gave me a smile that told me that, in what mattered all was well, very well. I was sorry to have caused her these difficulties but then, on reflection, it had been worth it. Perkins was beyond praise for my actions and un-fortunately took the time to tell me a repellant tale involving himself as a student, a Lady who was no Lady, a fence and a minute ill spent, all of which got him into trouble also, but of a different kind.

More study

In the evening we could see the famous 'Berlingas' or 'Burlings', a small group of rocky islands off the Portuguese Coast and the Cape of Carvoeiro, covered by nesting seabirds, and circling above them in the thousands a mix of terns and black and the white-capped noddy.

Thursday 6 October

Our ship met while coming up the Tagus a Portuguese dispatch boat flying the dreaded yellow flag of cholera[17].

On the Tagus River short of Lisbon where the William Fawcett anchored. I-II-9

The Captain and the surgeon conferred with men in the boat, and soon announced to the passengers that there was a possibility of cholera in Lisbon brought there by a Portuguese merchant newly arrived from Goa. That those passengers who wished to do so would be put off on the riverbank near Almada and to do as they pleased or they might continue onto Cadiz or Gibraltar.

Later, another boat arrived carrying the British Consul in Lisbon a Captain *{Army}* William Smith came out to confirm that there definitely was a suspicion, perhaps, maybe, of cholera in the city.

The wind also abated and left us standing in a perfect calm so we anchored and those passengers who wished to proceed rowed ashore as stated. It was nearing evening that we raised our anchor and, using the current of the Tagus, made our way back to the Atlantic where we spent the rest of day crawling off a lee shore. I was sad not to see Lisbon and, had time permitted, I would have wished to see the remains of the three lines of Torres Vedras[18].

There was a fine meal supplied that night, it being a lovely *Lingua de vaca a Portuguesa {Portuguese ox tongue}* served with cucumbers and tomatoes. It was a meal fit for a Portuguese king. I was permitted this night to restart my nightly strolls with Millicent on deck, endlessly circling, as usual. I find that at the ends of these I cannot remember a thing she or I said, only that I enjoy it thoroughly.

As other nights, 'we four' worked, till past midnight drilling on the languages.

Friday 7 October

In the morning I assisted Perkins who was directing Mr Little's navigation exercises. He is doing much better being drilled over and over again and can now state the mathematical formulas from memory. His navigation is a study in exactitude.

After our refreshment we returned to more study, Perkins and I march one another around the deck using Persian commands. The crew and other passengers think we are complete dolts. Perkins declared himself tired and I spent the afternoon with the crew re-learning the names of sails, ropes and other nautical terms. I knew them but I knew them in Danish for many of the whalers had been from the Frisian island where Danish held sway.

Just prior to supper we sighted on the horizon a British Frigate but we could not make out her illustrious name.

I happened to encounter Danae who announced stiffly that she would not speak to me in the future. She did so in the hearing of her Mother and other sisters. I could only agree to her commandment but it left me puzzled given her previous actions.

Supper itself was as bad as the previous night fare had been delightful. We were assaulted by a type of smoked salmon in aspic; revolting. I instead made a meal of a broth than contained floating bits of vegetable flotsam and jetsam and stale loaves of bread soften somewhat with a touch of lard and butter. This made me a more tolerable meal than the main course.

In my walk with Millicent I asked her about Danae's action but she could not explain it. I felt a chill upon my spine. I hoped for Gibraltar on the horizon. My father had always said that one could deal with a problem in three ways, accept it, move away from it, or kill or solve it.

[Editor's note: Driscol came back at some later time and amended the line above adding a 'four', then scratched it out and wrote 'three' again]

I finished the book I was reading with some happiness for I had not enjoyed his description of Pompeii. I have always made it a point of honor to finish any book I begin but the last I had found torturous.

The United States Navy frigate USS 'America' in full sail and racing the French corvette Circe. I-II-10

Saturday 8 October

We are in the Gulf of Cadiz. The horizon filled with sails and ships. At least forty are in sight, including a French, Spanish and British man-of-war. Later in the afternoon, we passed by something I had not previously seen before; an American warship which came up from astern us and, in passing, the Captain sent his compliments and had them returned by the frigate's commander, a Captain Wilkinson, who spoke to us using a speaking trumpet. The *United States* was a fine ship, rated at 44 guns but she carried over 50 and she had her full suite of sails out to include skysails.

The French razee Circe. I-II-11

Shimmins suggested she was making 14 knots with all her sixteen hundred tons and she had a bone in her teeth *{a line of white water at her bow}*. He joked that she was either at war or her Captain like to run his ship hard for no reason. We soon had our answer for at a spot on the horizon was a low cloud bank and out of her came a French ship on the same course as the American. The Jonathan was two miles ahead of her. It turned out to be the Frenchman *Circe*, a particular ship, a former 44 gun frigate now

razeed {having had the upper deck cut away} to a 28 gun corvette. Remarkably, we determined she was making nearly 14½ knots and at this rate would catch the American if racing to Gibraltar, or it would be close if they were using Cadiz as a terminus. After these greyhounds had passed us our staid 6 knots seemed rather pedestrian and Perkins stated we seemed to have set our cadence to a slow march.

The Germann sister's had spent the day knitting and sewing a variety of things. I only noted then that they had no maid which led me to believe that the husband's work in the east had not enriched them but also that I was not a fortune hunter, I thought it odd that I had not once thought of this point before.

Sunday 9 October

We made landfall on the Spanish coast and ran along the coast to Cadiz. As there are no passengers to land, the ship must only get close enough to see if a flag of a certain colour and shape has been raised on a building in the city. By late afternoon, we worked our way to the point we needed to be and Shimmins, telescope in hand, declared no flag in sight, and we have no need to make the port. I regret not visiting the famed port for one of my maternal Danish uncles had been pressed gang into the British navy in 1803, while he was in Bristol. His new home was the British frigate, the HMS Minerve, Captain Brenton commanding it was then captured when it went aground off Cherbourg, France in July 1803. As he was not British and the French needed seamen he ended up on the French warship, the Argonaute 74.

[Editor's note; The French did not use prefixes like the British did with 'HMS']

While on that ship he survived the battle of Trafalgar only to be taken prisoner by the Spanish in 1808 when Spain and France went to war and the French fleet in Cadiz was compelled to surrender, blockaded there ever since Trafalgar by a vigilant British squadron. Again, by not being French and knowing the use of cannon he made his way into the Spanish forces soon afterwards[19].

A map of Gibraltar and environs. I-II-12

111

Chapter III

From Gibraltar to Malta

Africa, Gibraltar And Despair - West Africa Rice With Ground Nut Sauce -
A Friday Of Shooting, Bombshells And A Skirmish With The Infantry -
Millicent - By Maltese Speronara To Ceuta And Alger (Algiers) - The Xebec
From Texas - Escape From Algiers - Jellies, Leatherbacks And A Fracas -
The Melee - Respite And Regrets - A Profound Gain And Loss

========

Africa, Gibraltar And Despair

In the late afternoon, we made Cape Trafalgar. The sight of Cape Trafalgar, the scene of
Nelson's greatest victory and glorious death, awakened strong emotions in the bosoms of all
the Englishmen aboard and there was much comment and commotion over our being there. I
made no mention that my maternal relative had fought - against his wishes - with the French
fleet, although three from my paternal side had also been there; one as a sailing master,
another as a mate and the third as a volunteer.

We sighted Africa off our starboard side and debated if the mountain in sight was Mount Moses
{Jebel Musa}. Catania said it was. A new continent was at hand and this thrilled me
immensely, even more than having passed by Trafalgar. All the passengers came up again and
crowded the deck to see this. I was able to stand behind Millicent and, in the momentary
press; she extended her hand behind her. I grasped it and we played 'fingers' for a while as
we chatted as if nothing was amiss or un-called for going on between us. It was deliciously
sultry, sinful and un-seen.

There was no moon this night but we could see the lights of Gibraltar. The Captain decided to
anchor off the Spanish town of Tarifa and await the morning. Even by starlight, the white
buildings of Tarifa shown as a pale white triangle against the darker hills.

I cannot believe the first part of my journey is nearly complete.

I took Millicent on another endless stroll on the deck where we discussed flowers, cookery,
and I tried to explain, prompted by a question she had asked, on why so many people had
been excited by seeing Trafalgar, the main event of the Napoleonic Wars at sea - without
gaining any success in gaining her understanding of its importance. She confided in me that
her voyage to the east is part of an arrangement by her father to marry her to one of his
associates in Calcutta, a man nearly twice her age. She and her sisters are all to be expended
in marriages to elderly men. She, Danae and Prudence are to be sacrificed, not for God's help
in defeating the Ammonite as was the fate of Jephthah's daughter[1] but to gain favour amongst
her father's peers and superiors. This revelation left me irate and hopelessly angry but I knew
well my position and I could do nothing to help her. I spoke with Perkins whose stance on the

matter of Millicent and her father's plans infuriated me further. He acknowledged my helplessness and offered up only the salve of 'there were many other women to be wooed'. Sleep escaped me that night as mad schemes wandered thought my mind involving eloping with her to America. Kidnapping her and then taking service amongst one of the armies of the German principalities that proliferate along the banks of Rhine or taking her back to Eccles, and abandoning my hope to see the east and becoming an explorer for the plodding life of a farmer or merchant. As dawn came, I had to be cognizant of the fact that I could do nothing and at that moment, I envied those who can lose themselves in drink.

Monday 10 October

We arrived at Gibraltar. The great rock arose before us, a pillar of Hercules' gateway to the

Gibraltar seen here from the Spanish shore to the west of the fortress. I-III-1

western sea for the ancients. For me, it stands as my gateway to the east. As we came in with the light of dawn, we could see that the mount resembled a lion couchant; a British lion, crouched not at the feet of larger Spain but guarding its territory with all its leonine majesty.

I watched with interest as the ship came in to anchor and to see how they did so being as they were a steam ship's crew managing the ship under sail only. I had seen some sloppiness when they had anchored in the Tagus. All the officers and men were sent to their stations. The passengers commanded all; passengers and crew, to preserve a perfect silence for at this moment our berth was amongst a thick tangle of shipping and an un-heard command could bring disaster. The studding sails were taken in, the burtons off the yards and the jiggers off the topgallant yards in a masterly manner. They send the booms and sails down from aloft in good time too and staffed the fore clew-garnets, buntlines and leech lines. The mainsail hauled up as the ship was going free.

Men were already aloft to deal with the topgallant and royal clew lines while others stood by to furl the sails snug, and square the yards by the lifts and braces. Other hands stood by the fore tack and sheet, topgallant and royal sheets, halyards, weather braces, and bowlines.

Men by command then began in the topgallant-sails and royals to furl the sails, and square the yards by the lifts and braces, hauling taut the many halyards as we neared our goal. Other seamen moved to manage the topsail-clew lines and buntlines, weather braces, jib-downhaul, and spanker-outhaul. The helmsman eased down the helm as we slowed and neared our selected spot. The acting captain commanded the men to haul down the jib, haul out the spanker, and when the topsail was lifted, to clear away the sheets, and clew them up. As this occurred they let go the halyards, clewed down, and squared away the yards immediately. The spanker-sheet was hauled aft, and when our headway ceased, they streamed the buoy *{putting the buoy in the water before the anchor is let loose}*. As the W.F. began to slow Shimmins' ordered the crew to let go the anchor. The crew then brailed up the spanker, crotch the boom, hauled taut the guys, light-to the cable, and as fast as she would take it, until a sufficient scope was out, then the stopper set. His last orders were to send the boats' crews aft, to lower the boats down. Let the boatswain go ahead to square the yards – clear up the decks and with that the order for silence was lifted and the passenger and myself gave a cheer for their masterly handling of this most complicated of seaman's task.

The Fawcett was anchored in good time in the manner I described above and we were disembarked by the lowered boats, all the available quays having been taken up for shipping, which was more valuable than mere us bringing passengers. As tradition demanded, those families with women debarked first, Mr Barrow and his new bride being the first to leave the ship with her sister in tow. In passing he invited Perkins and I to a supper a few days hence, to which we happily agreed. Perkins observing that no sane bachelor ever turned down an invitation to supper, for not only would food be served but a more valuable commodity would be there.

I thought he was talking of women and asked him so. He said, 'Yes but not as you think.' I thought he was referring to middle-aged married women. I accused him of debauchery in this regard but he let this pass and explained that such women, middle-aged married ones, were a storeroom of knowledge about all the un-married women in an area. 'You need but remark that you were in 'ERNEST' about the finding of a wife and within a day they would know of every suitable woman from miles around.' That was valuable knowledge, which I noted here thusly for future reference.

[Editor's note: Driscol put two penciled stars next to the entry above]

Several hours later, we made our way to Gibraltar. I observed the Germann's also took their luggage off and leave, with Millicent waving to me and later Danae added hers too. Prudence took no notice of us as they rowed off.

Once on shore, Perkins and I made our way to the appropriate offices and we both expected that no word would have yet arrived on how we were to proceed. While in those offices, I made inquiries as to where my regiment, the 52nd, was. I already knew that, during the period I would arrive at Gibraltar, the Regiment, which is stationed there, would be partially in Portugal and some men here. In the first case, they were there to officially visit and train with their Cacadores friends *{Portuguese light infantry with whom they had fought the French during the Peninsular War}*, while un-officially they were there to represent the British Crown's support of the regency of Maria II of Portugal, who was just seventeen at the time.

The only men left still at Gibraltar were a rump detachment and I obtained directions to find them. They were sharing barracks with the 2nd Battalion of the 60th Foot, the King's Royal Rifle Corps, known to all as 'The Green Jackets', and also at Gibraltar were the 68th Durham Light Infantry Regiment of Foot, the Faithful Durhams and the 81st Regiment (of Foot). They were in the West Casemate barracks.

As these were nearby, I went immediately and to my great disappointment found that my fine regiment was represented here by a broken down and badly aged corporal who had command of six men who had been too ill or made insensible by drink to make the journey to Portugal. I shared a few words with them and left them to their duties, which, as far as I could discover, were none. I was greatly saddened to have missed meeting with officers from my regiment.

Perkins, having smiled on my diversion, next led me to the Governor Generals Aide-de-Camp and produced his Letter of Introduction, which the man took with little interest until he noted from whom it came.

[Editor's note: Although it cannot be proved, the letter was probably from the Commander-in-chief-of-the-army or one of his staff, which rated it as being 'stellar' in its importance. A lieutenant with such a letter would be treated as a VIP]

I suspect he had not thought that an Engineering Lieutenant and a no accounts Ensign would have a letter from such a man. He promised all assistance, which consisted of our direction to check back with the shipping clerks the next day.

He related to us that the garrison orders were such: To remain in uniform at all times and in strict conformity with his majesty's Regulations.

[Editor's note: this was a change to the tradition of officers not on duty to wear civilian clothes; this was because Gibraltar was a garrison subject to attack at any time]

We were reminded that those civilians we did see such as the Town Major and all workmen and other inhabitants were never to be given orders by us unless the garrison was under attack. We were then given a litany of rules dealing with what not to do in regards to revenues, illness and other matters such as our duties during an attack, fire or storm. At the end, we were given a small pamphlet by General John Pitt the 2nd Earl of Chatham called <u>General Regulations and Standing Orders for the Garrison of Gibraltar</u> which covered all of this in some detail he had written this in 1825 when he had been Governor and his orders still stood.

We did hope that the Spanish would not attack and considered they were involved in a civil war that was highly un-likely however; the French were always a concern.

[Editor's note: Perkins and Driscol were very lucky, see full footnote on what they missed[2]]

Despite the lessons, Perkins and I were both delighted over the feel of England here, despite so many foreign people and the setting. He noted the women, of course; how they were long legged, some freckled; and many shades of hair colour abounded, from red to black, coupled with rosy white faces - somewhat a change from the darker skinned women of Spain and Portugal. The rest of the people were brown and dark haired Italians, and lighter skinned Spaniards; both of whom seemed of small stature. There were also weather creased mariners, sunburnt Irish and English soldiers, pallid skinned Jews, a coffee coloured Indian, and a knife nosed Moor with blackened skin and, if one were to believe the tales, a blacker heart.

I was feeling desolated over the fate of Millicent but, as I was on firm ground again, I enjoyed a fine piece of beefsteak with Brand & Co's condiment in the Garrison's mess. Un-fortunately, there I found no pleasure, for their newspapers and magazines were all older ones.

The meal was a good moment at last; for although we were not in England, this Gibraltar was a small part of England and I was glad of it. The shop names are in English and the food, may God be praised, is too. However, the folks are an extrinsic mix, as I noted above, and I sat on the terrace and watched the Spaniards who had come in from countryside to buy or sell begin to make their way home again.

I indulged this afternoon a passion of mine; at home, our Christmas celebration would always have rare oranges from the Azores as a special treat on Boxing Day. I rarely got more than a few slices but now I ate five at one session - very satisfying.

At half-past five, the evening gun sounded from the top of the mountain. Patrols of infantry swept the streets and the gates of the fortifications shut. No Spaniard is allowed leave to stay in the fortress at night. It was Perkins and I alone for supper, set in a forlorn and empty mess for the officers of the artillery garrison were in Spain, chasing after pretend foxes, it would seem. We made the best of the solitary supper and used the time to practice the names of everything in the room first in Persian, then Arabic - with much consulting to our dictionaries. At half-past nine a gun sounded that was the signal for all soldiers to return to their barracks and all seamen to their ships, and all marines to drown themselves, or so the story goes - or to their duties if they still retained their senses.

Stillness came over the place, and Perkins and I, having found the Officer of the guard and learned we could walk the ramparts - if we followed the following garrison rules:

The line wall of Gibraltar. I-III-2

All respectable Inhabitants can walk on the Line Wall throughout the Garrison; you may go on the Banquettes, look over the Wall, but are not to mount upon the Parapets, or enter the Embrasures, or stand upon the Guns or Carriages. We must also not stand or pass nearer than fifteen feet of a guard and under no circumstance speak to or order him to do any task.

We digested this and without causing an alarm, proceeded to do so; listening to the crash of waves against the seawall and the faint sounds of music and hilarity aboard the many ships anchored close inshore protected by the mole. We went down to the lines of fortifications that sever Gibraltar from Spain and, in the distance, could hear the cry of the Spanish watchmen across the sands: *Ave Maria Santissima;* the Spanish armies' version of 'All's well". We made our way back to our quarters with some difficulty. For in the dark, the nature of Gibraltar took on a forbidding face, with one expecting it to fall on one's head if one walked too loudly. In passing we found the Royal Artillery picquet being formed it consisted of the Subaltern, one Sergeant, one Corporal, one Bombardier, 1 Drummer and four and twenty Gunners. They looked to be sharp and intent on their duties

Tuesday 11 October

It was reveille at first light, by the beating of drums that announced the new morning and not the cannon for which I was prepared, as an active garrison the entire force was dressed and under arms to prevent a surprise attack. Again, it was Perkins and I at a solitary breakfast with an east Londoner for a steward who brought us a good plate of eggs.

I cannot believe it! For we found today, at the offices of the shipping clerks that we visited as soon as they opened, that our instructions had arrived in the post carried by the *William Fawcett* herself. We are instructed to take any passage we can arrange to Alexandria - for we have *Carte Blanche* in this regard - travel by land to Suez and then by HEIC steamer to Bombay! So, of the three possibilities we now know our fate.

Our path is chosen but how shall we do it? Perkins had gone out to India by sailing ship around the Cape in 1832 and had done the same when returning to England on this last trip. The way to the east is open but we do not know the manner of the way.

Of the original passengers only I, Perkins and Catania will go on the Mediterranean path, with Catania headed to Malta. We had found Mr Gregorian and although he was destined to go to Malta, he was happy to await for some more traditional way - but he wished us well, as he planned to stay a few weeks in Gibraltar to have a look at their cistern. He gave to Perkins and I a publication he had written on ancient water systems. Perkins would have thrown this away but I retained it for its paper alone, as it was full of calculations and references to classic literary works, and all but unreadable - being duller than dirt - but was printed on one side of the paper only, making it valuable for hasty work. *{paper was expensive in Driscol's time}*

All the others will wait for an East Indiaman to make their way by sail to India; a voyage of three to six months. We shall miss southern Africa but will gain Egypt and the central Mediterranean. Perkins and I agree that it is a good bargain indeed. We bachelors are housed in officer quarters of the garrison and the bed is better than the swinging hammock aboard ship and I have a Batman again - shared with four other officers, artillerymen stationed at the fortress but who are off on some lark in Spain, and we get a meal not influenced by Portuguese raised Goan cooks. This would be a paradise for some and not so untoward for me if it were not for the heaviness of my heart and soul for Millicent. I shall also miss Beer, who has been of great value to us in our learning Persian and Arabic. We find that we are on rations which cannot exceed, even for officers, one pound of bread, one pound of meat, either salt beef, pork and fish and one pint of wine. This to ensure the garrison larder is never depleted below having one year's supply of food for the garrison should the fortress be taken under siege.

At Gibraltar, I posted my voluminous mails; many letters to my parents, one each to my brothers (to Mark in particular hoping that we will soon start our games again[3]), sisters, four to Karen, two to Marguerite, one each to Philomena and Patricia, another to the regimental mess and a few others to selected acquaintances. I wonder what post there will be for me many months in the future at Bombay, for it is that address all correspondence to me will gather during this outing. At Gibraltar are artificers and coal for the Fawcett and she will have her paddle wheels remade, the required expertise not having existing at Corunna. Her crew moved to a receiving ship. I looked at acquiring Duperre. The crew consider her their mascot and will not give her up even for gold. I am frustrated in love again, it would seem. Dash it all! Such a fine cat even if named for a frog Admiral.

Little is to take the test for his certificate of navigation in two days so I bury my heart in the

small garden in the back of the quarters and Perkins and I assist him through the day on his navigation maths.

'Downtown' Gibraltar showing the exchange and chapel. I-III-3

In the later afternoon, we went into the garrison town, bought fresh dates, and went to a street outside the Alameda gardens were we could hear a band playing. We spent some time looking over the bay towards the white mound that was Algeciras. The purchase of the fresh fruit made our expedition a success.

We heard a succession of cannons firing, thirteen in fact meaning a Rear Admiral had come into port and we heard too his return of the salute with the same amount of guns but then another shot.

Our meal is again in the nearly abandoned mess of the garrison artillery to whom we were to take our rations while quartered in Gibraltar. The garrison artillery's officer of the guard, the only man left back, was not to be found and the stewards would only say that he 'had duties to attend to'.

Perkins made an un-endurably rude remark as to what that duty was. I asked him again how an officer and son of a bishop could say such a crude thing? His reply was instructive and fully constructed by way of grammar and logic to be irrefutable: it was, of course, short, impossibly crude and said with the broadest of smiles.

We found that the rest of the garrison was in Spain but, officially, no such word could be spoken as it was a private matter of the unit in question. I thought it odd that the garrison of Gibraltar was denuded in such a way. At the end of our meal their officer on duty, a young Ensign of my age whom Perkins had made his very un-couth jest about and burdened with the protection of this vast fortress, came in from his duties, stole some of our bread without asking, made a butter sandwich and left us in peace, having not said a word or acknowledged our presence - the uncouth swine.

After the man left, Perkins mocked him by having a pretend discussion with him, he playing himself and a chair the un-fortunate officer. In this performance, Perkins asked him in some detail about the extent of his 'duties' and he then moved to crouch behind the chair, and, in a whiny voice, gave out all the un-printable but choice details. This was so brilliant that I and the two stewards fell into laughter so deep we could not stop. My chest hurt so much after this that I could hardly breathe. We gave each steward two pence to 'forget' this performance.

That evening while we walked about we came to the entrance to one of the main magazines and were firmly and frightening challenged and correctly told to scarper off immediately or be placed under arrested. We did so!

Wednesday 12 October

Perkins and I have realised that to wait for appropriate shipping may take days, if not weeks. So while we have in hand an expert in such matters, Mr Catania, we must ask him the best way to find our 'way' to Alexandria. Gibraltar is a small place and a few questions led us to track him to the private Jewish home he was staying at and found him, not dressed in the English style clothing he had affected on ship but clothed in the long robe of a Levantine Jew. His appearance was odd but his smile was welcoming and we soon gained his assistance for he, himself, would finish his work here in a few days and wished to return to Malta and his family *post-haste*. He was now in the house of a 3rd cousin. As we suspected, he knew of a way to move east far faster than the shipping clerks of Gibraltar, whose supposed expertise would butter no peas.

Perkins and I had hoped to gain a Spanish ship in Algerciass *{Algeciras}* across the bay from the fortress. Catania, however, had a more adventurous proposal, which he explained to us over an eastern meal of cinnamon rice, chicken and spiced vegetables, using his hand while we took up our cutlery. He proposed we take one of the food boats out of Gibraltar, for Gibraltar had no source of food, of course, and imported its daily needs from Africa. Catania hopes to make for the city of Ceuta, a Spanish enclave on the Moorish coast, and there we could expect to find a French ship to Alger *{Algiers}*. The French had invaded that land some years ago and were in constant search for rations for their army, and from there we would go on to Malta. I learned and noted that the term he used, the Arabic name for the Straits is *Bab el-Zakat {Postern of charity}*.

He assured us that once in Malta, transport to Alexandria would be a simple matter; either on English, Austrian, French or Sicilian vessels.

To this we agreed but Catania would take no payment and instead asked that we demean ourselves (his words) to act as his escorts, for we were no longer in northern Europe and a Jew could expect to be insulted, robbed or worse at any time in these places we were to travel. He would take, instead of payment, the support of our pistols and Englishness, for our nationality gave us great protection against any casual act of aggression. To this, we heartily agreed and set the day of Friday to set off. Perkins noted afterwards that we were about to set sail on a Friday again. We laughed at the superstition but it made me wonder.

We spent the rest of the day with Mr Little and were engrossed with his studies for the Marine Board examination. I decided not to visit the Germann's this evening. A decision seconded by Perkins, who did not relish another mortal trouncing by Miss Prudence in the ways of wooing, which she insisted he was doing wrong, much to his displeasure.

Perkins and I went to dine with the Barrow's. We found our way there in the afternoon and, having made a thorough reconnaissance of the route, we returned to our quarters to idle an hour or so away before returning in good time. Perkins refused my request to go as early as I would have preferred. We arrived, and greeted by Mr Barrow's staff, all Negroes from West Africa. I had met few of these types of men and found them interesting. Barrow, I soon learned, was formerly a Navy man and had served in Africa for some years before. I also learned that he had been invalided home by fevers. He had recovered and entered the trade he now did. It was a small informal party; just the happy new couple, Perkins and I, a few of the Barrows' friends and associates, and Mrs. Barrow sister's family. The conversation was limited but the meal quite a delight for they had African dishes I had never tasted or heard of before. We feasted on a chicken dish that Barrow called Sierra Leone chicken a West African dish made up of one fowl, with the bones removed, and placed in a groundnut {peanut} sauce. I found it most agreeable and asked for the recipe, which was given to me by Barrows who was pleased for my having asked.

===

West Africa Rice with Groundnut Sauce

(Also known as African Peanut Chicken or Sierra Leone Chicken)

One started with a large whole deboned and cut up chicken, a white onion, some groundnut oil, six tomatoes, some flour to thicken it, two ounces of nut paste and a handful of shelled nuts which have been roasted beforehand. One then boils the chicken, fries the onions in the oil, then places the boiled chicken with the onions, add in the tomatoes, nut paste, and flour. Then add some salt into the chicken's boiled water and cook until it was well reduced, then add it back into the main pot with the chicken and add a hand full of roasted nuts

===

We received a small quantity of foo-foo, a dish made from African yams pounded into obedience with a dollop of palm oil. These two prodigious dishes came mixed with some ordinary vegetable dishes of Spanish or English origin. Mrs. Barrow was very happy and at one point cornered me to ask of my chances with Millicent. Un-wisely, I told her the un-varnished truth, which she pouted on but said that she wished her and me well. The evening's 9th hour gun fired and the Tattoo was beaten well and the honeymooning couple seemed anxious to rid themselves of their guests. We soon found ourselves alone, again, on the ramparts of Gibraltar, overlooking the sea studded with lights of the ships at anchor and in the far distance, the paltry Spanish lights too.

Thursday 13 October

A cool day in Gibraltar. Mr Little came early and reviewed the operations he would need again for his examinations. He offered Perkins a tidy sum to take the test in lieu for him but such foolishness would be the ruin of us all and we gave the man a bit of Dutch courage to 'buck him up', as the Americans say - something I learned from Mr Vadeboncoeur. We escorted him to a nondescript building next to the 16th century 'convent' *{Government House}*, a yellowish building that was once a Franciscan friary, and deposited him well armed with knowledge and the tools of his task, and agreed to meet him four hours later when his test should be completed.

We had yet to tour the 'rock', as the garrison calls this place, so we did so. In those four hours, we toured the galleries cut into the rock, made friends with the Barbary apes at the Queen's gate, examined the Moorish castle and viewed the hazy shore of Africa with my binoculars. At the appointed time we made our way to meet Little and were wetted by a passing rain that started as a light sprinkling of water but in a moment made Perkins think we were in a tropical forest or the lens of Lincolnshire for we were drenched thoroughly in that moment. Saddened and sodden, we pushed on, passing others who were equally as trounced by the un-expected rain as ourselves.

The test was completed. Little and seven others were outside pacing with nervousness as their efforts were graded within. He thought he had done well and a clerk soon announced the verdict of the eight takers. Only Little had passed. Having dropped that bombshell on the poor men in the courtyard, the clerk retreated with no ceremony except to pass to a very happy Mr Little his certificate of navigation, who took it with the gravity of a man taking a crown. He invited us to dinner and I presumed, had he been a woman he would have offered to bear our children for he was beside himself, having failed the examination thrice before.

[Editor's note: See Appendix I-II for an example of the type of examination Little would have taken]

The former convent where Mr Little stood for his examination on navigation. I-III-4

He knew a place to go and to it we made our way. We made our way to the place Little mentioned passing as we did through a flood of red and blue-coated British men, the infantry and artillery of the garrison who seemed determined to prevent us, by their crowding, to prevent our advance. However, we did force our way through in time. It was a small establishment and Little and Perkins found a good brew to linger over, and I obtained some limed and sugared water to my satisfaction. The meal was the freshest sardines *{Engraulis meletta}* still wet from the sea, grilled within our sight on hot coals and well covered in garlic and salt and an accompaniment of spinach, onion and garbanzo, or the common chickpease to me, and some indifferent bread of the Spanish type. We passed the afternoon away with Little, who outlined his plans to one day head a great shipping firm. He assured us that he would reward us when he had accomplished this. We shook on this but privately Perkins and I thought Little would do well to find a fat English wife and continue to be a pursuer, for he was good at that.

We had been invited (commanded, actually) to attend a Governor's supper that evening. For this, we engaged our Batmen, who were two rather surly Scotsmen but who also, to their honour, were most diligent in their trade and our uniforms were soon gleaming and ready. We approached this supper with some dread, as the Germann's might be there and Perkins, by his own confession, had never been so overwhelmed at his attempts at petty seduction than by Miss Prudence Germann. She seemed immune to his own self-assured irresistibility to women. While he found himself wishing to have her affection, she seemed only interested in the playful scorn of his manly efforts. I dreaded seeing both Millicent and Danae. Thusly, preparing for destruction, we awaited our joint doom.

Under my direction, we arrived well before the proper time and the butler kept us in the outer hallways until a more appropriate time. Perkins glared at me for some time because of this. The Butler a hard eyed Greek had nothing for us but a pleasant distain. For us and him both knew that the butler of a reigning Governor General outranks an Ensign and Lieutenant who had arrived far too early by a wide margin. The first guest to arrive, also too early, was the American counsel; a Mr Sprague and wife. They were from Boston and we conversed with them. He was an intelligent man but his wife was the dismal and dreadful sort. As we had a half hour or so, we told them of our journey in the *William Fawcett*. When we mentioned having travelled with an American artist, the Consul took interest in this and, having asked us a number of questions, he told us to our shock that that man was probably a reprobate named Mr Custard - not quite a criminal but no friend of the Consul or any honest American. His wife who spoke Dutch called him a *land-louper {vagabond}*. She explained, without being asked to do so, that it meant someone who ran from his country either to avoid punishment for a crime or to avoid a debt. Both Perkins and I resolved to check thoroughly our baggage when we returned.

There were some ninety guests; mostly garrison officers, naval officers, public officials, three Spanish officers and a man in a resplendent uniform who turned out to be the Captain of a newly arrived Chilean man-of-war. He was obtaining obsolete cannons from Gibraltar for future use in what many saw as an impending war between Chile and the new states of Argentina and Bolivia (the newspapers called it the Confederation) especially after the action in August of the Chilean's capturing of three Confederation ships. He seemed a swaggering fellow and of Irish stock but Spanish speaking. There were a swirl of women but all seemed married or well escorted. The music was modern pieces; the latest from Chopin, his Grand Polonaise Brillante, and later I recognised Schumann's Fantasie in C. There was dancing prior to supper I was told his was not un-usual as the style in hot climes was to dance first in the heat therefore allowing supper service when the temperatures were cooler. I made a successful night of it and did not have to dance a single step. There was also the good news that the Germann's were not there.

Supper was less interesting than the people and, again, I ended up between two women who talked on and on about people and actions of no interest to me. The main course was a chaudfroid of chicken that was eatable but nothing more; and the following *Petit Nougats aux Violettes {a desert of nougat flavoured with violets}* I found odd to the palate and left it un-finished its aftertaste made me long regret the tasting of it.

After supper, the women left the men to their cigars and brandy or, in my case, some nuts and tepid water.

While involved in this culinary exercise and awaiting a fitting time to leave, a garrison artillery officer made his way across the room, un-steady and probably drunk; and it was none other than our own annoyingly silent man and officer of guard of the mess hall. He became involved nearly instantly in an argument with the visiting Chilean and knocked him to the floor with his fists. The South American was game and rose up un-checked, and lashed about, striking some half dozen of the other military officers before this bull could be tamed. The hosts were mortified and apologies were made, and all was well when, not twenty minutes later, the same man attacked the now equally drunk Chilean again. I learned later that the *Araucanos {a term for Chileans}* had been insulting early in the afternoon to the British officer, in his language, to the memory of British women and, worse yet, the British Army.

Seeing here an opportunity to escape this dreadful scene during the confusion, Perkins and I headed for the door, a decision made by both of us based on common sense and not communicated between us - only to be confronted by the Governor General himself and his staff struggling with the Chilean whose drinking had released an Irish Demon's strength. The aide to the Governor ordered us to his side and we were tasked with a mission. 'As you are not of our garrison and this man has some disagreement with members of that garrison, I charge you to return this man to his ship and report back to me when you have accomplished this mission'.

Perkins and I found ourselves out the door and out the gate and deposited in a rush of men with the drunken Chilean, an Irishman with a Spanish temper; a mongrel breed ones does not wish to encounter often. We realised that, at this point, we did not know his ship's name or where it lie, but did recall in general were the landing port was. We questioned the man to his particulars, the name of ship and where she might lie at anchor. His response was to kick me and punch Perkin's in the chest.

Perkins' then disabled the officer with a strong blow to the jaw. We found that he did not long remain disabled but continued to swing his arms and fists while cursing England, women and us, sometimes in good English and the rest of time in violent Spanish. Perkins responded with a swift kick to his privates, repeated three times until the effect came to his sodden brain. He collapsed and we took to dragging him hither. He threw up several times, soiling Perkins' and my trousers. Perkins, a most sensible man usually, was cursing violently. I remarked that at least we had been able to leave that dull supper. To this, he laughed and we dragged the man until we encountered a Sergeant's roving guard. We soon had the Sergeant overawed and his four men carrying the Chilean while we held two muskets each. The lout was deposited at the quay and, most fortunately to us, we found his ship's boat crew ready and waiting.

We handed the sodden remains of their officer back to them and they seemed almost reluctant to claim him as he had recovered somewhat and was kicking, shouting and punching about in a wild manner. He regained his wits, poised for a moment, and demanded to know why we were dragging him through the streets in such a disrespectable manner, to which Perkins replied,

> "SIR! You have taken in a bit too much brandy and were placed under arrest for being drunk and generally disgusting. We are returning you to your crew. Now goodnight to you SIR!"

We waited until they had disappeared into the darkness then dutifully reported to the Aide-de-Camp. He was with the governor. As we approached, our blouses ripped, our trousers stained with vomit and dirt, for the Chilean had dragged us down several times, we snapped to attention and saluted. The Aide and Governor could not repress their laughter but gave their many thanks for our actions. He explained that the garrison officers had been near to doing fatal violence against the man and that we had prevented a diplomatic incident or even a murder. We excused ourselves but, as we were about to exit, the Adjutant of the garrison artillery also thanked us and invited us to luncheon the next day, with a ride into the Spain side. I would have told them to go to Hades but Perkins accepted - although before he spoke, he spit out the blood from his mouth for he had been the victim of our drunken bundles prodigious right fist.

We smiled and left; I, nursing a badly kicked shin and a shoulder all but torn from its socket, and Perkins, dribbling blood from his cut mouth down his chin and over his blouse.

We roused our Batmen and gave them the remnants of our uniforms. Despite our pains and the hour, my friend and I spent several hours un-packing and examining our entire luggage. It was our opinion that our luggage had been well searched, much opened and resealed but nothing taken except at the end when I noted that one of the bottles in my medical chest had been open. It was the one than contained laudanum and I found the medicine was gone. We found the medication replaced with plain water coloured with wine. This turn of event was certainly odd indeed.

Perkins and I spoke about the possibility that Mr American had been a spy of some sort. Perkins brought up Catania, as well. Could he, too, be a spy? We thought not, for how could he know our mission? Perkins was suspicious but we had let nothing out about our true goal and we decide early in the morning that Mr Custard nee Vadeboncoeur had been an opium fiend in need of the drug in my chest.

Spanish Bustards what Driscol went hunting for in Spain. I-III-5

A Friday Of Shooting, Bombshells And A Skirmish With The Infantry

Friday 14 October

A messenger brought us to wakefulness far too early for Gentlemen. It was from Catania who entreated our pardon for he was delayed and asked if we could depart on Monday and if this would be agreeable to us? It most assuredly was and we sent back a reply to the affirmative. As soon as that messenger departed, another showed up, this time held by an anxious but arrogant Chilean midshipman; his rank guessed from his youth and uniform. He informed us of our challenged nature, to wit to a duel, spoken in excellent French. He gave us a card showing the man in question was Capitán de Fragata Sergio Delgado O'Meara, commander of a corvette called the Concepcion. Perkins replied in fine style that the challenge to a duel should be delivered to the Aide-de-Camp of the Governor-General, and we told the lad his name and where to find him (or so we hoped) and he left somewhat diverted and even more un-sure of himself than before he knocked on our gate.

Perkins and I went back to our beds.

Later in the morning, our Batmen had done wonders and the uniforms were back to their full glory but we were to go in civilian clothes there being an exception to the rule of officers always wearing their uniform and that was when they went into Spain. A groom appeared with horses saddled and bridled and we were soon mounted and led to the Alameda parade grounds where the rest of the garrison officers had met for a ride and shoot. I have with me Ascalon, and Perkins his father's double barreled shotgun which he had had William Chance & Son alter to percussion fire but it was too short of barrel for my taste, being only 32 inches in length and of 12 bore. The two of us were hailed as conquering heroes and the Aide-de-Camp rode up asking why in the Lord's name had we sent on that Chilean child to him? We had discussed in advance the plan of conversation if this occurred and Perkins was prepared to lay it on thick. The Aide-de-Camp did not disappoint us by saying the matter is closed by order of the Governor who had prohibited the Chilean officer from coming on shore again. He also ordered said officer to leave his Majesty's port as soon as his ship's business for the Chilean nation was completed. Dueling, of course, being highly discourage amongst the King's officers.

The rock offers no room for mounted excursion so we fell in behind the rest of the officers, for we knew now that it was a tradition to ride out in this manner whenever it was possible. My horse was a fine spirited Andalusian gelding bay of at least $16\frac{1}{2}$ hands and being considered a Spanish devil for it had two small 'horns' behind its ears. Riders told me this was a characteristic of this Spanish breed and the mark of a good horse, and he was a good ride and rather a tall horse, which I appreciated. We made the northern gate, crossed the Spanish lines with but a nod and a word of greetings, and the whole country was open to us.

They took us along the beach and into hills behind where we could see the shape of Gibraltar to our advantage, and view the other side of the rock with more clarity. We rode some four miles to a castle called the Castellar and onto the property of Mr Moscoso who, for a small consideration, allows the British officers to do some shooting. For other 'small fees', as the officers called it, the Spanish officials take no notice of another country's army officers riding armed into their country and shooting away at the wild life. The cost of this violation of sovereignty is about 1£ a month and $^1/_{10}$ of the birds or beasts bagged. We did some birding and I saw an impressive shooting ability by the garrison officers - should French fowls or Spanish birds ever attack them, this bastion of England will be completely safe. I manage to hit nothing at all, hampered somewhat by having only one barrel. On the last shot of the day, however, I was presented with a target of three and bagged two with luck. They were Spanish Sisons or what we call the Little Bustard, *Tetrax tetrax*. While I did not receive much praise for my marksmanship, Ascalon did receive many an envious comment. Perkins did well, taking a bag of an even dozen. These birds we donated to the mess.

We were back by the middle afternoon and had a passable luncheon with the officers of the garrison artillery, wary of the bird dishes. One un-wary Major broke a tooth on a lead pellet. A friendly lot but not one of them had been east although a few had served in garrison at Malta, Corfu, Saint Helena and other places. One man, old now for a Captain, had served as a boy on the islands of Saint Marcouf[4] during the time of the celebrated attack against it. He gave a good and lively description of that desperate fight against the French.

We made our way to our quarters but, still feeling restless, I went for a further walk, making my way to Frobes' quarry and spent some time there investigating the rocks for fossils and found instead a human skull in good preservation hidden back in a dark place. It seemed un-usually shaped but feeling it was no Englishman I took it with me. Perkins thought it was a good souvenir and that I should, in the barbaric eastern style, fashion it into a drinking cup. I thought of it more in the lines of a piece for my museum[5].

We had returned to quarters when another messenger arrived to tell us that there was a Lady at the gate. We hurried down and found Danae in a grey and yellow dress and matching hat. She seemed pleased to see us and seemed to be without an escort, and she gave us messages; one from Mrs. Germann, herself (to both of us), one to me from Millicent, one to Perkins from Prudence, and another from Danae, again, to both of us plus one other. She smiled and then left in some haste, declining my invitation to escort her home, while swinging her parasol like a broadsword at any dog or man who hindered her passage.

A reprieve, it would seem, had been issued; with Millicent, writing with Mrs. Germann's grace, inviting us to partake of a Saturday party at the Barrow's. Danae's message was more startling, as she wished our assistance in helping her to escape. I showed this to Perkins', who said it must be sarcasm, or worse, acerbity, for truly she could not be suggesting I would elope with her? Perkins' note from Prudence he would not reveal, only that he was astounded by her turn around - for he remarked that she seemed as contrary as a Belgian whirlwind. I had to ask what, pray tell, was a Belgian whirlwind and he seemed nonplussed that I did not know and came forth with a rambling discourse on recent Belgian history. It would seem he did not know what he meant either but I believe he was talking about the un-sightly tangle that was politics in that newly born country *{Belgium had come into existence six years ago}*.

We took up the last note written in French, and was from that Chilean officer. He suggested we were cowards and should redeem ourselves by meeting him in accordance with the Code Duello *{the code that many Europeans followed while dueling}*. The duel to take place in a field next to the amphitheatre which was located to the northeast of the hill known as El Rocadillo within the ruins of Carteia, some five miles inside Spanish territory, and we were to bring seconds. We looked at one another and sent the new message to the Aide-de-Camp, once again by our Batman. We thought it rather discourteous to send challenge notices by way of female acquaintances!

We ate that evening after four games of chess; two draws and a victory for each of us. There were more of the birds taken earlier that day but placed into pies. These - without the pellets - were quite well done and I ate more than I should. The Lieutenants I was seated next too were both from towns near York and we spent an evening talking over which was the better town to live, York or Manchester, but it was good to meet men from that area. They were quite impressed with my knowledge of artillery, something they had not expected from a Light infantryman but I told them as a lad I had memorised the firing tables of the standards guns - as they had too, if somewhat later in life.

A message came to us from the Aide-de-Camp, thanking us for being levelheaded and not raising to the bait the Chilean had offered, and that he would deal with the situation, again.

The conversation was going well as we were nearing dessert and, considering the quality and quantity of food so far, I was looking forward to it when the senior man made a discovery. The major observed that, counting the officers in the room and the 'guests' - us - there were thirteen officers sat down to supper in the mess a most un-lucky number, or so the legends go. A heated discuss erupted over who is most likely to die the results of being the un-lucky 13th man - and who is most deserving of this shortened life span. The discussion also rose as to who was the Judas in this which was, of course, the Major who had brought up the matter. It was resolved that the luck of each man should be tested by climbing up to the roof and passing over a narrow wall, and leaping a gap in said wall to another building. This seemed a fine idea and Perkins and I had risen when one of the Lieutenant's I had been sitting next to observed to the senior man,

"Sir, Ensign Driscol is not from this regiment, nor an artillerist. Certainly the tradition is not brought into force by the appearance of a mere light infantryman and this pointing to Perkins this engineer?"

He *{Perkins}* was both an officer and a Gentleman protested Perkins.

"Sir, now a woman or three have stated that I am not a Gentleman, but I do hold a commission in the Engineers and I protest this attempt at exclusion!"

This brought a roar of laughter and it was at this point the terms 'wall' and 'leaping a gap' came home to me and my fear of heights rose up in me like a wall of ice around my heart and intellect but there was nothing for it but to proceed boldly for the officers headed to the roof at a scramble. I was most fortunate that the night was dark and I could but barely make out that there was in fact a wall to walk but not what lay in the darkness on both sides of it. For once my fears were not triggered; with little concern I skipped crossed followed by a hopping Perkins and the others. The Major then cried out that, since our luck was proven, a sortie *{a surprise or sudden military attack against an enemy position}* would be called for as it was a necessity, which was met by a cheer from the artillerymen. They rushed off and, with nothing better to do, Perkins and I followed, leaping over walls and dashing down narrow lanes. It soon became clear as to our target; it was the infantry battalion's mess. We met and overran in a flash a befuddled Corporal's guard. What they might have made of thirteen officers without hats running thorough the street I pondered on later while writing this. We assaulted the gates of the infantry in fine style. The befuddled guard raising up only a weak, 'Sirs' as we ran by them.

One man, the Major, halted to reprove him for not using the correct plural, 'Gentlemen' and never the awkward 'sirs'. The rest of us swept on. Our target was the 81st Regiment of Foot, Loyal Lincoln Volunteers regiment. My father had fought with them at Corunna. With the puffing Major again in the lead, we burst into their mess singing a bawdy version of their regimental march, 'The Red, Red Rose', with much more expressive words. The Major and a Captain leaped onto the table where dessert was and a wild melee took place. Perkins and I had no idea what was occurring but we soon picked up the rules of the encounter. It was a game of rugby, aided by food missiles of any sort one could grab. This seemed impossibly mad and I made my way out having grabbed in one hand a fine raspberry bombe and in another a lemon tart. Thus well looted, I made my way back to my quarters, staying to the shadows should I by chance come across a more senior officer - my hatless, desert smeared uniform and disheveled appearance might gain his non-admiration. I made it back, recovered my hat and found Perkins waiting for me. Un-like myself, his uniform was un-marred and his hair neatly styled. We had a great deal of amusement over the actions of the officers. I found that once we had crossed the wall he had pulled up and made his way back - he did not want to be part of thirteen officers running about in Gibraltar. To reward his foresight I lent him half my lemon tart with him promising to return it the next day, if somewhat the worse for wear.

The galleries of Gibraltar where Driscol explored the fortifications and tunnels of that fortress. I-III-6

Millicent

Saturday 15 October

With not much to do, Perkins and I discussed the theory of phlogiston[6] when we awoke but we both agreed it had no merit so it was not much of a discussion. We went down to the port to view the shipping and saw a large Indiaman at anchor.

We also noted that the Chilean warship was gone. To that, we breathed a sigh of relief, for one more difficulty was done with.

[Editor's note: Driscol noted at a later date that on this date, unbeknownst to him, of course, the following note on an action of his regiment]

> I have learned by post that Major-General Sir Alexander Woodford, K.C.B. inspected three companies of the regiment in Portugal. I am happy to have heard of this great success and especially that my old company had done extraordinarily well - I am certainly glad to have heard that and I am doubly glad to not have had to go through it as such events are the height of boredom.

We made our way to the Barrow's but the party was in abeyance for the General Hislop, the Indiaman we had seen had come into port and those going around Africa to India, were making haste to board her. It would seem my comments to Mrs. Barrow had made her arrange the party for the benefit of Millicent and myself. We made our way to their locale but could not find them. After some moving about, marching here and there, we found them by sighting Mr Beer who was standing at the embarking point with his limbs crossed and a mixed expression on his face. He greeted us and pointed to where the Germann's were. He could see our confusion and said to go ahead and make our good byes for he was not going.

My last sight of Millicent was she in a launch rowing out to the General Hislop, she was too far off to shout to but she turned about and, keen-sighted, she saw me and waved most warmly. Danae did so also but with less vigour and even Prudence turned and gave a sedated departure wave. It took the launch at least twenty minutes to make the ship and Millicent would turn every minute or so and wave. We made inquiries and found that the ship had been loading since late yesterday afternoon and would soon weigh anchor as the flags at her masts showed to be true. I stood there for some time until the anchor raised and she headed out to sea. I finally lost sight of Millicent on the deck sometime after that. This took some two hours to do and during this time I could not leave the seaside. How I regretted not being able to have time to speak to her at the party so kindly arranged by Mrs. Barrow.

Beer came up later and stated that he was left behind and was to travel to India on his own money as he had had enough of Mr Magistrate Germann, to tell the truth. We told him of Catania's plan and he nodded his acceptance. He added he was still in the man's employment but the ship could not take any more passengers, especially those who were 'of his kind'.

We went to the Barrows and had a spiritless meal and I resolved to swear off women until I was five and thirty, rich and famous, and when I might have my pick. Mrs. Barrows was most comforting and nearly motherly in her concerns. Perkins took Prudence's departure with a mix of relief and sadness but he was soon commenting on the looks and possible lack of virtue in a woman he had seen at the Governors-Generals party. The departure of Prudence disturbed Perkins for nearly an hour and I believe, up to this time, she was the only woman to have hooked his heart mainly by his failure to hook hers.

We arrived back at our quarters to find two messages, one from the Germann sisters wishing us well and wondering where we were at, the other a later message hoping we might meet them to say goodbye. I was not impressed with the efficiency of the Gibraltar servant's messaging system. In the second envelope was another smaller one made from folded paper and in it, secured by a paper tab and lettered with a single 'M', was a lock of her lovely hair.

Perkins made the best of my mood by suggesting that although I might not have her hand, I did have her heart and, with the growing recession of my own hairline, I now had some hair to cover it with.

Later that day, another invitation arrived from the infantry battalion, offering us an entertainment that evening. We accepted on the general principle of never turning down a free meal.

The officer's supper was a grand affair and we heard many accounts of the night raid by the garrison artillery. They invited us to a Sunday hunting outing into Spain, and again we agreed wholeheartedly. Anything to take up the time as we waited for Catania and now Mr Beer.

Sunday 16 October

We awoke early and met with the officers of the 81st regiment; this group of men paying no attention to the Sabbath or church parade. We were led out of the garrison by the band which was playing the tune 'The Lincolnshire poacher', which I was made to understand was played each time the regiment rode out to do some hunting. We passed the overslaugh return parade to which twenty sergeants and seven and thirty corporals from each regiment were part of this. These men released from any duty with the regiment to take part in the garrison's guard during the next week, the men provided by each regiment in turn.

It would seem that the small area of Gibraltar did not allow for the keeping of a full stable and the same horses were used by all the regiments and staff stationed there. I traded the first horse I obtained for the tall Andalusian with the 'horns' I had ridden before. We were to hunt rabbits near San Roque and we entered an area of stunted woods that swarmed with blackbirds, finches, brown and green linnets, robins, thrushes and other common species but not a rabbit found. A six-foot snake that escaped our wraith startled one man's horse.

View of Gibraltar from San Roque. I-III-7

The brown hill town of San Roque, I learned, was where the Spanish inhabitants of Gibraltar had gone when the British had taken the fortress in 1704. The looted stones came from the ruins of Carteia, a Roman city said to have been built over the ruins of an earlier Carthaginian one. We halted for some time to water the horses and made our way up the steep stone streets to the Plaza Mayor and the summit. From there we had fine views: to the south was the sea, Algeciras Bay, the Straits and Africa with Mons Abyle beyond. Closer in, Mons Calpe *{Roman name for Gibraltar}* was well defined and seemed more an island than a peninsula. To the north were the Sierras in shades of brown, purple, pink and streaks of red. We took a moment to view the relics within the Church of Santa Maria de la Coronada, rumoured to hold all the Romanish treasures from the church lost at Gibraltar.

Having paid a small fee to the Mayor, we gained a guide and under his direction we went back to our horses and a short distance away we formed a line and advanced with pieces at the ready but again any *liebre {hare}* escaped us. While so employed, officers from a Spanish regiment came by mounted with lances, hunting *javali {boar}*. They were from the 6th Regiment of Infantry the famed *Saboya* contingent. They did so in full uniform and there was full-blooded discussion in French and Spanish over the advantages - and which was more gentlemanly: the hunting of *zorro {fox}* with dogs or spearing boar from horseback. A horn soon sounded and the Spaniards were off in a rush of hoofs and cries, and we went back to not shooting at hares. We discussed for some time why during a civil war a Spanish regiment would be in garrison here instead of fighting? *{This regiment had decided to be neutral}*

After a bad day of shooting, we made a hasty camp and the regimental officers, perhaps to make up for the day's bad sport, told us of greater hunts, for a few days ago they had been foxhunting over this same ground. A Lieutenant related a two-week hunt he had undertaken some months previously, which had the flavour of danger in it. He held that a distant ramble was better if associated with the chance of personal molestation and death. In this, Spain could provide for the countryside was seething with agrarian discontent and lawless peasants driven from their land by drought, debt or just making deviltry all made more dangerous by the civil war. You became the stalked party while out on the hunt. He spoke of the *contrabandistas {smugglers}* of the coast who permeate the mountains of Andalusia and who bring in all types of merchandise by conspiratorial arrangements with the custom officials - if they are not the custom officials themselves. They are also not above attacking a lone hunter or small party of any nationality. The propinquity of these brigands, real or imagined, often caused great inconvenience while hunting the more desolate areas. A meal was proposed but some of the officers decided to eat on the hunt and left us in small parties, and we ate olives, cucumbers and tomatoes as a fast repast. Perkins and I, not knowing the ground, stayed within sight of the camp at all times but found nothing but lizards, small birds and many insects. Finally, the three spaced shots of recalled were heard, the first shots we had heard in hours. It would seem the hunting had been as bad in the afternoon as it was in morning.

We soon gathered and controversies arouse one concerning a Lieutenant by the name Bursnell who had not appeared and other trivial matters. I remembered his name, as I knew a boy of the same name from Eccles. The signal made again and a wait ensued. It was debated and resolved that a search be made, and we were placed in a five-man party to search to the west. We did so, finding after a time a trail and followed it, one of the infantrymen being a fine hunter who could follow the trail well enough. We soon came to a large rock and found a Spanish style *alforjas {food wallet}* resting on it with its olives and bread un-eaten by man but well picked at by birds and insects. We shouted his name and, as the area was rising and rocky, the trail was lost. We spread in line and, moving forward, continued to shout his name at intervals. The good hunter and I made our way to a precipice that was nearly three hundred feet deep. Seeing nothing, we split; he going north and I going south. We had gone but a short distance when I came across a cocked shotgun lying on the ground near the edge. I raised a shout, and the other searchers joined us, coming at the run. The evidence was grim. Holding on to one of them, he peered over the edge of the *canon {valley or draw}* but could see nothing. Perkins found a way down that was not to steep and it was soon after that we found our man, for there on the rocks he laid. He had been smashed into splinters by the terrible fall and had been impaled on an outcrop of a large boulder. We found his trousers open and theorised he had been urinating at the edge of the ravine when he had slipped only to end up here. We placed his body in our un-used game bags. We climbed back up, seeing no way to move his body at the time. At the top, we fired a signal and an hour went by as the Regiment arrived, some of the men in shock at the happening for no officers had died in the regiment since the 1820's. A number of men went to find Spanish peasants, rope and wood to make a sledge to draw him up. The commander asked that we depart and he brusquely declined our assistance but we forgave him this as he clearly had been taken aback by the loss of his officer. We stayed, however, and it was near evening before we made the lines of Gibraltar once again.

A message was waiting for us from Catania who had found Mr Beer and who now joined our party. We would depart Gibraltar at dawn on Tuesday with precise directions given as to where to meet.

We studied Persian texts until we went to sleep. Perkins made an un-charitable remark before we put out the lamp in that he wondered if a remarkably crafty Spanish rabbit had pushed the hapless Bursnell into the ravine. He also told me one odd fact: I had not looked at the corpse in the face and he observed that that man was a bit shorter than I but still thin as a reed and had the same blonde hair I did.

Monday 17 October

Perkins and I packed up our belongings. Catania had mentioned nothing about supplies so we laid in about twenty pounds just in case. We paid our respects to the 81st but the funeral would not be until tomorrow. The commander of the Regiment apologised for the poor entertainment and, noting that I was a light infantryman, he added that he could arrange for my appointments here in his regiment should I so desire, there obviously now being a position free, of course. I declined most graciously but I thought that he took it with a frown. Why would one want to stay on a rock - a pleasant rock, yes - when the east beckoned? That there were no women here was also a problem, and I could not speak Spanish, nor did I have any desire to do so, with my mind filled with Arabic and Persian. I highly suspected that I would meet few speakers of Persian at this posting; although just to the south were a plethora of well-armed Arabic speakers.

While out we encountered the Baptism parade where children of the garrison are paraded in good military style along with their parents and taken to the Convent Chapel for the necessary actions to be done.

We walked again the streets of Gibraltar town, viewing the lives of those natural born citizens named 'rock scorpions'. We visited the Jewish synagogue and spoke with the Rabbi, using our limited few words of Yiddish and finding he did not understand Arabic. He was a tall, thin man who looked more like a Jew than Catania. He was well educated and spoke both delightfully accented English, sprinkled with Spanish terms, some French and Giffoot; a language Catania had told us of while aboard ship - it being a Jewish corruption of Spanish spoken by many in Gibraltar and the other sea-ports of the Mediterranean.

Neither Perkins nor I had ever been to such a place and he gladly gave us a tour. Perkins asked about his favourite subject, women and found that this gender was not allowed to worship here, it was forbidden, as it was a moot point to allow them into such a godly place as these poor creatures had no souls. The Rabbi noted also that the men often prayed to thank God that they were not women who, be it said, despite being angels are no gifted creatures. Perkins, in an aside, said that perhaps that explained Prudence - she had no soul. Nevertheless, I thought to myself that Millicent certainly did, and so did Danae who, had instead of a staid British woman's soul, had that of a female Spartan or perhaps a more feminine member of Thebes Sacred Band[7].

We toured Gibraltar again, having grown more accustomed to the people and sights for we saw more this time around. The exterior of cold stone was beginning to turn green as the hot summer turned over to the wetter and somewhat cooler autumn and the vines and creepers grew more luxurious. We saw numerous rabbits and birds but the convention was that no firearms might be discharged within Gibraltar except by military necessity. We made our way to Europa point, by way of Windmill Hill and O'Hara's Tower viewing the charming villas and pavilions then resting a moment on the point itself and wondering how many Phoenicians, Greeks, Carthaginians, Romans, Visigoths, Moors and Spaniards had stood here before, enjoying the cool breeze and the view of Africa.

Europa point and the southern end of Gibraltar showing Windmill Hill and O'Hara's tower. I-III-8

There was a light here for the benefit of ships for the east side of Gibraltar was made up of cliffs and several ships are lost each year against it when they are back-strapped. The ship driven round to the back of Gibraltar by the inshore counter-current and eddies of the wind re-directed by the rock, the strong currents detaining her there until she is either towed off, the wind comes to her rescue, or she is wrecked.

We went to see the locations of Jumper's battery, the location near where the British had landed to take the Spanish fortress a century ago. We wondered how this weak spot had been left so un-guarded by the Spaniards. We visited the gardens by Government house, which was a relief from the stony ground of the rest of the fortress, the Geranium trees offering well-appreciated shade, and we walked about, ending our tour at the bronze bust of Wellington set on an old Roman pedestal. There was a party of officers there enjoying an impromptu pic nik and we were invited to join the men they had sheet music and one said he would send me a copy of the music for some of the men had instruments and as they played it I found the music and words struck me greatly[8]

We were not use to the streets and at one point, we turned down a narrow street which looked to us to be a regular thoroughfare but narrowed even more, then made a dogleg after some thirty feet and abruptly ended in a high and closed gate to some depot or cistern terminating thusly into a cul-de-sac. We were amused by our joint folly. I declared Lieutenant Perkins' guidance defective and he defensively replied that he had been following my lead, from my front. We turned and made the corner again and nearly collided with a man in European coat and trousers with long blonde hair. He seemed startled that we were coming towards him and he seemed dissimulated. <u>We remarked to him in passing that it was not only us, who had been misled by the street, and walked on.</u>

[Editor's note: Driscol underlined the passage above in pencil]

We went up to some of the higher batteries, for I had an interest in the nature of their carriages as I had wondered how they had addressed the problem of the horizon depression or dip for their pieces of artillery. The problem was their angle must point below the horizon. The angle is that which the axis of a gun is laid in order to strike an object on a lower level. The depression required in batteries of a very elevated site like Gibraltar for the firing the guns at landing enemies or near vessels is so great as to necessitate a peculiar carriage. The carriage was different, the muzzle pointing downwards and the barrel rotated so the firing mechanism was at the bottom and in front of it were shallow pits so the gunners could work their pieces. I thought it a fine innovation by British gunners.

One of the Infantry officers had suggested a place to have our meal and we made our way there, it was a rather un-spectacular looking place but we had been alerted that this was but a facade and it served the finest Spanish fare in the town. Soon on wooden platters we were served a series of adobo dishes, finishing with a large piece of *lomo en adobo {tenderloin of pork}* and we announced it both very red and delicious. Before it had come *cazón en adobo*, a fish of some sort, and the best of all *berenjenas de Almagro {pickled aubergine, eggplant for Americansheadchee}*

The elderly owner of establishment, which was rightly named Jubaltare Rest *{the earlier English spelling for Gibraltar}*, was a former Spanish seaman who had served many years in British bottoms. His English was none too bad, and he said it was good that it was autumn now and, observing the sky, he could see that it would soon rain. He also said that in the dog days of summer not only did the sea here seemed to boil, but wine turned sour, the water was predominantly foul, dogs and Frenchmen grew madder and all other creatures lethargic while burning fevers and hysterics afflicted Godly men and women. As a good man of the sea, he had a barometer and thermometer on the wall and it registered a pleasant temperature of 77° for that hour, with the barometer beginning to drop as we ate. We left him the better part of a Cobb - 'Cobb' being the Gibraltarian term for the Spanish dollar. We nearly made it back to our quarters before we were completely drenched in an outburst of rain that seemed more like someone pouring a barrel of water over us than a good honest English rain.

We practiced our Persian writing that day, using the back pages of the pamphlet given us by Gregorian. It was admirable paper I must say.

We had a good supper, despite not joining the Garrison artillery's mess who were having some Ladies event - to which we had not been invited. I felt that was due to Perkins' wandering eye but I said nothing for I was happy to stay in our quarters and read. Our Batmen secured for us some delights. A ship had come in from Sicily carrying fruits and we found a small bag of oranges to supplement our rations of Spanish style bread, green and black olives, some detestable cheese and a good slice of a Portuguese type of honey cake *bolo podre de Estremoz.*

The original sheet music Driscol referred to in his journal only the front sheet has survived. I-III-9

By Maltese Speronara To Ceuta And Alger (Algiers)

Tuesday 18 October

We awakened before dawn and as the light broke to the east we found Catania and Beer, and conducted our welcomes in halting Persian and worse Arabic, aided at times by Catania in French.

We made our way to an un-familiar type of boat with a spur like bowsprit that, instead of rising, stuck out like a poorly made above-water trireme's ram. Catania told us it was a Speronara, or as the Maltese called it, a *Xprunara*. It was a small vessel of perhaps eighty tons when wet; having three masts, usually but ours only two, each with a triangular sail similar to the lugger tradition with its three-cornered sails. A large crucifix in the Latin style hung from her stern. She, for it was definitely a feminine looking boat despite its warlike painting, had a bright red and black hull with masts painted an un-settling shade of green. A young Maltese man came up to us at once. He had a ring in his ear and spoke rapidly in what we presumed was Malti the home language of Catania and the Maltese. In a few minutes, a deal seemed to have been struck or agreed to and Catania turned to us and said we were in luck for his countryman was to go to Ceuta, and if we found no French ships going to Malta, he intended to make for Alger for a cargo and there we could try again. The cost was minimal but we must provide our own subsistence. Catania was pleased that we had brought provisions and we readily agreed to all the conditions for we were now the 'owners' of the boat and the Captain asked when we would care to sail. He spoke poor but understandable French and we all agreed that now was the time and the crew jumped to their tasks like English tars at the word from their young Captain.

Our quarters were an enclosure of sorts made up of stout timbers and added to the structure of the ship at some later time. It was, however, firmly lashed to the ship's deck by strong rope and brackets of iron and covered with a waterproof tarp and had the shape of a tent. It was of limited space and was set up for sleeping only with the deck serving as a bedstead aided by some thin mattresses of un-known construction and fill.

There were sculptured mounds on the bulwark that made up the structure and, when I asked, Catania said they were a representation of the breasts of Saint Agatha. Another icon of some artisanship adorned the mizzenmast and that was of Saint Publius *{patron Saint of Malta}*. As Saints flanked us we would certainly find some comfort and safety in their presence, even if it was Popery.

Our luggage went into a hatch which smelled of fish just in front of our 'cabin-tent' and we did so with help from an Italian speaking crewman who spoke constantly despite none of us except Catania speaking the language, and he not well at all. Beer had volunteered to be our cook and he found the brick lined space to do so in the forward 'hold'. The ship contained hundreds of pieces of crockery and she hoped to trade for foods stuffs in Ceuta to take on to Alger where, as Catania had said before, the French would pay top prices for anything to eat - being good Frenchmen, all.

A fresh *datoo {the west wind of the straits of Gibraltar}* was blowing. The crew prepared the sweeps, for the ship was small enough to row out. She used her fifteen-foot long oars, which were soon un-shipped, and the ship began to manoeuvre with her sails still un-furled. It was the schooner's Captain, a Maltese of Italian origin named Scerri[9], who was constantly looking about him as he took his boat out of the harbour who noted that several men on the quay were observing our departure with some interest. We turned to look but could not see them among the crowded quays. As piracy was not a dead issue in these waters but as we carried nothing overly valuable the Captain thought it nothing but stated that his eleven man crew and two boys were well-armed and had only last month driven off a boat intent on robbery off Minorca. Catania, I could see, was concerned but would not express his concerns more than to dismiss our queries with a shake of the hand.

The crew was a swarthy bunch, having, to my mind, eastern eyes, black to brunette hair, and that muscular development particular to seamen. They all spoke Malti and a few were conversant in Spanish, Italian and Arabic, and one large man Turkish. All were young men and the two boys were nearly men themselves. As they rowed, they took up a chant and I imagined that the chant they gave out with might have been a song sung by the Athenian crews on their way to besiege Syracuse[10].

It would be around fourteen nautical miles to Ceuta and, once we had approached and passed the mole, the waves of sea began to rock the boat, which rode the waves gently moving up and down on them in a more musical way than the *William Fawcett* that had seemed to dig through them. The sails were quickly spread out and I could feel the ship begin to surge ahead. We had that *datoo* wind from the west, and it was to our quarter and we were soon making at least eight knots. The Captain had a shouting match with a Gibraltar fisherman who crossed his path too closely and amplified by vigorous gestures and shouts that were comedic in their intensity. The sea spray did not enter the boat and I asked the Captain in French what the name of the good ship was. It was the *Addolorata* which Catania said meant 'sorrows' and added that it probably referred to un-requited love, although it took a few minutes' conversation in French to determine exactly what he meant.

Perkins thought it a good name for a boat that would carry me away from Millicent's departure point. I replied that he was a poet at heart. No, he was more of a wordsmith than poet was his response. A few moments later, he noted he could not think of an antonym for the word poet. I suggested the word 'hack'. Which he accepted for a moment then announced that he was thinking of someone like Robert Southey, *{the Poet laureate of England at this time}* and to that I had to agree. We discussed his poem, Roderick the Last of the Goths, which we both thought terrible.

The sky was bright and clear and around us no less than three hundred sail of ships were within the circle of the horizon that we could see, almost all were small craft and for the first time no war ships were about except those at the anchorage of Gibraltar. Our course was set and we made our way across the narrows. It was difficult as we were cutting through the majority of the sea-lane's traffic; about 60% of the ships were inbound to the *Mesogeios {Greek name for the Mediterranean Sea}* or the Hinder Sea of the Bible. Catania told us that the Hebrew name was the Middle sea and Beer said in Arabic it was known as that, too but Catania disagreed and, after an exchange of good natured Arabic debate, it was decided that the true name in Arabic was *Bahr al-Rum {the Roman Sea}*.

I knew nothing of Ceuta and was surprised to find that the Spanish had a city in the land of the Moors; somehow, I had missed it in my reading. Catania knew it only by name and reputation it being one of the few ports he had not yet been too and, he explained, this was due to it having little to offer in the way of naval stores.

Driscol's Maltese Speronara showing the 'cabin' at the stern. The crude drawing taken from his journal and shows his faint skills as an artist. I-III-10

It was perfect sailing weather and we made our anchorage at Ceuta before noon. There were few ships in port and none that looked French to Catania's or Scerri's experienced eyes. We went ashore to determine the possibilities but immediately ran into difficulties with the Spanish officials who were mightily suspicious of two Englishmen departing from such a boat. I suspect they thought us deserters, which were the usual Englishmen they met. Despite our protests and production of our passports and our expired papers from Corunna we could not obtain a passage to allow us to view the town for the day. As it was, even an offer of a modest fee by Catania was dismissed contemptuously - a rare thing to witness; a Spaniard turning down a bribe. We returned to the boat but the Captain and Catania proceeded into town.

Perkins and I settled down and practiced our Persian, drilling one another on modal verbs. The port had little to recommend it. We had anchored a long musket shot from the city but inside the eastern mole. Further to the east was Mount 'Acho at the end of the Peninsula of Almina which resembled in some ways its sister, Gibraltar, but less pronounced. There had been some talk in the English press over the years of exchanging Gibraltar for this rocky place but I do not see

how it would replace that fine fortress. Gibraltar is un-surpassed in being a way to tweak the Spaniard's noses. There is little trade here, as the locals will not trade with the Spanish openly but much smuggling occurs: food and trifles for Ceuta and alcohol for the non-drinkers of Islam. From Acho, the city itself - Calle Real, we were told was its name - sits on middle ground and to its west rises another piece of high ground on which old Ceuta is situated and completely commanded by the fortifications on it. If that hill were to fall, the city could not be held. The Spanish had recognised this weakness and had pushed some miles farther on into Africa where three lines of fortifications existed to make any attempt to come near to that fateful hill would have to be paid for highly in blood; a price the native Moroccans feared to pay.

Ceuta the Spanish port located on the Moroccan coast. The view is from the North looking south. The Speronara would have anchored where the three-masted ship with bare poles is shown. I-III-11

The afternoon was aging when our men returned. Neither was in a good humour. The story was that we had just missed a small fleet of French victuallers that had gathered up all excess foodstuffs in the town and had sailed the morning before. More supplies, expected tomorrow and the Captain hoped to fill his hold with pressed dates or other bulk using the Mahaya - a brandy distilled from grapes, we were told - that filled the crockery that filled his ship now in exchange. I had thought the ship in ballast when I had first approached it but found that this type of boat rides high even when well loaded, so designed to never have more than a fathom of depth, allowing her access to many of the smaller ports on this inner sea.

The Captain apologised for his mistake and offered to refund our initial payment but we agreed that knowing of mercantile movements was not the reason we had hired him. The night looked to be dry and pleasant so we would wait the arrival of the commodities in which he was in need.

Catania observed that if we waited till dusk we could make our way to ashore. We, of course, inquired how this might be done, as the Spanish official seemed quite determined to prevent us. His explanation was educational. It would seem that at dusk a different man came on duty and if we were to go ashore not dressed as Europeans, but in different guises we would have no difficulties wandering about until the port closed. For, like Gibraltar, the Ceutans never allowed foreigners in their city at night.

Catania and the crew lent us the clothing for this adventure. In a short space of time we transferred ourselves from his Majesty's service to that of rather peculiar Moors. This accomplished by a bit of dirt and some local dress. All I lacked was a good knife - carried by all the Moors on this coast but the large Turkish-speaking crewman lent me his curved dagger, sheathed in leather and copper and having a fair edge. We awaited the coming of evening when the shadows of the night would hide our light eyes, perhaps also hiding the fact that Perkins looked like a painting of an English Gentleman and my height and definite northern European look.

With a great deal of excitement, we were rowed ashore, with Perkins and I speaking what little Arabic we knew between us. We landed at the quay and the official paid us no mind for he was happy to sit on his chair at his desk of casks, swatting at flying insects and smoking a square cigar. We found that the peninsula was indeed thin; only thirty paces brought us to the southern edge of the city where more boats were. We turned towards the west and made our way to the base of the hills. The town was un-usually clean; there were no Jews, Mudejares[11] and little to our eye of trade. Nevertheless, we toured about for a while, practicing our eastern swagger and even returned the greetings of 'fellow' Muhammadan who took no great interest in us. There was little light but after an hour or so we found a small place by the sea were couscous and grilled fish were served. Our Portuguese and Spanish coppers were most welcomed but we avoided drinking anything. We had smelled the fish, for they were kept alive in a large copper reservoir by the door. The place was full of men and no European could be seen. A babble of voices, some in Arabic but mainly Spanish, Italian and other languages, were being spit about.

I was chewing on the last piece of fish when Perkins bent forward towards me and whispered in Persian that I must listen to the men behind him. I did so, expecting some sharp expressions in Arabic, although we had found it nearly impossible to follow what these Moroccans called Arabic. I scratched at my ear and, cupping it, was able to pick up some of the words. For the place was closed in, dark except for four candles and open to the sea on one side. I thought I could hear Russian being spoken.

I looked at Perkins who raised his eyebrows and I returned it, and continued listening. We sat for some minutes but I could not make out what was being said with the clamor of others talking. I was frustrated in hearing what was said by a waiter who walked with the grace of a bullock across the creaking wooden floor, as the establishment was built out over the water and the sound of flies and the rolling up of the waves against the seawall beneath us. I could speak only a few hundred words of Russian and had not heard it in some years. I could make out a few words such as, 'I,' 'you,' 'we,' and other common ones but could make out no sentences. Out of a sentence of, say, ten words I could understand but two or three.

Perkins stood and I followed his movements as we made our way out. I took the time to look at those who sat behind him but they were in shadow. As I past, I caught sight of something; there was a paper out and it was lit by a faint candle that sputtered in the wind. It was what was in the man's hand, that device is what caught my attention; it being impossible to see what was written but the device, a pencil that he held, was a damning truth to me, which I noted, for I had seen the like before and Perkins and I moved on and out. We walked slowly up the street than moved to one side to whisper to one other in English.

He was concerned, as he knew it was a European tongue and I confirmed it was Russian indeed and that most likely spoken by one man who I understood to be a Russian or someone in contact with such. Perkins wished to know how I knew this. I told him of the pencil I had seen, for I had seen them in the Baltic and in the hands of my Mother's relatives. It was a square, black enameled 'magic' pencil *{mechanical}* with a square graphite point made in Nuremburg and manufactured for the Russian market exclusively. I told him briefly of my summer at sea in the Baltic, we had engaged a large cargo of that type of merchandise and taken it to Peter *{Saint Petersburg}*. We found it impossibly odd that Russians would be in Ceuta.

I felt again and reassured that my French pistol was under my robe. We made our way back to our boat. We found the crew waiting, as expected, and smoking something that smelled of rotted leather.

In some haste we came back to our ship. During this time, Perkins and I began to doubt what we had been agitated by. It may have been a Russian pencil, they may have been speaking Russian but Russians were not un-known in this part of the world. They were great seaman and I recalled that during the Napoleonic wars a fleet of nine ships-of-war under Vice-admiral Seniavin and an enemy of England at the time had spent a great deal of time in the Tagus before being dealt with by the Convention of Cintra[12].

We were soon aboard and whispered our finding to Catania but he, instead of dismissing our concerns as the flights of fancy of two young men overawed by their first steps in Africa, took our discovery quite gravely. He asked several important questions, the answers to which made all three of us - and soon Beer, too, was added in to cabal - concerned.

As we talked, a question came to my mind: Why was Catania concerned about Russians? He asked us first why were WE concerned about Russians Perkins explained that Russia and Britain were at odds on a number of issues and as military men we were always concerned as to why Russians might be in Ceuta. He, of course, made no mention of our planning for an expedition into Tartary.

I asked Catania why he was concerned. He had more of a general concern as he was carrying papers and bank draughts worth a great deal. He was not concerned that they were Russian but that they were dressed in the eastern manner and not openly European. For some time, the limited piracy in these seas had been led, not by the natives themselves, but often by renegade Europeans drawn to a pirate's life.

We puzzled over this for some time. We decided in the end to make sure our arms were at the ready and we would keep watch. The crew had settled down after a meager meal. The boat had two firearms, both flintlocks of un-determined age and one crewman was left on guard - for they had little to steal, un-less a man wanted to take the entire boat and for this reason they slept on deck and the Captain had the other firearm loaded and near at hand, and every other man a cudgel, pike or sword. Our Captain also had a larger firearm too but chose not to mount that small artillery piece, as he was afraid it would inspire someone to steal it.

We made up a second guard post and I was the last to take up the duty of guard, and was very pleased when dawn broke.

Wednesday 19 October

We all had a good laugh over our fright the night before and I began to wonder if Perkins and I had been completely mistaken in what we saw and heard.

The crew was diligent and the Captain was quickly on shore, and some hours later two *barcone {barges}* came out and our cargo was taken out and replaced with another. We took on tons of Tunisian botarga; the roe of the common tunny fish or mullet pressed and dried. It was very dry and reddish and had little smell. The Captain offered us some and it was surprisingly good with a touch of olive oil, some salt and lemon juice. It reminded me of salted fish; especially the sprat we had in England. I enjoyed the leathery texture and fishy flavour.

It came out of a Sicilian ship that had had the poor fortune to be naufragiated *{wrecked}* on Catalina Island just off the port of Ceuta. Normally the Captain would have taken two days to do the transaction but he told Catania that he had been told that men, foreign men, had asked about his boat. He thought it best to be gone. We had not told the Captain of our worries and this distressed us completely.

Perkins and I went forward and tried to puzzle out what it might mean. How could Russians know of our mission? Would the Russian even care? It left us completely befuddled but we agreed that once at sea and out of this port, we would feel better. We kept a close watch on the porters who assisted the crew in their hard labour but they were all locals and stripped to waist and carried nothing more dangerous than short three-inch knives. The high point of the day being when two of our men fell into the water and, despite being seamen, did not know how to swim. We fished them out with some good humour.

By late afternoon, we had a good breeze and our cargo was on board. There was no need for the sweeps and we fairly leapt from Ceuta. The Captain made as if going to Malaga and once night had fallen, headed back towards the coast of Africa. I felt it odd, Catania feared one evil, we feared another and the Padrone Scerri feared everything. He had related how small boats were sometimes lost to brigands or pirates who boarded them, killed the crew and made off with the boat and cargo - even in this modern day and age. We could see why Catania had wanted an escort, but who would escort us?

There was an active trade in this part of sea and we were rarely out of sight of another ship's lantern. It was some hours later that the weather began to turn.

I slept poorly, chaotic dreams of darkness and men in red, of pencils, and Slavic gentlemen with long blonde hair.

At the sight of a large approaching Felucca, a council of war had been held. After much deliberation, we decided our only hope against any opponent, should there be one, was to play the innocent merchantman and perform a violent ambuscade against any boarders. Our revolvers are still rare in this world, and this would give us a remarkable volley and volume of fire at close range. We would stay under cover until the enemy was at or on our decks, praying that any enemy did not sit off and shoot us into splinters with cannon - but if they were pirates, sinking or damaging the ship would be against their own good.

Our preparations were for naught. The large Felucca over took us and passed us in peace early in the morning.

The weather continued to deteriorate, we were soon presented with what Catania called a *trave*, in French, and fishermen in England called a *beam*. We were approaching a double line of gloomy and murky dark clouds which were observed to the east, and to which we grew nearer to at every moment. Scerri said it foretold of a violent storm and a change in the wind. I could hear Perkins stomach gurgle in protest and Beer did not look happy either both had not suffered greatly from seasickness so far.

We had been under easy sail but the Captain took a dislike to this weather and bore further to the north and added more sail as, like any Mediterranean Captain, he feared being driven on to a lee shore. The wind was still from the west but was weakening, the distant clouds were seen to have a luminous halo - a sure precursor to gales of wind, and stormy weather called by some a wind-gall.

We were some miles short of Capo des Tres Fourches *{Cape Three Forks}* in the afternoon when we saw a Xebec, or so Catania and Scerri identified it to us.

He had a good glass for a Maltese Captain and he and I watched the Xebec for a few minutes. It did nothing suspicious initially but it was odd in having every sail up as the local seamen tended not to rush about and then it was seen to alter its course to follow us.

It could have been that it was in search of news or information but that seemed a remote hope. She was larger than we by one hundred tons, and was certainly faster. Muhammadan raiders had used xebecs for centuries. She might carry cannon and could carry a crew of thirty men comfortably. Scerri began his preparations as agreed upon at the council of war. His men recovered from the hold a two-hundred pound swivel gun of Swedish manufacture, throwing a $1\frac{1}{2}$ pound shot I would suppose. They had a good supply of powder but only thirty stone shot and four small barrels full of iron musket balls, rather rusty, but sure to do some execution if used as canister. It was mounted on a pillar of wood just back of our 'cabin' loaded and covered with a scrap of canvas. Their two firearms were loaded, and given to two determined looking Maltese men. The others armed with various manual arms as noted earlier. Beer had no weapon at all so I lent him one of the two Colts and he gathered up a six-foot pike. Perkins, who also had his double-barreled shotgun, held the other American revolver. I had my French pistol and Ascalon. Plus, we all dug out our service swords which, despite the gaudy hilts, were sharp and serviceable. Catania had a twisted knife for his defence and would take up no other weapon.

As expected, our western wind slowly died away then replaced within an hour with a stronger wind from the east northeast or, as Catania called it, an *'aquilon'* wind.

The Xebec moved like a sea bird flying low over the water with her full suite of sails. She closed us rapidly despite the slowly dying wind. The four passengers had taken up a position within the sides of the cabin made of four-inch planks. The tent had been taken down, rolled up and placed along the top to provide us concealment and I was able to watch the approaching ship with my binoculars.

 It was Perkins with his more powerful eyeglass who noted the flag. He described it, as I could see it only as a fluttering of red, blue and white. The flag consisted of horizontal panels of red and white, and at its base a rectangle of blue with a white star. Neither of us knew what this might represent, Catania was sure that no European flag was of that type. By now, the ship was closer and we could make out the flag for it was an enormous one, probably 10-12 feet in length. Perkins and I discussed the mysterious flag and we both came upon the answer at the same time, for we both felt we had seen it before, but not in colour and it had been in the Times and other newspapers for some time. It was the flag of the new independent country in the Americas who were fighting against the Mexican Empire. It was, we thought the flag of Texas.

The flag that Driscol and Perkins' observed. I-III-12

The Xebec From Texas

The complete madness of the situation made Perkins and I laugh. Why would a Texas flag be flying from a Moroccan or Algerine Xebec? We explained this to the others who were not so up on the news of the world outside their own tiny slice of it. They had not, of course, heard of Texas, although Beer had a glimmer of recognition.

The Xebec had closed to a half a mile when she turned so we could see her length. She had a raised quarterdeck and amidships with five cannons ports which were open.

The weather's change caught us wholly by surprise, for so intent had we been on the Xebec that we had not noticed its arrival. It announced its presence by a lash of cool rain against the back of our necks. Within a few minutes, we were enveloped in the clouds that had looked threatening but now provided us with a place to hide from our larger foe. Or was it just an imagined foe? The wind was now strong from the northeast and Padrone Scerri redirected his bow to the southeast and, having reduced his sails, we moved on through the wind, clouds and intermittent rain.

We had a meal of the fish roe, olives and I opened that tin of corned beef I had purchased in London. It was excellent, I must say, even when served up cold. The aftermath of fear is often hunger and we consumed our meal under our re-established oiled canvas. Padrone Scerri did not find an offer of our reddish meat palatable. The swivel gun had been taken down and the charge drawn.

We practiced, as usual, our Persian and Arabic; one man asking a question in one language, the other to reply in the other. We did this for some hours.

Friday 21 October

For a storm, the series of rainy squalls we ran through that night had not made the sea rough and at dawn, we awoke at sea with no sails about. The Turkish-speaking mariner astonished us by being a Muhammadan man and he made his prayers on the deck in an easterly direction. I had not seen that before and observed his devotions with interest, however; I declined to ask how he could possibly determine an accurate *Qibla {direction to Mecca}*.

We asked Scerri why he carried a Muhammadan aboard. His answer made much sense. He often had to deal with Muhammadans and Turks around the French lake *{A soubriquet for the Mediterranean}* and for that a Muhammadan could go and do such that a Christian could not or feared to do. He was a good fellow and very passionate about his love. We asked what his love was and the answer was cause for much hilarity. For the man did love his black-strap, the dark country wines of the Mediterranean. I had tasted it in Gibraltar and found it completely wretched junk. As wine is forbidden to the true Muhammadan, he had found solace amongst us infidels - who supplied him with all the black-strap he could swallow. We found that instead of silver for his wages, he took so many bottles of the soul stealer instead.

During our time on the ship, the Maltese crew who, of course, were fervent followers of Popery, had conducted their rituals on a daily basis. In general, weather permitting, they had Morning Prayer just after dawn. At noon, an Angelus bell rung and ritual associated with it performed, along with a prayer, usually in unison together before their meal. In the evening, they sometimes did just a prayer but more often did a lengthier Ave Maria which, considering the circumstances, was often well sung. Four of the men, two sets of brothers who were more pious than the others, did what I believe were acts of contrition before sleep but, not understanding their language, I could not ascertain this with any certainty.

We decided to do some fishing as the tunny roe was beginning to be less delectable with each meal in which it participated. The Maltese, of course, had hand lines available. I had my packet of hooks and bamboo pole, and we soon had our lines out baited with bits of the botarga. We caught some seven fish in due course but Scerri and Catania were contemptuous of them for they were horse mackerels, *Caranx trachurus*; a dry, coarse, and un-wholesome fish very common in the Mediterranean but not deemed a fish worth eating un-less you were a Sardinian or a Frenchman, which, by God's good fortune, we were not.

We were un-able to tempt anyone to eat them and our culinary courage failed, too, so we cut them up for more bait.

In the hold where our baggage was, Beer found a scrap of a European newspaper that was in German. Scerri said it had been part of some packing used months ago when he transported pottery from Malta to Crete.

It was the bottom half from a newspaper dated August 14th 1828. I could read it with some difficulty but with Catania's help we soon had the news from what we discovered in the text to probably be a broadsheet from the port of Emden in the western part of Prussia. The Mayor was being honored for something neither of us were able to translate, it being hidden in a twenty letter long word. On the other side were some advertisements for women's clothes, and shoes and, of more interest, an article on the Chevalier Jean Auguste D'Angos who some five and thirty years earlier had made claims of having found a comet, one no one else could see. Some thought it was deliberate fraud, another thought he had mistaken a star cluster for a comet. One German was not sympathetic to the Frenchman's case for he wrote that

> *"d'Angos had the audacity to forge observations that he never made, of a comet*
> *that he had never seen, based on an orbit that he had gratuitously invented, all*
> *to give himself the glory of having discovered a comet"*

It was interesting that the man had worked in Malta for a time. Scerri knew him not but Catania was aware of him and his narrative and observed that the scandal had given a new word to the world, '*Angosiade*'; a term for an astronomical falsehood. This brought up our spirits as did the partial article about whether Jesus would come next year - obviously, he had not.

In the forenoon, the wind changed to a raw and strong easterly breeze, the full Levanter of legend and literature. We sailed across the wind in a close reach heading in the purposed direction of Alger.

Thus the day went, with periods of short rain but mainly the steady breeze from the east. The wind could chill you if exposed to it for some time. The crew had taken to their 'winter' clothing consisting of the same torn pantaloons and shirt but now topped off by a fez. This was the red cloth skull-cap which we had seen everywhere in Gibraltar and Ceuta. We continued to fish and were rewarded with a good catch of a three-foot fish we could not fully recognise but decided it might be a hake of some sort. It was added to our larder and feasted on with fried eggs from Gibraltar. Perkins and Beer delighting in the taste of its liver.

We resumed our Persian studies that night.

Saturday 22 October

There was a fight amongst the crew; two members taking exception to one another's presence. It was but a lot of noise and soon peace prevailed again. We were near the coast of Africa, hoping to make the run into Alger. We were passing and passed by the ships of all nations. We spoke to a Sicilian Paranzello, a small vessel, pink-stern with a lateen main-sail and mizzen, and a large jib marked with a large reddish cross. She had left Alger the day before and reported a large number of French ships in the harbour and outside waiting to make port. She also reported that pirates in *Lurcra's {small coastal craft}* and Xebecs had taken some smaller ships, and that the French navy was on patrol.

Some hours later we sighted a French Navy 20-gun Brig that had us hove-to after Scerri had raised the French flag in response to his challenge. The brig was a trim little ship named the L'enreprenant and commanded by Lieutenant de Vaisseau Armound who arrived by small boat with a well turned out crew showing the same sharpness in public display that one saw in the British Navy. He boarded us with two others; a sergeant from the L'infanterie de Marine and an Egyptian Copt acting as the Lieutenant's translator and *Trugman {dragoman}.*

The Padrone offered him and his sergeant a glass of wine - in actually glasses, something that had not been offered to us - and a portfolio-containing sheaf's of paper. These consisted of his licence, showing that he had not been to any port that was under quarantine, and a French issued licence that granted him leave to provide food for the French; signed, counter-signed, stamped and embossed with abandon. He also had his outdated Mediterranean pass; a document granted by the Lords of the British Admiralty to registered vessels of their colonial holdings, which was still valuable in some eyes to establish legitimacy. This was all looked at with little interest by the officer who handed them to the Marine, who handed them to Copt, who took to reading them with compelling attentiveness.

Our French officer briefly checked the cargo, and finally came to us, for we had been standing quietly to one side. Un-alike continental officers, British officers never wear their uniforms except when on duty or at social events where full dress is required. European officers wear a uniform at all times and we, of course, had on our civilian clothes. We greeted him in French and I added to his title the honorific of Mon[13], which he acknowledge with a smile and he was mildly surprised to find us on such a small ship. We exchanged what news we had. Perkins telling him of the piratical Xebec that had chased us to which the Frenchman nodded, noting that that was the largest ship he had heard of involved in such actions. A general conversation ensued with the Copt, Catania and Beer conversing in Arabic to one side while we, the three officers, spoke in French. The French Marine looked bewildered and quietly drank the two glasses of wine that had come into his possession.

Armound turned out to be a well-educated fellow from Perpignan and he had been to sea since he was a boy. He was of middling height, of squarish head and dark brown curly hair, and having a fashionable goatee with no moustache. His seafaring family was related by marriage to the Maurel family who were well known in Mediterranean commerce and shipping. He stated that several of their ships were in Algiers (as he pronounced it) and he was sure they would be travelling to the east. He apologised for not being able to offer us hospitality, as his duty required him to patrol and check the local sea traffic endlessly. He added a strong expression at the end of his monologue on selfless duty, and he added a good Gallic "*Mon Dieu*," said with mock intensity to end it.

Sunday 23 October

We are approaching Algers now that the Levanter had died off, replaced by a *Levanter Blanc* or dry wind. There were many ships about, most cruising up and down the coast waiting for a space in the harbour. We had raised at our foremast a flag given us by the good Lieutenant Armound, announcing that we had been checked and we had food on board.

Approaching Algiers made me remember kindly Duperre, the sea cat on the *William Fawcett*; for it was for the French Admiral who had bombarded and captured Algiers that he was named.

Algiers was said by some to be built in the form of a Roman amphitheatre, but the appearance represented to me, viewing it from some distance out at sea, was that of an inclined plane of white marble, coloured with veins of brown, in the shape of an acutely angled triangle. The slope on which it stood was so steep that almost every building was distinctly visible as you entered the port and the variegated colour of the roofs could be easily seen. The surrounding country was un-equal in its green beauty, which was spotted by large villas outside the walls where the rich relatives of the former Bey - and now the French conquerors - retire during the summer to escape the smell and crowds of the city. Seen from the deck of the *Addolorata*, it seemed an enchanting place despite its former reputation for the holding and degradation of generations of Christian slaves.

A small cutter met and led us to the south port around the Kheir El-Din pier. I had seen an etching of the town when Lord Exmouth had bombarded it in 1816 and its pyramid of white rising out of the sea is memorable for its imposing and picturesque aspect, as I have written above. As we came in we could see that both harbours were full of small mercantile craft. The Padrone put down all three anchors in respect to the *Levanter* wind that continued to blow and which we were exposed to in this anchorage. The anchors only stopped us when we nearly drifted into a non-descript tartan, which is a small coasting vessel with one mast and a bowsprit, lateen-rigged. Much-spirited cries of despair and outrage were given and taken by the crews of both boats, despite no damage and no contact. We were finally successfully at anchor in the outer harbour.

There was time to spend on other matters as the French officer had made it clear that no one should leave the boat until a health officer made his inspection. Armed guards on the pier and around the harbour reinforced that statement.

Beer and Catania spent their time shouting questions and answers to the many boats around us, getting the news. As they were so employed, Perkins and I practiced our Arabic and did some fishing. He pulling up an ugly 3 foot beast that I believe was a *Lophius piscatorius*, the devil-fish of these seas, and called by Catania and the crew a 'fishing-frog' for reasons they could not explain but they did say it was excellent eating and so with little else to do we tried our hand at cooking the ugly creature. The ship's cook had his fire up making a meal, and we gave it to him to stretch their provisions and we got back lovely grilled fish. Certainly, we agreed that no fish had ever been better and we sat, ate, and watched the developments of the

French city of Algiers. The city was the centre for the French invasion of this barbaric land and the bringing of European culture to this former den of pirates, religious error and slaveholders.

A boat finally arrived some hours later and the chief medical officer of the port made his inquiries. He was small man, nearly a dwarf, from the capitol of Auvergne {Clermont-Ferrand} where I suspect they grow naturally small, or are excessive pruned when young. He did his duty but on his face there was expressed both his stubbornness and miserable view of his life in this colonial port. We had a short discussion with him; he recommended that we announce ourselves to the British Consul and a few other suggestions of what a European could do in Algiers that amounted to a recommendation of NOT going ashore.

We made our way to the shore by boat and with some directions delivered to us in Arabic from various surly storekeepers we made our way to the streets near the Bab el Oued where the Vice-Consul was said to live, but those that said it had apparently been lying. We found no trace of the English Consul so we wandered the streets and we ended back at the port, and walked along the seawall to the end of the fortifications near Bab Azoun. We found it hard to believe that forty thousand people were supposed to fill this city for we saw few about, and those few we saw were sullen and un-friendly; having been conquered by the French, they had little time for any European; and also having been masters for generations, they took to the yoke poorly. A few French were around but they did not seem predisposed to make Algiers attractive to visitors. We retraced our steps and made it to the highest part of the southern wall. The fatigue of this toilsome ascent was compensated for by a grand panorama of the city, harbour and the fortifications along the coast.

Disappointed, we made our way back to the comforts of the *Addolorata.* Padrone Scerri was back, as was Catania who had had business ashore. He had sold our cargo and bought another; a full load of barilla which is an alkali (*soda ash*) procured by burning plants. He said it was from Spain but there was too much here for the French to make use of so he was reshipping it to Malta for future shipment elsewhere for the making of bricks.

Scerri pointed out to sea and there were, about four hundred yards off, two other Maltese ships of the same Speronara build anchored. One, he said, was an old boon companion he would be visiting tonight. The other was a relative by blood whom he would pointedly ignore. He waited a moment to see if we would ask about why this was so, however, none of us rose to the bait and so, un-bidden, he launched into a convoluted tail of marriageable 2nd cousins, un-marriageable 1st cousins, cruel betrayal, knifings, bad food and a particularly shrewish sounding grandmother with a taste for rabble rousing.

He invited us to join him but we declined. He invited Catania and Beer, also but they, too, refused. He then asked if we would guard the ship as Algiers, as he said before, was a dangerous place and to this we agreed for he was taking with him for his visit most of the crew except the Turkish speaker, the two boys and one of the pious brothers who was ill in the hold.

Small Algerine boats plied the harbour selling all that a man might want. From them we purchased charcoal, chickens, fruit and vegetables, and soon had an excellent meal as night fell. From the many ships around us, there were sounds of seamen entertaining themselves with music, singing and dancing. We found out a great deal about Catania's family and his extensive system of commerce. He kept no books but had everything in his head; a mind, we found, that was prodigious in its retention of details. He left the boat with his men in the darkness leaving us with an admonishment not to steal the boat or let it sink.

At midnight, the others went to sleep and I took the first shift of guarding the boat, with Ascalon at hand. It was some hours later when I awoke Perkins. Just as I did the harbour that to that point was quiet ceased suddenly to be, for off in the distance, the sharp sound of the discharge of firearms shattered the silence. No flash was seen and cries and shouts were more imagined than heard. The French guard boats made their attempts to find the trouble but we could hear no more after the initial flurry, for no more firing occurred. Many hours later, as we strained our ears and eyes in the darkness, we were hailed by Scerri and the crew were soon aboard.

The other Speronara, that owned by his relative, had been boarded by men who had made demands in Spanish and French which the relative had decided that evening he did not understand. Taking them for robbers, his men had opened fire and had had it returned. The sky overcast and the moonlight had been indirect and fleeting so the action was confused but the attempted boarders driven off after a number of shots between the boat and the invaders, who had rowed in on a small craft.

Scerri said that the men had asked where the two Englishmen were. He also added that it had been a European, two, in fact, making the demand. We stayed up that night making plans.

Algiers viewed from the pier next to the harbour that the Speronara, *Addolorata* anchored in the 23rd of October 1836. I-III-13

Escape From Algiers

Monday 24 October

We found in the morning that Scerri's relative had weighed anchor and left the port before dawn. Had we not had Catania with us, I believe the good Captain would have left us in Algiers, for he was a merchant and complications of the variety we presented was neither healthful nor money producing for him. We had to wait for our time to do the cargo and our time at the quay finally did come. Perkins and I had to leave the boat as the crew and workmen needed all the room they could find to move out the fish roe and replace it with bags of Spanish barilla soda ash. I spent the hours with my hand in my pocket gripping my French pistol. Catania suggested that we pay the man more and we did, it being a small amount and the Padrone was once again our good friend. It took most of the day to remove the original cargo and replace it with the bags smelling of burnt plants and chalk. In our plans, we had decided to stay with the Speronara as switching to a French ship would place us in hands we did not know were clean. We found, to everyone's frustration, that although loaded and the wind being fair we could not leave, and permission to do so by the French was not forthcoming.

The full moon could be seen during the day, having risen in the late afternoon and I observed and pointed out to the crew a partial ellipse of that orb. They were not barbarians but took it as a matter of fact, the importance and wonder of celestial mechanics being of no interest to them. Perkins, Catania or Beer where little better.

We considered leaving port at night but the French officials had not completed the paper work, the all-important licenses. As it was the man's livelihood, we could do no more than wait on its arrivals in the morning - trusting to the many legends of Gallic competence in such matters.

Once it had become dark, we had been at the quay but had spoken to another ship that was quite happy to allow us to pull back with our sweeps and to take our place and thus gain an advantage for next morning's commerce. We were led out by our small four-man boat armed with a lantern. We made our way through the tangle of ships and anchor cables to a point at the southern end of the great pier where lay a French battery that was set up and well garrisoned day and night, something I had personally reconnoitered during the previous hours. It was here we laid our anchors. Scerri brought up his swivel and we armed as necessary. The Captain had also bought a cask of white soap up and used it to coat all the railing and the points of the deck where someone might make his way up to the deck from a boat or leap down onto us from higher up. We thought this ruse most clever. He had used the subterfuge before when entering Sicilian or Greek ports, especially on the Dalmatian coast where 'water fleas' *{swimmers}* who would steal aboard a boat to commit petty larceny or even more grave assaults that could be expected to bother the rest of an honest seaman.

We found, to our disgust, that the French gun crews were soon asleep and their previously well-set guards disappeared. We soon determined the method of the deception: We observed that prior to the inspections of the officer of the guard who conducted his duties punctiliously every hour. A sergeant would come before him and make sure all was well and ordered so that when the officer came he would find the men at a state of supreme readiness and would continue his rounds. The gun crews and watch would then go back to sleep to await the next arrival of the guileful Sergeant.

Noting this trickery, I determined not to fooled myself in the future when conducting my own inspections and would make a reminder of this. I had been officer of the guard many times and wondered if my men and done the same. Certainly, Sergeant Tomlinson *{a Sergeant in Driscol Company in the 52nd}* would have been capable of this kind of deceit.

[Editor's note: Driscol made a large star here and underlined the passage above, later comments - not included here - showed that he did come back and had remembered this]

The full moon was quite bright and there was not a cloud in the sky this night. A mild land breeze was blowing off the city, bringing with it the malodorous traits of Algiers with it. I could easily see the outline of boats some distance away and wore my spectacles.

[Editor's note: Driscol had remarkably good night vision, for he seemed to be able to see better than the average person at night, perhaps making up for his poor vision in the day. I have deleted here several notes of his regarding stories from his youth outlining this ability which are fragments only and hard to understand. An example of what he wrote down; 'April, second house, rock sighted with only partial moon, 110'. Etc.]

We had wound our watches in unison after our partial supper that night and it was at 3:05 with the arrival of the French officer that the trouble began. The officer, it would seem, had found fault with our anchoring so near his precious 24 pounders. The officer of the guard insisted we move fifty yards away. He seemed to think we were hostile Algerines with an explosion boat beneath our heels or we had fifty Berber cutthroats thirsty for French blood concealed in our holds and were preparing to overwhelm them.

He did not appreciate my command of the French language either - probably a Parisian by his superciliousness.

I roused Scerri, who had not been awaken by the exchanges of shouts, and we lifted our anchors then moored some yards father off, nearly touching a low-lying settee and thereby setting off a loud exchange between their crew and ours, for ships had no honest business moving around in an anchorage at this time in the morning.

It was all for nothing and what followed was an innocuous early morning notable for only a loss of sleep.

Tuesday 25 October

The exposure of our weapons to the sea air had caused them to begin to rust and we spent the morning cleaning and oiling the weapons, having drawn the charges. Discharges of weapons in the port being something the French looked down on, especially if committed by a *Rosbif, {roast beef, French term for the British the counter to them calling the French frogs}.*

Scerri, by supplication, finally obtained his papers and we rowed our way out of the mix of boats. We were caught for a few minutes by a current which swept us south down the coast but the good Captain soon regained control of his boat and we were soon under sail and on course for Malta. The Levanter was still blowing but with little force so we were close hauled to the northeast.

We soon came up on two ships stopped on the sea; a black and yellow painted Polacre[14] rigged in the manner of a brig but of un-defined nationality and a green painted Mistico, an odd-looking boat being a hermaphrodite. Scerri thought she was a Cypriote, as she was well-loaded with Grey-Friars[15]. Both had their boats out and were dead in the water.

An engraving found in Driscol's papers on the back of which is written the date that corresponds to the day he was off Algiers. He seems to have mistaken this image of a tortoise for the turtles he stopped to hunt that day. Tortoises of this kind being land animals. I-III-14

Jellies, Leatherbacks And A Fracas

We had made some five miles from Algiers for I have changed to the French spelling of Algiers from the previous Algers when we entered a vast bloom of jellyfish, jellies or sea-blubber which stretched as far as the eye could see. More to our interest were the sea turtles who were feasting on these species of *Acalephae*. It was for this bounty, offered up by God and nature, that caused the ships in view to come to rest at the edge of this startling sight.

For this, the crew brought the ship to a rest and made to harvest a few of the turtles with our permission. We had secured some food at Algiers but not much as the place had been one, where no food was supposed to be exported due to the demands of the French army. The small boat was launched and the turtle hunt was on. We decided that shooting them was not a good way as the Padrone said they might sink. A few were grabbed and one harpooned. The crew brought back four in short order; one a *Caretta Caretta* of nearly a hundred pounds and three smaller leatherback *Dermochelys Coriacea*.

Beer raised the alarm by his cry and his arm pointing urgently. Coming down towards us with the wind was a Xebec; the Texas Xebec.

She had approached un-heeded from behind the Mistico and was less than a mile off when the alarm came. The turtles were cast into the hold and the sails hastily raised. Scerri announced his attention to run towards Algiers, for we could still see the upper tips of the ridges above that port. The swivel was mounted and we went back to our previous plan with one modification: Scerri loaded the swivel with a blank charge and fired it as a signal as the sails raised. He also had run up his French flag.

The two fire-armed men nestled with us and we took down the tent and re-made our barricade, ensuring we left a space of some six inches to see.

I was trembling with excitement then as I am now as I record this.

The Xebec was running with the wind and was approaching rapidly. I studied her through my glasses. The long bowsprit had two men in it doing some action and I could see how narrow she was. The foremast being square rigged, her main and mizzen with a felucca rigged lateen sails, and a triangular gaff-top sail.

Our delay in raising the boat and turning-about towards Algiers had allowed the enemy, for that is what I supposed her to be, to close with us. The Xebec's ports were not open. Their tiller was manned by a man in blue with the ubiquitous red fez of this sea. To his left were three individuals; the largest was armed with a glass and he was peering at us. He had on a dark blue hat and cloak, and by his stance and size we took him for a European. Slightly behind him was another in the same style of hat and clock, and behind him a smaller bareheaded man with long blonde hair flowing forward with the wind. Perkins thought it might be a woman but the way he held a musket made us think not. The larger of the men held a sword with a gold hilt that flashed in the sun and the other a pistol and sword. The crew numbered some five and twenty men, with only four muskets in view and, like our own crew, armed with a mix of swords and pikes. The ship also mounted a short barreled swivel on a pillar forward of the tiller near the port stairs leading from the quarterdeck to the main.

It was Perkins who remarked that the man with the woman's hair was the same as we had met un-expectantly in Gibraltar. I looked again and could do no more than agree with his assessment.

Although the Xebec was much swifter than our merchant ship, the Speronara, with her smaller size and sweeps, was much handier. We intended to avoid her as much as we could and IF forced to by either her manoeuvre or use of cannon to allow them to board and ambush them as we could. We knew any use of cannon would draw the French coast guards.

Scerri fired another blank shot again, hoping the sounds would draw the French guard boats but none could presently be seen.

The Xebec swept past the mistico, for we had hoped she was really a pirate and would take the smaller boat, but she showed no interest in her and she still held her course. She had the wind behind her back but was angling away from us to get abreast then turn in at us, or so we speculated.

Scerri frustrated this by turning more to the west, not directly towards Algiers but slightly to the north of it. He did so that at this point of the wind *{direction of sailing with the wind}*, our boat was faster.

Perkins had taken from his luggage a package, which he made me to understand were his papers and our orders, and to this he added some of the rusty musket balls that were to be used with the swivel. If the situation became desperate, I was to throw it over board.

The Xebec ran up a string of flags. That it was a message was clear but neither of us knew the meaning of nautical flag code, for I had never read Popham's book on the subject. The large flag we had seen before was raised when the Xebec came within seven hundred and fifty feet of us. At this time, the men on the bowsprit also displayed another flag; one of dark blue with a white star.

We sailed along for some minutes and, having received no answer to her signals, the Xebec made her wants known in a more direct way. One of her ports opened and a brass three or four pounder was brought into battery and a shot fired. Where it went no one could tell. Perkins declared that it had been a blank shot; one meant as a warning to stop our running and come to.

The smaller of the blue clad men went to another port which was raised, the gun brought into battery and fired, and here the shot splashed forward of us by a good distance.

Padrone's response was to give the signal and the ship made a hard turn to starboard, ending only when the ship faced into the wind, falling into irons and we tacked.

The Xebec was un-able to follow this and she sailed past as her crew on the main deck with the guns had to move smartly to match the manoeuvre. The Speronara, having come into the wind, was brought further to starboard by the application of the sweeps we had run out but not used prior. We were soon in position to regain our speed at beam reaching while the Xebec was now a thousand feet away. She was half way through her turn to starboard but she aborted this and turned to port to match the *Addolorata.* We continued to gathering way waited until the Xebec had completed its turn to port. When she turned again she had broad reached the wind and was now headed roughly north west. We conducted our turn which this time the Xebec matched with perfection but Scerri to his credit now had the weather gauge.

[The weather gauge was crucial in sailed naval warfare it meant that ship was closest to the source of wind, being upwind of one's opponent and could more easily come down to or escape an enemy]

The Xebec's long guns could shoot, if and when he decided to open fire, three quarters of a mile but their balls had small effect. We were fortunate our enemy carried such an armament instead of the shorter ranged but deadlier effect of the 'smashing' carronades.

The wind slackened, and presently fell altogether so that we were forced to have recourse to the sweeps again. The failing of the wind seemed to us a reprieve as we could never outrun the Xebec with our sails but it also meant no arrival of French aid, and with our sweeps we could not out-row her.

Our sweeps were manned but we had only two out on each side, manned by two men each. The previously sick man was also up, glistening with sweat, having come up from his sick bed in this time of difficulty.

Scerri smiled like a tethered sheep found by a hungry bear.

The Xebec also had sweeps, something I had not been aware of, and these were soon out four to a side, with three men to each. They began to gain on us.

The smaller man in blue seemed to be loading the cannon all by himself, with the larger man and the one with blonde hair remaining at the tiller with the blue clothed Captain of the corsair.

Having closed to six hundred feet, the cannon fired at us as the ship rose with the waves. Where the shot went, we could not tell. By this, we could tell the man was French or Spanish trained[16].

So the chase continued; our rowing grew faster but slowly we were being gained on with an occasional shot from the pursuer. Scerri declined to return the fire. His small stone balls would have no appreciative effect at this range.

On the fifth enemy discharge, we took a small hit; a nice hole high up on our mizzen lateen rig.

It was Beer who made mention of the Polarce which with no wind had also taken to its sweeps but was moving slower that either us or the Xebec. I placed them about three quarters of a mile away. However, they were not moving away but towards us.

The Xebec was now but three hundred and fifty feet away. The cannon discharged and hit our hull above the water line, scaring the man who was taking a moment from the sweeps and was renewing the soap coating on the port side. It struck beneath him. He dropped his tub and tool but under a strong directive from Scerri went down below to put a wooden plug into the new hole.

At this point, a large splash occurred in the water between us and the Xebec, and a belated 'boom' followed.

A puff of smoke betrayed the firer - it was the Polarce who had fired and raised to her foremast the French flag, and the French Naval ensign.

The Polarce was armed and we could see now she mounted a long 12 or 18 pounder on a turn table mounting on the forward deck. A canvas had hid this previously. She was probably a French naval auxiliary. This brought a cheer from the Maltese and us too.

This cheered us up, and the Maltese crew gave another shout and the talk was of deliverance.

The Xebec came on. We could see that the blonde haired man now stood with his musket aimed at the ship's Captain. With them were six men, dressed differently, and Catania said were Moroccans. All armed with muskets and swords they must have been in the hold for we had not seen them before. They had gathered around the larger man on the quarterdeck who seemed to be shouting at us, using a speaking trumpet but we could hear nothing of what he said.

Much to our temporary relief, the smaller man abandoned his gun laying practice and joined the man we considered the leader. He took up a position behind the short swivel and turned it towards us.

The Xebec leaped towards us as we found that the entire crew, except their Captain, was now at the sweeps.

She closed to one hundred feet and the larger man tried the speaking trumpet again. It was French but we could make no understanding from it.

I peered at the man now with my glasses and handed them to Perkins, for I seemed to recognise him. Perkins agreed but neither could place him as his hat covered his features. Scerri, with a refulgence of a Nelson, had placed us into the light of the morning sun. It would be in the attacker's eyes as it came up, as it did now.

When the Xebec reached to within five and seventy feet, our instructions were restated and repeated by Catania to the crew. The enemy leader tried his trumpet again and here we could snatch parts of it in French. He was at a rage but his curses, blasphemies and oaths of our death made no sense.

Scerri was still standing exposed at the tiller. All the other men were either with us or at the sweeps. At his word, the sweeps were brought on board and the men took up their weapons. The Xebec's sweeps taken in and the boat turned. The Xebec, manoeuvering to lay aside us, came on. The quarter deck of that ship being some four feet higher than our own but our main deck being a foot of so higher than theirs. I could see the crew of the ship. Having abandoned the sweeps, they were scurrying for the hold or crouching beneath the bulwark.

Scerri yelled something in French that I took to be not complimentary to the opposing Captain's mother and the enemy swivel fired. The shot, a solid one, smashed through the barricade of our 'cabin' about six inches above the deck and plunged through it, and into the hold. The four-inch timbers of our barricade and the two inches of the deck being nothing to it. It was the first time I have been fired at on purpose and not by accident it is not a pleasant sensation.

Catania said it was deplorable that the builder of the ship had cheapened its value by using soft wood for the decking. I thought it a hilarious remark at the time and I tried to steady my breathing and wiped, again, the sweat from my hands.

With a thud that shifted our ship side wards, the larger vessel hit ours and began to rebound. The Moroccans came to the railing of their quarterdeck and presented, and fired their muskets in a volley.

Our two Maltese gunmen stood and returned the shots but with the range at only twelve or fifteen feet no shots took hold that I could see. We four remained hidden.

A period of silent took hold. The muskets had been fired and for what seemed a long time nothing happened but in truth it was but less than a second. Then with a shout the two blue clad men sprang onto our deck, followed a moment later by the Moroccans, having dropped their firearms and drawn their swords.

The smaller man who had discarded his hat and cloak was wearing a blue uniform of some sort, and armed with a single shot pistol and a cutlass. The larger man had also discarded his cloak and presented himself in a brilliant blue uniform covered with golden braid, also with a pistol and his gold hilted sword.

Sketch of the engagement between the Speronara *Addolorata* and the 'Texas' Xebec. In Driscol's outline the original location for it was to be in the Appendix as Map two but I have placed it here

Appendix Map two: Sketch of the engagement between the Speronara, Addolorata and the 'Texas' Xebec on the morning of 24 October, 1836, from an original by Driscol

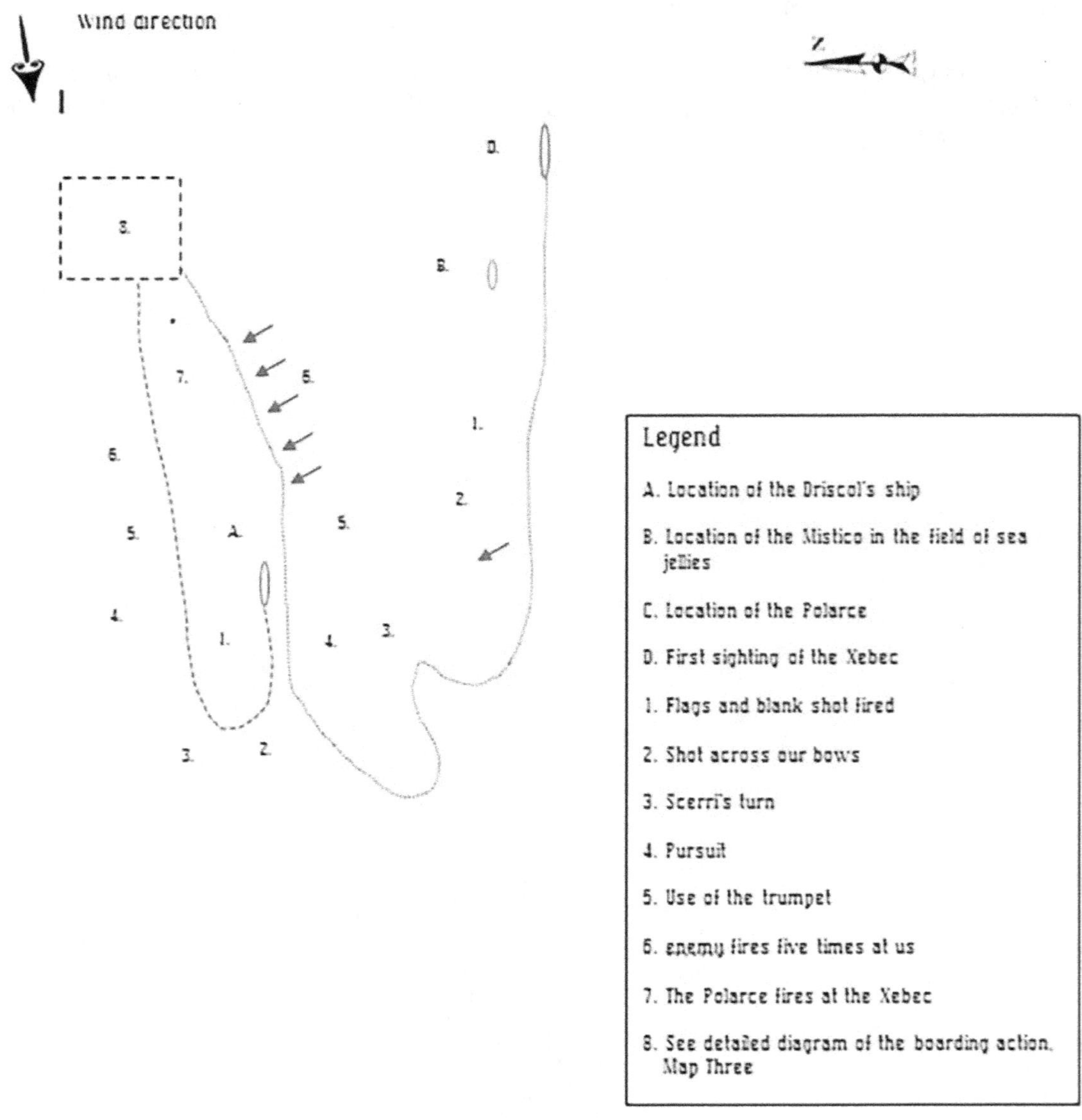

The Melee

When the men hit our deck they did not land as one body, the first to come onto our deck was the smaller man and he wore nailed boots and planted his footing well. The larger man in the glorious uniform did not do so well for he slipped and fell onto his arse. The Moroccans came across, also with less success; one, landing on our railing, encountered the soap. His legs shot out from under him and he landed on his buttocks with a large smack and fell backwards with a scream between the two boats and into the sea. The other attackers kept their footing but had to grab ropes, railing or each other to keep their footing, From behind them the man with blonde hair appeared along the Xebecs quarter-decks railing, along with ten or a dozen of the crew, not cowed or scurrying but instead armed and the intent to murder showing on their faces.

Perkins shouted as he rose up, "AT THEM!"

We rose up, my hands slick with sweat and my breathing rapid. The smaller enemy with the pistol had fired at Scerri who, a brave man, was still standing fully exposed on deck. He missed and turned somewhat to see our weapons come up. I had intended to deal with the enemy leader but the malevolent face of the blonde man with his brigands behind him drew my fire. I gave him the Ascalon 10 bore shot. I had loaded it with a tenth more powder and had placed a portion of buck shot in front of a solid slug. This I discharged followed a moment later with an aimed shot at the blonde man from the upper barrel. The shock of the 10 bore had knocked me off balance and my second shot was wasted. Firing a long arm on a moving deck at sea is not an easy task and until one has done it its complexity escapes one's consideration. The men around him were not just armed with melee weapons but also several muskets, and one of these fired at me. I could feel the touch of hot fire to my upper lip and a blow to my neck and shoulder. I tasted blood tainting my mouth, causing me to spit it out violently.

To my right Perkins fired both barrels of his shotgun into the Moroccans, who were already at the barricade fighting with the Maltese musket men and crew of the *Addolorata* who had come up from sheltering from the fire.

I had dropped Ascalon and drew my French pistol, and had already had my light infantry stirrup-hilted sabre in my left hand. The larger attacker had been un-able to gain his feet due to the soap we had spread and instead had scuttled closer like a crab, still on his buttocks; his feet splayed out before him. He fired at me. The shot stuck the edge of the barricade sending up a shower of splinters but somehow missed me. He swung his sword and the tip caught my upper thigh; a painful sting. I used my sabre to block a return stroke and in doing so my point was driven down and into his foot, pinning it to the deck.

A fusillade of fire broke out. It was my five-shot pistols and the two Colts, one in Perkins' hand and the other in Beers', whose fifteen rounds came out as a steady crescendo of sharp cracking sounds. One accustomed to single weapons would be left dumbfounded by its effect and I was not being fired at.

Perkins had engaged the smaller man, firing three times into him and I could see the shock of the struck man's face.

I had my own business. I had my opponent's foot pinned, his sword halted against mine, closer to his body and his pistol. One of the older single shot percussion types had been fired. He looked up at me, not in anger, nor in fear, but with grim determination. I fired all five rounds at the man, for I recognised him now. It was Capitán de Fragata Sergio Delgado O'Meara the Chilean Officer from Gibraltar.

Beer and Perkins, who had shot down the smaller man, also had poured their shots into the Moroccans when a shattering blast occurred behind me. I turned, stunned, and found that Scerri had fired his swivel into the mass of men on the enemy quarterdeck. What affect he had had I could not tell. I then turned back, switching my sabre to my right hand. I saw two Moroccans down, the others struggling against twice their number of Maltese, Beer and Catania. The Xebec had now drifted off by four feet or more. The blonde man was there and two grapples had been thrown during the fight and were now being drawn in. I drew out my second cylinder for my French pistol and, calming myself, changed it. This, something I had practiced endlessly in the last few days and I did it in a moment. I straddled the barrier and, seeing one of the enemy crew had reloaded or not previously fired his musket, I shot him in the stomach for he was now but eight or so feet away.

The enemy had not been prepared for our revolvers, for such weapons were very infrequent still. I stood there, with blood flowing down my lips, and to my mind calmly selecting targets from the men but a few feet away and shooting them. Firing as my father had instructed. Shooting at their middles. One threw a boarding spike but it went I knew not where. A body came flying from our side, one of the Moroccans, our strong Turk having seized and thrown him overboard. One of the Maltese twin brothers appeared with a leaf bladed short spear and used it to severe the grapple ropes. The crew of the Xebec, seeing the failure of the attack and un-moved by the shouts and remonstrations of the blonde man, fled from our own men, who had taken to throwing dropped swords and pikes at them across the gap between the two boats.

When our own Maltese regained their muskets, the entire enemy crew fled the quarterdeck leaving the blonde man and the Captain with the red fez. I stepped forward to shoot them both but forgot the soaped deck and landed on my back, losing my pistol amongst the bodies and blood. Perkins and Scerri helped me up and I found my pistol. The Xebec was now fifteen feet off and the crew was belaboured by their Captain to take up the sweeps or so we imagined, as his Arabic was hard to understand. I decided not to fire but the Maltese did so.

I turned to find the Polarce had come up and was now a half mile away. The Xebec would not be able to sit off and shell us with their three pounders for the heavier gun of the French auxiliary cruiser would make such an attempt un-wise - or so I thought. The other three ports were opened and as these guns were already loaded we had to go back into action. The broadside, even though fired from less than fifty feet away, whistled and screeched through the rigging but caused no mortal or material damage. I had left my binoculars on my chest during the engagement, so excited had I been I had forgotten they were there, they held in place by a leather strap allowed me to easily raise them up and view our enemy in some detail. They were reloading two of the cannons and I could see the blonde man berating them still. I also noted a large store of ready powder behind the guns: it would seem they planned to punish us severely for the defeat of their forlorn assault.

I could observe their preparation - their gun crews were un-skilled. I shouted a warning. Scerri had begun to turn the ship but the men were still stunned by the violence of the past minute and responded slowly to his commands to take up the sweeps. We got down and two blasts occurred, one difference than the sharp crack of the cannons we had heard before while the other was a softer shooshing whomp of a sound. I stood up and viewed the scene and found a cloud of smoke billowing up from the enemies amidships. I studied the situation through my glasses, finding at that moment that one of the enemy pellets had hit my French binoculars and dented it. This annoyed me thoroughly. The reloading of the cannons was abandoned and I could see that the blonde man could no longer be seen. As the smoke slowly cleared away, it became clearer what had happened. The farther gun, having been a century old or more perhaps, had exploded into pieces and in doing so had detonated the ready powder stored behind it and inflicted great loss on the crew of the Xebec. The flash had caused a number of fires in the rigging. A Polarce shot splashed into the sea again. This time nearer us than our discomforted enemy. The French gunners not being equal to the task, it would seem.

The Xebec had manned her sweeps, the Blonde man had disappeared and the ship was now a half musket shot distance off, and seemingly planning to speed away before the Polarce arrived or she, by an act of bad luck, was struck by the 18 pounder, for the French seemed to have no skill in their sea gunnery.

We watched as the Polarce chased the Xebec, who had turned to the north but even with her reduced crew she was faster than the Polarce, who none the less kept up a sluggish if steady fire at her.

I turned again away from the sea and saw the sickening results of this action. I suspect that the boarding attempt had taken no more than twelve or fifteen seconds to resolve yet it seemed in my memory to have lasted an age.

I wiped my mouth and found the back of my hand covered with blood, as were my neck and shoulder. I found Perkins' eye and he gave me a weak salute. For once in his life he was disheveled and splattered with blood; none of his own, or so he claimed. I found I had been hit by a blast of pellets; one each to my left collarbone, shoulder, curve of my neck and three in the upper arm, and there was a shallow sword cut along my thigh that had bled profusely.

The Maltese musket men gave the Xebec a two gun volley, more to clear the weapons than in any hope to hit them at this range. Scerri was trying to reload his swivel but dropped a stone shot, then an entire cask of rusty musket balls, which scattered about the deck coming up to dead and wounded men. Some of the more auspicious balls, luckier perhaps or un-lucky depending on your view, rolled into the sea and gained freedom from human servitude.

Beer, we found, had been wounded three times; once seriously in the leg by a musket shot to the thigh, some wood splinters in the area of his stomach and a sword cut to the his right shoulder. We found Catania under the body of one of the Moroccans struck in the chest by the Jew's asseguay Maltese knife. Catania's head was covered with blood and he was insensible. He seemed alive but I could not wake him and Perkins persuaded me not to use spirit of hartshorn *{smelling salts}* on him. We made him comfortable and tended to the others.

Scerri had led a charmed life and was un-touched by bullet, blade or the blood of the enemy, or us. Blood seemed to cover everything in the stern of our Speronara.

Our brave Turk had been done to death by a thrust to his heart from a pike; the Moroccans who had turned on them and not us had cut down two other Maltese. Perkins and I suspected they were ordered to leave the Europeans alone - perhaps Catania's white face had marked him as an Englishman.

Five Maltese were wounded to include the sick man who was now covered with sweat of his fever and the blood from two cuts to his head. He was lying on the deck moaning to himself in a slowly spreading pool of blood about his head, this we moved to staunch.

The smaller Chilean officer whom we took to be a ship's master or perhaps a first mate or perhaps the man's servant lived for some time but he had both lungs punctured by the rounds of Perkins' or Beer's Colt and he spent a few minutes fighting for breath in a frothy spew of blood before he expired. We found one of the Moroccans clinging to the boat; the man thrown overboard by the Turk, we thought. I declined Scerri's request to shoot him. The man, who could not swim, was forced off by blows from the blunt end of a spear. We paid no attention to his cries that soon ended as he drifted away. Another two of the enemy were seen floating near-by. Of the other four Moroccans, one was very dead by the blasts from Perkins' shotgun and another from his or Beer's Colt pistols, with the third apparently killed by Catania and another grievously wounded in a horrible way; disemboweled by one of the Maltese. A Maltese who had lost his brother slew him with repeated vengeful strikes of his pike.

The Chilean Captain was dead for I had shot him four times, the fifth bullet's path I could never discover. The first had struck directly on his chin, shattering his lower teeth; another had pierced the throat while the third had penetrated the sternum and the other was to his stomach. The one to the sternum had probably penetrated his heart. I searched his body but found nothing more than a good silver pocket watch, a silver cross around his neck that had one part of the cross bar and our saviors left arm shot away from the sternum shot. He carried nothing else that I could see in my quick inspection.

I found the experience of having armed and hostile men calling out your family name. For that doomed Chilean had done so, while they come at you with pistol and sword in hand does tend to sharpens one wit's most frightfully. It was a vision that I could not erase from my mind, as I stood there watching the Xebec move off and I resolved to assist the wounded if anything to keep the idea out of my head.

I sat when I found that my legs had begun to shake violently and I could no longer stand. I watched the Xebec rowing away, followed by the Polarce which took 5 and half minutes to reload its long gun. Inexcusable slackness in their gun drill, I thought, and then thought what a ridiculous thought to have when one had just killed a man and had been nearly killed himself

Scerri sat on the bulwark with me and we drank deeply from the *boracchio {wine skin}*, which I found disgusting but drank a draught for I found I had a great thirst. Perkins took some too. For once he looked so unmade, splattered as he was with blood from his head to his waist. I used the contents of my medical chest to aid those injured. We went first to the Maltese man who was down with the head wounds, his blood flow had been stopped but he was still and his eyes glazed. We turned our attention to the others.

I removed the splinters from Beers stomach, and his leg wound was cleaned and bandaged. My distaste for blood limiting my vision at times, as I fought again spells of blackness. It was lucky for him that the ball had gone completely through.

The Maltese dead were buried in their Christian way. We attended as we could but could not understand the service, of course. The Turk was stripped and thrown overboard. It would seem he had never been a very popular seaman. I wonder what his mother would have thought of the loss of what once must have been her sweet little boy.

Catania we laid on his mattress and we found by cleaning his head that he had a large swelling on left side and no other wound, the blood on him not being his own.

The rest of the wounded crew were taken care of but one man, even I could tell, would not live long.

We then cleaned and prepared our rifles. The stock of Ascalon had taken a ding when I had dropped her on the deck but it rubbed out nicely..

After some work, I had time to see to myself for my wounds hurt me abominably now. I opened the medical kit I had brought on deck prior to the engagement.

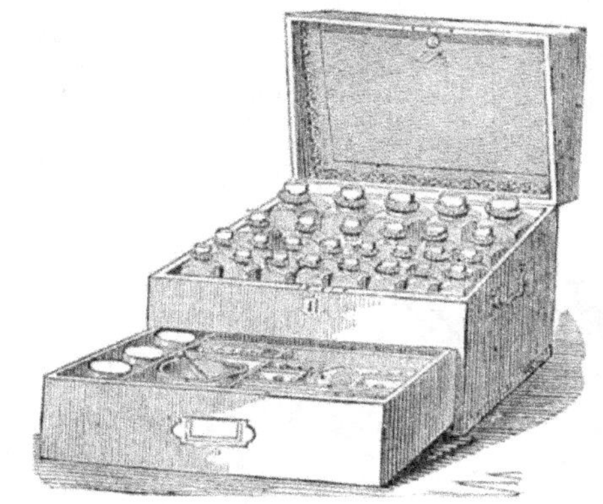

Driscol's medicine cabinet given him by his parents, it was 22 inches in length and 15 inches high. I-III-15

I looked with its mirror that showed that my upper left lip was still there but a bloody furrow starting at my Cupid's bow *{philtrum, the vertical groove under the nose}* to the edge of the lips had been made in it with the blood running into my mouth. Perkins suggested that I would have a most gallant scar but I decided then to grow a moustache.

The Xebec, with the Polarce in pursuit, moved on and off to the horizon; it escaping to the north, I believe, for I had grown indifferent to its' departure.

Diagram showing the melee between the crews of the Xebex and Speronara while off Algiers on October 24, 1836. At the moment of attack after the Moroccan volley

A.
B.
c.
d.
e.
f.
i
ii
iii
iv
v
1
2
3
4
5
6
7
8
Legend
A. Xebec
B. Speronara
c. Tiller or wheel
d. Mizzen mast
e. Quarters tent
f. Wooden pillar or fixture with swivel cannon
1 Driscol
2 Perkins
3 Beer
4 Catania
5 Scerri
6 & 7 two Maltese with flintlocks
8 Other Maltese crewmen
i Blonde haired man
ii Chilean Captain
iii Chilean Mate
iv Xebec's Captain
v Moroccan mercenaries and crew

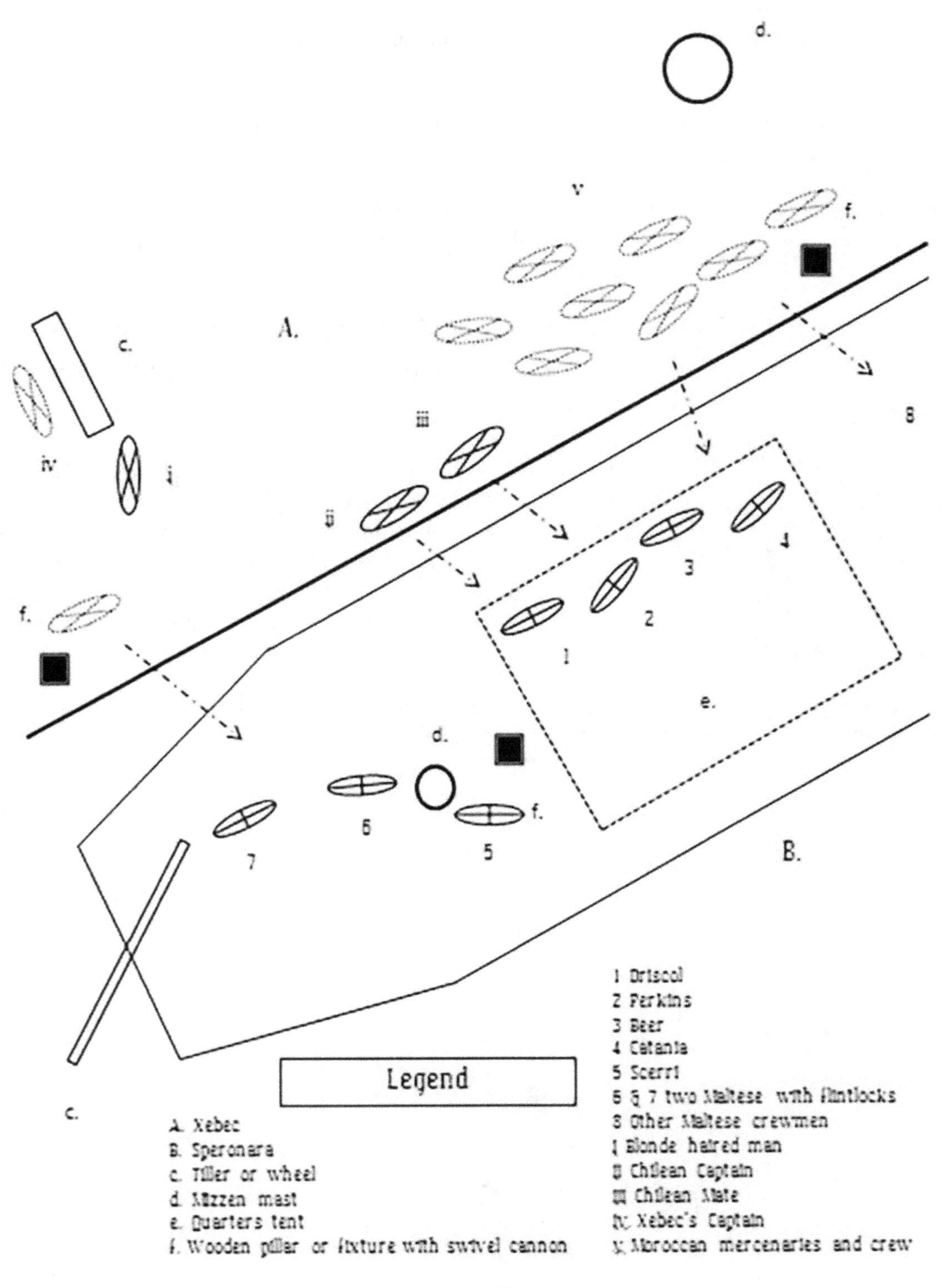

Map Three

Respite And Regrets

I sat on the bulwark of our 'cabin'; my shirt off, plucking lead pellets from my body while seated next to the bodies sprawled on the deck.

I thought to use my mirror and tweezers to pluck out the pellets that had entered my body. I could not face the thought of another doing it. Fortunately, none of them had penetrated more than a quarter inch into my body. This was frightfully painful, and I found that my right shoulder was badly bruised. This puzzled me at first as I had taken no blow there but as I worked out the pellets, I remembered that I had fired Ascalon from my shoulder, the weapon not being firmly seated in my haste; an inexcusable error on my part. I found the pain from removing the pellets helped to clear my head of my fear of blood.

Perkins searched the Chilean first mate more thoroughly, and found four Spanish coppers in his pocket, a feminine handkerchief and a folding pocketknife which he gave to one of the boat lads who had been standing silently as we burgled the bodies. I gave it only after a nodded agreement from Scerri for the boy, who was not more than sixteen, had fought well and still stood with his bloody pike, somewhat dazed it would seem, but he appreciated the knife of a man slain in battle as any lusty young lad would.

I turned my attention again to the ill-fated Chilean officer and saw that the wound to his stomach had not bled and, intrigued, opened his blouse and found a linen belt, which I recognised as a money belt similar to my own but this one was much thicker. I found that my bullet had penetrated his blouse and the linen of the belt with ease but had not completely punched through the belt, or so I supposed based on the lack of bleeding. I explored further, showing no respect for the body until I had removed the belt. It was soaked in his blood from his chest wound. Examining his money belt, we found it divided into small sewn pockets and in those, many pieces of silver and gold. I put this aside not quite comprehending what I had found.

The Maltese were not in a good temper from their losses in friends and brothers had been high. The clothes of the Chilean Captain and first mate were stripped from them, for they were valuable, and Scerri took his boots despite my sword thrust through the right one of the Captain.

The only man seemingly un-moved by this slaughter was the Captain of the ship, the young Padrone Scerri, who was perhaps too busy to contemplate the slaughter that lay on his deck.

Scerri had the bodies of our enemies thrown overboard. Perkins and I thought a service for the officer would have been in order but the Maltese would have none of it. With Catania not available to intercede, we decided not to press the issue. To them, these murderers were but pirates; a hated and despised breed, for the good Captain and crew knew nothing of our relationship with these two Europeans. We saw no reason to tell them otherwise, should we gain their anger for having brought this blood down on them. We gathered up a number of weapons, all of which we presented to the crew as a small compensation to their loss.

The Chilean officer's gold hilted sword would bring a good amount, for it was a Toledo blade and would be worth a great deal in compensation to the families of the men lost - except the

Turk. The crew would not accept it and returned it to me as a sword won in battle. Scerri also noted that the blade was inscribed - limiting its value. I had not looked at the sword closely. It was un-deniably a fine blade; an older one with a touch of dried blood on the tip - my blood. The blade was finely etched with the name of Tighe O'Meara and had been presented to that man at 'Tourcoing'. I suspected it was his father's blade and that he had been one of the Wild Geese *{Irishmen who became mercenaries after the defeat of an Irish Jacobite army, later the term came to mean any Irish mercenary}* who had served in the French army, and had helped to defeat the British and Austrians at that battle in 1794.

I had a harrowing discussion with Perkins in English over the Chilean's search for revenge. We found the thought that the man had followed us to be complete and utter madness, and Perkins recommended that we must, in the future, be more aware in maintaining our distance from those with Latin temperaments and habits, and if we must deal with them in the future, we shall use greater tact and correctness. I could do no more than agree.

The ship continued to pitch gently in the calm for an hour or so until long after the Xebec and Polarce had disappeared over the horizon, an occasional distant 'boom' signaling the chase.

The decks were doused and holystoned to some cleanliness. In doing so, a crewman noted a line of musket balls embedded in the deck. Perkins and I found that by the angle of the strikes, they had come from when the Moroccans had fired their volley and, by using one of the pikes, we determined that those bullets had passed over our heads by a small distance - inches in my case. As a light infantryman, I knew that we had been saved not only by the movement of the sea but by the natural tendency of men to shoot high when aiming 'downhill'. The enemy had aimed at us as we crouched beneath the 'cabins' walls and obviously they had seen us.

While we examined these wounds in the ship's deck for we were happy to do something to distract us - Scerri was a man of business and was interested in the money belt. It was now dried out in the Mediterranean sun and stiff with blood. Scerri, knife in hand, had shredded the money belt. Stacking coins on a moving boat can be difficult but, by using one of the mattresses, he did just that; piling them up by their type. There were some twenty kinds; his hand full of silver, bronze and copper piaster, shillings and others but it was the gold pieces that drew our interest. These were Frederich d'ors worth 17 shillings and 6 pence, Louis d'or, Portuguese Joanese, a heavy coin in Arabic *{Tomond?}* worth 3 pounds sterling 7 shilling each and a large number of Spanish Pistole. Scerri had a good idea of their value and in his view the one hundred and seven coins in his piles before us was the equivalent of 132 pounds sterling.

[Editor's note: Driscol made nearly 8 pounds sterling a month and Perkins around 10 so this amount was worth about a year and half in pay for Driscol]

Scerri, by weight and eye, divided the coins into piles; one for himself, one for the ship's owner, and separate smaller ones for his crew; or, if they were dead, for their families; smaller ones for the two boys; and a large pile for us, he pointing at myself, Perkins and the disabled Beer who was lying next to us in some pain.

We motioned to Catania for he had received nothing, and I suspected he intended to leave out the Jew but Scerri surprised me by shaking his head and pointed to the owners' pile and then back to Catania - so Catania was the owner of the ship! This, he had not told us, but for some reason I was not overly perplexed by this.

I noted tears in Beers eyes and he replied positively to my query if he was suffering and I had found own pain had reached a crescendo too. I found and removed from my medical chest my glass container, which I had bought in Gibraltar to replace the drugs stolen, I suspect, by the American Mr Custer. I gave one of the small, slightly sticky, green pills to Beer, four to Scerri for his men and broke one in two for Perkins and myself; he, while not wounded, seemed to me to be in some distress nevertheless.

Perkins took up the money and we divided it amongst ourselves, it coming to some 14 Sterling 6 shilling in our estimation to each of us, and I had the sword, too.

I then took the pill, which was bitter to my taste, and washed it down with bad wine; two bad tastes at once. As we sat, the sails flapped and in a few minutes the calm was gone, replaced by what the Padrone called a *Tramontana*, a harsh north wind. A peculiarly cold and blighting wind it was, too. We crawled into our makeshift cabin and drew the tent over us, there being no wish to erect it. Slowly, my pains resided from me, but my throat felt odd. I felt good and the world seem brighter now. The crew had returned to being seamen, the sails were set and the Speronara headed east. I fell to sleep with pen in hand as I write this.

[Editor's note: There were several drops and smears of blood on this and the proceeding pages]

As a child, I had dreams in which I thought I was awake but then would come into some situation that was impossible, vile or fanciful. I dreamt this way again after I fell asleep. I was a boy again and visiting my father's friends who live in Liverpool. From their house, one could see all the way to the sea. In the dream, I awoke from my sleep and went to look out over the distant sea. As I did, a legged serpent, a leviathan, emerged from the water. I would have said the distance was less than a mile, but not by much. In the moonlight, I could see it clearly and felt the cold fingers of fear seize me. It then looked in my direction and I could tell it was staring at me, impossible at that distance and it began to make its slithering walk in my direction; its lizardly body crushing houses and trees and scattering their remains like pebbles before a boy. As it grew closer I tried to move, to cry out but I was frozen in place.

I felt pressure on my arm and a face appeared but it was light and with a start I awoke for it was Perkins' hand on my shoulder. It was late afternoon and he was once again himself; in fresh clothing, clean-shaven and not a hair out of place. Perkins observed that I had seemed to be suffering from a nightmare, or in this instances an 'afternoonmare', and thought I should be awakened from it.

My father's damning words, echoed by many others, came back to me, 'An officer is always on parade'. Falling asleep after a battle probably would rate high in his list of misdeeds.

My wounds did not ache but my limbs did tremble so. Yet I shaved in seawater and restored myself to some acceptabilty in appearance. Again, as the minor wound to my lip would prevent shaving, I decided (again) from that day forward to have a moustache.

He announced that the opium we had taken had made him appreciate the story of the Odyssey more, as now he understood in part the tale of the lotus-eaters. While discussing the Odyssey, which Perkins wittily remarked that the sagas plot was, "To Ithaca by way of everywhere from Troy, except actually going there." his first such attempt at humour since the attack.

Beer was asleep and Catania remained insensible. We forced some water down his throat but he did not revive. My medical book suggested that he was in a coma and I showed a quote from the book to Perkins 'from any cause affecting brain insensibility which terminates in death'. He agreed that Catania might die. The book also held out a hope that recovery was possible but the reasons for it were not fully understood by medicine. What was recommended was what we were doing; he was resting and we kept his face covered from assaults from the sun. I had recalled father's stories of badly wounded men made blind by being left lying mistakenly in the Spanish sun for too long.

Perkins observed that perhaps we should have conducted a *sectio cadaveris {autopsy}* on the Chilean; perhaps his madness would have shown in his brain. We discussed this for some time but, having examined the situation - all of it again, we decided that the blonde man, even though he did not look Russian, might have been an agent of sorts. At the last we also thought perhaps we were silly children and all that we had experienced was nothing more than a 'woman's nerves' and that the Chilean's excessive need for revenge for his bruised honour had been the source of our happenings, nothing more. We decided that we would continue in our way, not mentioning our true goal, and from Malta we would go incognito, or using the Indian term "*in Mufti*," as non-British officers, easy for me not so for Perkins who looked solidly English.

We also decided that we must report the incident but would do so only as an attack of piracy and the two Europeans being described as Muhammadan deceived renegades a not un-common occurrence in this sea.

[Editor's note: Driscol would write three times of this action. The first, a one-page summation to his mother, in Danish, very sanitised and didn't mention his wounds except to say 'lightly injured with no danger'. He wrote to Karen a more dynamic account, and he and Perkins would agree to write up a report on the matter which they did and that - in part - appeared in the Times]

We were hungry by then and, despite the slaughter in the morning, by late afternoon the ship had regained some of its calm. The harpooned leather-back and one of his brothers we cooked up. The man chosen to cook them did so in an un-usual way; he did not break the shell as I had seen done before but instead cleaned out the offal using one of the leg openings. Both were soon cooked up within their own shells and the broth from it given to the wounded. My portion was several pieces of flesh and some polenta. Perkins and I wolfed this down. Beer was sitting up and he ate his meal with us. He was in good spirits but our un-conscious friend beside us put a pall over our conversation. He was glad to have been in the fight, for his life had been a literary one until then. He said that he had always feared that he would be let down by his terror in any such incident but we assured him he had acted as well as the historic English Infantryman and that his blood had been true to him. He added that he thought the nobility of his Arab ancestors; conquerors once of much of the world, had added some spice to his English blood. We found this to be a good jest and most possibly true.

The Padrone joined us for supper later, bringing with him a container of honey, which we spread, on cold pieces of polenta. I found it difficult to eat, as my tongue has swollen some along with the side of my jaw.

We headed towards Malta again and decided to avoid any other ports until we arrived. He did say that the shot that had penetrated our hull had also struck one of our four water barrels and asked that we refrain from too much consumption. Perkins was dismayed, as he seemed to wash his face on a bi-hourly schedule. We, of course, agreed but voiced concern for the wounded.

Scerri was of our same mind that there was nothing we could do for Catania; he was in the hands of his Talmudic God. Should any of the others develop fevers, we could make for Sardinia or Sicily but not any of the North African ports.

It turned into a lovely evening and Perkins and I talked of Greek myths and heroes into the night, and quoted parts of the Iliad to one another.

I also took from my luggage two bottles of spirits given to me by my father to bribe the Tritions and other minions of King Neptune. I would have encountered them had I gone around Africa. These I presented to our captain and crew and they appreciated them for it being something they rarely were able to savour.

[Editor's note: Driscol would have used these as bribes to avoid the "passing the line" ceremony run by the crew of crossing the equator - something best missed by young officers]

Before going to sleep, Perkins and I cleaned and reloaded all of our weapons. We found reloading the Colts was very difficult. I remembered at that moment that this was Saint Crispin's day and the four hundred and twenty first anniversary of the Battle of Agincourt.

Driscol & Perkins' error: The left flag is that of Chile while the flag to the right is the flag of the Republic of Texas. One can see why they might mistake one for the other, especially as the only illustration of it they would have had would have been from black and white newspaper articles. He never mentioned this error in his journal. I-III-16 & 17

A Profound Gain And Loss

Wednesday 26 October

I was awakened by the bustle of men, of animal-like sounds and the brightness of lanterns. Some trod on me and I thought we were again under attack. Befuddled, I cried out to Perkins what was the matter.

He replied that Beer was suffering an apoplectic fit. It was just past midnight. His body was distorted in pain and blood poured from his ears and nose. Nothing we could do. Nothing at all he died less than a minute after I had awakened. He would have died in his sleep un-noticed but his thrashing about like a fish on shore had awakened Perkins and the men on watch.

We were left devastated by this most recent loss. We had no words to convey our feelings. We left his rites and burial for the morning.

I was next awakened from what I thought was but a moment of sleep but it must have been hours. A ghastly apparition staring down at me. It took a moment for me to realise that I was seeing Catania, distorted by the swollen side of his head in flickering light of a lantern. He was wondering what had happened!

Perkins and Scerri were awakened, and much cheer was gained by the return of our eldest passenger. I gave him some of the opium for he said that *Raqib* and *Atid* were sitting aside his shoulders and pounding on his head[17]. He could remember nothing of the fight, his last memory being of the Xebec growing nearer. We praised his bravery in killing one of the Moroccans with his knife. I returned it to him, for which he smiled grimly and I thought for a moment he would throw the blade overboard as he seemed at one point to begin to do but then reconsidered. The news of the money belt and its treasure he seemed un-interested in, giving falsehood to the stories I had heard of Jews being only interested in lucre. He was deeply saddened by the death of Beer, who lay covered next to us awaiting dawn and his interment in the depths of the sea. By the glare of the lantern all this seemed un-earthly and strange.

He ate a little and went back to sleep, seeming addled and confused by the situation, and not aided in gaining clarity by the opium.

At first light we secured a piece of canvas and, with some rough work with a boltrope-needle, made a cocoon like sack. From the ships bilge we secured several pieces of heavy rubble, rough stone work used to ballast the ship, to weigh it down. With such rude equipment, we had a short service for Warren Salem Beer. Catania performed a viaticum, placing a small coin in his mouth owing to traditional superstition that was, I believe, a follow on of Charon's *obol {the coin placed on the tongue of pagan dead}*. In the honour of his full heritage, we did the main part in English, with a quote from John 3:6-8, which Warren had, on occasioned, quoted before.

That which is born of the flesh is flesh; and that which is born of the spirit is spirit.
Marvel not that I said unto thee, Ye must be born again.
The wind bloweth where it listeth, and thou hearest the sound thereof, but canst not
tell whence it cometh, and whither it goeth: so is every one that is born of the spirit.

Perkins said a Hindu prayer in the Tamil dialect and Catania, looking drawn out and weak, gave out a portion of the *Salat-I-janazah {Islamic funeral prayer}*; for although Warren had been born a Christian, it seemed right to mention his other heritage too. He was committed to the waves at a little before 7 am. We then secured his valuables and luggage after having shifted through his papers until we found the address of his family in Bombay, India.

Despondency was the order of the day, Catania being given compresses of water cooled in the depth of the sea to bring down the swelling of his head. It was at high noon that one of the sails on the horizon gained our notice. It was not the Xebec but a 20-gun brig who soon showed herself to our French friend the L'enreprenant, commanded by Lieutenant Armound who fired a gun to leeward.

She came up to us after we had lowered our sails. He was soon abreast of us and asked if we had seen the Xebec again, for he had had intelligence from his Polarce about our fight the pirates had escaped, of course.

We gave him a brief description of the fight, Scerri adding the fact that two renegades in European clothes had lead the fray. Armound commended our valor and his ship's doctor - really just a glorified medical student - came and checked our wounded but could do nothing more for them. We did have some wine, as did his Marine Sergeant, who drank an entire bottle in the flick of an eye. He commended our skill in defeating the attack and we let him fire three rounds from a Colt the ease of their firing astounding him. He turned back towards Algiers with a loud '*bon courage'* and a salute.

More turtle and I have found that I do not care that much for its taste.

Thursday 27 October

No entry except for the date

Friday 28 October

Early in the morning we passed our first land since leaving Algiers. Padrone Scerri told us it was called by the French Galitons de l'Est, some small islands which are north of the lands of the Bey of Tunis. To my eye they looked stark and isolated.

Catania was much better but his head was still swollen and he has taken his third opium pill. He says that we should arrive in Malta on Sunday, if not sooner.

When the ship was in the vicinity of the island called Qawsra *{Pantelleria}*, the ship undertook a ritual; taking out a bottle of wine, a type called *passito* made on that island, and it was passed around, each man taking a drink. I tried it out of respect for the Maltese crew but found it objectionable for its taste but liking it for its having a sweetness that one could find pleasant - were it not tasting of wine. It had been four years ago that the ship had nearly been dashed to pieces on the northern shore of that island and each time the crew passed the island, now ten nautical miles to the southwest of us, this ritual occurred.

Late in the day we sighted a British warship anchored and, as observed by Perkins, doing survey work. We had Catania direct us closer and were soon in communication with Lieutenant Commander Thomas Graves, RN *{Royal Navy}* of the 14 gun 'bomb' brig of 380 tons, H.M.S. Beacon, doing as we thought; survey work at this spot off the coast of Sicily where the infamous disappearing island is said to sleep under the water. For it was at this location that the Isola San Ferdinando, San Ferdinandea or Julia Island, had come up out of the water only to subside again several times during the years[18]. He said that as we were going to Malta would we agree to take his post? To be more precise, he wished to have letters given to Major Charles Bayley who was both Inspector of police and the Lieutenant-Governor of Gozzo and from him to his daughter Frances Sarah.

We did so but, as both sides wished to continue in what they were doing, we agreed to meet in Malta should fate so arrange it, as Lieutenant *{Commander}* Graves intended to complete his survey in a few days.

We were underway again and Catania, who was much improved, told us of his first visit as a young man to Marseille, France and his being taken to see the various sights of the city. In the church of Saint Victorie was a large stone coffin said to contain the remains of the seven sleepers of Ephesus[19]. He told the anecdote because he kept falling asleep and the last few days had seemed like a dream to him. He was better but still dazed, it seemed to me. He slept a great deal and at times seemed unable to understand our queries about his health. He slept more that day and, like a cat, preferred to rest in the sun.

In the early evening after our supper. Turtle once again, which fortunately for both my sense of taste and my soul was the last of them for each time I ate it I had bad memories of the fight in that sea of jellies from hence the turtles had come.

Catania fell into the sea when going to the head. His cries brought us to his rescue and I dived into the sea to secure him and keep him afloat (for he was an indifferent swimmer) until ropes could be thrown to us. I found the dunking in the sea refreshing. It was the first time in four years I had entered the sea but the salt of the sea made my wounds burn with hellfire.

That evening we were pestered to distraction by an infestation of fleas. We resolved it by soaking the mattresses in the sea and leaving them to air in the rigging. It was a hard night on the deck but better that than constant biting for these Mediterranean fleas, which were harder in their bite than an English one - the bastards.

Saturday 29 October

At sunrise a shout was raised and all awaken for to our south was the first sign of Ghawdex *{Gozo}*, the companion island of the Maltese chain. The crew became quite animated; crying out and jumping up and down. We came to understand that although they were Maltese they were in fact all from this smaller island. Even Catania had been born on that isle but was the only one not to live there now, for he lived in La Valetta. Catania seemed much better and the wounded crewmen all managed to rise up to see the sun coming up next to their home. It was a cheering sight to them, and to us, too, for it meant no more fleas and no more worry about Xebecs and crazed Chileans and especially something to eat beside turtle. We steered nearer the island, heading for the thirty fathoms line. With the rising sun, the wind had freshened and we were soon off Marsalforn a fishing village on the north coast. The fishing boats were out in force; beautiful blue boats with stripes of orange and red, some five and twenty in length with a bow and stern, of the same construction and both higher than the amidships. They seemed like water birds on the sea and not manned vessels. They bobbed up and down in rhythm with the sea. We passed through some twenty of them, many whose crews waved or made coarse jest - or so Perkins and I conjectured. Catania waved a few times to men he knew. The island consisted of grey, red and white rocks covered incompletely by short green vegetation. There were many steeples marking the village, most of which, if not on the edge of the sea, were perched on the many hilltops. One crewman came up and hugged Catania, pointing to some headland with great vigour. Then he ran off to do the same to the other crew.

Catania explained that the man had a woman who would be his wife when he returned. His wedding was long planned and he had pointed out the place on the rocks where he had sinned with her when she was not yet the woman who would be his wife.

A more somber point in this parade of happiness was a fishing boat with three men; full of happiness, initially, but who soon became sad: the father and brothers of one of the men killed. They stood silently after the news had been conveyed to them, watching the Speronara as it sped on.

Catania explained the way the crews of the boats worked. He said there were four crews who each worked the boat for 2-3 months and then return to their lives ashore or as fishermen. Only Scerri was a professional seaman and he and another Captain shared the boat in turns. Scerri, when he was not at sea, was the manager of the warehouses on Gozo.

Catania, knowing our interest in the mythological, pointed to the place where it was said was Calypso's cave *{From the Odyssey}*.

The sun had come up more and we could see that the sea near the island was turquoise and inviting. Since my involuntary swim to save Catania, I had a wish to swim in the warm sea again.

A British Brig-of-war *{Brig-sloop}* was coming up from the channel between the islands, passing a smaller island called Comino. She was a proud sight with the sunlight in her sails. As far as the eye could see, one saw shipping covering the sea.

Chapter IV

Malta To Alexandria

The Speronara Addolorata Comes Home To Malta - The Governor-General's Ball -
Maltese Diversions - Bouverie's Pronouncements - Hooga Booga - From Malta To
Egypt - Complaints - Recovery And Nonsensical French People

========

The Speronara Addolorata Comes Home To Malta

Saturday 29 October (continued)

We soon came up to the city of Valetta and dutifully impressed by its fortifications. Fort Elmo
is immense and the whole harbour looked impregnable from sea attack. The city sat on a hill
known as Xiberras between the two arms of the main channels. We came directly into the
main port filled with spars, masts and ships of many nations, making for the Marsa Musceit
{Marsamxett harbour} and the private quays in that portion of the city.

Several men could be seen hanging in gibbets *{gallows where pirates, were hanged on public
display}*; we were told by Catania. I was surprised to see it, as the gibbeting of sea bandits is
outlawed in England for two years past. It was a macabre welcome but I thought that Sir
Alexander Ball, buried in a traverse of the bastion upon which the gibbet stood, would have
appreciated the demonstration of British resolve.

There being no customhouse in Malta, we had only to await the arrival of the Board of Health
officer. Our crew put up the square yellow flag to request same. He duly arrived after only an
hour's wait. For an officer of the Board of Health - Duinsforth was his name - he was a rather
un-healthy looking old man. He boarded us near the *Lazaretto {the quarantine station}*.

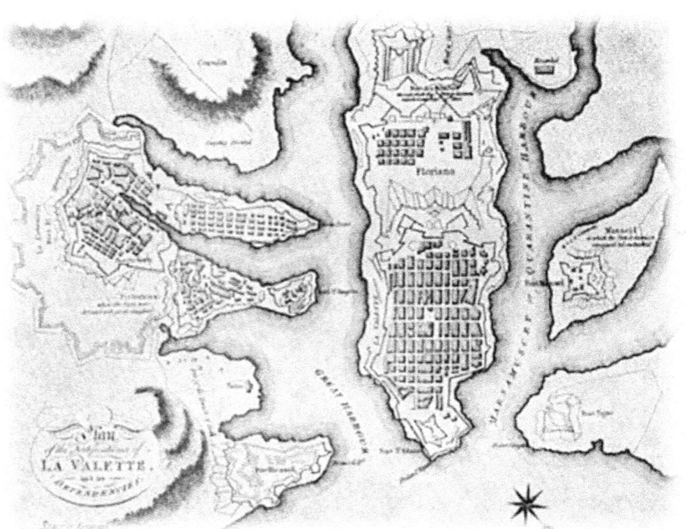

A map view of Malta harbour, Driscol would stay in the central peninsula for most of his stay. I-IV-1

As he inspected the ship, he came across the wounded crew and soon had our story of attack by pirates and our desperate defence. As a young naval surgeon during the Napoleonic wars, he took an interest in our tale. He checked the men and found them healing well and no sign of gangrene or inflammation, and he soon issued us our *pratique¹*. This was the first pratique whose granting we could follow, as it was in English, of course. He gave us a good day in a loud voice I would not have expected from such a weak looking body. He sounded almost like a Yankee in his briskness. He also gave us directions as to whom, where and when we could present our report of the attack, and the death of those under the protection of the British Crown.

Boatmen soon appeared and, as the *Addolorata* would have to wait some time for her berth, Catania, now much more animated than before, found us a boatman he knew and liked, and we soon loaded his small boat with our luggage. Another boatman tried to interfere by claiming some preference and insisting on a higher rate for the hire. After some colourful shouting and waving of hands, he was sent off, and we too departed, followed by a second boat filled with Speronara crewmembers eager, it would seem, to get ashore.

The reason for these men to follow us soon became apparent for the porters of Malta are a troublesome breed, not particularly civil and not easily satisfied with the meaning of the word 'no', in Arabic, English, French or the Maltese language. Catania dispensed with them all using a remarkably sharp tongue. They were demanding 6 d for a simple portage but they would not get such a hire from us. Ridiculous.

The Port of Malta seen from the Great Harbor.
I-IV-2

We found the docks full of passengers from a ship newly arrived from Naples, along with those travellers from an Austrian ship which had also just arrived from Trieste. There was great contrast between the pale-faced British, German, Dutch, and French men and women, and the natives. So many pale European faces mixed with those of the natives, bronze-coloured from the sea-air and sun of the Mediterranean. Ladies dressed in stylish if cumbersome travelling dresses, Englishmen moving along with a practiced nonchalance, Germans holding themselves up as staid and not really in an eastern port, Dutch looking at the sights in open amazement and Frenchmen leering, as always, at the women. British bluejackets were about expressing sharp swearing words in every sentence. Within the press were also groups of Greeks, Turks, Egyptians, Maltese, Italian, and Albanian workers. There were Indians from the east in their robes and turbans, and having black glowing eyes. Beside them were orange and grape-selling local women whose cries for custom were loud and stringent. Yet more foreign seamen, in outlandish costumes, fishermen, porters moving portmanteaus and boxes, and the touts from the neighbouring hotels calling out the names, virtues and rates of places to seek comfort. Amongst all the pandemonium black-eyed beggars beseeched one and all for dying grandmothers and wounded fathers and shoeshine-boys demanded trade from all who wore shoes. All this seething mélange crowded the stone pavement, moving up and down along the quay and seemingly coordinating their efforts to block our passage, and mine in particular.

We nearly, just nearly, made it out of this maelstrom in good time but were delayed by Perkins who found he needed to speak, not just once but three times, with different European young Ladies. Catania went on to his house with our agreeing to meet at the ship at noon the next day for by then in should be at its berth and being un-loaded.

Four of the crewmen assisted us in moving our luggage - a task not helped by the steep streets and stretches of stone stairs. We made our way to the appropriate office where our bona fides were confirmed. We were offered three choices: to be quartered on the accommodation ship in the harbour, at the barracks - but the clerk said they were frightfully occupied - or to stay at one of the hotels with the Crown taking up 65% of the charge. We took the option of a hotel - somewhat more expensive but we felt we deserved it.

We made our way at last to the Hotel D'angleterre but they were filled to capacity and they suggested the Grand Hotel to which we made our way and at which we were most welcomed, and they charged but 8s 6d a day. On its first floor it had a French style café, the 'café de la Reine', which had a slate up, showing what was available in the way of food, that caught our hungry eyes. We took a two-bed suite that looked over the harbour and which was spacious, very clean and had a good breeze coming in off the port and sea. We knew that it would be a good place for as soon as we arrived a lovely brown-eyed maid brought us, with compliments of the management, flowers and a plate of chocolate biscuits, figs and cool water which she offered us in a most pleasant manner. She filled the room with an intoxicating perfume, of lilacs I believe. If there had not been so many flies, it would have been perfect.

We bought our crewmen bottled Italian beers, which none had ever had before, and sent them back with our thanks and appreciation to the Padrone, as they were needed for the hard task of un-loading the ship.

We made our way down to the cafe. It was early but we placed our orders, nonetheless, and waited impatiently for we had too much money and too much of an appetite, for the food had been limited on our voyage since Gibraltar. We made a meal of Poulet a la Provencale; a much anticipated and appreciated fried octopus, for I had read of octopus in classical Greek texts and wished to try it. If one ignored the obvious, it looking like tripe. It was succulent in the extreme. The green salad with vinaigrette was our next favourite, as was a piece of beefsteak broiled with olive oil and sprinkled with thyme from Crete; somewhat tough but glorious in it being beef and not turtle. The chicken arrived last and the poor dear was eaten down to the bones, and, having died for our sustenance, we honoured it by sucking the bones dry, leaving not a drop of juice, sauce or skin. Having been complete gluttons, we sat for a while, digesting and topped off the meal with a slice, a thin one, of lemon cake that was simply superb.

We reviewed the garrison, discussed which regiments were stationed where and, most importantly, where we might get invitations for dinner. Malta had five infantry regiments, the 5th, 59th, the first battalion of the 60th which we had seen at Gibraltar, the 70th and the 93nd. The latter, known as the 'the thin red line', was well-known to have pretentions of greatness and it was said that the officers had egregiously poor manners. So no meal would be wanted there. The 70th and 59th, or The Glasgow Greys and "the other whose nickname no one could remember", had reputations for being good but phlegmatic. That left the former the 5th, the Fighting Fifth, where one might find a meal in good company.

We would have visited them but on our way, Perkins recalled an un-pleasant altercation with a member of that Regiment who, during a game of cards, had failed to honour the payment of his signed chit. So, defeated in our plans, we decided, to carry out our errands instead. We received at the port office the address and name of the shipping agent who the admiralty had sub-contracted its arranging of passages to; A Mr J. Davidson, of whom we went in search of after that substantial meal. Passing, as we did a number of shops, we delayed to make purchases. I restocked a number of items from my medicine chest, sadly depleted in some items from the action against the Chileans. I added to my chest some Moxon's magnesian effervescent powder in bottles, lemon and kali powder, a package of bandages, and more Seidlitz powder, too. I purchased a tin canteen of two quarts volume. I also added some prepared dry French mustard, a tin of Harvey sauce and arrowroot.

We found after a mighty search the esteemed offices of the agent whose clerk explained that they expected the French passenger ship *General Sebastiani* to come into Malta on her way to Alexandria in four to five days. She was not steam powered, but considered capable of getting to Alexander in three days in good weather. The cabins were relatively cheap; Perkins and I could have separate ones, near to one another, but not adjoining. Perkins insisted on this, as he had noted before that I snored too much and too noisily, and that he hoped never to conduct a night attack with me in attendance, even with my acknowledged cat like ability to see in poor light.

The clerk was a good fellow and he patiently explained our options, making it seem like he was helping us out as a friend, telling us things he must have told a thousand other travellers before.

The French ship was equal to any British ship, one of which would arrive in a week or ten days, or even later, from Gibraltar - which would have been us had we waited in Gibraltar, had we done so Beer would still have been alive. The French ship was preferable from the point of living, civility and cleanliness but these positive points were outweighed, in the clerk's mind, by the lack of servants and stewards who spoke English. The prevalent habit of serving French dishes at meals and all manners of Gallic impertinence in the matters of the serving of tea - which was not done at all. Instead one being served with absinthe or wine OR we could wait for the Gibraltar to Alexandria packet which, coming a week later, was noted for timeliness but also for the ineffectiveness of its galley crews to keep hunger at bay.

It was his final comment sealed our choice; the British ships had hammocks and the French feather beds.

Perkins and I looked at one another and selected the *General Sebastiani;* the clerk harrumphed our choice and directed us to another clerk who did the French Levant line scheduling's. He did make it a point while filling in the forms and making lists that some complaints had been made about the service on the *Sebastiani.* One; that some women of questionable virtues had been seen aboard her, and two; that Jews were allowed to travel in the main cabins, and thirdly; that instead of tea being served for breakfast, one would be forced to drink hot chocolate.

I liked the idea of the third point while Perkins the first. There would also be some bother about the baggage. All baggage must be distinctly marked with the passengers name and designation, and written in French, of course. Additionally, no single piece of luggage could be more than eighty lbs. and must fit within the dimensions of two feet three inches for length by one foot and two inches for breadth and one foot two inches for depth. Luggage larger than this was placed in the hold and not the cabins.

Seeing our raised eyebrows, he handed us a card from a company in Malta that made just such portmanteaus of this description - the profiteering swine.

Our travel billet would allow us an allotment of two-second class cabins, or we could pay 2£ 8s more and obtain two first class. We did so, of course, both of us later admitting that using the blood money from the Chileans seemed suitable.

We went travelling around Valetta looking for the shop to make luggage acceptable to the French, which we did in short order for this city was organised on a grid. Having found and ordered sufficient kit, we realised we had no accurate memory of the size and status of our departed friend Beer's luggage. We made our way back to our hotel and did just so, having not opened his luggage previously other than to find his family's address.

Perkins explained that in India, all the personal affects and luggage of a man lost is searched prior to it being returned to his family. I found this puzzling and asked the why of it. He said that it caused distress to the family and the regiment to have found in an officer's luggage or diary mention or evidence of disgraceful behaviours. He noted that he had found French etching of a disreputable subject amongst men's belongings; diaries where the men would list their liaisons with native women, their worship of onanism, and other un-mentionables to include compulsions towards that which should not be mentioned.

We found in Beer's luggage none of that, for he kept no journals but we did find that he did have a bundle of letters from his wife. For his young son he had purchased an exquisite set of lead soldiers in the style of the French and British at Waterloo. One hundred and sixty four figures, the boy in me appreciated them and Perkins and I fought a mock battle on the floor of our quarters. My brother Mark would have appreciated them greatly.

The rest of his luggage was clothing; two English dresses for his wife and a smaller one for his daughter. Several bundles contained scarves and more clothing that is feminine. Nothing that we thought might cause embarrassment, except for two bottles of Scotch of a rare name, 'Auchentoshan', and inferior quality - or so Perkins declared because of its triple distillation, instead of the conventional two distillations, which left it with a high spirit volume but a bit sweeter and a more delicate taste. This, he declared, made it suitable for elderly French women and invalids. There was no address for his employer but we thought a letter addressed to Magistrate Germann by his title would find him with the sad news. We did find within a shoe some seven and thirty pounds worth in gold coin. This we split amongst ourselves for safekeeping. We always wore our money belts, heavy now with the treasure from the Xebec.

Our new modified baggage came and, having repacked those things we would need on a daily basis into our new Frog approved luggage, we then considered what we might do for the rest of the day.

It was now Saturday afternoon and, as the Health officer, Duinsforth, had suggested, we could meet with no official appointments until Monday when we would present our reports to the office suggested to us. We spent some time writing out our reports on the incident, for such is necessary if men under British protection are killed.

We were imposed on by a messenger from the Governor-General's aide, inviting us to an entertainment that evening in the honour of his appointment. Major-General Sir Henry Frederick Bouverie GCB, GCMG had taken over this position just some weeks ago and his 'reception of acceptance' was that night. Some orderly or Aide-de-Camp was quite efficient, having found two newly arrived and obscure British officers to invite.

Malta harbour showing the quay where Driscol landed. I-IV-3

The Governor-General's Ball

Our dress uniforms, when brought out, we found infested with fleas and we spent several hours killing them off with irons heated over a candle.

My wishing to be early and Perkins desire to come fashionably late had us compromise and we arrived on time. It was located in the ballroom of the Auberge de Provence. We were introduced in time to the General who seemed interested in our movement to the east. After some time spent on exchanging pleasantries I mentioned that my father had been in the right centre column under Vandeleur at Vitoria and to this he was delighted for he had been a young officer in the Coldstream Guards that day in the left column. He did not, of course, know my father but we spoke of the campaign for some time when he must have noted that Perkins had not partaken in the conversation so he asked what his father had done during those decades of war. Perkins replied that while the General and young Driscol's father had been keeping Boney from invading England, his father, a Bishop, had kept the Devil out of Westchester. That caused a great deal of cheer amongst the General and his hangers-on. He invited us to join him and his staff Monday evening for supper, as he had much he would like to discuss with us but his duties as host required his immediate attention.

I asked Perkins why his father was a Bishop, for he had not mentioned it before, and why he seemed so lacking in religious fervor.

This I did not quite understand and I had him repeat it three times, but then he excused himself to speak to the many Ladies in attendance. I could then write it down exactly as he had said it.

I had found that they had Cherry Heering, and with this in hand to avoid nettlesome stewards attempting to give me some wretched drink, I moved about, avoiding conversations with some success, for who would wish to talk to a young light infantry ensign with a struggling moustache not quite covering a striking scar across his upper left lip? I found a cluster of excited people in one part of the great hall and found a delight there: ice. Ice added to sherbets for the taking. I found the ice was of two types; one from America, of the Wenham *brand {from New England lakes}*, and some from the Italian Alps shipped here from Venice. I obtained a dish of Pomegranate sherbet that I found most agreeable. I was in search of Perkins to tell him the news of my discovery when I was approached by a naval officer who came up and introduced himself as Lieutenant George Playdell Webster of the H.M.S. Rodney, a 2nd rate now at anchor. He was a jolly chap and he must have thought me someone of more prominence. He was soon joined by a group of other young naval officers, most off that great ship or burdened with some pointless beadledom *{bureaucratic}* job ashore. I was listening to the 'news of the day' when one young midshipmen mentioned that he had heard a ship had come in and had reported an attack by pirates.

The word 'pirates' is a word that will inflame the martial passions of any young naval officer, particularly in the time of peace, and an animated discussion soon arose. As I finished my sherbet, I mentioned that the ship in question was the one I had arrived on this morning and pointed to the purplish scar on my upper left lip, one of my wounds.

This made me the centre of attention for some time. I told the abbreviated fairytale Perkins and I had agreed on. No mention of the Chileans; they were to be lowly European Muhammadan turncoats. I told the tale four times. Each time I finished, a new arrival would ask what he had missed.

Another older well-dressed man in the uniform of a Major of a regiment I did not recognise came up and asked if we had reported this. I explained our conversation with Duinsforth. He in turn introduced himself and he was a man we sought. For he was none other than Major Charles Bayley, the Inspector of police and the Lieutenant Governor of Gozo; the man who we were to deliver the letter for Frances Sarah from that lonely Englishman we had found afloat off Sicily[2].

I had the letter with me in hopes I might find him at this party, or at least a man who knew him, and presented him with the letter from Commander Thomas Graves, RN, which he was most happy to receive. He asked that I remain in place in the manner of an order and not a request. The spirit of the conversation had died but my new friend Lieutenant Webster, who was small as an outsized jockey, and his companions had an idea for a crusade of vengeance.

As in many posts and ports, there were rivalries between ships, regiments and departments. It was the H.M.S. Rodney's cross to bear - or the junior officers thereof - to be in conflict with another ship, a miserable 3rd rate whose French sounding name had been twisted into an amusing and vulgar pun. It would seem that some weeks ago, on the first of October in fact, at the fete celebrating the change of Governors-Generals, a number of midshipmen and younger lieutenants from that other ship had had the audacity to dress up like women to prompt embarrassing scenes and actions from the swains of the H.M.S. Rodney at the party, much to the great laughter of all - although not to those so tricked. This had all been made worse by the great enmity already shared between the Captain of the Rodney and the Captain of that of the other ship, for, as young Lieutenant Commanders, they had both chased a lucrative French prize during the Napoleonic Wars and the Captain of the Rodney had suffered the fate of being left so far behind that he had not gained a shilling from the endeavour.

An entertainment began but, as it was an Italian *castrato {young men castrated as boys to retain their childish voices}* singing some ghastly opera, my new mates and I declined the torture. The naval officers had been, since that torturous moment, all wind and piss in attempting to come up with a suitable revenge. Rejecting, reluctantly, a massacre most bloody as not being cricket.

They were determined to embarrass their rivals but they had not yet thought of a way to do so. It took some time to gather the full story of this crusade of revenge for it came from the mouths of humiliated and discomforted navy men, and they were pained so much by their shame. We were soon called into supper, before the tale had been completed. As usual I was given the arm of a middle-aged woman who wore enough perfume to discomfort a humming bird. My comment to the hostess that I had been ordered to remain where I was was dismissed by a feminine wave of the hand; here she outranked all.

I availed myself of the food, which was fulfilling of the fantasies I had had aboard the Speronara, enjoying a nice piece of ham; a food that, naturally, we had not partaken of on a Jewish owned ship out of defference to her master and not having any supply of it except in tins.

I was eating away and having a good entertainment within my own company, thinking of Marguerite, Millicent and Patricia, when the woman next to me asked who I was and if I had liked the earlier singing by the *musici {polite term for castrato}* Giovanni Velluti.

I replied that I had not gone to listen to it, as in all honesty I found such entertainments disturbing. She was most interested to know the why of this, while I was more interested in eating more of the dish before me. I said that the idea of listening to an *evirato {another polite word for castrato}* so weakened me that I would not dare to attend even one performance and that I had been particularly enraged by the actions of a similar 'man' by the name of Consolino who made clever use of his delicate, feminine features in London. He would arrive at homes disguised in a dress then conduct a torrid tryst right under the husband's nose, the poor cuckold and his servants thinking his wife's visitor was a woman.

This shocked her into an un-speakable condition, whether from the use of the word, 'tryst', 'cuckold' or trying to image a liaison between a woman and a castrato, and I returned to my peas, carrots and delicious Italian ham.

The supper was mostly good, if somewhat Italian in its creation, and not fully to my taste. I had had Italian food before and found it again to be too cheese filled to gain my full appreciation and attentiveness.

The slender and proud gentleman across from me was some form of medical man and, after I quieted the woman, he began to annoy me. His details I have forgotten but he regaled me with more details about the health prospects of Malta than I was interested in. His one-way discourse was full of observations about the pervasiveness of asma (asthma), lingering bronchitis, scrofulous distensions and eruptions, dyspepsia and hypochondriasis - and how he treated all these disorders by (in my mind) an over-active use of expensive therapeutics and excessive billing for his services which caused his patients to be cured of their present ailments by their dying of starvation, as he had taken them for every shilling they had.

The Ladies soon left us to cigars and brandy - or, in my case, water and biscuits. The man near me asked what I thought it might have been that we had been eating. One Italian dish had been presented that I could not recognise, as it was covered in some layers of cheese and a red sauce. I replied that I thought it might be goat scrotum en croute. This drew some laughter.

In this situation I found one man who, like myself, was enjoying no smoke and only water. I introduced myself and found he was a British merchant from Canada of that stock who had once been Americans but, after the rebellion, their loyalty to their King had caused them to move to the north. We discussed the state of the States and, in our discussion, he had a titbit of news I found rewarding.

A race between an American Frigate and a French warship from the Azores to Minorca had been won by the Frenchmen. I mentioned that I had seen off Cadiz the American frigate and the French ship in question. He had with him a satchel and from it he presented me with something from England. He did not sell it, but instead loved it and was evangelical in his desire to spread it world-wide. It was a confectionary of solid eating chocolate made by J. S. Fry & Sons, a British chocolate producer. It was bits of chocolate coated in sugar that I found lovely and I retained an additional one for Perkins. We shook hands and talked for some time though now I un-fortunately cannot recall his name, or what line of commerce he was in or the type of merchandise he sold.

Perkins was further down the table and had been speaking with some infantry Lieutenant Colonel but we soon joined back up and he announced that the entire female contingent of Malta was married, soon to be married, a whore covey, a group of toffers planning to be engaged, or walking out with someone; and all uglier than a Mancunian bunter *{a particularly loathsome type of prostitute}* - he adding that descriptive phrase just for myself. It would seem his whore pipe would not be in use during this visit. I congratulated him on his failure, which he took well. He did say that he had found Frances Sarah quite lovely but that his entire conversation with her had been his attempting to answer her detailed questions about the condition and look of her fiancé whom we had found surveying off Sicily.

We were soon gathered up by the naval squadron and taken on a tour of the docks. This moonlight walk had a purpose for the officers saw in us, two young officers who were soon to leave and were not known to their enemies, as the tool in which to extract some revenge. One of the men was a son of an Earl. A fine fellow, I must say, for when we protested that any action by us might lead to some difficulty in the future, he came forth with an offer; an offer which, if it had been voiced by any other than this silver-tongued devil, might have led to strong words. He made it known, in the most polite terms, that should we be able to trick their foes, in a way yet un-known, at a time in the future, he would be glad to reimburse us most handsomely for our time in the performance of such callings.

We spent a joyous evening coming up with one un-workable plan after another. All failing to come to fruition by the obstacles of physics, decency (the naval version of decency being less than ours), un-lawfulness, something that might be deemed actions un-becoming an officer, too elaborate for we had only a few days left in Malta, too insulting to religion, or too insulting to a higher officer.

An idea, however, had come to Webster, who had a friend who worked as an aide to the Port Captain. A group of dignitaries, an official party made up of Moors, Arabs and Turks from Tunis, was to visit and be shown the marvels of British power. The H.M.S. Ship-Who-Was-Not-To-Be-Named had been selected as one of the ships to be toured.

He felt that in some way we could make use of this to gain their revenge, but it must have been growing very late or very early for our watches had stopped, we having made it a practice to wind them before going to bed each night.

 Perkins and I walked back. I was conscious of the fact that we were completely un-armed but the streets were safe, it seemed, as no one was about, even drunken seamen. We wished to get some sleep, as we would need our wits about us to avoid the church parades of tomorrow.

Waterfront of Valetta. I-IV-4

Maltese Diversions

Sunday 30 October

We circumvented the task of attending church by our simply not waking up in time. It was avoided but not the Month of the Rosary. We found out from the staff that what sounded like a battle between cats and dogs with drums and cymbals tied to their tails outside the hotel was the Maltese celebration, a cacophonous procession for the *Il-Madonna tar Ruarju {Lady of the Rosary}*. Curse these loud demonstrations of error, Popery and poorly played music.

It was two hours before noon when we found, thank God, that the hotel had a gay Sunday tradition of providing complimentary hot baths to its guest if they would tip the attendants. We did and indulged ourselves fully, Perkins commenting on my fine selection of scars from the insult of bullet and sword.

We made our appointment with the Speronara crew. They lined up and, in our own way, we 'inspected' them, giving each man a small sum in our appreciation, and they gave us three rousing cheers, for they held that our swords, pistols and shotguns had won the day against the 'pirates'.

We were invited to visit Gozo, which we promised to try to do. Catania asked us to dine at his house that Tuesday, which we accepted, and he added that the Maltese called their islands, 'The flower of the world' and it was best to breath in its scent deeply. He looked much better now, dressed in the long flowing garb of his race and not the white trousers and shirt of the rest of the Maltese.

In his asking, he made it clear he would not be offended if we decline his invitation but we, of course, accepted; free meals never being turned aside by lowly paid bachelor officers. Perkins had wondered earlier if we might be invited and if Catania might have any comely, dark-eyed daughters. I had reminded him of that Moroccan whom our mild mannered Catania had knifed to death with a single thrust. That had made him frown somewhat.

As we stood with Catania discussing his plans, he scowled and pointed discreetly at two European men dressed in the northern Italian manner that were walking slowly down the quay, showing a great interest in the un-loaded cargoes. He whispered to us that they were two men best avoided and he added, with great venom, the word *Safranschau.* He explained that they had once been inspectors and enforcers of purity in spices arriving from the east, tracking down those who would seek to foist counterfeit pepper, saffron or mace on the good people of the west but now, centuries later, they had become enforcers of other things[3]. It was his opinion that they had been corrupted by all that skulking around the Middle East for centuries and their focus on purity had led them down darker paths and a more intense fanaticism. We asked but he would tell us no more about them.

We decided to tour the town aided by suggestions received from Catania and others at the gathering last night. Catania had told us that the Grand Hotel[4] had actually been the location of the Knights of Saint John's treasury. Perkins thought the cream colour of the cities stone made it look somewhat like Bath. I had been to Bath too and agreed but the grid of streets reminded me of towns built on the ruins of Roman plans.

We ascended the Street of Steps, which both of us knew from the line,

'Adieu ye cursed street of stairs'

Lord Byron had written this in his 1811 poem, the *Farewell to Malta*.

We walked down then up the Calle San Juan.

We found Saint John's cathedral, whose facade would make someone wish to take a whip to the architect responsible. The interior was another matter indeed; the choir was by Bernini himself and depicted the baptism of Jesus while the ceiling was adorned with scenes from the life of the Saint in question. The floor was a marvel of jasper, agate and more precious stones, and midst these were the tombs of the Knights of the order who had held the citadel of Malta against the Turks. We had arrived just after the morning service so we could wander about without being bothered by queries and offers of services.

The Rue Saint Jean which Driscol called by its Spanish name, the Calle San Juan. I-IV-5

The Knights of Malta had been organised by languages; these were the famous eight Auberges of France, Italy, Provence, Castile, Aragon, Auvergne, Germany and Bavaria, and each of these had a chapel which ran parallel with the nave. The door to the stairs, which led down into the crypt, was un-locked and we descended to look upon the tomb of L'Isle Adam, the first Grand master in Malta. When down in that dark place, I had a momentary worry about meeting the grinning, long blonde haired man from the Xebec, his face full of malice and his two hands holding oversized revolvers. I breathed a sigh of relief once we had come back up into the main church.

Having admired the inside of the church, which was as creditable as much for its art as its somber quality *(as the exterior was not)*, we left and emerged back into the street by a side entrance where we saw that it was a dead-end-street with an enormous ancient stone covered with inscriptions, some archaic and some more modern. We could read the Greek and Latin names and short phrases. Being inspired to leave a message to those who might consider us ancients in 2,000 years' time, we did some carving[5] around five and half feet from the bottom of the stone so that we might be away from other carvings. We then wandered about for some time, ending back at the café where we consumed in good order another goodly meal in the French style - another dish of the *Poulet a la Provencale* which we had had the day before and which we agreed was equal in wonderfulness to the declaration of love from a rich and comely young woman.

We visited the Palace of the Grand Master and, despite it being Sunday, gained entrance by the payment to the Maltese guardian of the grand sum of 1 Grani - a worthless copper coin used in these islands. The ground floor was taken up by the kitchen and the former chapel once used by lowly Protestants but long since replaced by a more suitable church. In the upper floors we found the armoury containing some eleven thousand muskets from modern to archaic, and many types of arms from the days of the knight to present. One piece of armour was inlaid with gold. The conservator, for he had appeared with hand out and mouth open, was the suit of armour for the Grand Master de Rohan. There was a gallery of fine paintings of sea fights, knights and mythological themes, and many tapestries on a variety of subject matters. We found the observatory with its wonderful panoramic view of the town where one could see both harbours in some detail.

The fountain in the Grand Masters Palace's lower Courtyard; Neptune's statue. I-IV-6

We were disappointed to find that we could not buy our way into the garrison library, for the key could not be found. Thinking this was a ruse to obtain more money, we departed. We stopped for a time at a number of shops. At Mrs. Muir's Stationer we purchased more ink, as this journal that I write each day is written upon thirsty paper and it must be given the drink it desires.

Feeling quite like a wealthy mogul, from another stall I also purchased a well-made embroidered muslin shawl with gold and a blue silk for my mother; one in the eastern style each for Marguerite, Millicent and Patricia; a curiously wrought crimson one for Karen and two green ones for my sisters. Perkins did the same for the women of his family. We then found the offices of Mr Zammit, a custom house agent who, for a small charge, would forward these packages back to England. We also deposited our copious supply of post to him to forward back to England and other parts of the civilised world. In that post were two special letters from me: one to the Colt Company, commending them on and recommending some changes to their fine weapon. And another to the French designer of the pistol; again, commending and recommending, and congratulating him on his product. These presents, letters and their postage cost me a South American dollar from Mexico, worth about 4s 4d, and a single Maltese coin called the Scudo, which is valued at about 1s 8d. I received back in change 8 Tari and 14 Grani which to my eye looked valueless.

We found the newsrooms of the Union Club in the same vicinity where we had enjoyed the ball the other night. They were most welcoming and we looked through the collection of papers. We found there copies of the Times only one and twenty days old, which we thought remarkable. It was good to read an English newspaper and I reviewed the headlines of several French publications. The world, it would seem, had gone on doing its nefarious business while I had been at sea.

Monday 31 October

"A sufficiency of absinthe can make a good man a knave but it takes a bad officer to make a good man a complete cad - that, or a whore with a fetching smile, or a friend who snores too much".

I awoke to that wisdom from Perkins who had threatened me in the night with murder most foul if I did not stop snoring. I did point out to him that I snored while asleep and such a performance was beyond my abilities to control. He thought it damned rude that I would or could not! He vowed to write Millicent and warn her of her future life without sleep. He was so annoyed that he demanded that I purchase breakfast for him. I did so out of respect for his greater age and rank, and that he had one of my loaded Colt's in his luggage.

We went about our work as soon as it was time for the bureaucracy to awaken to a new week, sharpen their pens, gather their inks, stamps and embossers, and prepare to deny our every need and request. We made ourselves known at the office of a Major, late of her Majesty's 1st Bengal European Regiment[6]. He looked to be a fat, un-healthy and un-pleasant toad of a man. We introduced ourselves and we were completely taken aback by his response. He was the most pleasant and cultured man I had yet found behind a desk. He was genuinely pleased to have met us and had been informed of our presence by the other officer who had ordered me to stay in place at the entertainment on Saturday.

We mentioned that we had a report dealing with a pirate attack. He offered us chairs, tea and cigars. I partook of the cigars, as they were a good brand, for future use as a gift. He accepted our report read it over in a deliberate manner and called out for a navy man to join him. The naval officer was badly burnt *{pitted by small pox}* Lieutenant Commander, he asked the obvious questions, which we answered. Both men were puzzled by why a pirate would have attacked such a ship as ours so close to port - and in day light.

[Editor's note: see Appendix I-III for an article printed in The Times on the attack]

It was their experience that small boats were taken at times but usually at night by men in small boats. On a rare occasion a pirate would attempt to take a very valuable prize usually with an easy to sell cargo but of what value to a pirate was a small Maltese ship carrying barilla in bulk?

He questioned us on our cargo and shipmates. When we mentioned Catania, he and the Naval officers nodded their heads.

"Ah, that is the clue to solve the case", they said nearly in unison. We said nothing but agreed having decided not to complicate the matter by bringing the Chileans into it.

It was their opinion that the Jew was probably transporting specie *{gold or silver}* and the pirates got wind of it. With that solved, he wondered who these Europeans might have been. We did not know but we had recovered a sword from one of them and I handed over the weapon to the Major. He examined it with great attention then returned it without comment and gave me a look that said he was envious of my acquisition.

We made out a secondary report on the death of Beer, signed it, and the matter was done. He then invited us to sit awhile, for he had spent four and twenty years in India, having left only recently the year before due to ill health. He had un-expectantly recovered enough and had taken up this secondment as the deputy adjutant for the Fortress of La Valetta, for this was as far east he ever intended to go again. The man I had met earlier *{it is unclear who Driscol meant}* was the actual adjutant and our man suggested he was always too drunk to come in on Mondays.

He told a number of interesting stories of his time in the East, spoke a touch of Tamil and Bengali, and told us once how a French correspondent had called him, in print, an empty headed Hindoo hating, tea drinking, Mussulman *{19ᵗʰ century spelling of Muslim}* loathing, missionary swatting, limey bastard. He had objected to being called a limey bastard, as he knew who his mother was and she was a most truthful woman who told him his father had disappeared during the wars, and that he did not like limejuice. He made that last pronouncement in all seriousness. We were un-certain whether to agree, offer our condolences or laugh, so we did all three.

Having finished our business here, we spent the rest of the morning and early afternoon walking about the town making our way to Sliema. Here we viewed the out-sized residence of a local Russian banker known to the locals as the Kremlin. I thought we should bring in one of Napoleon's nephews and have him burn it down, as it was an un-sightly building. The views of the harbour were worth the walk and we built up a good appetite. We also went to the Malta Fencibles, a local regiment, and viewed their display of weapons.

At Perkins' demand, we did not have *Poulet a la Provencale,* much to my regret. He insisted that we have Italian style food, which was also served at the cafe, and ordered for us a *Bistecca alla Fiorentina* and any regrets I had disappeared. For first time in months I enjoyed a steak. It was toothsome and I had no need to uncork my Brand & Co sauce. (a sauce dear now to my heart and tongue) It was what we would call a porterhouse steak; a cut I had not had previously but Perkins knew it, and it combined the fillet and strip steak together. It had been perfectly grilled over charcoal and its preparation was simple; olive oil, copious salt, a touch of lemon juice, some pepper and a few sprigs of rosemary. I noted this down, as I intended to reproduce it in India but Perkins deflated this idea, saying the local beef there was not up to this type of dish but he did recommend that if I did try, to invite him to the attempt. The owner, seeing we had eaten his fare with great gusto, offered, on the house, a small dish of stewed lamb which he called *Ossobucco* that was nearly as good as the Tuscan style steak. We found out the owner was, of course, a Corsican and had a passion for Italian dishes; this one was a specialty of the Milanese and was made of veal shanks braised with vegetables in white wine. We applauded his chef and I thanked Perkins for the choice. I had disliked the Italian pasta dishes but found in their meat some fine fare.

At Perkins' demand, we did not have *Poulet a la Provencale,* much to my regret. He insisted that we have Italian style food, which was also served at the cafe, and ordered for us a *Bistecca alla Fiorentina* and any regrets I had disappeared. For first time in months I enjoyed a steak. It was toothsome and I had no need to un-cork my Brand & Co sauce (a sauce dear now to my heart and tongue) It was what we would call a porterhouse steak; a cut I had not had previously but Perkins knew it, and it combined the fillet and strip steak together. It had been perfectly grilled over charcoal and its preparation was simple; olive oil, copious salt, a touch of lemon juice, some pepper and a few sprigs of rosemary. I noted this down, as I intended to reproduce it in India but Perkins deflated this idea, saying the local beef there was not up to this type of dish but he did recommend that if I did try, to invite him to the attempt. The owner, seeing we had eaten his fare with great gusto, offered, on the house, a small dish of stewed lamb which he called *Ossobucco* that was nearly as good as the Tuscan style steak. We found out the owner was, of course, a Corsican and had a passion for Italian dishes; this one, which he shared with us was a specialty of the Milanese and was made of veal shanks braised with vegetables in white wine. We applauded his chef and I thanked Perkins for the choice. I had disliked the Italian pasta dishes but found in their meat some fine cuisine.

A display of weaponry of the Malta Fencibles Regiment as seen by Driscol at Bouverie's Headquarters. I-IV-7

Bouverie's Pronouncements

We read and studied our written Persian, writing out military style orders in that language and passing them to one another to see if the other could determine our meaning, until it was time to join the Governor-General and, as he was military, we wore our dress uniforms. We arrived in due time and found it would be a small affair; just the General himself and eight of his staff and associates. As we were by many steps of ranks the lowest of the low we found ourselves not ignored, but the centre of attention. The reason for this was soon apparent.

The great man had not finished his business, for Malta was a major port and had one hundred thousand inhabitants and many were the details that must be discussed, so the General did so and in a great an animated style. When we arrived they were discussing the Courts-Martial of a Lieutenant Frederick Greengoode, Royal Marines, of the H.M.S. Tempest, on the charges of his being willfully disobedient, neglectful and contemptuous of his duties and senior officers; for, while officer of the deck, he had gone ashore without permission, failed to inspect the guard, appeared on deck without his coat and behaved in a 'haughty manner' towards his senior officer. He had, of course, been found guilty. Now the matter of the moment was the nature of the penalty. Some suggested dismissal from the Royal Marines, a loss of rank. They decided instead on his being dismissed from his ship and placed at the bottom of the seniority list - this leniency being granted as he had been drunk 'for reasons that were understood to be grievous'. As to what that meant, neither Perkins or myself were bold enough to ask.

Then it was to us. The governor asked if my father had worked for Major Scovil *{Scovell}* and I replied that he had for a time. That made the General thump the table and pronounce that he was glad he could recall my father and then he picked up a piece of paper, showed it to the port admiral to his left who then passed it to the commander of the garrison who passed it once again back to the Governor-General.

'Most particular Mr Perkins', he said.

I was at this point very happy that Perkins outranked me for instead of a social supper we seemed to have stopped into an inquisition. The Governor-General and the three naval officers were un-happy with the report they had received from the man formerly in the HEIC 1st Bengal European Regiment, the deputy adjutant we had spoken with that day. He felt - and his naval staff agreed - that the entire epic had not been told. There we were, two junior officers; one man and, if the truth be told, one frighten boy being looked at skeptically by eight senior officers.

Perkins rose and began to speak. He was, I had noted before, a charmer of women and he could also, as he demonstrated now, be a charmer of men. He related our meeting with the Chilean officer in Gibraltar, the various after incidents, ignoring our panic over Russians in Algiers and our belief that the good officer had pursued and attacked us over a manner of honour.

Major-General Sir Henry Frederick Bouverie regarded this, nodding his head in some agreement then announced to us, "So you believe it had nothing to do with the upcoming expedition"?

Perkins and I just looked at one another and put our best questioning looks on our faces. The General smiled and added that he respected our discretion but he was an associate of Lord Ellenborough and was aware of the letter written by William <u>Hamilton</u> *{see Volume II, Chapter VI for the details, Driscol also underlined the name Hamilton}*. He was fully aware that Perkins was on his way east to set up an expedition to enter Central Tartary on a matter of some importance to the Crown.

We agreed as fast as we could.

He then switched back to the matter of the Chilean's. He thought it best that the officer's death should be reported, as inquiries might be made and our shipping interests in Valparaiso should not be compromised by any scandal. He suggested (and I use the term loosely) that we were to bring the sword to his offices the next day and there it would be returned, with compliments, to our Consul General in Valparaiso. The general said he knew the Consul General, the Honourable John Walpole, and would write him to find the bereaved family and return the sword to them, or if not successful to turn it over to the Chilean navy for them to deal with.

To this, everyone nodded and we did so also. He thumped the table again and ordered our supper be brought in, and it was in good order.

Five of the men in the room had been to the east and we had long discussions over the climate, food, women and the best way to avoid dying un-pleasantly. I could not remember all that was talked about that evening. For we had roast lamb and I ate far too much, now how an over full stomach can cause one's memory to forget details I cannot understand nor explain however, Some of the recommendations we received were:

1. To wear flannel next to skin in all seasons and to never remove any part of one's clothes while perspiring or for the sake of mere coolness.
2. To never ever, open a window especially if dew was to be expected.
3. To give up any ideas about pursuing any walking sport or violent exercises for exposure to the sun's heat had proved fatal to many thousands of Europeans. riding, however, was recommended.
4. We were reminded to never travel in the hour after sunset nor in the hour prior to sunrise, unless on military service.
5. To never sleep or sit while in wet clothes, always ride or walk until dry.
6. To avoid at all costs acidulated drinks, fruit juices or sour wines.
7. Sleep as much as you can and never take time away from that action for study or the vices of society.
8. We were also enjoined to face sickness with a stiff upper lip and not complain.
9. It was recommended that we keep moving on one's journey, and never to loiter on the way, disregarding sickness and fatigue.
10. That cleanliness, cheerfulness, regularity in living and avoidance of all annoyance would serve us well.
11. That in tropical countries the exuberant vegetation produces miasma[7], prejudicial to health and to trust to an observance of regimen, well-grounded faith in Providence and its sufficiency of its power to protect the Godly man from all dangers.
12. To avoid the pernicious custom in hot countries of taking copious beverages at all hours of the day, whether it be lemonade, wine, sangaree or beer, as it promoted excessive elimination and sweating.

13. To eat the simplest foods, to avoid a variety of dishes, to abstain from local foods that would cause one to perspire and to avoid those fruits and vegetables we were not accustomed to

It was a good evening yet I felt like a young boy who had been bombarded by thoughts and suggestions from a room full of uncles who, knowing what they know, had tried to give helpful advice but in the end just confused the poor child. Confused we were, when we left in the early hours and made our way to back to the Grand Hotel.

We discussed for some time the fact that our expedition was no secret at all. Perkins thought we might change our titles from Lieutenant and Ensign to 'End Piece Pawns'[8].

That evening I had a restless sleep for I dreamed of Chilean sword-armed raiders who took from me my Tuscan style steak.

Tuesday 1 November

We awoke early and as soon as was practical I delivered up the Chilean sword, both relieved and sadden by its loss. Perkins thought it was better to be done with it and I agreed once the transaction was completed.

Having the day free until our supper with Catania that evening, we made an excursion. We hired a clumsy looking Maltese *caleches* styled carriage from the Hotel and were soon on our way out, having decided to not eat breakfast, as we were both still digesting last night's lamb that, although tasteful, had elected to avoid being consumed by our bowels without a fight.

Perkins and I drove out through the walls, guided by the words we had heard the night before. We went out to Floriana and visited the botanic gardens. We went on from there to Citta Vecchia, a small town that lies in the centre of the island and known as the *Notabile* of the Arragonese kings. It was once a larger place but the rise of Valetta had destined it to be overlooked and abandoned by the fashionable folk. The cathedral was modest but was said to be built on the site of the house of Publius, the Publius of Saint Paul's fame. There was also a cave where the Saint was supposed to have lived but I found that idea fanciful. We avoided the catacombs and instead rode out to the highest point of the island called Mount Benjamin and was six hundred feet above the sea. Others had been there before us as there were many tombs said by some to be Carthaginian. This took my interest and we later found the valley of Boschetto the only place on the island that had standing trees and a stream. As we had not brought a pic-nic, we went back into town to attend to this at Catania's this evening.

We found at the hotel a grandson of Catania, there to convey us to our supper. We followed the lad to his Grandfather's house. From the grandson we found that Catania was the stately age of eight and forty and he a masterly eight and one quarter.

When one approaches Catania's 'villa', as he styled it, one would think a ruffian might live in it. Certainly no robber would show any interest in that hovel. It had the appearance of the lodgings of a poor man, for the structure was surrounded by a severe seven-foot wall of rough stone in poor repair and without stucco or ornamental. However, once within the gate one finds he is in a garden and when one enters the villa he is in eastern splendor. The plushest rugs adorn the floors and walls, brass and silver is the metal of all items in sight. Catania was glad to see us and, much more, the wounded man we had known on the

Speronara, his hesitations and confusion, was gone and he, himself, announced his being healthy and sound as the Houses of Parliament.

[Editor's note: at this time the ruins of parliament were still being hastily repaired and the rebuilding effort would not occur until 1840, so the 'houses of parliament were not very healthy or sound at that time but the phrase had a traditional meaning]

We had a meal with many dishes I did not know nor had I heard of. *'Soppa ta l-armla'*, or 'widow's soup'; his wife and servants had made this in celebration of her not becoming a widow. It was made of a mixture of vegetables and eggs. There was also a dish with rice and chicken livers. I do not care for liver but I ate some to assure no insult was conveyed. I do not recall the name of that dish or the one that followed, but the main dish was cooked lampuki, a type of small fish found in the waters of Malta.

We mentioned a number of our adventures and Perkins told of Lieutenant Webster's search for revenge. Catania seemed to know everything that went on in Malta but infighting between the various ships in harbour had not come to his ears. When we told him that we might need to dress up like Tunisians, he offered up his services and after dinner showed us some of his supplies. In his commercial dealing he often needed to disguise himself as a Muhammadan or westerner, for these two types of men can travel in and out of places a Maltese Jew would do well to fear. We spent the afternoon with his four sons and families who came to visit, as did his three daughters and their families, and we soon lost all track of names. At the end of the day, we stood at the gate making our farewells when Catania asked if he might speak with us alone. So, out on the street, he made a request of us. He needed to go to Cairo. As we were going that way, could he accompany us there? We told him we would be most pleased but we did not know enough about the overland part of the transfer from Alexandria to Suez to know how close to Cairo we would be, or how much time we would have. He dismissed this with comments that he would be certain that he could proceed alone if necessary and he had some idea that we would go to Cairo first before having to make the effort to go to Suez. We were gladdened to know our journey on the *Sebastiani* would not be alone.

We were so full of food that both of us felt somewhat burdened, like a soldier with a 68-pounder cannon ball in his haversack. It was late afternoon when we came back to the hotel. We both decided that we had been eating too much.

We had just laid down and were both commenting to one another that we would probably not need to eat again until India, when a knock came. Perkins wanted to act as if we were not there but I got up, for reasons I do not understand, and I made sure I had my French pistol behind my back before I approached the door and enquired as to who it was.

~~It was Lieutenant Webster. He was animated, eager and he had a plan.~~

[Editor's note: The above line had been overwritten by another colour of ink but the century and half or so that had passed had been unkind to the later ink, which allowed the more durable Indian ink to show through.]

Wednesday 2 November

We checked with the shipping office this morning and were told that no news of the *Sebastiani* was known. As we were getting ready to leave, a boy came into the office to announce that

the *Sebastiani* was off the port and signaling. The signal was long and we waited for the flags
to be read. They told an interesting tale:

"Sebastiani in collision - Phelypeaux to stand in"

It soon was revealed that the sister ship to the *Sebastiani*, the *Phelypeaux*, would take her
place, as the original ship had been struck by another French ship in Leghorn *{Livorno}*. As the
ships were built in the same manner by the same yard and by the same man, no changes to
the billets would be needed. The ship would sail late tomorrow morning. The agent estimated
the tide would be suitable around noon. We could board anytime this afternoon.

We made our way to Catania and told him the news. He had arranged a second-class
passage on the ship and would meet us there the next morning. For our part, we returned to
the Hotel, packed our belongings and those of Beer, and waited for some hours until we could
enter the ship. As we waited, we conjugated Persian verbs.

The *Phelypeaux* was named for a pioneering French commercial seaman by the
Christian name of Jerome. His ship was a fine one, painted white with black masts, rigged as a
barque *{bark}* and of nine hundred and sixty tons, four times as large as the *William Fawcett*
but without steam power of any kind. Our cabins were relatively spacious. We split Beers
luggage between us. As we had been advised, our heavier luggage was placed in the hold but I
secured my weaponry and, more importantly, my books in my cabin. The cabin smelled of
fresh paint, varnish, wood oil and green timber.

View of a British warship about to receive an unusual visitor. I-IV-8

Hooga Booga

~~We made our way then to Lieutenant Webster's quarters ashore for they had rented a small house that was in poor repair but had a view on to the deck of the 3rd rate ship-of-the-line that was to be the target of his revenge.~~

[Editor's note: The line above was also struck out, under the same circumstances as noted previously, and three newspaper clipping had been pasted into the journal. A fourth was also added but had been lost.]

[First clipping. Written in pencil on the clipping: From the Times column, Naval and Military Intelligence, page 4, November 23, 1836]

From our Naval Correspondent in Malta. 3 November

It has been reported that an incident involving the H.M.S. _____, a third rate of his Majesty's Mediterranean fleet, and first thought to be a diplomatic misstep has now been reconsidered as an elaborate hoax. The matter has caused great consternation in the Admiralty and diplomatic circles and occurred during the visit of his Excellency the Bey of Tunis.

[Second clipping, which has written on it in pencil: "From the Times front page, November 25, 1836"]

BOGUS VISITOR HOAXES FLEET

~*~

A ruse suspected

~*~

With details of the deception by an eye witness
who observed what happened and is printed with
his permission

~*~

All of England is laughing at the expense of the officers of an unidentified warship of his Majesty's Mediterranean fleet. It has been dependably conveyed that this diplomatic episode occurred during a diplomatic visit to Malta by Mustafa ibn Mahmud, Bey of Tunis and the 9th in the line of the Husainid

Dynasty. His Excellency had arrived aboard the H.M.S. Hanover carrying his entourage of 120 souls with some said to contain both European and African slaves.

It has been reliably reported that a request had been made on the day of their arrival to a 3rd rate in Valetta harbour to provide both a tour of the great ship of war and a luncheon. One of the younger Princes, or Beylet, named Ansa would be visiting the ship and that all arrangements for a tour should be made and that they should receive every manner of close attention. The message reportedly came from the Governor-General's office and had an official looking stamp and a scrawled signature. It also included a recommended French menu, for the 3rd rate was well known to have aboard her one the finest French chefs on the Captain's staff. The Captain of the ship was also informed not to attend the Governor-General's fete being planned to entertain the visiting Bey, as his full attention must concentrated on the task at hand, to ensure the full satisfaction of Beylet Ansa.

Our informant tells us that at the appointed hour an outlandishly dressed group of men in a wildly painted boat approached the waiting guard of honour on the quay.

In it was a man in the formal evening dress of a high official and four Arabs or Moors. The Englishman in the formal dress declared himself to be none other than Herbert Holmonde, deputy assistant in the Corps Diplomatique and interpreter for his Excellency Ansa Mustafa Muhammad Muhamet Mahammad ibn Mahmud, eldest son and heir of the ruler of Tunis, to be the 10th in the line of the Husainid Dynasty. It was remarked that the official was a handsome Englishman with an educated manner of speaking.

This elder son of the Bey was reported to be tall thin man of dark skin, long black hair and partial beard for despite his height he was not quite a man, more a grown boy. He was accompanied by his lackeys, three rather disreputable looking men with black bushy beards, poor hygiene and darker skin that he. The Prince, as that is the terminology given him, wore a sky blue robe, had a leopard skin half cape, a dark cloth over his head and wore a silver studded belt which held several knives and leather pouches, and his feet were shod with silver chased leather scandals. The rest of the men wore long brownish robes, blue turbans and patent leather boots with long square toes in the Italian style.

The Lieutenant in command gave the Prince a smart salute and welcomed him to the cutter of his Majesty's ship H.M.S. _____. This was translated to the Prince by Mr Holmonde, who responded with a loud and cheerful Hooga Booga!

The Lieutenant was not prepared for the royal guest to bring his own boat and it was crewed with smartly turned out Maltese in white trousers and blouses, and each wore the traditional long Maltese caps. Mr Holmonde stated that the Prince would follow the naval Lieutenant to the ship. This was done in some style, a band began to play as they neared the ship.

The Prince was piped aboard. A suitable salute was fired with blanks, eleven shots to be exact, and they were expertly timed. The Prince and his party gave back loud shouts of Allah Akbar, Booga Booga and Hooga bin Booga!

The Prince was able to navigate the rope ladder up the side the ship without difficulty, then the second diplomatic incident arose. A Lieutenant offered his hand to guide the Prince up the last steps but this was slapped away with a loud cry of Hooga ali Booga. Befuddled, the man withdrew, with Mr Holmonde smoothing over the difficulty with a sharp word to the naval officers that a non-Muhammadan must not touch his Excellency, as he considered the touch of an infidel on the skin of his exalted self as the same as a blow would be to an English Gentlemen. The first incident had been the music, as followers of the Sunnah sect of Islam music was forbidden to true believers' ears, Mr Holmonde explained.

Apologies were given and accepted. Our witness states that the Captain of the ship was presented and the Prince stepped forward but mistakenly took a Royal Marine Captain for the Captain of the ship until this was corrected by Mr Holmonde. Once that had been sorted out and the real Captain identified, the Prince handed him a dried up object on a fine silver chain. The Captain accepted it but seemed unsure of what to do with it. Mr Holmonde was there to whisper that it was dried heart of a lion and to avoid offence he should put it around his neck. Informed of its importance, he did so, to many cries of Hooga and Booga and the striking of chests and stamping of feet by the Tunisians. One of the Tunisians whispered into the Prince's ear and he turned to face the First Lieutenant of the Ship and handed him a smaller version of the first dried thing on a chain saying Booga, Allah, Hooga. Mr Holmonde again explained that the second in command was also being honoured by being presented with the dried heart of an African leopard.

The tour of ship proceeded, halting at one point when the Prince's entourage stopped to relieve themselves on the quarterdeck artillery, much to the misery of the Ship's officers and the suppressed amusement of the crew.

They were on the lower deck looking at the 32-pounders, when the Prince suddenly turned and approached a middle-aged sailor and spoke Arabic to him, for that man had some of that tongue and had greeted him, and he and the Prince spoke for a moment. The Prince turned and snatched the dried leopard Heart from the second in command and gave it to the sailor and then hugged and kissed him on the forehead, for he was a small man. This left the officers of the ship in a state of some confusion.

Mr Holmonde explained that the crewman had spoken Arabic to his Excellency, greeting him in the proper way and was thus a deserving man for the reward as he knew the language of the Holy Koran.

The tour continued we are told by our witness, showing off the fighting strength of one of Britain's wooden walls, with the visitors reported to have been spitting on deck in unison at the signal of said Prince. Mr Holmonde explained that this was the highest honour that the Tunisians could provide. One of the Tunisians attempted to strike flint in the darkened powder magazine even producing at one point a bottle, and a Chancel's match. This was prevented — forcibly, of course — as such an action could have touched the many tons of powder in the magazine, with Mr Holmonde apologizing for the excess of enthusiasm from the Tunisians amid the great consternation of the ship's officers.

It was then observed by our onlooker that the two of the Tunisians seemed unable to retain their balance even with only the slight swell within the harbour. Many times they tread on toes, upsetting the officers. Many so struck, reported that they were particular vile smelling and their hands very unclean, leaving marks of an unacceptable nature on parts of the officer's uniform not to be mentioned.

The tour was completed and while waiting on deck for the luncheon to be served, the Prince gave compliment after compliment on the state of the ship, crew and its large cannons to the Captain and its officers. The Prince then made a number of remarks about the Midshipmen, which caused diplomatic incident three. These comments were taken as complimentary until Mr Holmonde translated them fully to the British Officers. It would seem the Prince's father kept both kinds of Harem's in his palace; one of the most ravishing women but also one of gadymedes and he had wondered if the good Captain would care to exchange some of his young men for those of the Bey's this evening? This caused a near collapse of the diplomatic visit but the good Mr Holmonde did well to calm the Captain, his officer and the midshipmen, explaining patiently that these Tunisians were Moors and such horrid things were common in their blighted land and he asked that the Officers display their Christian forgiveness for this wretches' comments. This was done and Mr Holmonde thanked them for this and remarked that Tunisians were so far into heretical belief that one of their feet must already be in Hades as he spoke.

When the luncheon was to be served, the Muhammadan Tunisians suddenly announced that it was time for Dhuhr prayer; one of the five prayers demanded of those in submission to Islam. Rugs were demanded and provided, and for forty or more minutes a scene of wailing cries and the issuance of Booga Hooga and other exclamations were made with the Muhammadan's doing their prayers in the direction of Meccah. The meal was then finally joined, somewhat cold, unfortunately.

The last and greatest diplomatic incident then occurred. Our observer was not so honoured as to be at the table but has reconstructed what occurred by speaking extensively with his shipmates.

The luncheon was going very well with the Tunisian's seeming to know and accept the European taste for wine and they toasted the King, through Mr Holmonde, but then they showed great preference to the French Fleet. The Prince asked his interpreter if he might speak to the cook. This unusual request was, of course, honoured and the befuddled cook was brought into the Captain's great cabin.

The Naval officers were astounded to hear the Prince complement the cook on his duties and his food, and he asked in detail about the food, which had been served, in poor but passable French. All of the naval officers, of course, could speak French, and the Captain asked the good Prince why he had not spoken French before. The Prince replied that "you are English" and he thought Englishmen spoke English and Frenchmen French. The Prince then asked the good Captain about the dish he was eating. The cook said it was 'jambon', and the Prince ask from what animal does that come? The Captain said that it was pork, a hog when the word pork appeared to mean nothing to his guests.

The Prince then asked in his own language what that meant to Mr Holmonde, who answered them sheepishly that it was forbidden meat!. A complete riot then ensued, with the Tunisians spitting out the food as they began to yell in French, to threaten war, to perform an immediate emasculation, with tweezers, on all the ship's officers and immediately demanded to leave the ship, as they had been fed unclean meat and must immediately purge themselves of it in fear of their souls. They were pursued to make amends but they were in a savage rage and before the Officers could apologise for the oversight – for Mohammedan's, like Jews, may not partake of pork in any form – the Prince and his men, calling the Officer dogs infidels and much worse in French, for it was found that all of them could speak the language, made for their waiting boat. Where Mr Holmonde made a last effort to recover the situation and to prevail on the Tunisians to accept the good ship's officers apologies but it was not to be and shouting to the Captain that he would go with the Prince back to his father and try to stop a war from starting. The glamorously clad group was soon rowing away. The ship's boat, loaded with repentant officers pursued them to offer more apologies but once the Maltese ship had left their passengers on the quay they were seen to move quickly into the town and were lost to sight.

The Captain, much concerned marched at once to the Governor-General disrupting the ceremonies then on going and a terrible scene occurred which has been well reported on by this papers, which ended only when the Bey of Tunis most definitely declared that his son, not named Ansa but Abdul was not in Malta but in Tunis and that the name being used to describe him, Ansa, meant goat.

The Admiralty has stated that they have fully investigating the affair, which is now thought to have been a prank. The dried

'awards' given to the Captain and others of the crew were found
to be the dried organs of a sheep.

[Third clipping which has written on it in pencil: From the Maltese Gazette, November 12, 1836]

It has been stated by the Governor-General that the investigation of the 'Prince Ansa affair' has been completed. It is reported by a senior officer in the Malta staff that a Lieutenant aboard the H.M.S. Rodney is suspected as being the organizer of this ruse and that he had also been dressed as one of the Prince's lackeys. To these charges, the Lieutenant had stated his complete innocence. Notwithstanding his pronouncements of blamelessness, an arrangement was made in which he admitted knowledge of the incident but not culpability. he was reported reprimanded and our source holds that rumors to the effect that his punishment was limited to 'being struck three times on the hand with a goose feather and told to not do that again, please'. He was also ordered to write an apology to the officers and crew of the H.M.S._______, which he did willingly after being assured that no further actions would be taken against him. This letter of apology has come into the hands of this publisher and is not so much a letter of apology but a detailed list of each embarrassing action and adding each time that he was sorry that this had happened or been done by others. It was said the apology was eleven pages long. The Officers of the ship in question were not thought to have agreed with such leniency and have called for another investigation to determine who the Prince and Mr Holmonde were and proper punishment delievered.

A very fanciful image made of the 'Tunisian Prince' and printed in the Times, virtually every detail is incorrect. However, this copy of the newspaper picture was found in Driscol's papers. I-IV-9

From Malta To Egypt

Thursday 3 November

We are waiting to sail off to *Rhakotis {ancient Egyptian name of the city of Alexandria}* in our cabins and between us, we are looking at what fortune has brought us, for packages have been delivered to us by a smiling man, who shook our hands and wished us a good voyage. The packages were four, with two for each of us. The smaller two contained a 12" long sterling silver ink stand, one with a stag and the other a boar, showing the finest craftsmanship, with four crystal ink wells, with associated pens and accessories set with in a silver repoussé mahogany box made by Timothy Renou, a famed silver smith. We were both impressed. I had been given the stag but Perkins fancied it more than I and we exchanged; I rather liking the boar more, so I was happy to do the exchange.

The second, larger and heavier pair of boxes we opened to find it contained a gold chased English-walnut case. It contained a pair of matching percussion dueling pistols of .63 calibres and two smaller pistols of .52 calibres - these being for each Gentleman's "second", or associate, who would be present to observe and ensure the possible death-match met the standards of fair play. The two sets, which were identical, were made by Phillip Bond of London. The larger pistols had octagonal barrels measuring eight inches while the smaller 'seconds' were less than five. The case also included complete set of tools; such as bullets moulds, cleaning rods, and an un-usual dual-compartment powder flask which holds a few of the lead bullets as well. The beautiful cases were lined with brilliant green silk and came with a tooled leather-carrying bag.

We thought that the ink set was worth at least £7, and the pistols £25-40, for they were simply magnificent. We both had the thought to sell them but they were so exquisite how could we? I resolved to retain the boar inkstand and sell the pistols, as the single shots were outdated and I did not expect to be in any duels in the near future. I had the French revolver and I had found that it served me well, and I did not need another. Perkins' observed that we now had between us seven pistols and two long arms. We were so well-armed in fact that perhaps we should turn pirate!

Catania found us and he thought us mad, completely senseless - but we had finally left Europe - for Malta had been declared part of Europe by an act of Parliament during a debate over pay and allowance for those stationed there and not as the Middle East where the rate would have higher.

[Editor's note: If it were not clear and Driscol did removed any mention of it from his journals. It is highly suggested that Perkins and Driscol were the Prince and translator who in modern language 'pranked' the British navy. Readers should keep this in mind when viewing their future actions]

On the door of our cabin was an interesting sign in English and French[9] that greatly amused us.

We informed the steward that we were *ill {emphasis added by Driscol}* and had food brought to our cabins. I moved to eat with Perkins in his cabin. The stewards, after a gratuity for dealing with annoying Englishmen, brought us all that one might need. Fresh bread, *Potage Celestine {celery soup with leeks and potato}*, and *Saucisson en brioche {sausages baked in dough}* and, to our added enjoyment, a plate of *Les Croquets Denison {Walnut and Almond Puffs}*; the last five of which we had to take out our American cards and play a few hands to determine who would get them. Perkins gained four and ate them with overstated relish. I ate my lone one with less enthusiasm. The meals were good and at a rate of six Francs per day for two meals, with the additional cost of one Franc if an afternoon tea was wanted.

We heard the evening gunfire, for, like Gibraltar, Malta was a fortress and those without a special purpose expelled from its fortifications and patrols made sure nothing was amiss. It was now that we waited for cries to announce that the ship was to depart. Soon our diligence was rewarded and we made our way out of the harbour, late but still going. We had small sidescuttles and these we looked out of, changing places every few minutes as the glass was four and half feet above the deck, making it awkward to do so and only some eleven inches in diameter and not of the best glass.

The French ship finally made it from Valetta and we were on our way to Alexandria. ~~Once we had left the harbour we decided we had 'recovered' well enough to brave the deck and we went up but only after another scrubbing session for me using salt and vinegar to remove the last of the stain from my moustache and skin, my skin was quiet raw by now.~~

[Editor's note: the line above was marked out in the manner discussed previously and all other such instance in this chapter have the same explanation]

A sailing ship is so much finer to travel in than a steamer, especially when one is on a large well-founded ship like this one. The sound of the wind and movement through the water was pleasant to the senses. Unlike the Speronara, which tended to float over the waves, this vessel cut through the seas as had the *William Fawcett.* Perkins observed that this ship attacked the sea like a column of French Grenadier's while the Maltese boat had been Hussars, always moving with the terrain. I countered that it had been more like light infantry, moving over the surface with less speed but quieter.

The passengers were about half English, a quarter French and the rest other Europeans; with a few Turks and other Easterners, only one of which was not in western dress. This Turk was in a turban, slippers and robe, and was followed everywhere by a gigantic Negro servant who must have been nearly seven feet tall. We speculated that he was probably a eunuch from the puffiness of his face, which was crisscrossed with a pattern of scars. The sun set behind the island nicely and we watch until Malta and the sun had fallen into the sea, I found that I was beginning to sweat and not feeling well at all. Was my immunity to seasickness coming to an end? I turned to Perkins who I found was in worse shape than I. We made it to our cabins and our beds. I declined that evening to go to supper and bid the Steward to not bother me again, but I did ask him to check on Perkins. He did and reported him ill and feverish also. I asked that the ship's doctor attend to us, for I felt like a hot blanket had been placed over my head and sweat was beginning to pour off me - yet at the same time I could not get warm. The French doctor came in time. For the life of me I could not understand his accent as he was a *Francitan {A speaker of Occitan, the southern French dialect}.* He was reassuring and left for me a good supply of water, an extra basin should I become sick and I believe I successfully persuaded him that I did not want to be bled - the savage. ~~So we went from pretending to be sick to the real article.~~

201

Complaints

Friday 4 November

I did not eat in the morning, as I felt generally un-well but did make it to dinner having a fine plate of buttered noodles and fried rabbit. After this, I went back to my cabin, finding that Perkins had not risen at all that day. I found the pitching of the ship restful as always.

Did nothing to celebrate Guy Fawkes Day. I was not up to it. The best I could do was to place my finger in my mouth as I had done as a child and withdrawing it quickly to make an enjoyable popping sound.

Saturday 5 November

Sickness has kept me to bed this last day. Catania has been kind but mainly I have lain there sweating and regretting whatever it was I had done to deserve this. The French doctor had tried again to have me bled but I declined several times, for to see my own blood would cause me to swoon in my present condition. Catania said that Perkins' illness was worse and that a large number of the crew and passengers had also been struck by the malady. I was able to get up and make it to Perkins' door. He weakly acknowledged me and I got a smile from his sweaty face by accusing him of suffering from a bube *{venereal disease}*. I barely made it back to my bed which was still wet with my sweat. I put a duvet on the deck and went to sleep again as I was un-able to read. I awoke early in the morning and wrote some in my journal, bringing it up to this point.

My namesake was my Uncle David Perley Driscol who had been killed at the battle of Maida. *{a battle between the French and British 4 July 1806, in Calabria, Italy}* He had been my father's youngest brother and had joined the service. We were south of Calabria when I recalled him. He had been wounded at that battle from a shot that had pierced both his cheeks, removing all his teeth and had died some days later from putrefaction. He had been a Sergeant in the 58th (Rutlandshire) Regiment of Foot.

Sunday 6 November

Recovered my wits and health suddenly early in the morning of this day. I bathed as best I could and changed my wardrobe, deciding at the time that I would grow a beard to avoid having to shave at all and that it would complement my moustache that was coming in nicely. I combed my hair, finding that it would soon need cutting, and did my ablutions. I found the night steward, who was glad to see one of the passenger recovered. He said that about three quarters of the passengers were sick, and half the crew, but none had died and some few had recovered like I had. He found for me some bread and a thick slice of cold, well-done pork which a selection of grass *{vegetables}*. He provided me with a large portion of sweetened hot chocolate in a beer tankard. I was still not that hungry but I ate what I could. I found Perkins asleep and did not bother Catania. I went up on deck and the chill wind soon made me seek my thicker coat.

From the officer of the deck I found we were now off the south coast of Crete with the sea calm and as smooth as the finest silvered mirror as we moved along with a slight breeze. I had taken up my three-legged stool to the deck and spent the day there, being much refreshed by the sea, the wind and thought of Minotaurs, Greek heroes and exquisite pagan Goddesses.

We kept off the south coast of Crete for the entire day, the scent of land coming to us once the sun had risen, for we could smell the thyme that grows in profusion on Crete. Sunset came and the stars came out in their magnificence, and soon the sea itself turned to green fire. With the setting of the sun, a stronger wind had come and small waves had appeared and these burned with an emerald fire that stretched around the ship in all directions. The light was as bright as the fullest moon and we could see clearly, although everything was cast in a chartreuse glow. At this time porpoises made their welcomed appearance and their jumps made the sea red, for the *Stenella coeruleoalb {Driscol used the scientific name for dolphins while writing porpoise}* were pursuing fish and these streaks lead out to the horizon. It has been speculated that these sea fires are tiny creatures in the seawater itself but it is a wondrous and magical sight to see and I did so wish I could have shared it with Millicent.

The crew sighted the island of Konfouisi which lies off Crete and is the point where the ship turned to make a straight southeastern run to Alexandria, some three hundred nautical miles.

Catania, I found, was in his cabin, alive and with papers strewn about doing calculations and he had no time for me. Perkins was still un-well. I found that the French doctor had bled him twice.

I finally found my appetite and had *Boeuf aux olives {beef and olive stew}* picking out the few potatoes that blighted it *auberines en Persillade {baked eggplant with béchamel sauce}* and several other titbits; *crème au beurre a la meringue Italienne, {butter-cream meringue with frosting};* and I placed in my pockets a number of Spanish oranges for a later meal that night.

The ship's Captain has announced that tomorrow evening there will be a shipboard *carnival* with music, dancing, and the use of masquerade to celebrate the return to the ship of good health, but one must wonder where they think we might find a costume while at sea in the eastern Mediterranean?

I had an additional late supper dining well and in beautiful silence on a large bowl of *navets a l'etuvee {buttered turnips},* and some spare piece of meat which I doused well with my Brand & Co. sauce to make it more toothsome than it first tasted. I finally found my appetite, and I felt my body and soul were in need of food since my illness, and had

[Editor's note Driscol's writing breaks off here the sentence unfinished]

Checked on Perkins, and found him better and reading some French book which he said was a book on religion titled, *Justine ou Les Malheurs de la vertu*[10], which I had not heard of before. He said he had been gifted with it by one of the French Ladies. He held up another book that he was consulting, his French dictionary; saying there were many words in French he did not understand.

Recovery And Nonsensical French People

Monday 7 November

Perkins had recovered and he awoke me to go in search of food. We waited some time as the dinning salon was set up and then sat down to French breakfast. The room filled up well, there being quite a selection of people out now. There were omelettes to feast on, and we did. Catania emerged from his cabin to join us also and the chatter of the people around us was like a dunning, for the dining room was lined with mirrors which reflected the sound back; a lovely room for shipboard dining but deafening for conversation.

One of the French crew with a comedic long beard was acting as barber and I took him to his word that he could do so, and he cut my hair perfectly. Removing the curls that had begun at my neck and making me cooler in the hotter weather to come.

On deck, we passed through a small fleet of fishing boats who caught fish by means of two vessels towing a large net stretched between them, called by our Maltese friend a bilancella net. The next ship we sighted was a trading vessel of some one hundred and fifty tons which sailed by and which Catania named a Jerme, as the vessels out of Egypt were called. It was probably headed to Trieste carrying, for the wind brought us its smell, and our trade master declared that horrid scent was of atherine[11] and dried fish. Catania noted that the smell meant the cargo was rotting and it would sell for little. He knew she was bound for Trieste by the way the anchor chain was stored; for the seamen of Trieste do it like no others in world and they do so only to demonstrate they are returning home, a tradition or superstition of those men. Foreign seamen like these Egyptian did so also for superstition is rife amongst them.

The dinner meal was more like what I had expected on a French ship. The passengers had recovered from illness and seasickness and the salon on the main deck was teeming with people. I had secured a table in the corner and remained there during the afternoon, eating with Catania then Perkins, and watching Perkins move about, conversing with all and one - mainly women.

The dining room of the French passenger ship Phelypeaux. I-IV-10

The *'Carnival'* began and ended rather quickly: just some music that was ear piercing within the confines of the salon. There was some dancing which I avoided, of course. Catania stayed in his room and Perkins was in his element. As it was a masquerade, we had both come as English officers but I had given myself a much deserved promotion to Lieutenant. I carried the extra rank for the insignia of rank were my father's from the time he had briefly been an officer. I took them with me to use should I actually make or purchase the exalted rank of Lieutenant - should I ever amass the money to do so, as I owed still nearly £200 on my Ensignship.

I met two people of note. The first was a Frenchman from Lille whom I named *Mondamoiseau Folie {Mr Nut and Madness}*. He came in looking presentable but as soon as he had introduced himself and found that I was an Englishman capable of speaking of scientific terms in French and Latin, his pattern of voice and delivery changed. He explained that he was going to Egypt to take sanctuary amongst the pyramids, for he knew they had special powers to protect him from the many conspiracies plotted against him in Europe. It would seem he had proven that the propensity theory of probability proposed some three hundred years ago by Geralmo Cardano[12] was true. He held that whereas the scientific community and the many bastards in the universities had declared that a new century could never begin on Sunday, Tuesday or Thursday but he, Mondamoiseau Folie had proved them all wrongs, they were all botchers, blind to his studies and evidence in his favour. He was sure that all the academic doctors of the world were out to get him for his discovery, to both suppress it and steal it. After he had 'gained powers' by visiting the pyramids he intended to go to the east and find a Maharajah to fund his future research and protect him from the knives and looks of all those who opposed him. I purchased him a strong French brandy and excused myself, going to my cabin for an hour. I later returned and regained my seat and was about to return to my reading when I had my second visitation.

This was Madam Cosette, who seemed both angry and concerned over some matter. She berated me quietly for a minute or so, but she spoke so fast that I could not understand her; both for the rapidity of her speech and her accent. Once I had made her understand that I could not do the same for her, she slowed down and I found she was from Vendee and spoke that ugly patois which I had never heard before. Once she restated her declarations I found that she was asking if I valued my reputation, as she said I must not, as I seemed to associate with that Englishman Perkins; and that I ought, for prudence sake, to remove myself from his society or I would be tarred with not being in the association of a Gentleman. I had to ask what she meant and, it would seem, he was being forward with the Ladies. I also had to ask exactly how was he being forward. 'Monsieur he is using their first names!' She also seemed to think I was a German. I insisted I was actually English, pointing to my uniform but she did not believe me, saying I spoke French like a German *{i.e. badly}*. Having delivered her message and, seeing I was not in agreement with her pontifications, she, like a bird of prey, took off in search of more suitable and perhaps agreeable verbal prey.

Perkins rejoined me for supper, having on his arm the widow Madam Angelique of no more than two and twenty years of age. We had a pleasant evening. Her late husband had lands on Mauritius and she was going out to oversee there sale. At one, point Perkins left us and went around the salon introducing himself and speaking with the people at the various tables. He did not return for an hour or so and, meanwhile, I and Madam Angelique had a fascinating discussion about French politics and her great love for Louis Philippe. I found that she held that he was loved by all the people of France and they all supported his idea of *juste milieu {Just middle}*, a political idea of being just annoying enough to everyone but not enough for them to take up arms against one's self. *{He abdicated in 1848 and was the king against whom the barricades in June 1832 were raised in Victor Hugo's Les Misérables}*

Perkins' returned and gave the Lady and I the gist of his exploration amongst the wild fauna on board this ship. He had found out the most intimate details of the fellow passengers, which he then told me. Of the dozen or so he spoke of I can remember only six. One couple was married but not to one another and were escaping the natural hatred of everyone they knew by going to the Orient. The next couple were two men who were in a somewhat wildly sinful and degenerate arrangement, fleeing persecution for the liberal lands of Egypt; although as I understand it, such actions are punishable by death but still easily deflected by a small remuneration to the authorities. The third group was five men of a mindset so revolting I will not set it down. Another was a perfectly average French couple from Bordeaux who had decided to give life to their children by having relations within ancient tombs under the gibbous Moon during the north African winter. Fourthly, there were two matrons in their forties; their husband's dead, their children departed or out of touch, and going to Egypt to buy some children to raise up anew and perhaps to do better this time, (children could be purchased in Egypt for a small expenditure in Francs). Finally, a newly married couple on their way to Beirut to travel thorough the Holy Land as a measure of their honeymoon. They would have been the most conventional couple Perkins had spoken to if one had not been not quite fourteen and the other three and sixty, and the man the younger. He brought all the stories to me with a face and animation of speech that relayed to me that these were the most entertaining people in the world. I told Perkins in response that I had become somewhat discouraged by the Gallic race and told him that this race of men who fought at Wagram *{the famous French victory against the Austrians in 1809}* will be gone from this good earth by the end of this century.

I left the widow and Perkins to speak of other things and ate my last good French meal, as the Captain had announced that if the wind held we would make our port tomorrow. I enjoyed the pleasure of *Pain Francais {plain French bread}* spread with lamb marrow, some butter, salt and parsley and a number of *Mille-Feuilles a la fondue de fromage {Cheese Napoleons, pastry}*.

I began to read Barbara Hofland's Africa Described, in Its Ancient and Present State, which seemed fitting as for the second time in my life I approached Africa.

I remembered too late that evening that this was my mother's eight and sixty birthday. I wished her a silent grand day and thought back on birthdays past. She always liked fancy porcelains or glassware and her children often banded together to procure the best available and we would have a purely Danish meal. One dreaded dish from that was her salmon and onion cakes, laced with fennel and dill, which may have been admirable on some point of culinary importance but I always beheld them with the utmost horror. To counter-balance that were a number of sumptuous dishes that made me regret taking this journey away from her kitchen.

Map of Alexandria given to Driscol by the Manfred Schiffer much later in his journey. To the south east of the City you can see the Mahmudiyeh Canal he took Cairo. I-IV-11

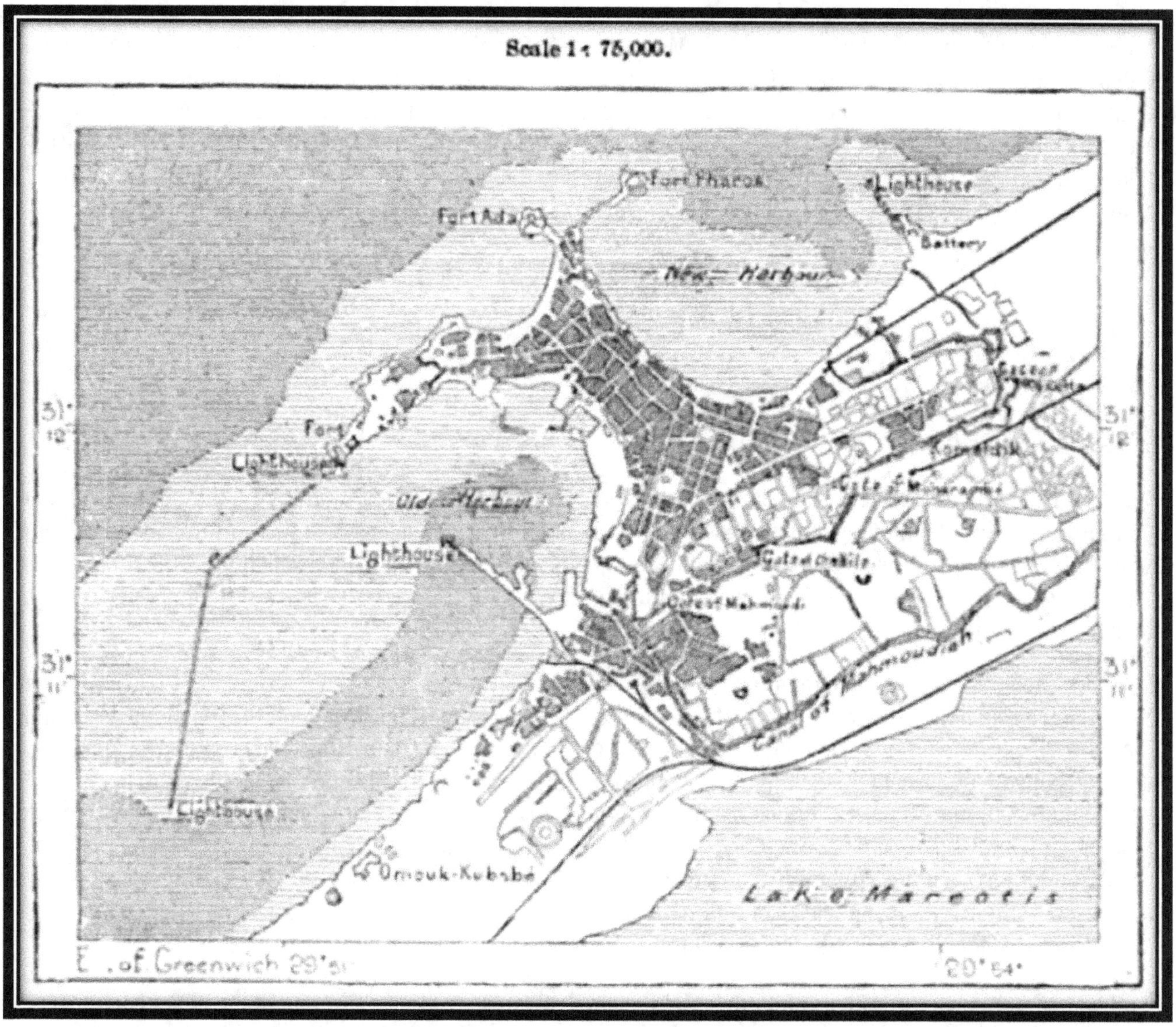

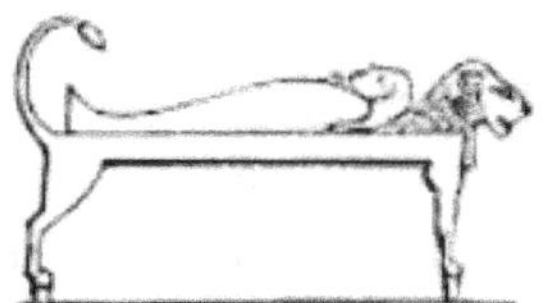

207

Chapter V
Alexandria To Suez

Alexandria; The City Of Alexander - The Mahmoodeeh Canal To Caire (Cairo) - We Enter The Nile - Cairo; The Victorious Capital - The Imaum Of Mushi Street - The Great Pyramids Of Geezeh - Skullduggery - Disguising One's Hair Colour- Table For The Cost Of Slaves And Commodities In The Markets; Cairo, November 1836 - The Schranschau Warren - To Suez Over The Desert From Cairo - Dusty Suez - The Atalanta; Ship Of The Honourable East Indian Company - Pontifications - The Most Senior Of The Most Junior - Alexander Anton Horne

========

Alexandria; The City Of Alexander

Tuesday 8 November

We arrived directly off Alexandria, demonstrating the masterly navigational skill of the French Captain but I was saddened that Pharos[1] was not there to greet us as it had the ancients. The city was low lying; so different from the hilly Malta, Gibraltar, Ceuta or Algiers. I had come to *Ifriqiya {Arabic for Africa}* finally, as I did not count Ceuta as truly being Africa as it had been Spanish territory for centuries.

Our ship was large enough to need pilots to enter the harbour, and we waited off shore some time before the small boat carrying them arrived. In the meantime, I swept the harbour with my binoculars, putting what I saw into the context of what I had read of this great city. The great 'T' shaped central peninsula was what most amazed for over the many centuries this had been built up, changing famous Pharos island from said island to a peninsula, of which some three thousand feet of land had been added. Ancient and medieval ships would come to Alexandria in ballast, for what could Egypt want in trade from elsewhere? It was said the fill for the artificial peninsula came from their centuries of said ballast being dumped here, discharging it into the harbour to pick up grain during Roman times and later the spices and other wonders of the east.

I had read too that no trace remained of the great library; a place where Euclid and Erasistratus had taught and Theocritus, Hipparchus, Callimachus, Lucian and Ptolemy, the great geographers, had studied.

As we came in under easy sail, the packet passed us from Constantinople a French steamer, the La Galissonniere going at a rapid pace. It was the first foreign steam ship I had yet seen. She was from Trieste and going ten knots if not more.

The coast was a series of sandy hills, dotted by windmills. One immense building stood out and Catania identified it as the palace of Said Pasha, the ruler's man in the city. As we neared the port, we could identify Ramleh, a place that the inhabitants would go for sea baths and escape the insufferable heat of summer. The ruins and inhabited parts of the city are a reddish hue, with green provided by many trees but even in autumn it seemed to shimmer in heat even though it was a pleasant 70° here out at sea.

A boat carrying the local officials arrived and a lively discussion that occurred between the pilots and the ship's officers in French, broken Arabic and, I presume, Turkish. It concerned the occurrence of plague in the city, but the news was good for none had died of that loathsome malady for a month.

The French officers had told us that the entrance into the port of Alexandria is considered difficult, something any French maritime officer would remember with regret. The refusal of Vice-Admiral François-Paul Brueys d'Aigalliers, the Comte de Brueys, commander of the French fleet to enter Alexandria caused them to anchor instead at the nearby Aboukir Bay. This action provoked, from the French point of view, the disaster of *Le Bataille d'Aboukir*, or, from the British point of view, the victory of the Battle of the Nile, at said bay in July, 1799.

The pilot boat, having left their man with us, departed with the many letters of introduction to the various Consuls in the port. The pilots were discomforted when they almost immediately lead the ship aground, which caused a great deal of shouting but it was but a temporary measure as the sand was yielding and the freshening Levant wind soon pushed us off, after some harrowing moments.

The southeastern harbour was full of ships. A few bedraggled Turks and Egyptian ships who were displaying proudly there Irish pennants, *{Rope-yarns hanging about on the rigging and indication of sloppy ship keeping}* were anchored there. Perhaps as tokens of sovereignty and as a demonstration of European trade, there were some forty Austrian sails, a similar number of English ships, and some others from Sardinia, Netherlands, France, Sweden, and Denmark, and, of course, the Neapolitan merchant fleet. Also, in the basin were four Egyptian built warships. The *Iskanderieh*, of 100 guns, and two 138 gun ships, the *Akka* and *Mehallet El Kebir*, and one ship of 80 guns, the *Beylan*. They could be seen in the basin Alexander's architect Dinocrat had designed for military shipping. A larger fleet could not be seen. Perhaps this lack of naval power was a lingering result of the battle of Navarino[2]. We were the second to disembark as the British Consul's boat came out quickly, manned by what appeared to be a leprous European, an Indian who looked as if he might soon die of consumption and an Egyptian whose purpose on this world appeared to be to compel all the other native rowers, of which there were eight, to be as surly as possible, and in this he was greatly successful.

Moreover, they were led by an Italian *Renegado {renegade, a Christian converted to Islam}* who greeted us in fine French and, having found the English passengers who would be making the continued passage to Suez, gave us our directions on what we needed to do. He would act as the guide for the seventeen of us so designated as 'passers'; those passing thorough Egypt on the way to Suez and the Orient beyond. The boat journey was directly to shore, some third of mile in a crossing pattern of small waves.

At the custom houses we paid a nominal baksheesh and our bags and Beer's were not checked, and showing the card we had been asked to display which characterised us as passengers to go on to Suez. Thus having exhibited the mark of the Biblical beast, we were descended upon by Arabs who fought amongst themselves to carry our bags. So rough was this donnybrook that I thought the portmanteaus might be damaged but they sorted themselves out with a tumultuous shouting of oaths.

These rude comments dealt with their competitor's questionable parentage and we entered into the town by way of a two wheeled carriage pulled by a pair of horses as near to death as I've seen equines before, outside of an abattoir. We first travelled through the Arab quarter of the city. Alexandria is roughly divided into three parts; one part for Arabs or Egyptians, a part for Turks and then a third smaller section for Franks[3]. Those of the first two classes who were wealthy enough to escape the squalor also lived in the Frank's quarter. The streets of Alexandria were muddy and filthy. The shops were open to the assault of wind, dust, and insects. In the Arab quarter houses lay broken, disheveled and mysterious to my eyes. The city's swarming crowds consisted of many Negroes, brown-skinned villains and white scoundrels, copious beggars and cripples of all conditions from the pitiful to the horrible, and the veiled women who seemed to move through this earthly purgatory like un-noticed ghosts. The Egyptian people were ragged and an un-healthy looking yellowish brown; the children as thin as sticks and almost naked, crying, shouting like banshees, running about like a disturbed nest of bees, and troops of feral dogs were all about. The stench here assaulted one. We were used to the sea with the occasional hint of bilge but here it was an overpowering reek; acrid, strong, pervasive. The odour of the east, which at first sickens ones, is then added to the visual disgusts one must see, puts one off of seeing more, slowly begins to be seen as a great show, an entertainment of life; and one either recoils from the east or comes to love it. I was of the latter persuasion although why I was escaped me at the moment of recording this.

The many dogs made it a point to torment the horses' legs but they, near death, ignored their nips and barks and soon brought us up from the shore custom house and quarantine station and into the city where the appearance of the land improved and where we would meet up with others taking the overland passage. Our guide, although dressed in rags he seemed competent, at least enough so to find the building where the Franks lived. Catania kept up a steady stream of observation. He said this was all normal and we were in no danger and that the east was like this. It was but a short ride of about a quarter of a mile to a more tranquil place.

There was a sign in German announcing that we were entering the *Franken Quartier* and that those non-Europeans who were neither servants or who had no business in the quarter should not proceed. Perkins and I wondered aloud how many Egyptians or Turks, let alone Europeans', could read high German written in gothic letters? Catania informed us that this part of Alexandria was called El Manshiya.

We arrived at the Consul's residence where we met Mr Robert Thurbern and his Italian wife, who greeted us as warmly as lost relatives. We were glad to get indoors as we had been under a steady assault by Egyptian larks *{flies}* who seemingly filled the sky. Above them were a wheeling mass of seagulls whose constant cries hurt the ears. We were informed that we would stay that evening with them and start out for Suez the next day. The bachelors were asked to entertain themselves while the families were given quarters. Catania, dressed as he was as an Arab, a wealthy one at that, decided that we must see the sights. There being nothing else one could do but swat away flies, and on which subject Perkins amusingly stated that we could not swot so we might as well swat[4] It took some time to explain this play on words to Catania.

We followed him but not before securing our pistols. The squalor was wretched, for how could a city founded by Alexander the Great on the foundation of the Ancient Egyptians have fallen so low? This is what had become of great Alexandria? In antiquity, it had been considered the most beautiful city in the world. I was sad that my namesake's city had fallen so low.

We made our way first to Pompey's pillar, which is some five and eighty feet high. We read on its side in Greek:

To the most just Emperor, tutelary of Alexandria Diocletian, the invincible, Postumus, the Prefect of Egypt (has erected this monument)

So the pillar was to Diocletian and not to Pompey. We found this interesting as many books make this mistaken identification. It was a lonely but lovely triumphal column made of red stone, perhaps granite from the look of it. I did remember a story about it and hoped that Commander Shortland's[5] steak was as succulent as my Tuscan one had been in Malta.

'Pompey Pillar' showing the ropes erected by the British in 1803. I-V-1

I wondered where the destroyed temple of Serapis might lie, for its location had been lost over time. However, Perkins was not well versed in the fate of ancient Ptolemaic temples so he could offer no clue.

We sighted another obelisk, probably the one called Cleopatra's needle·, and another large obelisk was lying fallen surrounded by the sand, broken masonry, pottery and rubbish, that lay strewn in all directions.

We returned back after we had walked down and viewed our next route, the Mahmoodeeh canal *{Mahmoudiyah is the modern name}*, which leads to the Rosetta arm of the Nile north of Cairo. The canal, whose banks seemed in fair repair having been finished sixteen years before, did not impressed us, nor did the Mareotis Lake which lay beyond it so we decided to return. We soon found that the tireless task of moving one's hands to defeat the hordes of flies that attacked us unceasingly caused us to sweat copiously. Walking in the soft sand amongst all the broken masonry left us tired and discouraged and we were therefore driven hence to retreat. I felt in a way like the Biblical pharaoh and the fourth Mosesian plague he had faced.

Perkins knowing my love of Caesar and my romanticising about the east, quipped at one point about my part in this excursion, "He came, he saw, he was un-impressed and left, and none noticed."

There was so much broken brickwork around, livid squalor, heart breaking misery, sick looking dogs and asses but some trees, at least, were lovely and I took joy in that. We went by an incoming camel train, which added a small amount of dignity to the scene. Not even Shakespeare or Marlowe could have made this setting appealing. One snaring un-lucky dog got within range of Perkins who, in public school, had been quite the player of football and he sent the cur flying with a swift kick. That had been the pack's leader, and the rest quickly ran from us. I could see from the strength of that kick one reason that Chilean might have followed us: for Perkins had dealt him three such blows to quiet his drunken trashing about.

When we arrived, we were assigned a room and faced another challenge: a well-dressed - for Egypt - Turkish official had joined the Consul and was assessing our charges under the authority of the Egyptian Transit Administration. We had to pay an additional 1s 4d for each cwt. *{Hundredweight}* of baggage over the proscribed limits. Having our own mountains of luggage and Beer's, we paid out the required sums but with little concealed ill-humour towards this extra charge which the Consul assured us was legal and required.

Perkins and I were in the same room and that we did not mind for we had plans for the moiety *{a share of something by two}* of our flies. Surprisingly, our room was reasonably clean and had a window with actual class in it, but it was broken. We secured a cloth over it, sealed it down with wax and proceeded on a campaign of extermination. We were as Cossacks against the retreating French in 1812. Hard-hearted and pitiless were we warriors. Over a period of ten minutes we killed every fly in our room. I thought the count might have been nine and thirty but Perkins insisted that the answer was two and forty.

Having made our room livable and finding the mattresses clean and not verminous, we rested, forcing ourselves to explain what we had seen to each other, alternating between Persian and Arabic - what one asked in Persian, the other then answered in Arabic. This we did until supper and tea, dinner never seeming to have arrived. I said supper and tea, however; they were served at the same time. The table was well set and we each had a native fan waver behind us to keep off the flies.

The meal was artless simplicity, for the Consul, his wife and their cook had the worldly good sense to know it was impossible to produce a truly European dining experience here. There was an Egyptian style *pillow {pilau or rice pilaf}* that was spiced with cardamom, which I enjoyed, and they served Arabic style coffee that, by its smell, I decided it must have come from one of Dante's lower tiers. As the pillow had vegetables, presumably a chicken and everything else one might want all in one dish, it was easier to protect one's meal from the ravages of family *Diptera {Latin for fly}*.

We were then delighted by the announcement that we would move that very evening to our boats. Given the un-promising view of Alexandria I cannot say I objected to leaving this fallen beauty as soon as possible.

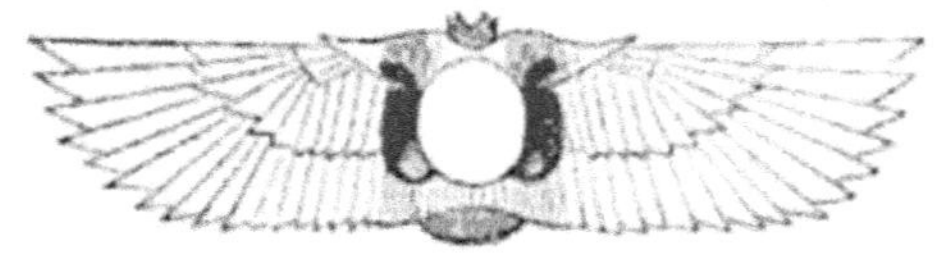

The Mahmoodeeh Canal To Caire (Cairo)

We were to be accompanied that night by the Vice-Consul and the *Cancellier {Chancellor or Consul's clerk}*, a fellow named Charles Sleane who I found amusing as I had grown up with a boy of that same name. I asked him about it and found that the man was a not-quite-a-Mancunian like me but from the south east of the city, from the village of Reddish and yes, he was a 2nd cousin of the person I knew. He had come out to Egypt in 1828, married a Copt *{local Christian}*, learned Arabic and joined the consular service. I asked what had brought him to Egypt at such a young age, for he was in his early twenties. He replied that he had felt the lure of the east and a need to view Holy Jerusalem but that, having travelled around the Holy Land, he had had enough, then fell in love by a happenstance in Damietta (in Egypt's Nile delta) and ended up here. It was good to meet him. We talked at length to try and find a common friend we might both know but we failed except for the previously mentioned relative. Somehow, in having lived in the same area for thirteen years or so, we had never met or had a mutual acquaintance.

The carriages had arrived. They were painted white and, dissimilar to everything else we had seen in Alexandria, in good repair. From a snatch of Arabic between Sleane and Thurbern, I gained the reason for our hasty departure: a hint of murrain *{a disease of animals}* was coming into the town, not so much a threat to the people but to the east some forty thousand cattle had died of it. The Consul feared for his horses so he obviously thought to save his transports while discomforting his guests and charges.

Perkins and Catania grimaced at the news of the reason when I transferred it to them.

There was also the American Consul, a Mr J. Gliddon, who was taking the care to check on his compatriots and it would seem all other Europeans. He was a kind, considerate man, fully versed in the nature of Egypt; a complete Gentleman for a man from that rebellious land.

Led by men with torches, we made our way out of the Frank's quarter and down Ibrahim Street or so a faded wall sign in Arabic declared. We reached a gate of sorts where a ramshackle guard was kept. Our valiant Consul did some diplomacy and we were soon though and on to the canal.

We travelled on to a place called Sharquah where we came to the boats. For once, Catania did not know the specific name for the boat we would be on. The name was provided by Sleane. The boat, or *dhahabiyya*, was some five and sixty feet long and had fine lines for a mere riverine craft. She was built of small pieces of wood instead of long pieces of timber that gave her a patchwork look. Her sides are low, her beam great, her draught necessarily slight and her stern high for distinction.

She was equipped to move in any of four ways, or in case of need one or more at one time. She could be poled or punted, rowed, towed or sailed. She had two masts with lateen sails; a huge fore mast and the other was located where a mizzen would be on a European ship. It looked odd to my eyes, as if the mainmast had been plucked out by some fuming Egyptian God, perhaps to be used as a toothpick after a meal of sacrificed Apis bull. The forward sail was called the trinkeet and her rear the ballakoon. Half of the boat was covered by a rectangular wooden deckhouse. There were four 'cabins' or areas separated from each other by thin timber partitions. Gauze or linen coverings for the outer walls were secured in the manner of a tarpaulin. On the roof is the place the passengers spent their time under a large red striped awning. The *dhahabiyya's* narrow cabins being a place of stowage for the passenger's luggage and sleep only, one would live on the deck. Of great importance were the several goolah jars. Set into wooden frames these earthen jars are porous and cool one's drinking water.

An image of a Dhahabiyya from forty years later but little changed from Driscol's time. I-V-2

Goodbyes and farewells were shouted to us from the bank by the Vice-Consul and returned from the crew and us. Our crew were five Egyptians of nondescript appearance who were poling her away from the bank as fast as possible. The crew, we soon found, were idle lads at most times but good river men when the need was there, otherwise they were thoroughly lazy, vain, quick to offence but generally good-natured, even boisterous. They showed little discipline and little courage and were often falling asleep; to which the remedy was to use a method I had seen on European ships of 'blowing the grampus' *{sluicing a person with water}*, especially on him who skulks or sleeps on his watch or while doing his duties. This dosing was demonstrated to us within the first ten minutes when one of the men went un-accountable.

There was another man who soon introduced himself. He would be our guide or *Cavass*. He was a large man, a bit shorter than myself but as stocky as Perkins with light brown eyes, brown hair, sunburnt face and certainly no Turk or Arab. He was called Sosana *{named after the Spikenard plant}*, a man from Circassia but having a Georgian mother. He had a badge of office that proclaimed his designation and superiority over the boat crews and held a silver-capped cane from which swung three shorter silver chains that ended in small disks which had the same ornament on them as his badge; a French Marshal's baton for Egyptian guides, it would seem. He wore a pointed red cloth hat and robes that could once claimed to have been a type of vermillion.

He would act as our guide and assistant to our boat, and the two others that would soon follow. He also wore a curved knife and I saw that he kept a loaded French style .69 calibres flintlock musket in the 1777 Charleville pattern. The five-foot long weapon also served as a flagstaff; adorned with an un-clean white rag, he waved it in the deepening dark to signal the other boats that our departure had begun.

We met our fellow wanderers, who were: One, a Swiss missionary and his wife on their way to Abyssinia to teach the Lutheran gospel. Two, a newlywed British couple; he, a covenanted Company Clerk (HEIC) having obtained a young cleared-eyed bride was taking her back with him to Ceylon. She was quite beautiful; a fact confirmed when Perkins devoted himself to learning everything about her. They had come down to Egypt by way of Trieste. Three, the last people were two well-educated and academic German speakers; one a Prussian, the other a Württemberger; scholars; one to see and record the ruins of the Nile valley and the other to draw the many ruins. My German was inadequate but they spoke fine French, though no English. The

Swiss couple was of German background but spoke French better than most Frenchmen of my acquaintance.

The Prussian artist (Hans von Klenze) made three-color drawings of his voyage down the Nile with Driscol. This one he labelled, 'Sosana, Abiad and my man Ali'. I-V-3

One of the crew, a lean and willowy fellow with a cleft palate, soon had tea brewed up for all. I dumped mine in the canal, apologising to *Iteru {the ancient Egyptian name for the Nile}* for doing so.

We waited some time for the other two boats to get behind us and, having reached a speed of a knot or two, the sails were brought into play and the cold wind from the north that had brought us into Alexandria with such dispatch in the morning took us away in the evening. We sailed along, the crew active with their poles to keep us off the bank when it began to rain. The canal was very shallow in parts and the crew could use poles to push us if necessary. This was un-expected, as it rarely rained. I had packed away all of my instruments but I presumed the temperature to be in the low 60's°. The rain began slowly and soon was coming down in a torrent. Perkins remarked that THIS was like the monsoon. So strong was the rain and the loss of visibility, that Sosana soon came to us to tell us we would moor for the time being in the middle of the canal until it stopped. He gathered us all in the deckhouse, having taken down the thin partitions, and it would seem he had memorised a speech, which he gave in clear French. He told of the twenty thousand fellahin, the poor Nile Delta peasants who had died in digging this 'ditch', as he called it, under the lash of the hated Turk, Hagee Osman. It had been built along the path of another older canal which had been built perhaps in the time of the Pharaoh's and repaired and rebuilt by the Greeks, Romans and most lately the Venetians. He explained our route would be exactly one hundred and sixty-six and a quarter English miles and depending on the wind we would soon arrive in Boolak, the port of Cairo - sooner than we expected - a curious turn of phrase.

There being nothing else to do, I went to sleep, and making sure that my French pistol was near at hand. I saw, too that Perkins had his Colt available, as did Catania, who had consented finally to arming himself. He was dressed well in the Arab fashion and he had also dyed his hair and beard a shining black but, not knowing the meaning and the status of types of dress amongst the locals, I could not tell if his clothes identified him as a Jew, but I think not.

Wednesday 9 November

I awoke with a start as something was lying astride my leg. A chill ran through me as I thought it might be a snake. So slowly, very slowly and with an excess of caution, I rose my head to find myself looking into the face of small kitten who had nestled down next to me and the boat blanket I had covered myself with. Where she had come from I did not know, for canal swimming cats are rare even in Egypt where once cats, it was said, were worshipped as they could do magical things.

I have always wondered why cats, a water hating breed loved fish. They certainly cannot catch them, what did cats do in the wild, sit by a stream waiting for a depressed fish to jump out and commit suicide?

There was at this time a piercing woman's screech. Perkins and I had been in process of dressing and we emerged from our cabin, armed and un-kempt. We soon found we were not under attack but the Swiss couple was enraged. It would seem that the insatiable curiosity of the crewman like many an Asiatic in the presence of a European woman arouses a great desire to see the un-attainable. To glimpse this beauty, a keyhole is often the way to do so, but where none exists view holes are driven through the wood in some quiet corner. Such was the case here and one sullen crewman had been found doing just that, though he had not driven a hole but instead removed a vice-nail *{screw}* from the wood work.

Sosana was suitably enraged and to deal with this he smashed the man across the face, which made the man stumble, blood flow flowing from his nose, and Sosana then kicked him twice; the second time propelling him into the water. I thought for a moment that he might drown but like the rat he was, he recovered and began to swim to the embankment fifty feet off. Seeing this, Sosana presented his French musket and asked the woman if he wished the man dead, wounded or left to swim?

Her Christian forgiveness came to the fore and the man reached the bank and without looking back, ran up and over it. His worldly property, a small raggedy bag, our captain threw into the canal and Sosana made it a point to distribute his pay to the other crew, berating them in Arabic at a rate I could not comprehend, for they must now work somewhat harder at their tasks. Their first task was to drive a copper spike into the offending hole and bend back the point flush with the planking.

I found after this excitement that the rain had stopped and the boats were moving slowly forward, it being just after dawn and the wind having died down somewhat. I found Sosana, musket in hand, keeping an eye out. Behind us, in the darkness, I could dimly make out the other two boats. I greeted our guide in French, which he returned with the slightest of bows and a smile. He said to my un-asked question that the wind would soon rise again and that we should be in Caire (as he called Cairo in the French) in three or four days.

The canal moved between elevated ridges of sand thrown up in its construction. Vegetation had taken over some of the banks while others were still bare. Rising above that ridge was the mound of an ancient town. We had moored that evening near the ruins of Sehedia, named so by Strabo. We could see regular sixteen-foot walls, of which there were some fifteen in parallel. Our guide said that the ancients had kept boats here and that these were galleries in which they were contained. While the left bank often showed ruins, the right condemned to hold only poor villages built with Nile mud. These were desperately poor villages filled with the hovels of the fellah; grey boxes of dried mud, roofed with dried palm fronds and other vegetation. The hovels grouped by disorder without a discernible pattern. Many of the villages were surrounded by dovecotes *{pigeon-houses}*, often in better repair than the fleapits their masters lived in. For the pigeon is a much-respected visitor to a wealthier Egyptians plate. In some places, these pigeon houses are so many that they make up what seems are separate villages. They are often three or four times higher than the fellah's own house and resemble at a distance giant beehives. Midst them, women in long faded blue robes carrying ancient looking amphorae on their heads would come to the canal to gather water.

We had a sparse breakfast consisting of olives, cheese, cucumbers and somewhat stale flat breads. Sosana spoke of a break in the canal which we had passed in the night where the British, wishing to connect the lake of Mareotis to the sea, had done so, allowed us {British} to bring boats into that fresh water lake and to discomfort the French during the siege of Alexandria some five and thirty years ago.

As Sosana predicted, as the sun rose so did the wind and we were soon moving along at some speed. The banks of the canal were very green, lush with plants that I did not recognise and dotted everywhere with small villages. The Canal was a trip of some monotony for the ridges alongside the canal prevented us from seeing the countryside with any ease. The scent of the canal was one of foliage, dust, and flowers, especially the red lotus, which was rare but occasionally seen. The stench of manure would tell us when we were near a village. Then we would move further down the canal to catch another scent, this time of wood smoke. These scents would mix but more often we moved from one to another then the patterns repeated in endless variety, flowers, foliage, manure, smoke. Papyrus reeds were becoming common along the banks of the canal for it was now becoming another branch of the Nile, then it would be/become a true canal, despite Sosana's claim that there was actually a lock where the canal entered the branch of the Nile at Afteh.

In the late afternoon, Sosana said that due to our hasty departure last night, he had not been able to provision the boats as well as he liked, as I had already heard. Our fare had been rather meager so he pulled into a small town called Kairoon which was devoted to glass manufacturing to purchase fresh provisions and gain wood for our fires.

Sosana and the crew in discussion with villagers for needed supplies. Sosana is standing with his musket and the three other crew are with their backs to the viewer. I-V-4

I declined Perkins suggestion to wander about the village. I sat instead with Catania and discussed his life. He seemed a very happy man. As of yet, he had not told us why he was compelled to come to Cairo. He declined again, saying only that he had business in Cairo and a matter of some concern that he would inform us of later once he had the full details of it.

I made an experiment using a glass jar of two quarts capacity I drew up some of the water of the canal and examined it. In the sunlight it had a yellowish tint. This seems to match in some regards the colours of the soil in some parts of the canal. I left it to settle as I wished to see how much sediment it contained.

The Canal widened here and as we sat moored to the bank, we were passed by several barge boats on their way to Alexandria carrying foodstuffs, some of which Sosana bargained for, obtaining several sacks of some item. Perkins used this word 'sack' that I had not heard before. He said it was not an un-common one among those he had grown up with.

Provisioned and well stocked with live chickens, a goat and one sheep, plus several 'sacks' of vegetables, one of grain and a pottery urn full of freshly pressed olive oil, we made our way back into the middle of the canal and proceeded along as the cook made more detestable tea and ended the lives of several chickens. The Swiss woman found this distressing, I had to presume she had led a very sheltered life or had grown up in town, or had wealthy parents. I wondered how she might do in the wilds of Abyssinia. However, she was so attractive and charming, I forgave her, her mild weakness. Perkins was no longer enamoured of her, announcing her as a nineteen year old with the wit and mind of one of nine, and so she was; for I had spoken with her to gain some idea about what Abyssinia might be like but she knew nothing about where she was going. I did, but feel it un-wise to tell her of the savagery she approached.

The canal was lined with trees in parts with both the Turkish and Arabian (Dog) sycamores and many mulberries, with lotus trees; also common was the mimosa, the tamarisk and accia. The banks of the canal were rich too in water fowl, grey herons, shovelers, comorans, ergets, gulls, whiskered terns, and, of course, ibeses. To add to this were flights of golden orioles, sunbirds and flamingos and a number of other birds I did not know the name of.

The chickens had not died in vain for Sosana soon announced a special first meal for his guests: *Sherkasiya {Circassian chicken}.* This I found both tasteful and interesting as it was the chicken cut in half and boiled in water with walnuts, almonds, hazelnuts which I normally dislike but which were good in this stew. It had plentiful amounts of Hungarian paprika, which I had heard of before salt, onions, and a handful of butter - all of which, after being, cooked was made into a rich sauce that covered a large mound of rice. There were vegetables but I did not like the look of them. The chickens were not only appreciated but I observed that the flies, not as numerous as in Alexandria but still prevalent, would not land on the chicken. Sosana said that was because of what he called Cayenne pepper, which had been mixed with the paprika, which I was not aware of. He could not, however, explain what it was or how it differed from regular pepper. After some discussion, I found that Cayenne pepper was another name for Guinea pepper. The meal was spicy and well taken.

I found my new cat friend would eat it also. She delighted in the chicken skin particularly. Sosana had no idea where the cat had come from and he seemed one of those dark souls that does not care for the queen of small beasts for he offered to cast it into the canal should anyone find it objectionable, however, the Swiss Lady and I came to her defence.

After dinner I read as best I could but I would often stop to watch our progress down the canal. Perkins and I both said at the same time that inland water travel by boat was far superior to ocean travel. However, I only partially believed that, for the surge of the sea, the movement of the boat and the salty smell I did truly love but this was not a bad way to travel either. I asked Perkins in Persian whether we could do this in our expedition to Tartary. He said that, yes, there was a notable river, the Oxus. I then remembered it too from classical sources. He thought that was good idea and we would have to see if that mode of travel would be possible at some point.

The lanky Egyptian cook, who had done marvelous things with chicken equipped only with his rudimentary gear, was also the master of the Egyptian musical instrument, the sistroid angle *{tambourine}.* In addition, he was a dancer of the Saraband; a boat dance of the Moors of Africa. I found he had once been a seaman but had taken to the canal boats when he had married to see his family more often.

Catania, Perkins and I gave lessons in Arabic to our Prussian, Württemberg and Swiss friends, our British couple keeping out of sight most of the time - so are the priorities of newlyweds, or so I was told by Perkins. I could imagine such a trip with Marguerite, or Millicent or especially Patricia for her red hair still stirred in my memories.

The Mahmoodeeh canal and the villages that flanked it. I-V-5

We Enter The Nile

Thursday 10 November

Another pleasant day for we are now in a branch of the Nile itself, the Rosetta, the *Bolbitine* of the ancients. We had passed the town of Afteh and the locks in the night, and Sosana assured us that we had missed nothing for the inhabitants of that place were said to be *ignorami {ignoramuses}* who had nothing but dust to eat and daughters who made even a dog with two back ends look alluring. We had also passed by the town of Fooah, which we were told has so many *mosks* {mosques} because of a labyrinthine of quarrels between the leading families, each building its own house of worship to avoid having to pray with its centuries old enemies. We had also gone by the ancient city of Metelis, a place where the pervasive red cap called the tarbooshes *{tarbushes}* were made.

He also mentioned that we had gone past the shrine of *Shekh {sheik}* Ibrahim Dessoke of Tanta, a man of some importance in the religious annals of Mussulman Egypt. Catania had not heard of him so his un-importance to the greater world was underlined.

My experiment had been partially successful: the glass jar had at its bottom a thin layer of sediment but the water was not completely clear. I found it was a $\frac{1}{4}$ (inch) of sediments on the bottom when I measured it. However, I could not see any excess of growths in it.

I spent the day taking in the many ruins. It was sad that we could not stop. Perkins, not feeling his chipper self, had spent the day with his arms across his head. Catania and I got more into Arabic phrases and, in particular, amusing ones. I practiced a dozen of them until the accent was correct and, much to my delight, the crew understood and laughed at them. I feel more of the Orientalist than before. My first humourous phrase being:

They said to the camel-bird (ostrich) "carry a load". It said, "I cannot, for I am a bird." They said, "then fly." It answered, "I cannot, for I am a camel."

I spoke at length with the Germans, despite my weakness in Deutsch. I found Herr Schiffer very interesting as he and I shared an interest in *archaeologia {Latin for what would become known as Archaeology}.* We discussed the ramifications of the famed Rosetta Stone and the controversy with its translation.

I received an invitation to become an antiquarian. He was envious of my knowledge of Arabic and ability to speak with the crew; however, I pointed out that I was a rank amateur and he was associated with the famous Tübingen University. Schiffer noted my constant writing into my journal and wrote in it his address in the Kingdom of Württemberg. He also had a request: once I was tired of the Indian east, to come to the Middle East and explore the ancient civilizations. I must say I was inspired.

Manfred Schiffer, Keplerstrasse, Friedhof Haus, Tubingen, Kingdom of Wurttemberg

We shook hands on it. I call him a scholar but he was eight and twenty at that time. The other man, the Prussian, I did not see to eye on. Finding I was part Danish, he seemed to want to provoke an argument with me over the status of Duchies of Schleswig and Holstein[7]. My declaration that I was an Englishman cut no mustard with him as it seemed he wanted me to surrender these Duchies to him personally. I broke off the discussion. Schiffer later apologised for his colleague who was a man who had been refused entry into the Prussian army due to the 'irregularity' of his parentage and was full of more arrogance than usual for a Prussian or, as he said, he was "too proud."

[Editor's note: Driscol never mentioned the Prussian by name probably for the reason above. He was not a noted artist as the quality of his images in this chapter show. He was the younger brother of the much more famous Leo von Klenze a German architect of renown]

We had to pass the mound that was, I believe, the legendary city of Sais but Sosana would not consider stopping. He was a man with a mission: to delivery us to the port of Cairo as soon as he could. He would do this at any cost. He would have been a good man to lead an assault on the breech of an enemy city, for he would take that city or die trying.

Perkins has recovered somewhat in the evening, suggesting I give our Prussian friend the 'Chilean' solution, in regards to the conceited Prussian. I had to agree that I had considered it as a possibility. He also cruelly pointed out a number of turtles and small land tortoises threatening to land and bring one back for supper.

[Editor's note: The above is the best I could do with the comments Driscol wrote. As to what they meant is harder to understand; it might be that the 'Chilean solution' is to either kick them or shoot them, as had been the fate of the Chilean naval officer. In the other sentence Perkins seems to have been teasing Driscol about his dislike of turtles as a dish for dining]

Animals were rarer but we did see some mongoose with their young and most striking was the sighting of a five-foot long *amelanistic {albino}* Nile Monitor of the family *Varanidae* who was eating a large striped mullet as we passed. The Egyptians thought the white lizard was a bad omen. We saw also a hawk of some type take a water bird nearly the same dimensions as him; he struck it and it fell crippled into a large date palm tree along the edge of the canal, the rest of struggle being lost to our sight.

The evening meal was the best yet and for me the best part was I was able to sit next to the Swiss woman who I found smelled faintly of roses. I did my best to keep up with her idle comments.

We were served up the young *chevon {kid, goat}* who was cooked up *en ragout* with many vegetables, eatable this time, with buttered rice and freshly made flat breads.

Catania amazed us in speaking excellent German to the Germans about us. The British couple sat quietly. It was only later I determined that the British couple could neither speak French and certainly not German, so for him and her they were in the midst of foreign speaking foreigners.

The Swiss women pointed to shore at one point at the large beasts there whose glossy black-gray skin made them to her hideous, saying that they were such ugly cows. Considering the superb quality of (Confederation of) Helvetian *{Switzerland}* cattle, which I had seen, I could understand her point. However, Catania explained that they were not cows but buffalo, or in Arabic the *Ghamousah {Gamoosa}*. The myth is told that after Allah made the useful cow, the devil came to have a look, burst out laughing, and declared that he could do better even with his eyes shut. God took him at his word. The devil set to work and produced the Ghamousah; useful and flavoursome but ugly.

Later, Sosana came to the men one at time to say that this section of the Rosetta flowed through the Libyan Desert and that sometimes, rarely, the Beedoowin *{Bedouin}* came down to the canal to fire upon or assault the boat traffic and that we should be on guard. We secured our firearms and other weapons, as did the crew, and remained watchful, for beyond the canal's levee we could see low sand dunes shimmering in the distance. No one was seen; neither Bedouin raider nor peasant, except an Egyptian woman driving her flock of goats to drink at the canal's edge. Our false alarm soon came to naught when darkness overtook us. Sosana said these Bedouin were a lazy lot and never attacked at night and in the Arab fashion considered the day ended and a new one begun and it was now Friday for them, a holier day than most, for this nomadic Arab ends the day at sunset and not as we do at midnight.

Friday 11 November

There had been during the night a strong wind from the north northeast and our sails are full.

I was awakened by the call to prayer from a mosque we were coasting by at the moment. It was just before dawn so it was the predawn *Fajr* devotion. Sosana is up as always, for it is the holier of the weekdays for the Muhammadan; as our Sunday is to us. Our missionary couple is quite observant, as our crew had not prayed before in the Muhammadan fashion before this morning. Sosana said we were near Nigeeleh, which I could not associate with anything written by Herodotus or Strabo.

Perkins had recovered. This was the third time I had seen him so stricken by a pain he called 'the spear of fire' that he said at times penetrated his head for reasons he could not understand but as he aged the pain has becoming less and the attacks fewer.

[Editor's note: the next page is smudged and unreadable, as the page seemed to have been drawn on by a child with a crayon. I suspect he was explaining Perkins symptoms, which sound like what we call today a migraine]

We were proceeding along when Sosana attempted to take a short cut by going inshore of a sand bank on the west side of the Rosetta Nile. We ran aground gently, for these boats, while flat bottomed, sit down two or three feet and it was with a great deal of exertion that we did get her off after an hour or so. The crew swam to the nearby bank, assembled a small group of locals, paid them a pittance, a single coin for them all, and by their combined efforts coupled with the crew of the other two boats. We were soon freed and Perkins and I threw the fellahin a number of our smallest copper coins that made them dance in delight, the children scrambling to find them amidst the sand and reeds. We had to go with the current down a mile or so then we could continue our voyage.

The Rosetta Nile in the autumn light was a truly magnificent sight. We sailed on making some seven knots I would have wager on, the wind overcoming the current of the river by a great margin.

It was a pleasant day on the river. I played some chess with the good Wurttemberger, winning two to one loss. Catania watched the game with interest. He had never played and seemed resistant to learning to do so. Perkins and I doing Arabic lessons to help our German friend to learn some required statements.

Saturday 12 November

It was Perkins who first sighted the pyramids rising up to our south east. They seemed so close but I knew them to be far. They appeared ethereal, vague and airy like, seeming to float beyond the palms to our front along the Nile while we could see them rising up behind. I estimated we were some five and twenty miles from them and Perkins thought it even more distant. Over this, we disagreed and he asked why I was so certain on my estimate. I told him that, as someone self-schooled in measure and use of artillery, I could estimate ranges easily. He protested that I was a light infantryman. To which I replied that I was by necessity but I had trained myself in the arts of artillery, range estimation being one of its qualifications and I hinted that I had a magical ability. To which he, of course, asked about. I said that I had been gifted with a calibrated eye-ball. He thought my statement presumptuous but witty.

We passed into the Nile proper at what Sosana called the cowbelly where the great Nile splits into two to embrace the delta. Sosana went into pains to point out that the river was very high. Usually it reached its peak in late October but it had not started to recede yet. This had given rise to fears for the dykes that weaken over time if kept wet for too long. As we entered the river, the full scale of its current acted against us, slowing us greatly.

[Editor's note: For the first time, the journal has in it an 'absent-minded drawing'; for that is what Driscol called it. He had drawn a number of three dimensional triangles (i.e.; pyramids); two sides facing outwards with faces drawn on them, sometimes with captions. We would call it doodling but that word was not known to Driscol. Doodling came to mean what we consider it now just in the 1930's before that it was a term to denote simpletons or the actions of such. See Appendix I-IV for a sample of his 'doodling']

I had prepared for this by having some fishing tackle out and was soon trolling the waters in fulfillment of my childhood objective to fish these historic waters. I hoped that in the future I would be the man to search out and answer the great question.

[Editor's note: Driscol is probably referring to the question of the source of the Nile that was not resolved until many decades later]

We were nearing what Sosana announced is the harbour of Cairo. I was trolling, my bait, a lure made of chicken feathers, was strongly taken, and the fish put up a sturdy fight before I secured him. It proved to be a *Lates Niloticus;* a Nile Perch. The pharaohs themselves had once eaten this fish. I had only seen line drawings of one before but in person, they were silvery with a blue hue and a dark brooding eye ringed in yellow. It was a small one, just 18 or so inches, but I was quite proud of it. I presented it to Sosana who was happy to see his future lunch but I felt we would make port before that happened, however; happily, I was quite wrong. The boat soon found it could not make way as the wind had shifted un-expectedly to the south and lost it strength too, so it and the following two boats made their way to the west bank and anchored to wait for a friendlier wind and not the one that blew straight into our faces. Sosana said that the river current was far to strong to row against in this part of the Nile, the current being some 3 to 4 knots here *{5 miles per hour}*.

So anchored, we had our late breakfast made forthwith and I received a large portion of my fish. I was quite happy with this to have completed a childhood dream. It would seem the ancient Egyptian Gods must have smiled on us for no sooner had our luncheon been consumed - bread, cheese, olives, cucumber and my bit of fish - then the wind came back up with a vengeance and from the right quarter but only for a moment and then died again.

Frustrated in his cruising designs, Sosana decided to entertain us, for he was good at that. He made mention of a palace we could see near Boolak *{Bulaq}*, he pointed it out to us on the western bank of the Nile. It was once the habitation of Ismail Pasha, who it was said was a son by a concubine of the ruler Mohammed Ali. His gave him a task and dispatched him to the lands of the southern Sudan where he met with the Negro kings from whom he ordered a levy of men be made for his father's army. This had been a custom for many centuries but this harem-raised man knew not of the world and its ways. Instead of a months' time to raise the men, he gave the Ethiopian king but three days. When this chief, by the name of Melek Nimer, requested a longer period in accordance with tradition, Ismail insulted him in front of his men and struck him a blow on the face.

The wily Nimer dissembled his feelings and asked forgiveness for his slight. He invited the Pasha's son to pass the night on shore for he come to the meeting by boat. A barbaric entertainment was provided, laden with spirituous drinks. As the Pasha and his men lay insensible in their tents, a great supply of reeds and brush were piled up around them and they were set alight. Surrounded by flames, those few who burst through this circle of blazing fire were speared and thrown back into the bonfires.

The zephyrs seemed to have listened to the frightful story for the winds became strong again and providentially from the east. We made our way towards the port. We scurried with some speed across the great river and soon pulled ashore on the harbour beach of Cairo.

Bulaq was formerly an island in the Nile but the channel filled now with therefuse and night soil of the city's inhabitants or so we determined by the distinct smell surrounding the place.

Cairo is the only city along the Nile which lies on the west bank of the great river. That shows it is a city formed by it Asiatic conquerors, for no Egyptian would build a city there[8].

The river port of Cairo, Bulaq. I-V-6

We tipped Sosana well, as we did too the cook for he was a true prodigy. I was also happy to see that the Swiss woman had made up a web bag and imprisoned my Egyptian cat friend. It would seem he would be taking a journey to Abyssinia. I hoped they did not eat cats there.

We were glad to be on land again as the boat, although comfortable, had been too small for me to walk or pace. We had been forced by the size to just lounge about. I think best when I can pace.

Catania remarked that it was un-fortunate we had come to the Cairo at this time for Ramadan was but a month away and the festivities were a sight to see.

[Editor's note: Driscol may have written about the Canal trip while in Cairo as some of the places, times and locations don't match up well with the historic route, he may have jumbled up the sequence of when he was where and the timings]

The Qalat Salah ad-Din Salah (Saladin's citadel) of Cairo located on the Mokattam hills within Cairo. This image is of the site after Driscol visited for when he was there the Mosque of Muhammad Ali shown atop the hill and center left was not yet completed. I-V-7

Cairo; The Victorious Capital

The name of Cairo came from the Arabic term for Mars that, like in many cultures, is deemed a planet of war, or in Arabic "El-Kaher" or 'conqueror', hence the term Mars-el-Kahirah (The Victorious Capital), which in time became just El-Kahirah and from that the more common western pronunciation of 'Cairo'.

Patrick Campbell met us at the docks, a Lieutenant Colonel in the Royal Artillery, the Consul-General and his Majesty's agent in 'KY ROIE' as he pronounced it, and his acting vice-consul Mark Piozin who was an intelligent man who seemed to speak the language of everyone aboard the boat.

He came with tidings which he considered bad but which Perkins and I thought good and this was that the Consulate and associated housing was full but that we would be quartered with our compatriots who resided in the city. The next tiding was supposed to be bad news also but, again, Perkins and I favoured it. There had been no word from Suez as to the arrival of the steamer from Bombay. Additionally, the post packet had not arrived from England by Trieste, Marseille or England; a requirement that must be met for the passengers to be transported along the 'line' to Suez, for both passengers and mail must be sent at the same time. We were obligated to wait in Cairo - a fate we both wished to have. His good news, however, we treated as bad - terribly bad. This was that we would be obligated to check with the consulate every day once in the morning and in the evening.

Donkeys were provided to take us to the Consulate. The baggage was loaded on carts and guarded by Poizin and a group of fearsome looking Janissaries who accompanied him. We took to challenge the multitudes of Cairo. "Cairo;" as that was the way Poizin said it should be pronounced in English and not in the French manner of "Caire" which I had been using previously.

We arrived and received our orders along with an old Turkish dragoman designated to take some others and us to our quarters, which in our case were to be with a retired British Missionary couple. After we left the good Consul-General, our cart and a solitary Janissary following closely, we plunged again into the throngs of Cairo. We made our way for some time when Perkins stopped our guide to discuss some matter while I took in the street life of Cairo.

A handsome Turk in red tarbooshe and the darkest black beard went by, followed by a turbaned Arab clothed in an un-soiled blue striped robe, then a fine featured Greek or Cypriote carrying a heavy load on his back, followed by a wild-eyed Bedu from the desert in dirty rags but openly carrying a spotlessly clean and cocked flintlock musket. A swarthy city Arab who was clutching some fruit like it were gold, ebony skinned wooly-headed fellows carrying bails of cloth that was twice the bulk of himself being led somewhere by a small Egyptian boy going somewhere in the maize of small and twisted streets of the city. All of these people were walking about incommoded by the swarms of flies that testily attacked all and sundry. In Cairo men do the part of women's work. One sees them doing laundry, fetching water and shopping for food this was happening all around us as we travelled through the city. I was enjoying and trying to listen to the babble of voices in the street when Perkins tugged my sleeve to regain my presence. He said he had made other arraignments. As I cared not, I neither commented nor reacted but thought that a retired missionary couple would be as lacking in entertainment value as dead monkeys in a crockery shop. We headed off again and after some time making our way through the crowded streets through narrow lanes and alleyways of immeasurable irregularity and filthiness arrived somewhere that our guide seemed quite satisfied to have found, from there after a brief stop we plunged again into the teaming streets. As we went along, a few of our fellow travellers being deposited in a hole here, at a gate there, or sent bewildered into a larger building with hastily spoken instructions. We finally came to a side street, turned and the dragoman directed us to the entrance of the Hotel du Nil. At first, it seemed to have a well-deserved name, for no one was around. The man who finally greeted us, a bird like half-Savosian *{Duchy of Savoy}* and half-Bavarian by the name of Enrico Friedmann had recently established it. Perkins spoke to him as I arranged the movement of the baggage. I noticed that on the walls were framed lithographs from Le Charivari *{a French illustrated newspaper of the time}* and this sight of civilization buoyed my spirits greatly.

It was not a hotel in the true sense but more a large Arab house with striped stonework. Slatted wood baloneys adorned the upper floors and it had a traditional garden overgrown with orange, palm and lemon trees. We were directed to the back of the edifice and there stood a wall which was some nine feet tall that separated it from the Hotel proper. In it was a gate of iron covered in blue tiles and looking to weigh a good ton, and substantial enough to stop a 12 pounder shot but it opened with a fingers touch from the smiling guide. He arranged for our baggage to be deposited in a small garden where a fountain trickled and three fruit trees and a palm bloomed along with many flowers and several old amphorae. Several beautiful birds were in bamboo cages spread within this garden. On one side was a large bougainvillea that clung to the north wall and seemed to be trying to encompass the entire house.

An old Negro with a flat-countenance and a flabby, un-healthy appearance came. He salaamed and greeted us in French that greeting we returned in Arabic, to which he returned to us an even larger smile than before. Perkins said he had arranged for two rooms and he hoped I would not mind lodging by myself. I did not, of course, by Jove.

As I went to my room up a flight of stairs made of limestone there showed here and there what I recognised as chiseled Egyptian hieroglyphics. I marked this as interesting because this building was obviously built of ancient Egyptian masonry and I wondered what great things these stones had seen. I thought that they would be thoroughly un-impressed with just two junior British officers.

I was soon comfortable in a middling room with three windows high up on the wall barricaded with thick wooden bars, and a rope bed with a clean and comfortable looking green matelas *{French style mattress}*.

Perkins appeared and said that he would prefer to rest a bit and that we should have a dinner here then walk about fabled Cairo. This sounded acceptable and loving my solitude for small boats are full of annoying people I relished being anonymously alone for a while.

I then thought of Millicent, secured a book to read and was soon happy, but I also reflected on what the actual situation was here in these lodgings and what Perkins had REALLY arranged.

The servant found me at the appropriate hour sometime after the call to noon prayer.

He led me to a verandah where Perkins sat with an un-veiled woman of mid-thirties age, black hair and pleasant features. She introduced herself as Madame Maysoon in fair French and she was the owner of this house. I greeted her in French and Arabic. She was the daughter of a long

line of Coptic descendants said to have come from the line of Greek hetaerae *{courtesans}*. Her father had been a French officer with Napoleon's invasion of Egypt. He un-fortunately died at the siege of Acre of an honourable wound. I however did not believe a word of it. She had some sort of association with the Hotel du Nil which was sketchy.

Perkins' courtesan Maysoon, Probably drawn by Perkins himself for the image was found in Driscol Journal. I-V-8

Despite my reservations I found her enchanting - she being the first courtesan I had met but I must say I found myself somewhat un-comfortable in her presence. The meal was purely Egyptian, except for the wine which was a Medoc from France.

We had fool mudammas or as Perkins later said of it, "a foul breakfast", served covered with chopped boiled eggs and olive oil, fried cheese, chickpeas, lentils and a number of other well-spiced vegetable dishes. The only flesh consisted of pieces of cold chicken doused in a sauce of wine and lemon peel.

Nevertheless, I did my best to remain sociable and hungry, but my eagerness to see Cairo made me want to leap up, aided by my feeling of awkwardness in this situation and to scarper *{run away}* from that veranda and wander about in ancient Cairo.

Perkins soon finished and we were off. I decided to play the silent hero, and not to act like I had heard men do in such situations as explained to me in the officer's messes of the 52nd, 14th, 81st and the Oriental club where one makes a scene for being placed in a 'compromising situation'. Instead, I decided it was best to present a false bravado and make statements showing one's cavalier attitude to despoilment in the type of place I now lodged however, this was the east where such things were more acceptable and there was certainly no one going to wag their finger at me.

We had with us a sketch map of Cairo made by Catania that showed the principle sights. He had gone to live in the Jewish quarter and we had agreed to meet that night at the Consulate at our designated eight in the evening bed check.

Cairo has an irregularly shape, with it being spread some two miles along the river. The population is perhaps two hundred and fifty thousand souls, of whom more than half are followers of the Prophet. Sixty-five thousand are said to be Copts, the ancient Christian population said also to be of the blood line of the Pharaoh's themselves, some six thousand Jews, perhaps seven thousand Europeans (to include Greeks), three thousand Armenians and held to contain a mix of some five thousand Catholics of all nationalities. There were also some twenty thousand slaves, mainly female. The others were the remnants of the Mamluks. Not to mention the other actors in this vast eastern stage; some of the notable performers were the Negro eunuchs, Abyssinians and other wild men from the region of the Soudan. Where we lived was buried in the alleyways of the medieval city while the Consulate was located within the central area of the European quarter, or as Catania called it "Frankenstan," or more properly the Hart el Frang; near the al-Azbakiyya gardens where the booksellers gathered.

We came across there a Frenchman, a Monsieur Laurentine, who sold books and newspapers and we obtained an English paper - the Times, of course - that was only five and a half weeks old. One interesting item in it was an article from South America: the Piratini Republic had declared its independence from the Portuguese so there was a new de facto state that had come into existence on September 11th of the year. The paper stated it was in the area formerly known as the state of Rio Grande do Sul, once in the Portuguese Empire's province of Brazil. We favoured the news that there was a new country and we both thought if they would need a British officer to be the general of their armies[9].

As we toured Medieval Cairo, I saw the truth in what others had written. No race has been given such a gift at the skill of masonry as the ancient Egyptians, and coupled with a rage to build great things the Egyptians were bested by none at this. However, their being conquered by the Arab has twisted that noble ability and blended it with the Arab's modest interest in building and un-fortunately with their peculiar lack of concern in a building or construction once built. The Arab is magnificent in his indifference to maintaining his great works. While the Egyptian built stone work that has lasted ages, the Arab has no interest in the solidity of his work. Their constructions are raised quickly, in a hurry, using whatever method affords the finest look in disregard for reliability and without a concern for their future use. Often of lovely design, they soon come to ruin.

Near us was the Mosque of Amr ibn al-As, the oldest mosque in older Cairo. Catania had strictly instructed us on the protocol of such a visit and we were repeating his words to ourselves of the steps in Arabic that we should take as we made our way there. We arrived, removed our shoes and asked the first Muhammadan we saw if we might enter. He was a good choice as he was a wealthy merchant and was quite pleased by our speaking Arabic. He even acted as if he could fully understand us. He took us on a circuit of the sights within this great building. His name was Ansar. He was quite happy with what he called 'his mosque' as it had been enlarged and rebuilt a generation ago. He said that it had been the first Mosque in Africa and had originally been built as a twin to the original mosque in Mekkah *{Mecca}*.

He indicated two pillars which were close together and legend has it that a man who has never told a lie can pass between them, for they will open for him and close behind. The fate of the liars who try this is to crushed - slowly. He showed us too the *Qibla {direction to Mecca}* and other areas of interest and in particular the stone column that the Caliph Omar had whipped out of the holy city of Mekkah ordering it to walk to Cairo, which it did and where one can still see the marks of his whip on the stone. Lastly we were shown a well that he insisted was connected to the blessed well of Zamzam in the same Arabian holy city. He had grown more and more excited as he showed us these things and asked several times if we wished to become monotheist's. We declined his fine offer and with many words of gratitude, we were able to make our exit. So quickly did we move that some forty paces later Perkins had to stop for he found he had put his boots on the wrong feet.

Some have alluded to Cairo being the pearl clasp that that holds together the fan of land that is the delta. This might be true but it was a somewhat shoddy pearl, its exotic appeal notwithstanding. The locals and Catania called the city *Masr*, 'mother of the world'; set in the land called by the Egyptians *Misr*. One can disparage Cairo, as I have at times, but it does have its many charms. We were walking, somewhat lost, when we came to a scene that I wished I had had the skill to paint. We were in one of the larger open avenues, some fifteen feet wide at the end of which stood a Mosque's dome, with spiraling minarets, to each side, the street was flanked by two-storey houses with the upper stories projecting over the street and protruding from it were web like wooden structures.

Mashrabiya in Cairo. I-V-9

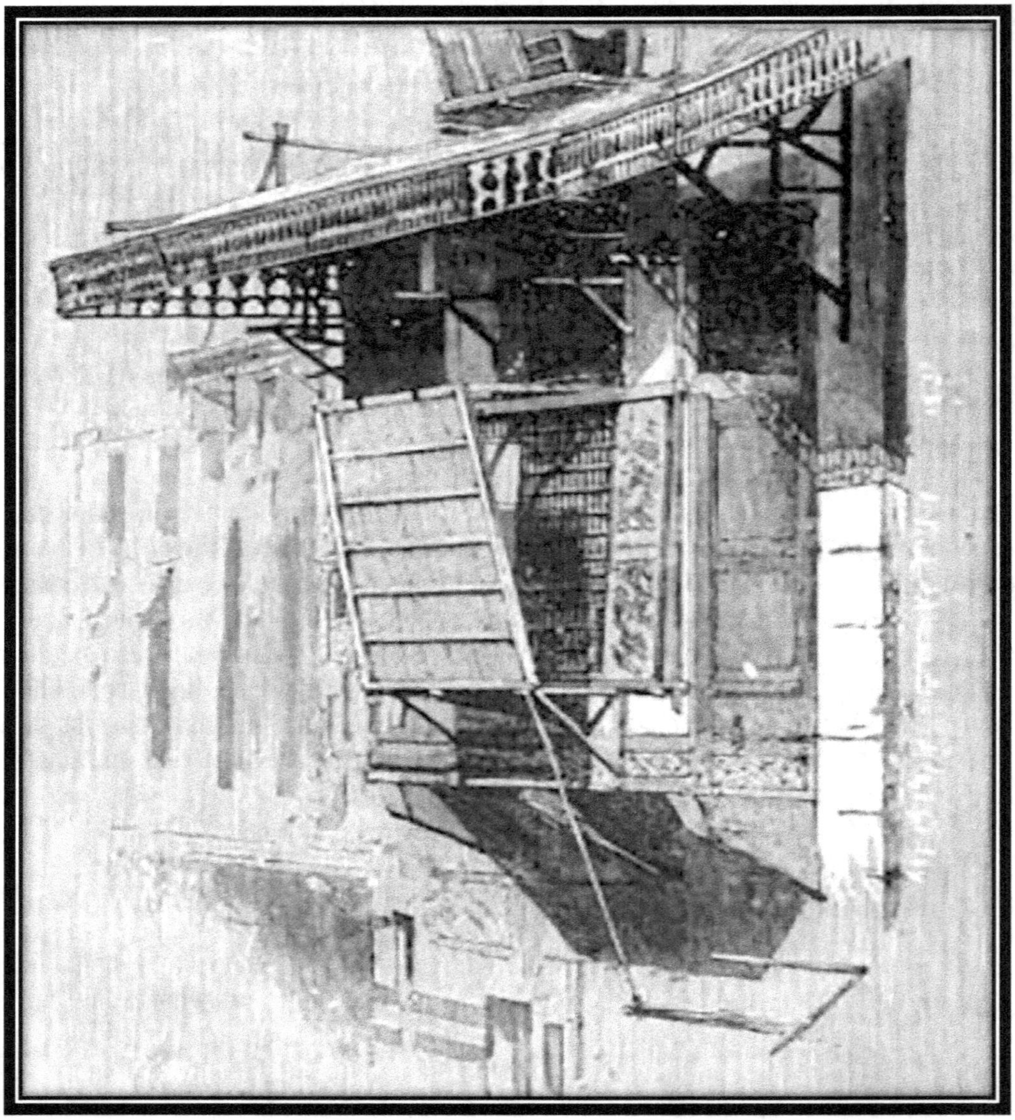

The Imaum Of Mushi Street

Perkins, the braver of us, asked directions and what the wonderful wooden window covering were called from a better-dressed and elderly Egyptian who turned out to be an Imaum *{preacher}*, and he told us we were on Mushi Street. He was pleased to speak to us, as are most Arabic speakers when you address them in their language. The windows, which we had seen briefly at the Hotel du Nil also, he called '*mashrabiya*', and are made of wood and allow women to sit inside and view the world without being defiled by being seen by strange men. As we had a friendly soul to talk to, we asked him the way and he elected to take us to our destination if we would tell him of the west, as he had heard many tales of it but and had never spoken to a European before.

He was a fatherly, happy man who seemed to know everyone for he received loud greeting wherever we went. We crossed a canal and he soon brought us to a street that led up to the citadel.

I have been un-able to recall the entire cascade of questions the Imaum hurled at us. Among the cavalcade of inquiries were whether the King of England was a Muhammadan ruler. When Napoleon might return to Egypt? Was it true that the earth went around the sun? That all the European nations paid tribute to the Porte in Constantinople *{Driscol always used this word instead of Istanbul as the name of that city}*. Whether it was true, there were places in the world where the sun did not shine and other places where it shined all the time?

The Imaum of Mushi Street, drawn by Perkins. I-V-10

We had answered them all despite it taxing our limited vocabularies. The good Imaum spoke only the Egyptian version of Arabic and we did what we could. He was delighted that we knew some quotes from the Koran and for this reason he wished us to submit to Islam. We avoided that by saying we would have to ask permission of our fathers before making such a decision. This he accepted as a wise statement. His name was Ahmed El Maher.

Before we left him he had found by his questioning that we were but hours arrived in Cairo and gave us a useful lesson. The streets had many shops and he showed us how Cairenes bought something. He did so by demonstrating it:

The typical Egyptian is completely ignorant of the phrase 'time is money'. A trader, if you show an interest in his wares, instead of stating a price or asking what you were looking for, will offer you a seat and some tea, coffee or one of those cigars one must discarded rather than smoke. He will show you his merchandise or help you find what you need later. When you are shown his wares you must not like it or ask the price. In the east, one does not come into a shop and buy what one needs. It is more of a social exercise in how to gain friends and accomplish very little while expending a great deal of time. One must wait until after inquiries to the health of his family, his cousins, the price of milk and the hopes for next year's crops. Then one may ask the price of something. He will quote a price some five times higher than it can possibly be worth. To which you must express your disagreement, repeating the Arabic word '*La*' *{no}* many times. Saying that word repeatedly is an excellent way to do so. You must do so with vigorous indignation. If you are bold, you may suggest a price that is often ten times less than what the item might be worth. The shopkeeper will then react with astonishment and plead that he has so many children to feed, etc. You must now leave. He may follow and offer a lesser price but usually this charade must go on for several days. He may even agree at some point to a price then, when the parcel is tied up and you pass the money, he will change his mind and you are back to bargaining again. Perkins seemed to have a feel for this but as we did not have the time for such pleasures, we just put down a sum, and if the merchant does not take it, we leave. Catania having given us the actual prices of commodities in Cairo.

We thanked him but he declined an offer of a small sum. My view of Cairo and the Egyptians was changed by that one man and the twenty-minute walk we had through the streets of Cairo. For the east, it would seem, had entered my soul, helped by that small curious man. He seemed to have affected Perkins in the same way, for he apologised for the arrangements he had made without my knowledge or consent and offered to move to the old missionary's if I wished. I said that he need not mention it as I found it deliciously wicked and if I felt a need to repent I could move to other quarters without disturbing his blissful, if paid for, utopia. He wheedled me to consider the possibilities of such an arrangement with Karen, Millicent, Marguerite, Patricia or Danae. I protested that he grew too bold and we both strode off to the citadel.

We saw the tombs of some of the Mamluks who are of the present Pasha's family and a Roman ruin that neither of us knew the origin of[10].

The citadel appeared closed to visitors, or so the stern faced Albanian mercenaries seemed to convey. They seemed to speak no Arabic so we admired it from the outside and made our way back to the Nile, coming after a time to the tip of the island that lies just off Cairo and where the famed Nilometer, or 'al-Miqyas' in Arabic, is situated. An old man was sitting inside the structure where the tunnel brought water in from the river and he showed us how the pillar was marked to show the level of the river, and he told us what it meant.

The river now stood between the marks for disaster and abundance. We could not see them but the old man of the Nilometer said that other markings, hidden by the waters, were indicative of plenty, happiness, suffering and hunger. Below the last mark of hunger one could imply famine and catastrophe. A fine piece of ancient Egyptian technology[11] and I was impressed at having seen it.

As we were walking back, we found our sketch map of Cairo would not do as we had no idea where we might be. We determined that we must find the British Consulate and from there the Hotel Du Nil and then Maysoon's house. As we walked on, we knew we could not be totally lost as we could always find the Nile again.

[Editor's note: Driscol wrote the following in Danish probably as a draft to send out a letter to his mother and others]

As we walked, we began to hear a din in the distance. A shouting and a word being repeatedly said in Arabic. I took it to be 'trample' but Perkins thought it meant 'stepping'. We were soon in a square that was full of people and our squabble over the meaning was soon moot, these people pressed up against us and we were trapped. Even with my coins secured within my money belt, I was concerned for my other items. I kept my hand out of sight and on my pistol. We were near the College of the *Durweehses {Dervishes}* and witnessed a stirring sight.

The afternoon prayers finished and a Sheikh, it would seem, wished to demonstrate the loyalty of his followers and the powers of Allah. He did this by calling for his supporters called, we believed, *Durweesh {Dervish}* to demonstrate the power of their faith. The Sheikh was mounted and clothed all in white and had on his head a turban of deep black to show that he was a Sayyid; a descendent of Mohammed the prophet. He sat majestically on a horse of average height and weight and I mention this for it will become important later. We had come into the square after many rituals had occurred and the followers had laid down in the square, some forty or fifty of them, side by side, on their bellies with their foreheads resting on their crossed arms. All were chanting the name of Allah, while nearly everyone else in the square was saying the word we had heard before. Some of the standing men were beating on small drums and this went on for some time until the Sheikh gave a signal and ten or more un-shod dervishes ran at speed along the backs of those lying in the square, exclaiming to their God some prayer. I was surprised to see the Sheikh ride up; however, he did not dismount. Instead, he tried to guide his horse to move across the backs of these men. The horse, a sensible animal, hesitated; for a horse will never step on another creature, Not out of kindness but in fear of losing its footing. The horse was urged and pushed and finally did so and, finding there was no danger, walked with a high pace over them all. He did so to great cheers and cries to the Arabian God for as he passed over the men they jumped up and joined the parade.

This example of faith; of devotion and rejection of physical pain was successful, for none of the men appeared injured even though they were each trod on by a horse and man of great weight. The ceremony seemed to be ending so we went back the way we had come. We came across a Levantine who spoke French but he did not know where the British consulate was, but he did know the location of the French one, for we were standing just outside it when we asked him. A knock, a query, introductions, much explanation and we were off. We were well on our way when shouts were heard coming in our direction. We hurriedly moved to the side of the street for that was what the other city dwellers were doing. A carriage came at us going at speed, led by two mounted sons of Ham dressed in a way one would expect from an extravagant Italian opera but also armed with gilded sticks which they swung with force at any one in the way while crying in Arabic, "Run away! We come! Out of our way! Make way! Make way!"

We pressed ourselves again the wall. The two men swept by, followed by the carriage and preceded by two other men who could only have been eunuchs, and we realised we must have sighted a woman of the Pasha's '*harim*' or other notable.

[Editor's note: Driscol's journal has an entire page here missing. I suspect that a letter had written on that missing sheet]

We arrived at the Consulate, found that nothing was new and from there, after two wrong turns, we returned to the 'paradise' that was Maysoon's.

We went out at eight and found that the Consulate knew nothing, again. There was a man with a message from our friend Catania. It read that he was detained and would join us at the Consulate in the morning and in case we departed before then, he wrote a long paragraph in thanks of having known us.

Tired out, we had supper by ourselves, Maysoon not joining us. We had a more substantial meal; a stew of artichokes and lamb (I added artichokes to the list of foods that I would put a question mark in regards to any future eating) and some roasted root vegetables I could not identify.

We had for entertainment a *psylle* or snake charmer who did his best to divert us. His Egyptian Cobra and puff adder did look dangerous but we could tell that their mouths had been sewn shut. A point noted by a Gentleman in the Oriental club to be on the look for. Nevertheless, it was a distraction and a finer bit than some Greek jugglers who were more Greek than jugglers. They could not understand neither Perkins' Greek nor mine something I had heard of before that being the modern Greeks could not understand their fore bearer's language at least not the way we pronounced it. One of them was literate and he could understand some, but not all of the ancient Greek words we wrote though.

I spent some time engaged in a small war with several cockroaches that had invaded my papers and journals during the day. I was victorious but I have to say that they died gloriously.

I read late into the night and when I slept I dreamed of eastern harems, flower gardens with flowing fountains and of a veiled woman whose face I could not see.

The Grand Mosque visited by Perkins and Driscol. I-V-11

The Great Pyramids Of Geezeh

Sunday 13 November

I decided to sleep longer and linger over a bath taken in a large tin basin with tepid water. I met with Perkins and we made the Consulate on time where we found there was no news, which was good news, Catania was fashionably late in the eastern style but greeted us warmly when he arrived. He had completed his business in Cairo and wished to entertain us this day. For this he had hired two carriages, a bevy of servants headed by a giant of a man for a Dragoman to guide us, for he intended to take us to the pyramids. That had been our hope for this day and since he had already arranged it we accepted with thanks. Catania had looked worried the entire time since we had left Malta but now he seemed a freer spirit.

He told us that we would spend the night at the pyramid's *mise en scène {stage}* but to this application Perkins would not agree, so it was decided he would ride back on his own in the evening. We took a barge across the Nile, met up with our men near the Jewish quarters whose narrow streets were smaller than those in Cairo itself. We could see the pyramids clearly and there were equestrians about, camels and small herds of buffalo. We passed fields of sugar cane and purchased a few strands to refresh the servants and ourselves.

The carriage's roof was too low for me to sit comfortably so I selected a horse to ride. I chose to ride, not an Arab, but a peculiar breed common to this country. It was short, not more than fourteen hands high, short necked and small headed but well shouldered and with heavy legs. Perkins said in Persian that the same observation applied to our accompanying Egyptians, which was quite quaint. She was good tempered and docile but had the ability to lash out with her hind hoofs without warning at any dog that dared annoy her nearly un-seating me on several occasions.

We made the village of Geezeh known to the ancients as *Ipersioi*. The village was in ruins. There were only carcasses of houses, bazaars and palaces but with some wretched cafés still in existence. Saw the ovens where since the time of the Pharaohs eggs were hatch. The Dragoman, whose name in Arabic meant 'Giant', said that eggs were cooked for eating not in the ovens but by the friction of the air, caused by the locals using a device like a sling to rotate them over their heads until they were 'cooked'. It was also said that this method had come to them from the Babylonians. I took all this in with a bit of skepticism and a grain of salt the extent of Sicily. Locals offering their services swarmed over us but the thunderous voice and use of a whip by the Dragoman soon dispersed the throngs of hangers-on who were most aggravating. One old woman, having grabbed my thigh, beseeched me endlessly with cries for *backsheesh {a gift of money, a tip}*. The Dragoman drove her off with a touch of kindness and the crack of his whip. As we left the village, a new hovel was being built on the outskirts. The rubbish was not cleared away but instead the hovel was assembled from the wreckage around it and the family soon had a place to live amongst the stray dogs, vultures and other vermin.

We came in time to Cheops atop a limestone ridge, which was still partially buried in sand as was the Sphinx. All around lay broken stones, masonry and pottery shards.

We were left to wander the site with the Dragoman to accompany us while the men set up our tents. The silence broken by natives who stood off shouting out offers for their employment, for goats for eating, pimping for a covey of non-reformed magdalen's *{Prostitutes}* in which not one was a looker and other noisome chatter.

[Editor's note: from his sketch and description it would seem the tents were placed near the great pyramid and in the shadow of the three satellite or as Driscol called them in a later letter the 'Queens' near the location where much later the smaller G1-d pyramid was found]

I found that I cared most for Mycerinus' *{Menkaure's}* pyramid, which was the easiest to go around. I also found that the remaining outer layers of Cephren's pyramid were also of interest. The Dragoman had but to raise his hand and I soon had three men to assist me in this task. They were somewhat surprised that I did not wish to ascend the greater pyramid but this one, but they certainly knew there way here too. I was all but lifted up to the point where I could see the stones of the cladding. I studied this for some time then made the discovery that the view was magnificent and that my fear of heights came upon me like a tree falling I felt I had been dashed with chilled water. I was quite happy to be carried back down again I had found the view exhilarating. Perkins was not into climbing pyramids and I decided not to try the other one as I had felt a great reluctance on the mere offer. I did, however, walk down to the head of the Sphinx and later gained the top of Mycerinus' pyramid which I could do almost myself. Fortunately, my fear on this pyramid was much less and I was able to see a great deal, even to the lesser pyramids to the south of us at Abooseer, Sakkara and Dashoor.

We found that the temperature was 72° at its height and that around eleven in the evening it had dropped to 67°, a very comfortable atmosphere for Egypt. I used my Saussure *{hygrometer}* to measure 59% and had we the time I would have brought out my Troughton's *{Troughton & Simms survey equipment}*.

The tents were up by now but before our early supper, it was decided that we were to enter the great pyramid. We secured candles, a lantern, and multiple ways to light them and some water bottles or *goolehs.*

We made our way up the massive stones of the great pyramid to the entrance in the side of the tomb, interestingly off-centre, which seemed odd considering the claims of great accuracy in the making of the pyramid by Smith and others. We ignited *{our torches and lamps}* with some effort and with the Dragoman leading with his lantern, followed by Catania, myself then Perkins and another man carrying the second lantern. I thought they might have needed to leave a trail of breadcrumbs. Perkins thought that clever but countered that *fellaheen* would follow behind us and pick them up. Such was the state of the poor here that we moneyless officers could stride about like Nabobs.

We went into the cool and darkness along a sloping decline of some five and seventy feet. We found the bypassed granite plug done so by tunneling around it though the softer limestone, a few rough steps, and one emerges into the great gallery. All the stone is incrusted with salt and the upper stones darkened by soot. We made our way up this sloping passage with some difficulty but reached the place where four portcullises of granite once protected the room beyond. The dimensions of this grand room being five and thirty by eighteen by twenty feet, it to me had a feel of grandeur. This chamber was of granite and at the end of it laid a sarcophagus of red granite, much broken. The Dragoman took up his large wooden mallet and struck it a blow, which reverberated around the chamber like a bell. I found this all fascinating and we explored further, finding niches and crannies elsewhere. We emerged from the dark coolness of the pyramid into the warmth of a sunny afternoon on the plateau with Cairo and the Nile valley spread out beneath us.

When we emerged, there was a singularly odd creature at the pyramids, a Scotsman, who was yelling with passionate anger at them and our guide informed us that this lunatic came each day to do so; he also seemed upset with some Arab Gentleman but I could not make out the name clearly. The lunatic named Bampot MacKreighton stood each day by the great tombs screaming at them that he would soon do empirical scientific tests to show Atlantis built them twenty thousand years before. It would seem Plato's date was also wrong by ten thousand years or so. He was stark naked except for a teacup strapped across his loins and held there by a ragged cloth, a *havas*. He seemed to foam at the mouth like a mad thing but I must say he was more an object of humour than concern. He could talk coherently if he chose to and told us he was from a small village called Oouttacontec.

[Editor's note: I could not locate such a place in Scotland perhaps he meant Oldmeldrum in Aberdeenshire?]

Poor addled creature! He also had a small mongrel dog with him who seemed to spend his time barking at carvings, 'Bampot' insisted his daft dog whom he called 'King' could read the ancient language. When we asked how he knew this he looked at us with surprise and told us that his dog had told him so. One last thing about the man, I had mentioned that he had secured his privates in a strapped on teacup but I must say that his having left the teaspoon in there looked damnably un-comfortable.

[Editor's note: Inspired by Driscol's description of the mad Scotsman I was able to find out that he had come to Egypt some years before as an engineer. He was to have worked on the irrigation system but he was profoundly inept and he demonstrated that he had no such experience or education and dismissed on the spot. Like a small minority of European's the east drove him mad. Major General Richard Vyse one of the British explorers of the Giza plateau was the last to note his presence in 1837 - his ultimate fate is not recorded]

Having violated the tomb of the Pharaoh, we dined on eggs, a portion of roasted goat covered in tahini *{sesame paste}* and some bread in the French style (which one can obtain in Cairo and is much better to eat than the flat bread of the present day Egyptians).

We ate for a long time, for there was great deal of goat. The servants and the Dragoman would take none until we were finished and they removed it to finish it away from us. They supplied us with a lavender flavoured pastry, which gathered no praises from Perkins, and I then ate some dates then a Baklava cake, which dripped in honey, and nuts that was well received by us.

We explored some more and I found the top of an even smaller pyramid beyond Menkaure's which I walked about then over the ruins of what I suspected were once temples, remains of other fallen pyramids and rock cut tombs.

We saw at the end of the day a string of men and camels approaching from the west. This Catania identified as a slave caravan from Siwah. They had brought up from Central Africa a group of poor niggers headed towards Kirdasa, a slave processing station near Cairo and this plateau. We estimated some three to four hundred slaves were in that column escorted by a half dozen armed Bedouin. Catania explained that these languishers were designated for sale in northern Africa. They were to be allowed to rest for some time, cleaned, taught a few phrases in Arabic and then marched on to Benghazi and places to the west. In Cairo some of the boys would be sent south to be emasculated.

Evening came to the necropolis and we had more food, pigeons baked in pastry in a style known as 'hamam mashi', or stuffed. I did not care for preparing a pigeon this way and, the spicing being anomalous to my penchant.

The stars were brilliant and the moon shone down on the four thousand years of history. The Dragoman told many stories in French of ancient Egypt but I did not care to listen. I just stared up at the stars. One of his stories did interest me, and that was of a more modern legend of a giant white snake that would issue out of the tombs here, making a great hissing sound, terrifying the locals then disappear back into the ground. The snake they called *Al Hanash*.

Perkins headed off in the dead of night, led by a servant holding a lantern to return to his Maysoon. Catania had remarked that the Hotel Du Nil must be a nice place. It was, especially if you did not actually stay there or a woman awaited your return.

I asked, and Catania told me of his reasons for coming to Cairo. He had three reasons: he considered himself an 'eastern' Jew; because of this he practiced polygamy, and had a younger wife and a family here in Cairo. He had come also because of a call by the Jews to a concave on what to do about a Mister Joseph Wolff, The Jewish community now considered him a threat due to his continual attempts to convert Jewish communities.

He had been in the region for some time and a discussion had been held as to whether to engage him in theological debate, ignore him or visit God's wraith upon him. He told me more about the man who seemed quite dynamic in his efforts. He had acted as a Christian missionary in Egypt for the Church of England and even to the most Jewish of Hebrews those who lived in Jerusalem.

I found it impossibly odd that Catania discussed the work of a Christian missionary with me in a negative tone. Did he not know I was CE *{Church of England}* also?

The decision that he was yet another trial sent by God was reached at a meeting in Cairo, and it was thought best to ignore him. I had the oddest feeling that Catania would have, had the decision gone to the extreme possibility, asked us to assassinate him. I was glad that difficulty had been avoided for that I would not have done. I had one or more men's lives burdening my soul already. I certainly did not need to add a Church of England missionary even if a former Jew added to it.

[Editor's note: Joseph Wolff was a Jew who converted to Christianity and explored the Levant and Central Asia trying to convert all the Jews he found there. He was looking for the lost tribes of Israel and wrote numerous books on many subjects]

His third tale was even more bizarre…

[Editor's note: the page is torn in half here and that section has not been found in his writings but he does take up Catania's third comment later in his journal under the sub-chapter 'Skullduggery', below]

Sleep came late to me that night for I had decided not to lie in the tent and took instead a thin blanket to lie out on the sands, which were still warm, and watch the moon disappear behind the great pyramid.

Something small scurried over me in the night but I slept on. A smiling Perkins who had come back out at dawn awakened me and I found the entire camp up, packed, loaded and ready to go. Somewhat embarrassed, I quickly gathered myself up, for I had slept well, it would seem. He had wisely checked with the Legation, as we had been somewhat tardy the previous evening but there was no reason for concern. There was as of yet no word of transport to the east.

We paraded away from the pyramids and as we went back towards Cairo. I kept finding myself drawn to turn and look again at those massive piles of limestone masonry. I had to say that the idea of studying them more and the ruins of the Egyptian Empire was strong and I recalled the offer by my friend Schiffer, the Wurttemberger academic.

We then made our way to the city, discharged the men and we went on to a Hammam a large one by the Bab e Shareeh gate and called, I believe, 'the Tumbalee', where we were introduced to the vapour bath. To me this seemed like the Roman style of bathing, so it interested me in that regard. We disrobed and sat around in a warm room with towels not much smaller than a Roman toga. Perkins and I both gave small Latin speeches, which we both had had to memorise when we were in school. His was something by Cicero and I quoted a shorter one from Caesar. Having developed a good amount of perspiration, we went into a still hotter room. I told Perkins about Catania's confessions (I did so in Latin) and he was suitably amazed at this marital status. A boy came about splashing us with cold water then a more disagreeable procedure occurred where we were washed down by an elderly hairy Turk - that I could have done without. He did something called a 'massage' which I found pleasant but again I did not enjoy it being delivered by a man. Perkins suggested I could obtain the same from one of Maysoon's female assistants or a suitably trained Danae.

We merged from the baths very clean, rested and I have to say I had another item to add to my growing list of that which I liked about the east.

Our clothes had been cleaned and were neatly presented to us. We dressed and Catania asks us to grant him one more boon. I thought this might be the case and I was ready for whatever it might be in would prove to be interesting. We made our way into the constricted passages of the Jewish quarter and, after ducking through and under low lying arches, up crumbling masonry staircases and down fetid smelling alleyways, we came into a residence that was entered into by a great iron bound door that was scarred, burned, chipped and blackened and was at least six inches thick and probably older than Methuselah. This portal was guarded too, by two strong looking and well-armed men we took as Semitic.

The Pyramids of Egypt in 1836. I-V-12

Skullduggery

In the room was a rough table, some chests, and a large silvered mirror. Catania had us sit and he explained his need for our help. He spoke again of the three reasons he had come to Cairo and said he had resolved two but for the third, he was in need of a darling Englishmen or two.

Perkins asked, impertinently, if he intended to grind our bones for his bread. Catania did not understand this allusion, so we had to explain for we both had it memorised and, saying it together, we gave out our rendition of:

Fe, Fi, Fo, Fum.
I smell the blood of an Englishman,
Be he living, or be he dead,
I'll grind his bones to mix my bread

This tale of giants from our English childhood he had not heard of before. After we had finished our explanation, he smiled gently, and nodded his head. There was no sign of annoyance crossing his features but I knew that it was there, perhaps he was wondering if we were still boys?

He continued, saying that we knew of evil giants then? Laughed and then continued.

~~The third difficulty's solution had been present to him when he had aided us in our actions on Malta. Our great success at that had inspired him to consider a similar solution to his present quandary.~~

[Editor's note: The above and been inked over but recovered]

He asked if we remembered the Safranschau? We did not and he took us back to a time on the docks of Valetta and had us recall his pointing them out on the quay of Malta near the lazaretto. We did recall them after his exactitude in prompting our remembrance, two men in European dress I had also written about that in this journal *{Chapter IV Malta to Alexandria - Maltese Diversions}*

Men of this organisation came from many backgrounds and he was ashamed to say that some were even Jewish. Their existence was shadowy but they dealt in those things that are best kept out of sight. Many were the rumours he said of what malevolence and venality they supported.

Near here, he said the slave trade[12] continued, somewhat out of sight now from Europeans but still legal and sanctioned by the powerful within the Ottoman Empire and endorsed, of course, by Islam itself. The Soonee *{Sunni}* clerics of the El Azahar *{Al-Azhar, the preeminent place of Sunni learning in the Muhammadan world}* holding slaves themselves, many have mothers who were once slaves.

The most highly prised slaves were not the commonly found Negro but the rarer white slaves; especially Georgian and Circassian girls, wanted as concubines for the *harim.* Some of these had been obtained by raids or kidnapped and sometime taken captive by raids between rival clans but most were farmed out by their parents as a method of survival for both the family and the child. Once they reached a certain age their parents sell them. The formerly well-established trade network would then move them to the slave markets.

He said formerly because the problems began some years ago when the expansive Czar conquered Circassia and Georgia causing the supply of Mamluks *{white slaves}* to plummet. The demand remained, however, not only in Egypt, but elsewhere in the Muslim world. "As a man of commerce I know," said Catania, "that when the supply of something, anything is restricted, prices rise and that rise inspires ways to increase the supply."

These white slaves would go to Constantinople and were then brought into Egypt at Alexandria, attended by eunuchs who use the exclusion of members of a *harim* of an important man to avoid any interference or notice of the exchange.

These white concubines were the privilege of the vice-regal families and the wealthiest Turks, plus a few Egyptians who had somehow retained their wealth during the centuries of pillaging by their Ottoman occupiers.

The trade from the north in this commodity has dried up but some are still obtained by the old network and from the daughter selling fair-skinned peasants of Anatolia.

Also important to this trade but from sources to the south were light skinned Abyssinian girls. So popular are these that many of upper classes are born to them. So prevalent, in fact, that they are called *Habashi* and can be found throughout Egyptian society.

There is, of course, trade in men too, for servants, rarely for agricultural work, and oftentimes as soldiers. Additionally, some ill-starred boys are transferred to places in upper Egypt where great evil is done. Every year, four hundred eunuchs are sold in Cairo or sent elsewhere within *Dar al-Islam {the region of peace or where Muhammadan's rule}* and they are said to come from village centres in upper Egypt inhabited by Coptic's who are knowledgeable in this specialised trade. They are not restricted by their religion, as in Islam, from conducting mutilations of this kind. All Egyptians eschew these villages and their tainted trade but the trade continues both for the money it produces and by the weight of tradition.

"You may ask why Christians would do such a thing," Catania said to us, and he looked at us in silence for some time then continued. "The answer, we believe, is that they are not Christians or of any religion that follows the precepts of God and these centres are run by the same Safranschau under the guise of being Coptic monks and a doctor is thought to be charge; a Jewish doctor, it is thought, much to our shame." Perkins then asked what Catania would ask us to do.

"I wish you two to take on a role: that of a wealthy buyer and find if these Safranschau have seized Jewish women for sale or are using male Jewish children for their eunuchs. Male and female children have disappeared in our communities across the region for a decade or so since the Russians have all but broken the white slave trade paths up north.

"I must ask you to do this for us. As all of us Jews here in Cairo are too well-known. Moreover, any attempt by us to interfere would bring great troubles upon our people here and elsewhere in the east. We ask only that you see if Jews are held in this way and then tell us, for the rumour and tales about it are forever flowing to us. If we can know, for certain, then we can take action."

Perkins and I asked in unison, "What actions can you take?"

"That which Jews have always done: we will try to purchase them back or influence the rulers to smile on our side in any negotiations to end these transgressions against us. We have influence in our own way but we cannot openly attack them."

He said he wanted Perkins to act as a European renegade *(converted to a Muhammadan}* and secretary to a wealthy Mussulman interested in concubines and eunuchs for his *harim*. Catania apologised for the un-intended insult to his higher military rank and greater age but the fact was that he looked too European and English to carry the part of an eastern potentate. While I had an un-common face, not so European and one that could come to a man whose father was an Arab, Berber or other easterner and a white concubine.

Catania explained that taking up a disguise was easier here because light coloured eyes were not un-usual, the presence of generations of white skinned slaves making light skin, hair and eyes more common and un-remarkable. He also told us some about the situation here as we dressed and had our beards tinted, for we had agreed at once to the venture.

[Editor's note: the unknown editor added a later pencil addition to the journal in the margins of two pages. This follows:]

==
Disguising One's Hair Colour

To colour one's hair, moustache and beard in the eastern way:
$^1/_3$ ounce of gallic acid mixed with
1 ounce of acetic acid
1 ounce of tincture of sesquichloride of iron
Dissolve the gallic acid in the tincture of sesquichloride of iron and then add the acetic acid.
Wash the hair thoroughly before applying. Apply the dye to either gain a colour of black or a lighter shade of brown

For black, apply the preparation when the hair is moist. For brown hair apply when the hair is perfectly dry after washing

Apply the dye to the hair using a fine toothcomb or soft bristled brush

==

As we dressed, Catania provided us with more information on the slave trade. A middle class *harim* was populated by a wife or up to four wives who had first place in power within it. Then there are the female slaves, white or Abyssinians concubines, Negro females for servile work. Thirdly of free female slaves, usually the children of the master's family from the previous generation of concubines. A high-class *harim* would be the same but might have eunuchs who, if present, would have top place in the hierarchy, perhaps not in truth, but by social custom.

He explained we would go into Mufti then be sent to a place to meet an intermediary, for an un-aware middleman had set up a meeting between the two said characters we would be that afternoon. We would go in disguise and make our discoveries. We would insist on seeing the 'merchandise', learn who sold them, and in the style of eastern bargaining make no commitment to a purchase that day. We would then return, making sure that none followed and meet with

Catania and give him the information. He offered a very large sum to do this but Perkins dismissed it out of hand.

"You make a poor Jew my friend Catania for you give away your money to freely."

"Not so," said he, "for in certainty I love my wives and children more, my God and people even above them and I but cherish money below my love of food."

I would not have been so presumptuous in declining such a sum as fast as my friend Perkins did for he came from a well-to-do family *{Driscol came from a modest middle class one}*. While I had two-hundred pounds sterling I owed on my commission hanging over me like the legendary sword of Damocles.

Catania provided us with a list of prices for slaves and other common products. In the time we had known him, it was the first written document we had seen by his hand.

[Editor's note: The original Arabic sheet has been translated and is shown below]

===

Table For The Cost Of Slaves And Commodities

in the Markets,

Cairo November 1836

Type of slave or product	Cost in Piasters	Sterling	*Modern dollars**
Female Negro	1,000	£10	$1,300
Female Abyssinian	2,500	£25	$3,250
Eunuch	3,000	£30	$4,000
Female Circassian	15,000	£150	$20,000
Male Negro	700	£7	$900
Male Circassian	6,000	£60	$8,000
Horse	50	£5	$650
500 lbs. of rice	200	£2	$250
Sheep	5	£5	$65

The price was also modified by the age and this was classified under the categories of Baligb (mature adults), who were sold at discounts up to 50%, a slave over forty being all but worthless. Sudasi *{teenagers from 11 up to 15 years of age}*, up to 75% more could be paid for these if female and handsome Khumasi *{children}* at the given price or somewhat higher.

**[Editor's note: in 1836, 100 Egyptian Piasters equaled approximately 1 pound Sterling or $130 US Dollars in 2015. I have added the value in US dollars for comparison purposes. All number are approximate and rounded]*

===

In the east it was thought that a slave bought into a household as Khumasi would become a member of the family but it took time and money to raise them before they could be useful. Such a slave became more reliable and loyal than older ones as they would feel an attachment to the family having grown up there.

Catania told us that the intermediaries had said that interpreters would be there to aide in speaking to the merchants should the need so arise.

Therefore, decided and done. I was to take on the role of a Moroccan man of great birth but of *Imazien {Berber}* blood as an excuse for my great height and poor Arabic. Perkins would be my European secretary a great luxury to have and an indicator of great wealth. Perkins, of course, will be a Frenchmen who had converted to the faith of the prophet the French being particularly weak in that way.

I was dressed in great style with purple and green vestments, the conspicuous silks sewn with seed pearls. I took on a headscarf of the Berber type and Perkins sported a large green turban and flowing robes. With my moustache and beard, I began to look rather rakish. Perkins also carried with him a Koran, as was deemed seemly for the newly converted. We obtained each our *tasbih* from Catania; mine of lapis lazuli and Perkins of a more common stone, this 'rosary' consisted of nine and ninety stone beads for these stand for the names of God or Allah as the Arabs label him.

I had with me my French pistol, my extra cylinder and 5 additional rounds. Perkins had only his Colt. I again regretted not having a good knife. As we needed such to complete our costume, I was given a Moroccan style Koummya; a curved dagger in the style of the more pronounced Omani blades. I secured that in my belt, concerned that it might be snatched away as it was made of ivory and silver with two green stones set into the pommel. Perkins received a smaller and less ornate version than mine, a fact I chided him over for a moment or two.

My skin was darkened by the application of walnut oil and soot plus a prominent *zebibah {prayer 'bump' that observant Muslim's have on their foreheads}* fashioned and coloured on my brow by way of herb based paint that stung somewhat in the most masterly way. Perkins was also so adorned but with one less conspicuous. Some trousers and slippers out of Galland's *Kitab alf laylah wa-laylah* or Arabian night stories *{Antoine Galland translated the famous book; 'One thousand and one Nights' Driscol did not finish the sentence but the meaning is clear he was dressed in a fashion he considered to that of the Arabian nights}*. Lastly, we were drenched it what would seem to have been rose water, for fragrant perfumes were worn by the wealthy and not so wealthy in the east.

Two Jewesses aided in this and Catania said they were relatives of his. Both had lustrous black hair. Catania spoke to us of the vocabulary we might need. Both were also very pleasant to view.

A female slave is called *ima* in Arabic, *abd* for male, *Khasi* for eunuchs. *Esra'elawi Falasha {foreigners/exiles}* and *ayhud or yahudi* for Jews. He also gave us a phrase to say to someone we might think was Jewish. This was the morning prayer. We learned it in Arabic as best we could, learning also how to say it differently if speaking to a man or woman.

'I thank you, living and eternal King, for returning my soul within me in compassion, great is your faithfulness.'

Once I was dressed like a Prince from a Spanish opera and Perkins as a scoundrel, a complete one, I thought and I told him so, and added that I thought he might keep to that manner of dress in the future. He replied that I would address him in the future as Lieutenant Scoundrel, sir or he would have me up on charges of disrespect. I replied that I might bring counter charges against him of conducting himself as to bring disgrace on true scoundrels everywhere, especially in Parliament. He called me a Radical and I returned to him he was d__ Tory.

We nervously did as instructed. We left by a series of small alleyways and dark covered ways being left near a mosque which we recognised, having seen it earlier when it had been pointed out to us by Catania. It was to here we would return. We did as good slave buyers do and headed for the well-known area that this deed was done. The Mosque as a starting location was well chosen as we need only walk down the crowded street and we would come to where we would meet our intermediary. Perkins, as my servant, walked ahead, making sure that none caused my path to be obstructed - being exalted and all that.

Entrance to the slaver dealer's villa. I-V-13

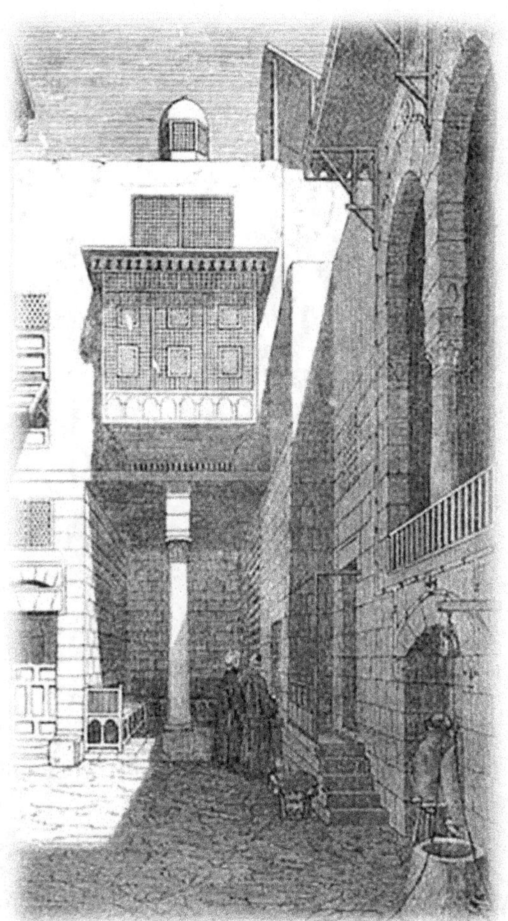

It was now early afternoon, the sun was casting shadows about, and rare cumulus clouds were in the sky taking more light from it. We made it to our point and accosted by a Turkish man who spoke Arabic well but in a dry sultry way, which I found hard to follow. We saluted one another in the Mussulmen's way, introductions were made and he bid us to follow. There were narrower pathways, but now they were on inlayed floors of granite and limestone. I thought it would be a long confusing walk but we emerged into a small square with Roman style arches surrounded by three-storey buildings. The arches were startling large at the ground floor but diminished as they rose to the top. In the centre was an archaic Greek style fountain with a bronze God contributing his share of water to the basin. I thought this odd as Islam has a prohibition against the display of the human form. The square was small, perhaps five and thirty feet on each side. We halted a moment and our intermediary left us with much obsequiousness towards me. The air here smelled of lilac and citrus.

Soon a man, an older Arab of dark complexion and marred by the pox, appeared. He was dressed all in shining white and wore the white turban of a Sayyid, a descendent of the *prophet {this can be black or white - traditions differed}*. He wore around his waist a green sash in which was placed a long curved dagger - peculiarly with a gold sheath, *{gold is forbidden for male Muslims* *to wear}*. We again went through the litany of phrases that constitutes the customary greetings between the co-religionist in the Middle East.

We went under the arches and found in the darkness of the shadows an alcove richly decorated with pillows, copper ware and another trickling fountain. Made comfortable I was queried about from whence I came and how he might help us.

Perkins explained that I was a wealthy man from Fas el Bali in *Magrib {Morocco}*. When I completed the Hajj I would return home and there I would marry. I therefore wished, while in Cairo, to obtain that which was needed for the finest *harim* I most assuredly deserved to have.

We gifted a drink of scented water and offered various costly perfumes but we accepted none.

Perkins outlined 'our' needs: we desired three *Sudasi* concubines; one each Negro, Abyssinian and Circassian; two more of each of these groups but *Khumasi* for servants and perhaps a *Baligb* eunuch or two could they provide these?

Where Driscol and Perkins in their guise as slave buyers viewed the slaves. I-V-14

He smiled broadly and said that his Excellency (he meant me not Perkins) had a fine plan but that there were limitations to what he could provide. Sadly, he did not have a Circassian Sudasi but would a Khumasi of white skin, from elsewhere be acceptable? We said we would consider it. He had a selection of Negro and Abyssinians in all categories but alas he had no Baligb eunuchs. Just a few Khumasi and Sudasi. Again, we said we were disappointed but would view the selection before deciding.

As is the custom, we had tea (revolting rubbish) and worse coffee to follow that despicable fluid was damn near poisonous by the addition of cardamom, so vile as to make a thirsty buzzard fly off.

Following that arduous endeavour, we some *luqma {Turkish delight}* was presented. These were very good and I had had some once in the past. I made it a point to eat not only those served to me but Perkins' supply also, as he ignored them while he asked questions about the qualities of the un-seen slave girls. He certainly was playing his part well as he showed a keen interest.

After more morsels, discussion of the markets in commodities other than human, of Arabic poetry to which our human vendor seemed knowledgeable and to which we could only match him by bringing up Persian poetry which both delighted and alarmed him; the Persian poetry being from the distasteful land of the Sheeah *{Shi'a}*. These Sheeah were heretics thought by the Sunni progeny of the prophet to be the lowest of the low. However, as we were considered to be nothing less than completely un-educated barbarians considering where we were from, and not being an Arab this was acceptable.

At long last we were allowed to inspect the 'wares'. These were first African children, boys and girls but we soon made it clear we were not interested in the boys. The Abyssinian girls were very beautiful for I had not seen one before. They were of slight build, fetching with long fine limbs, short curly hair, deeply brown eyes and, to my slight, having a delicate constitution. I asked about this but the vendor, who had never given us his name, said they were resilient, lived longed and stood up well against hard work, disease and childbirth.

The manner of their display was for them to approach us from the lighted courtyard, pausing a moment to wet their lips at the fountain and then approach us. The vendor would stand and remove the robe they were surrounded by. He would then comment on their charms. I found this un-comfortable but mesmerising to watch. I could not help but think of Millicent, Marguerite, Danae, Patricia and even Karen in this regard.

The eastern way is to find fault with anything presented for sale. We therefore commended on all; noting the bad teeth, blemishes, large feet, posture, roughness of their elbows or Perkins, the scandalous man, saying that their bosom's were either too less or too much. I forgot for a time why we were there, as one forgets what we were watching was sinful. It was very entertaining and distracting in a sad way, as any young man will say if presented with Ladies un-clothed for his viewing. But at the time I enjoyed playing the lecherous *harim* builder.

The situation. I-V-I5

The vendor had, of course, kept his best for last. He presented a woman very different from the others; somewhat older, perhaps her mid-teens with dark black hair and fair skin. Un-alike the Negro and Abyssinians who seemed to take the situation in a calm way, she was discomforted by the procedure, one could tell it from her eyes. We went through the discussion of her charms, belittling that which, in truth, was not and noting flaws where, there were none. It was while Perkins and the vendor were in heated debate about some aspect of her appearance when I said the phrase learned from Catania, to her. She was but an arm's length away. We were, of course, not allowed to touch that which we did not own. She made no reaction so I said it louder.

To this, she did react, before her eyes had been downcast and resigned. Now she looked at me, the first of the women who had done so, for bold women were not cared for in this market. Seeing that Perkins had the Vendor well ensnared, I turned my face from them and using my right eye, I winked. She was puzzled I guess and I suddenly grew afraid that she would speak when I clapped my hands to gain the attention of the vendor and asked what else he had to present. This caught him off guard, as I had been rather remote, commenting only occasionally the entire time but was, at the moment, deeply engrossed with Perkins. I had not spoken much as I had been hampered somewhat by a hammering heart for such views were too much for, as my father would have described it, a 'properly raised Englishman who feared Gods anger'.

He soon had brought in a boy who shambled in. To my horror this was a eunuch. A poor Negro. My feelings of revulsion I had had in Malta over the castrated singer were nothing to this. However, the poor lad seemed a pitiable specimen and I waived him away. Two more met with my disapproval but then a swarthy but white boy came up to be seen. He was a bit larger and had the look of a castrate about him, or so I thought based on what little Catania had told me. He did not look Jewish but I was no expert in that race or its characteristics and physiology.

I felt most un-pleasant in his presence and he soon was sent off. We expressed our general dislike for all that we had seen but - again using the eastern way of purchase - we asked if we might return the next day - perhaps then the vendor might have something better we might wish to buy?

The Vendor was all smiles and condescension. He had seen Perkins' face and his liking of two of the Abyssinians and the black haired white girls were plain. The vendor suggested that when I married perhaps I should provide a concubine for my servant? but then I had probably been smiling like a gawking fool myself I was glad to find I had not been drooling.

We complimented him profusely on his hospitality, the loveliness of his establishment and made a vague agreement to meet at some point the next day.

We had moved at this time to the fountain. I was ready to go but Perkins, whose Arabic was more ready and capable than my own, was discussing hydrology with the Arab slave master - who seemed un-usually knowledgeable in this area.

I finally stepped on Perkins foot and motioned that we must go. He agreed with a nod and we turned to follow our host out.

It was late afternoon now and the shadows were lengthening and the passageway out was darkened. As we neared, someone came out. Surprised, both parties stopped. The man who had stopped us in our tracks greeted us and moved to pass us by. Perkins, to his credit, regained his wits before I, saluted him in Arabic and he gave me a push and we began to move again and here I made a mistake I blundered into the man and instead of saying the standard Arabic phrase blurted out in clear English, 'Pardon'. I realised with a chilling wave of fear my horrible error and pushed on after Perkins.

For a moment I thought the mistake had been un-heard or not understood but then from behind came a shout, "WO KOMMST DU HER?" *{"Who are you," in an old style German}* in a manner that spoke of questioning, anger, confusion and threat.

We did not look behind. With me following Perkins we ran at full speed, having pushed our host aside with some violence. So fast in fact, I lost both of my slippers in the first few feet. We emerged into the street to find a donkey caravan in our way but we turned towards the mosque. The crowd was thick and we were dodging people as we ran.

In retrospect our prank or reconnaissance had gone far too well, as a well-known military maxim stated; 'If there is nothing wrong with your plan or its execution, that means you are approaching disaster and the longer Mr Disaster is not met, the worse it will be.'

Perkins shouted to me in English, "Who was that?"

"A man; - I did not see him well in the shadows," was my breathless reply.

The street we had come down from the mosque to the slave market was straight. My friend and I had never engaged in a race and I soon found I was the faster runner than he was. I turned into a narrower alleyway hoping to lose our pursuers.

We dashed into an area of butchers for there were flies and skinned animals hanging from hooks everywhere. I was finding that running and keeping track of where to go and not outrunning my friend were becoming difficult but we could not flee side by side due to the crowd. The crowd did not seem to take kindly to two wealthy well-dressed men sans turbans and head scarf from running amongst them yelling to one another in an un-known language. I had not had my blonde hair dyed, just my beard and those portions of my hair that might show so I would have looked particular too. I had, while running, been trying to find within my voluminous robes my pistol. I took a moment to do so, to await Perkins and see who pursued us, but there was no enemy in pursuit that I could see. I grabbed Perkins' arm as he came up. He was puffing like a winded horse even after a run of just four hundred feet.

I said, "No one is following. Perhaps they are trying to cut us off?"

We moved on but we soon learned why they had not followed the alleyway of butchers went nowhere.

Perkins and I both cursed violently and looked about for a way out. The butchers thought we might be lunatics but were looking on puzzled, and doing nothing else. It was not good to be in place where everyone has arms thicker that my leg and a well sharpened blade in hand and were experts at killing and dismemberment. A clever Bishop's son {Perkins} came up with what to do. He ran over to a window that was inset into the wall; jumped up on the abundant sill and as the roof was only some six feet off the ground made it to the top in one motion. I saw what his intent was and joined him. At this level, the roofs spread off into the distance. Most of the houses here were one-storey in this area of Cairo. We shouted for glee when we saw the mosque, which was only three or four hundred feet away. We made for it hoping that the roofs would hold our weight. We thought they would for Catania had mentioned that in the summer time most people slept on the roofs for the coolness.

So thinking this, we ran along the rooftops, getting some notice from the people below. Perkins, who was now leading so that I would not outrun him, suddenly plunged out of sight, having found a hole where no hole should be. I half stopped myself and looked down and found him looking up at me. A moment later, I jumped down to join him and he ripped down a tattered rug and we were out in the street again. It seemed to me that it headed in the general direction of the mosque. We turned a corner and there we could see that the street would join another that would lead to our meeting place. I took off my dagger sash and placed it over my head and Perkins found another cloth to do the same, for only a slave walked around with his head bare. Perkins grabbed my arm as we caught our breaths. We had been running perhaps for two-minutes and were breathless. He whispered in my ear that we needed to make sure we were not followed, so as to not expose the meeting point. We made to do some distracted shopping within sight of the mosque. We did so for some minutes, counting to ourselves to five hundred, for we had left our pocket watches behind. We separated and made our way casually to the stall where our Jewish co-conspirators had left us previously. We stood for some time idling away our lives, nervously talking with ourselves when a friendly voice behind us asked us in French to turn to the left and walk.

The roof tops of Cairo, a representation of what Driscol and Perkins would have been running across. I-V-16

We did so and after some two hundred feet, we sighted one of the lovely ebony haired Ladies who had assisted us so long ago it seemed. She did no more that look to her right and we followed her eyes. In we went, and found to our great relief Catania who looked like an angry father who finds his boy home late and no money in his pockets, drunk and with no good excuse.

We told him of what had occurred. I was able to say that the woman was a Jew but could not be so sure of the eunuch-boy for I had not had an opportunity to use the phrase on him. He did ask after we had reported why we had run out of the slave market?

We told him we had been discovered and pursued but he told us no one had come in pursuit. We were embarrassed by our panic but besides befuddling the slave vendor perhaps, no harm had been done. That we had garnered a great deal of attention in our wild run was sure but this was Cairo, where the fabulous, ludicrous, un-common and peculiar was a daily occurrence.

Catania was most profuse in his thanks. I, for one, was glad the adventure was over as my under clothes were soaked in sweat both from our excursion and fear. My mouth tasted foully of copper.

We un-dressed and our was appearance brought back to normal. My beard was too dark so I had it shaved off but after a great deal of attention my moustache became blonde again. My praying blemish also left a mark, like a healing bruise. Catania had no difficulty forcing me to keep the Moroccan knife, which I did, and the tasbih. Perkins accepted his, too, but not the knife. Catania, when Perkins was not looking, dropped into my hands ten sovereign and ten half sovereign coins, which I appreciated greatly. We gave one another a silent nod of acceptance. Perkins would remain pure in his chivalrous declining of payment and I would not be quite so poor.

We spoke with each other at some length why we had been detected; while I had spoken a word in English the typical Arabic speaker will consider such a word gibberish. That the man had recognised it and replied in German meant he was a European. I had not seen the man clearly other than he had on Turkish dress. Perkins had met him closer up, having done the dance of misstep; where two men awkwardly try to avoid one another. He was sure the other had been a European, certainly someone had shouted out a challenge to us in German.

I asked was it the blonde haired man from the Xebec, but Perkins was sure it was not. Yet I had my doubts. However, we were quite happy to have pulled off this escapade, despite the disaster at the end. Catania thanked us again and also for not shooting everyone in sight, which would have occurred if we had not been so frightened by that thunderous German shout behind us.

Catania pleaded that he must speak with the elders and leaders of the Jewish community and that he must leave us now. We sadly made our farewells with our good companion Catania. He returned once again Beer's pistol, which became Perkins' second again. He gave us a package to give to Beer's son and he lectured us for some time - father to his sons, as it were - on the trials and tribulations we might find in the east. We made our promises to write him of our journeys to his residence in Malta and when we came back to England, to visit him. He blessed us in Arabic and his own Maltese tongue. We shook his hand with great warmth and he was gone.

I dressed as normal. Perkins took on the guise of a Mamluk, for his face had been clearly seen and un-disguised. So he and I, a European and he a Mamluk Dragoman, made our way back to Maysoon's by a circuitous route. We toured around a bit more of Cairo. We felt as good as we did physically, for the success of our adventure had left us fully invigorated. Our souls were however, burdened with sadness from our parting with Catania who had made our travel across the Mediterranean, interesting, possible and rapid.

We purchased some oranges from the celebrated dealers in such things. From Catania we had learned that the female orange sellers' peripatetic promenades were not only to sell oranges but other commercial possibilities. The hostility of many Cairenes was directed at them for this, not for selling oranges, of course; nor for their prostitution but for the scandal of following two trades at once. This plurality of trades was particularly scandalous it was simply not done in the east.

We also found a man marching to his death by the loss of his head; his crime was for accidentally killing an ox by dropping a stone on its head as he repaired his house, or so said a sign around his neck. It would seem that the pagan rules still protected the ancient Egyptian Apis bull[13] and the Arabic sword was the method of punishment used by the vengeful Egyptian Gods.

We were near the Consulate well before eight and found Sleane who said that we would begin our journey tomorrow. Perkins celebrated this by having a slash *{urinating}* on the side of the Consulate, for we would have preferred to remain in Cairo some days more; Perkins for Maysoon and another massage and the lure of the pyramids I had sighted to the south for myself.

We came back to Maysoon's where he found his doxy. I ate in my small room to allow Perkins un-fettered time with his purchased but temporary wife. He probably ate better than I did for I was given some foul stew which I rejected, and in Arabic demanded a chicken well cooked, this I received in short order, a dinner of dried apricots and fried chicken with sesame, which sounded, smelled and looked better than it tasted. Having eaten, I began to write these notes trying to remember the conversations but I was distracted.

I felt insecure in my room for there was no way out except by the door for the high narrow windows precluded an attack or escape in that way. I barricaded my room door to make my worry less. I made sure Ascalon was loaded and ready and my French pistol near at hand. I had time to look at my new knife. I found how the rivets were set and removed them and the handle to find the tang with a touch of rust. This I cleaned away. It was a fine Sheffield-made blade and had forged into the tang the motto of the Company of Cutlers in Hallamshire, *Pour Y Parvenir a Bonne Foi {To Succeed Through Honest Endeavour}*. There was no mark of age or manufacturing date but I think it was one of the trade blades made in the 18th century. It was already razor sharp but the handle a bit 'bright' for my needs and too small for my hand. I took from my luggage a small thin leather wallet that had once held a thermometer and I tied it with a leather cord around the green stones in the pommel or butt. That fitted nicely and it felt better in my hand. As for the ivory and silver sheath I decided to replace that once I arrived in India. I was now well-armed, fed, if badly, and secure in my fortification within the city of Cairo. I could now return to recording our adventure within the slave market of Cairo.

[Editor's note: after Driscol's time efforts were made to alleviate the slave trade[14]]

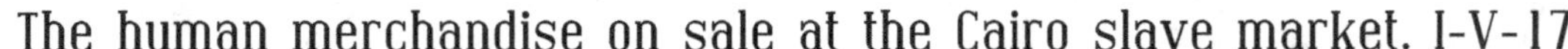

The human merchandise on sale at the Cairo slave market. I-V-17

To Suez Over The Desert From Cairo

Tuesday 15 November

We assembled early in the darkness in the pre-morning chill and I thought Perkins would have long drawn out goodbyes that I might have to suffer through but Maysoon made no appearance. A cart appeared and we soon found ourselves, too early it would seem, where we should be outside the Consulate. We were preparing to wait when a swarm of Egyptian rabble appeared - what their intentions were initially unclear but they swarmed over our cart and having been unsuccessful in keeping them away from the luggage and fearing they intended to steal - Perkins drew, cocked and fired his Colt into the air. The blast shattering the calm of the morning, for until then nothing had been said, whereas the majority of the beggars made off but three came at my associate, perhaps thinking he had but a single-shot pistol. I had drawn my pistol and made to fire but hesitated, moving from my point of aim from the centre of the first man's body to his feet, and fired, the ricochet making an ugly sound in the morning off the stone paving. They halted with sheer terror showing on their faces, thought better of their villainy and made off in some haste. The guards of the consulates, large Janissaries, joined us and the small street was soon cleared and regained its peaceful nature.

Soon everyone else came in; the missionaries, etc. The carriages or vans arrived and we were loaded up. Sleane explained that the trip was by stages. It was two and eighty miles from this exact spot to the receiving station at Suez, and we would make it in one movement. No sleep and stops only for the necessary and two meals. We were lucky, he explained, taking the vans which would take fourteen to sixteen hours, for in the summer camels or dromedary were used but these took from fifteen to four and thirty hours to accomplish the same trip. The vans had four horses and it was Perkins and I in one with our copious luggage. Most others carried three or four persons. Having assembled into a column of six such vans, we were soon off. I had asked Sleane about brigandage and he said that was very rare now but the vans would be joined at the first station outside Cairo by a patrol of mounted men who would ensure us of no Bedouin surprises. He wished me well and I thanked him again for his many kindnesses. He then added that he would be here four years later when I returned. We made it a point of agreement to meet again. I said goodbye to him with an especially effected thick Manc accent and he bid me farewell, also in the same false voice.

The way we would take was the same taken by the Indian post, for we were to join it on our ship and this path was called the *Derb el Hamra,* a path that would later join up with the more historic path which was called the *Derb el Hag,* which had been taken by travellers for thousands of years. We were soon out of Cairo. I saw no escort but later we found five rather rough looking customers following us to one side to avoid our dust. We were soon in the desert where only small acacia trees survived. It was the immensity of this desert that first struck me; it was vague and infinite, threatening and beguiling. I had not known a more magnificent and primaeval sight, for the desert was like a sea and only a knowledgeable man could travel it just as the sea is, which by its sense of bareness causes one to think it must be challenged only by a seasoned sailor. I resolved that I would become in time such a man who, when he next saw a desert, would not think how impassable it was but to think how soon I might conquer it and have it recorded on the maps of the world. I thought the following passages were very stirring when I wrote them but in reading them again I think I might be laying on the prose and rhetoric too much.

[Editor's note: Driscol struck out and re-wrote the last two sentences a half dozen times. I put above only his last two efforts]

We passed through an area covered with petrified wood and another where thousands of ground snails had emerged from the desert's surface said by the shouting driver to drink the dew. We saw a group of Moors and Arabs on horseback leading a number of camels. It was too disorganised to be a caravan but whatever it was, we coated them with dust as we moved thorough them at some speed.

There were everywhere the bleached bones of camels, horses and sheep mixed with sand, dust and stones all stretched out dead under the blue sky and relentless sun, whose glare was hurtful. It was not hot this November day but I could and would not believe that man could travel here in the height of the Egyptian summer when the temperature could rise to 118°.

Perkins seemed lost but I regained his attention by asking some questions on the state of training in the Indian army which I had thought about the previous evening. He listened to them and said, "Four things the Indian army can do faultlessly: one, is to breed excellent officers and sergeants by not training them, two organise funerals, three put together a frightfully complicated parade, four fight a military action against impossible odds and win it in an understated and practical way."

What more need be said! With that, he lapsed back into his thoughts and by his wistful expression; I could see he missed his Coptic-French courtesan.

We passed a station used by Muhammadan pilgrims and the bramble trees nearby were still covered in rags from their last passage, for it was here they discarded their normal clothing and took on the special ihram cloth for the Hajj. We would go some distance and then change horses. There was dust, desert and dust, and yet more dust. Following my father's advice I had not drunk since the night before and stood well the vibration of the vans, although he had not come this way and had made and left India by boat around the Cape of Good Hope.

The stations were run by Italians, Greeks and other non-Arabs and were terribly efficient, as long as a native was not the one to do the work. Arab women brought us water and it was vile despite bringing it from the well of 'Joseph'. Those responsible to do so did the task with the greatest lassitude, spending their time gossiping with one another and making us wait some time before they could be bothered to hoist the water jars to their heads and deliver it to us. The well was nothing but a hole in the ground with a nearby tomb used by the locally hired guards to oversee it. We usually had only a few minutes time to wait at the stations but this time we were delayed some fifteen minutes by their indolence. As to why it was called Joseph's well I never discovered, nevertheless we were soon off

The jarring was too much to allow reading. One's head often violently hits against the side of the van or, for me, I often struck the roof and worse I pitched against Perkins repeatedly. I would not have minded had it been the Swiss Lady from the canal boat but his body threw off clouds of dust when we regularly collided. Therefore, we crossed the desert in discomfort, seasoned with dust, thirst and a continuous bruising.

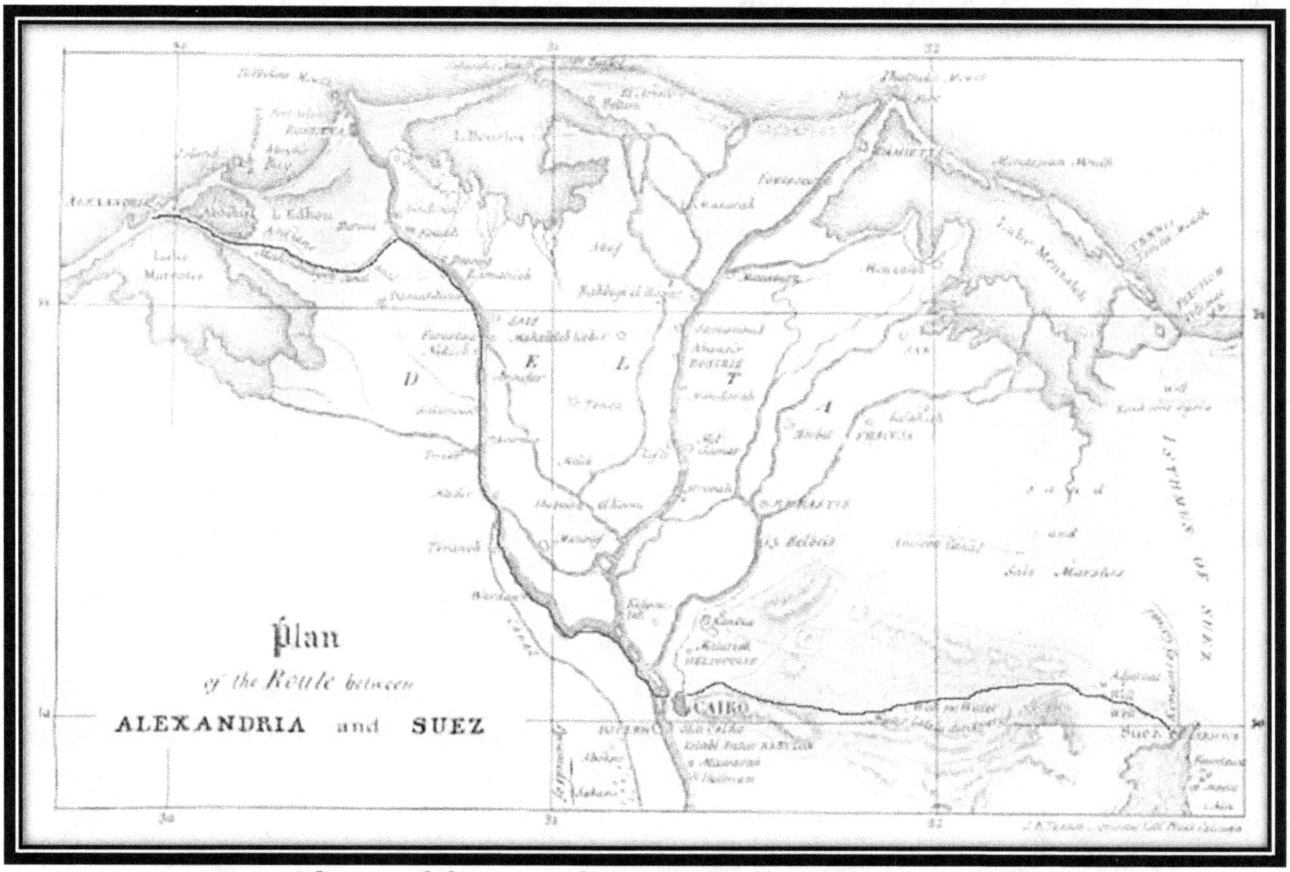

A map with a red line to show Driscol's route to Suez. I-V-18

Dusty Suez

We came to the end of this tiring dusty journey at the beginning of the evening. The environs of Suweis *{Suez}* or the *Clysma* of the ancients, were monotonous and barren, and the city had few lights to mark its presence but by then I cared not.

Had Lord Wellington himself stood before me and declared that I would and must that minute pick up my sword and defend the honour of England and its womanhood from a horde of pillaging despoliators and to do so I must retake that journey. I would have said, "Let them have their way, dear Duke, for I must first have cool water, a bath and sleep. I would gladly face, un-armed, an oncoming column of French grenadiers, smelling of garlic and sardines and bristling with bayonets than face that journey again."

The city was full of darkness, dust and un-clean Arabs and dirtier Egyptians, many sheep and goats but what any of these ate defied my powers of intellect for there was nothing here to eat. The climate was so dry and land was but stone, sand, dust and more dust. I suspected the dust itself was covered in minute dust. The town was built on a sand bank which lay between two deserts, the one I had just crossed and the mountains of Arabia to the east and the salty Red Sea.

The town was a collection of hovels and of no interest whatsoever. Its only illusion of importance was its port, for there one could take a ship to the east, and the other was its Biblical connotations. There was no green, only a few straggling trees that appeared to be nearing their long overdue deaths. In some we had seen goats which had worked their way up onto their lower branches and were nibbling at the shoots there. I named them *Hircum Aves {goat birds}.*

It was here that some theorised that the Israelites had escaped from the Egyptians by Moses' dividing of the sea. I believe the state of current Suez refutes the idea that the ancient Egyptians under Pharaoh were destroyed here. I believe they came, they saw, they were dismayed and followed Moses to find the land of milk and honey that he promised his own people too. For in Suez there was nothing to inspire an Egyptian to fight; to flight yes, but not fight.

We were met, of course, by the Suez Vice-Consul; a certain Mr Manoli, a lubricious fast talking Italian whose most outstanding feature was that I did not have to see him more than once. We could not see the port as of yet but he suggested that we might go to the bazaar since we were here and could buy provisions or anything else we might want. None took him up on his offer and we were soon led to our dreary lodgings.

I spent a restless night in a small room with Perkins and two other nondescript Englishmen we did not know nor cared to know about and I believe they felt the same. Everything to include every inch of myself and my every crevice was covered in dust. As I lied there, I felt I was still shaking even as I lay on the pallet, so shaken had I been from that momentous journey that for the first time in months I felt the tugging at my heart for Eccles and home. Perkins said he thought that he had dust even upon his soul, for even that felt rough and un-steady.

Perkins told me an interesting tale that his family had been long in the business of the Church and it was rumoured that his father was descendant of Thomas Wynter. I had not heard of him so he explained that Mr Wynter had been the supposititious son of the infamous Cardinal Wolsey by his paramour Miss Larke. So he said, he came from a long line of religiously tainted bastards. I wondered later what those two other Englishmen might have thought of our disrespected discourse!

I arose early as I awakened highly stimulated by a passing dream and made my way to a small rise near our dwellings that overlooked the port. The port was three quarters of a mile away and in the early dawn, I initially could not make it out. Behind me I could see the ruins of a Roman {Ptolemy era} aqueduct.

For in the harbour were not only Arab Dhows, but also Egyptian Dungiyahs, the large Jellbas and those large coasting boats of the Red Sea so famous for their shallow draughts. There were the plentiful trading vessels of Egypt the Jermes that were everywhere in the Mediterranean, and even a lonely and lost looking brig with the Portuguese flag at her peak.

I took out my instruments and notebooks and found Suez was at latitude 29°, 57', 30" N and longitude 32° 35' E from Greenwich I could not take a sun sight of course but instead verified the information that I already had. The temperature was 74° and it would rise to 81° at noon, the barometer was steady and the hygrometer pointed to it being abominably dry.

There was also something I must see, to see waiting for us, for there should be ship here for us. She should be an Indian Navy's paddle steamer. I wanted to see her, to be the first to sight her and to verify to myself that she existed. It was that which I sought and that which I had dreamed of that had awoken me. As I stood on that hill overlooking the port of Suez, that is what I looked for among the numerous craft, and I soon found her, for she was there, she was there indeed, with steam up and I recognised her from her likeness in the Times {newspaper} many months before. She had left England for the east last year and I had carried her portrait with me from London. It was her, I was certain but I nevertheless checked the view in my binoculars several times with the newspaper sheet I had with me, lighting a match to see more clearly and it was most certainly her.

I could now no longer claim to be travelling to the east for I had arrived and before me lay my magic carpet that would take me further, further into the east.

The HMIN steam sloop Atalanta in her English style black and white paint. In the Indian Navy she was repainted with a buff colored hull, red upper body and tan masts and a dark red colouring at her water line. I-V-19

The *Atalanta*; Ship Of The Honourable East Indian Company

Wednesday 16 November ± :

We came aboard the ship taken over there by a collection of shabbily built and maintained small craft. She was captained by Commander Henry A. Ormsby, FRS *{Fellow of the Royal Society}*; a noted scientific geographer, linguist and scholar who had been on several notable expeditions. As the *Atalanta* had been built as a warship, she was rougher in her trim than the other boats I had travelled in. I received a small cabin on her starboard side about the size of that I had had in the *William Fawcett*, a somewhat larger sidescuttle and, marvel of marvel, a porcelain basin instead of a tin one. I was certainly travelling in high *prétentieux {pretentious}* style. Perkins obtained accommodation on the other side of the boat. Her purser was a most harassed man that day, for he had a boarding and quartering plan but no one seemed to be happy with it. He had assigned our cabins by the ordering of our surnames by alphabetic chance. So I was soon in my quarters while Perkins, with that ghastly 'P' at the front of his surname, had to wait to be gifted a cabin that was somewhat larger than mine but which we filled with our departed friend Beer's luggage. I spoke in passing to the Captain in Arabic, and he was pleased to have me do so, for he too was a linguist and had travelled in this region for some time. I was astonished to note that he spoke Arabic with no error in its pronunciation. He was even able to say the hard to reproduce fricative sound *kh* familiar to German-speakers which I could not do properly - yet.

I was introduced to nearly all his officers. The first Officer was a Lieutenant Perkins and we found by tortuous comparison that he was my friend Perkins' were second cousins once removed. Where Perkins was devilishly handsome, this First Officer P_____ was a dull slack faced hard-featured and un-prepossessing man.

[Editor's note: To avoid confusion I will use the device of calling this other 'Perkins' P_____]

While Perkins discussed with his long lost cousin what tomfoolery their great, great, grandfathers might have been up to, I found another officer in a uniform I was not familiar with and I introduced myself and met one Ensign Horne; a good fellow, who was the gunnery officer, despite not having a naval rank and that he had not a thing to do in port while loading passengers. He was most pleased to show me the ship. He was used to the task and being inordinately proud of his ship, for she was the first of a new class of steam sloops for the Indian navy and was therefore looked upon in wonder and admiration wherever she went. Hundreds and thousands of people would come to see her in port in India, for she was home ported in Bombay.

However, I did not understand his rank or uniform and I wondered if I was being made a fool of as the man was certainly no naval officer, for a few questions dealing with the ship showed he was by education an artillerist and not a seaman. So I expressed my puzzlement to which he laughed offered me his hand again and said he would explain but that he would show me the ship first, for she was more important than he.

The *Atalanta* was a new kind of ship; a steam sloop launched less than a year ago at London. She was a sloop because of several reasons: one, in the Royal Navy a vessel that is ship rigged or having three masts is so called by that term depending on the rank of the officer in command.

Thus, a vessel may be called one thing when commanded by a captain, in this case a ship or frigate – the next time she will be called a sloop, because she is now commanded only by a lesser being or in this case, a commander, this ship itself has not changed, just the rank of her skipper.

The next reason; two, was because in the 18th century, a British navy sloop-of-war had a single deck that carried less than eighteen guns.

The *Atalanta* fulfilled both of these requirements; she had three masts and was deemed ship rigged, yet she was built as and sported a barkentine's rig in port. She also had less than 18 guns and commanded not by a post Captain but a commander. She was therefore a lowly sloop instead of a mighty frigate and her engine granted her the additional title of 'steam'. In the Napoleonic Wars she might have been considered a post ship *{a small frigate}*.

She displayed her smartness with a buff coloured hull, red upper body and tan masts and a dark red colouring at her water line. She was of 617 tons, a side paddle steamer, with dual 210 NHP *{Nominal Horsepower}* British built engines; launched in 1835 she could make nine knots under steam and fourteen under sail and steam. She carried four smooth bore muzzle-loading cannons of Dickerson's design. Firing a 32 pound solid shot and one eight foot long 54 cwt *{3 tons}* 8" *{200mm}* or '68' pounder, smooth bore muzzle loading cannon which could fire a 56 pound hollow iron shot or more suitably a 48 pound explosive shell with a bursting charge of 2 pounds and 11 ounces of powder. Her shells were set to explode by use of a standard common metal style fuse, for now this was a necessity as we were to go to a place in our God's domain where I imagined piracy was still real and even large ships were in some danger.

Horne was quite surprised that I knew as much as did about that fine gun, her weight of shell and other minute detail. I explained that I had taken up with the light infantry as a matter of tradition and a lack of lucre but had studied the intricacies of gunnery for many years. We discussed the ramifications of the experiment aboard the H.M.S. Excellent[15], which had been changing the way artillery, and firearms were viewed.

We had not gone much beyond the main deck and that wonderful gun and were debating the delicacies of a metal fuse versus the more customary Moorsom's made wooden ones when we were alerted by the loud voice of a mate.

Pontifications

The Captain of the ship was desirous of speaking to the men aboard and after some time we found ourselves assembled aft, Ensign Horne and I having to, reluctantly, cut short our discussion of armament. He, the Captain, welcomed us to HIS ship, introduced his principal officers then laid down what we were later to refer to as 'Ormsby's Rules'

I.	That our ship would remain at anchor at Suez (or Suweis as he pronounced it, the proper way in Arabic) until another important passenger arrived, hopefully this evening, with our departure to occur as soon as possible afterward

II.	We were reminded that we were now on a military ship of the Honourable East India Company and would follow the rules, traditions and timings of custom. That we were to wear our uniforms - if in the military while at sea and full dress for dinner

III.	We were to conserve water at all times, for not like England we were now in a drier part of the world and water here was a resource that one could not waste

IV.	We would then make for the grand city of Bombay but were enjoined by said company *{HEIC}* to make port at Djidda *{Jeddah}* and Mokha *{Mocha}* to pick up dispatches. After Bombay, this ship or another would take those passengers on to Calcutta and other ports further east

V.	He asked that all persons aboard stay aboard and not venture into the town - that caused some tittering in the assemblage for there was no reason a man in control of his senses would go to such a fleapit

VI.	That despite his relatively low rank, he was in command and while at sea and port his judgments on the movement, discipline and actions of said ship and crew were his alone, passengers of higher rank were invited not to attempt to overrule his authority

VII.	He wanted no talk of pirates in front of the ladies and children. Yes, there were pirates but they had not attempted to take a ship of this size in generations and he would not allow the gentler sex to be vexed by speculations on this matter

VIII.	He also warned of the perils of shipboard romances. A third of the passengers were un-attached, just engaged or to be engaged Ladies who were aboard to join their husbands or soon to be husbands in India, and that they might all consider us as their elder brothers, and, having said that, he would not allow any non-Christian or un-sightly 'arrangements' to be made

IX.	That ship church services would be held and that attendance was mandatory

He let those pronouncements sink in amongst us all - it amused me to think of what Perkins, standing to my right, might be thinking. He soon let me know. Perkins bent forward and noted in my ear that he was indeed, most amused, for he suggested that on Sunday, the good Captain would read to us from his Bible in his shirtsleeves, for while he was in uniform he recognised no higher authority. I pointed out to him that there had only been nine commandments so he had less authority that he who had given us ten.

Then invitations to join the Captain at his table were also given, again alphabetically arrived at but those selected were from the un-loved men who were without family and I being a 'D' *{for Dunce as Perkins quipped}* I was so invited. He returned to his cabin to sulk I suspect over the squashing of his hopes for a shipboard romance, or two or three.

Captain Ormsby surprised me and made mockery of my mockery when he continued with another three sets of rules. Detail pronouncements on matters of timing, use of the head, and who could, and who could not go into the rigging.

The Most Senior Of The Most Junior

He then asked whom the most senior of the most junior officers was from amid the passengers. That took some sorting and it, of course, derived upon me. I was the most senior, with some eight months in grade, there being six more junior ensigns, sub-lieutenants and coronets. Damn what right mess might this be, was my first thought.

I was informed that I had the great honour of being designated a King's courier and would take over the guardianship of whatever was being couriered and then to safe guard said important matter, paper or item until I could deliver it to the clerk of the British Consul in Djedda, to a Mr Jacoul Youssouff.

I was informed that whatever it was would be delivered to me by a charge d'affaire from Cairo and that at some point I would need to return to shore prior to our departure. He then added that I would obtain for this special duty a recompence of an additional $1/52^{nd}$ of basic monthly pay per each full day I was so selected.

Oh Glory.

I arrived early for dinner, as is my way, and found the ship's Captain's cabin to be large and austere. However, the bells wrung, announcing the time, and who were soon seated. Two junior officers who both had family names starting with 'F' both also arrived after the bell, and were soundly berated for their lack of timeliness and discourteous behaviour to the others. Before we began, a steward spoke with the pursuer who wrinkled his brow and spoke to the Commander, who then spoke to another, who then spoke to the Pursuer, who then directed a query at me.

"Ensign," he said, "our Lieutenant Easily is indisposed and I recall that you came aboard with another. What was his name?"

"Perkins," I replied.

"And is this Gentleman a bachelor?"

"Yes."

"Ah, good. Do you believe he would join us late for dinner?"

"Yes, he would," I answered, and so Perkins came to the A, B, C, D, no E and two boorish F's dinner. He later threatened me with a slow and painful death for having done so.

It was well laid out, consisting of a goodly piece of beef, well cooked, two curries, one of which I recognised from those heavenly days at the Oriental club in London and a few new dishes. The conversation soon became animated after the standard toasts to King and country and the rest demanded by tradition.

Perkins, who was seated some places away from me, said that 'he wish the women on this ship were as beautiful as the dinner which had been laid out for us', in Persian of course.

We were both surprised that amongst the talk of horses, ships, weather, the entertainments of Bombay and the price of caulking, another voice added, also in Persian, "Yes, that indeed would be heavenly."

It turned out to be the same Ensign Horne I had discussed the ship's artillery with who was cater-cornered to me. Perkins and he had not met and soon an animated three-way conversation was going on between us. We had only just identified each other and learned that we could speak Persian when we were stoutly reminded to not talk shop while at the Captain's table, NOR to speak rude and outlandish foreign tongues; and so stymied, we looked at one another in hilarity and fell to eating, like the good little junior officers we were.

After a good meal, a tradition of the 'first night at the Captain's table' was pounced on us. Each man who was not of the ship's officers was to rise, make a toast, and state his name & regiment, his place of birth and how many years he had been in the east.

There was Captain Abbot who toasted the regular British army to whom he was returning from a two-year absence in England, where he was happy to report he had failed to make a match in marriage and was returning as a contented bachelor to his garrison in Bangalore with the 62nd (Wiltshire) Regiment of Foot. He had eighteen years in the east and was from Belfast.

This drew some mild applause and a reminder that he had not spoken the sequence of announcements in the right order.

Ensign and Cornets Batesmen and Connelly, whose details I do not recall but who were newly commissioned with less than sixty days of experience, toasted the Prince of Wales and something else and were labeled 'Johnny Newcomes' of the first order *{men new or to be new to India}*.

Lieutenant Downey was from the 11th Regiment of Light Dragoons and, like myself, coming east under the special secondment. He had no time in the east and stumbled though some nonsense about a toast to the Church of England.

I was next and announced who I was, made a flippant toast to wine which the officers of the *Atalanta* seemed rather attached to.

> *"The wine bubble winked at me, and said,*
> *You will miss me sir, when you are misled or dead."*

However, I was dismissed as yet another un-experienced 'gryphon' *{new man}*.

They could not, of course, make any such remark about Perkins who had served in India for some time and his toast was notable. The commander brought me to task for my writing it down after he said it. He said:

"I especially admired three classes of people; men, old women and children and that he had enjoyed his dinner so much that he raised his class to the meal, his host and those I especially liked"

This speech was met with some somber appreciation and I must admit I only later understood what he had said and how he had indirectly insulted the host.

After that tortuous session, dessert was brought in and we rose up to speak and drink champagne, for that is what was offered but I had none. Restrictions on the subjects on which we could speak were lifted. Perkins and I were soon in conversation with Ensign Horne. We found his Persian to be more advanced than ours in the matter of vocabulary but we thought we had him in the manner of pronunciation. To this, he agreed and he told us how he had come to learn Persian. He had been recruited into the second British mission that was sent in 1833 to train the Persians. He had tried to teach them the actions of the modern artillery and had organised four batteries for the sorry lot. Those Persian officers he was supposed to help, as he called them, 'the lazy louts' who saw every attempt at improvement as a means to enrich themselves at the Persians government's expence, however, had obstructed him. Having found his advice disregarded and any control over the pay, rations or promotions of the batteries he had formed would be denied, he resigned his position after two-and-half years.

Perkins asked if he might be up for an adventure involving a need for Persian speaking officers? To which he replied with a question.

"In this adventure of yours, might I be able to ride at the enemy with my sword in hand, or will I be putting alcohol over butterflies in glass jars, or shall we be travelling in the areas where un-washed heathens have not yet met a proper Englishman with the intent to gain knowledge of said land so it might be righty placed under British dominion?"

Perkins replied to this saying, he hoped the later would occur in time, sir, with perhaps some of the second and, if need be, the first.

He consented to join without another thought and we had our third man.

There are no known images of Horne at the age in which he joined the expedition but this is of his younger brother who in later life is said to resemble him highly. I-V-20

==++++++++++

Alexander Anton Horne

Ensign, Bombay Artillery

On duty with the Indian Navy

Horne was the youngest son of Ackerley Maynard Horne, Esq., of a good but insolvent family; his father being a lawyer of many talents, one of them not being the law. He was born in the county of Devon near Barnstaple, on August 7th, 1813. His mother was from Portugal and from within the circle of English families by the name of Massey, a name well known in the Port trade. He received a modest education and his family, after many years of a middling income, came all at once into an inheritance which allowed him, at the age of 17, to enter Exeter College, Oxford. He was of poor academic habits in his family's chosen field of law and left after his first year. His family fortune had then taken another downturn in the meantime but he was able to gain an entrance to the Royal Military Academy at Woolwich. Horne attended, despite having a great yearning to be a cavalry officer as his father and uncles had been in the wars of Napoleon. He however had no way to obtain such a costly commission or meet its high yearly cost. He also had failed in his attempts to enter Sandhurst for this same reason. Woolwich, or 'The Shop' as it was commonly called, produced in him a 'good officer of artillery'. He was considered by his peers to be a flawless equestrian and, had his purse allowed it, he would have gained an entrance into the horse artillery. He was second in fencing at Woolwich and considered one of the best shots; this skill plus his horsemanship making him a formidable hunter. He was described as being of middle height at 5' 7", weighing 14 stone; sturdily built; a square head topped with the luxurious pitch black hair of his Portuguese ancestors; bright, intelligent, flashing brown eyes and a smile of perfect white teeth; somewhat bow legged from a youth spent on horseback. In India, he would pursue with a passion the hunting of boar on horseback with a spear. He joined the Bombay Artillery in 1833 but soon volunteered and joined a British mission to Persia. He returned and rejoined his regiment selecting to act as a 'marine' and artillerist aboard the ships of the Indian navy. His mother having been Portuguese, he knew that language fluently and Spanish too, and, of course, French. His Greek and Latin were not deemed remarkable but his Persian, although crude, was effective. He did however have a condescending attitude towards the Persians, Arabs, and Indians, which for some un-fathomable reason they seemed to favour. His ire was not just directed at the eastern races, for he equally held all natives and Europeans in low contempt, essentially everyone in the world who was not Englishman like himself, was a target for his displeasure and a pointed comment.

===

We talked of his being aboard ship, and he explained that the Company *{HEIC}* had not seen fit to spend the money to provide its own navy with a sufficient force of Marines. Therefore, an arrangement had been made by which the Bombay Artillery, charged as it was with the defence of the port and rarely going on inland campaigns, would provide its men a good group of men Horne added, not damn niggers as some of the batteries were native manned to the navy as need be, and so he was here.

Our good Captain, who said that he had just heard a comedy-tragedy from Captain Abbot that bore repeating, interrupted us. He spoke of a notorious duel that had taken place in India in the 18th century.

It took place after the First Carnatic War in May 1749 when two men, each artillerists, who had slandered the other with allegations of cowardice and worse. The duel was done in the following way: Each man was strapped with his back to the muzzle of a cannon with one's hands free and the cannon's set wheel to wheel, hub to hub but pointing in opposite directions. The method of the duel was that each man was provided with twelve matches to light and throw at the other man's cannon, which was loaded with a full charge of powder and primed with an extra-long fuse laid out atop the top of the barrel. So each man had twelve throws plus a glass of wine to drink or throw at the burning match of his own barrel should his luck be poor and his opponent's good.

The man stopped speaking at that point and was immediately bombarded with the obvious question of what had happened; who had won? To which he replied, "Well, it was May so the Monsoon soon spoilt the fuses and the Governor threw both of them in prison and, as they would not reconcile, he sent one to West Africa and the other to China. Where they continued the duel by post for many decades inside each mailing would be a consumed match."

The second in command then interceded that another tale must also be told about the journey of the *Atalanta* to this spot.

She sailed from Falmouth on December 29th making for Bombay. She was damaged in a storm off France in the Bay of Biscay - something I could relate to - with her paddle-boxes and jib-boom carried away and so stricken, she stopped at Teneriffe for eight days to repair damages. From there she steamed to Cape Town and made her destination after one hundred and six days being greatly delayed by the Monsoon weather, a gale of wind near Mauritius and again delayed in obtaining supplies on the African coast. She had been at sea for sixty-eight of those one hundred plus days, her delays being due to weather and the requirement to coal.

I added to this that the ship, *William Fawcett*, had also damaged her paddle boxes. This started a spirited conversation on the un-suitability of seagoing ships to be 'saddled' with paddle wheels as they not only reduced the ability of a ship to sail with the wind but they were fragile and liable to damage from the sea - not to mention what enemy fire would do to such fragile constructions.

[Editor's note: I have removed a discussion by Driscol with himself about the merits of paddle wheels versus screw propeller - he decided that the propeller, despite being so positioned as to be damaged in grounding would be the way forward. I have left in a shorter digression of his below, a table on the subject above and much to his interest[6]]

I found the officers of the *Atalanta* to be an odd lot and Perkins and I soon made our farewells and arranged to meet with Horne at the main mast to continue our conversation. He and I soon took the discussion off into areas that Perkins was un-interested in. *Why he would not be interested in the very thought-provoking fact that to fire the 8 inch cannon cost nearly one pound a shot or more specially 19s 3¼d {about $125}*

Cost per round of 8-inch naval shell fired

	s.	d.
Shell	5	$4\frac{1}{2}$
Moorsom's wooden fuse	5	0
Charge, 10 lbs. powder at 7d	5	10
Bursting-powder, 2 lbs.	1	2
Box (containing same)	1	11
Total, including box	19	$3\frac{1}{2}$

Awakened, in the early hours of the morning, I went back on shore to that cursed Suez and there I met the courier from England, he had come by way of Trieste. He would go no farther. I had to make my way at the wharf though the gully gully *{tricksters and magicians}* men. The eastern courier had come on the *Atalanta* and he had an additional satchel to take to the ambassador in Constantinople, thus the need for me. We met under lantern light and it had a conspiratorial atmosphere, as if we were to plot the assassination of a French Cardinal in some convoluted but fiendish way. The courier from England gave me his satchel, and the Courier from India gave his to him. We all shook hands. The man from England sighed, took hold of himself, turned and headed back to England. The Indian courier went with him as they would both journey, as I had, to Alexandria before he would turn north, and I turned to go to India, satchel in hand and bound eastward.

========

End of Volume 1

An Officer of the Crown:

The Middlecombe Expedition to the Aral Sea in Turcomania and the Khanates of Independent Tartary, 1837-1838

Reminiscences of an English Ensign's Journey to the East in 1836

========

The Germann-Debly sisters whom Driscol met on his voyage out to India, Prudence, & Danae

Driscol's beloved Millicent the third Germann-
Debly sister

==

Editor's Preface notes:

1. Hookem-snivey, a term meaning deceitful or sneaky but in this context probably means taking advantage of the situation.

2. The Danish colony in India.

3. Samuel White Baker. This man took up the hunting of game armed only with a knife and used dogs to run the beast down on foot. Driscol felt this was a more 'sporting' method of hunting.

4. Latin and Greek for note taking. Fortunately for us, Driscol was compulsive in taking notes.

5. Johnson, P. (1992). *The birth of the modern: World society 1815-1830.* Harper Perennial.

6. The vessels in the whale-fishery were obliged to bear those with no experience to gain their tonnage bounty in accordance with the British law of the time. The British wished to increase the number of seaman who could be Whalemen besides those in the North Frisian Islands of Denmark, for in time of war they might not be available to continue this valuable trade and the majority of 'English' whalers came from those foreign islands.

7. His regiment's insignia was the famed Light Infantry bugle. The instrument became the badge for the light infantry regiments because of their dispersed deployment voice commands could not be used and a complex series of bugle calls were created to pass information to the light infantry while in battle

----

Chapter 1 notes:

1. Pedasos was named after Achilles' third horse, from the Iliad. Pedasos, despite being a mortal horse, served Achilles along with the divine Xanthus and Balios. This was Driscol's third horse in his life and the first one he had bought himself. As a boy, his first horse had been a Welsh pony and a rare Perlino, a cream-colored horse with blue eyes, whom he named 'Lune', after his own Danish nickname. His second horse was a large grey Connemara pony whom he called 'Beast' and which had kicked him a number of times until Driscol learned to mount him from the other side.

2. The East India Company, the private ruler of India at that time. Also known as the Honourable East India Company, 'the Company', or by its initials HEIC.

3. Mirza Mohammed Ibrahim. A Persian employed as a teacher of Persian by the East India Company at their college, which would later be called Haileybury. At this time he was 36.

4. "Oxbridge:" A term meaning those who had graduated from either Cambridge or Oxford. A rarely used word until many years later.

5. "Jeweled rice:" A much beloved Persian rice dish of spices, fruit and chicken.

6. Minute by the Honourable T. B. Macaulay, dated the 2nd February 1835. This would lead to the displacement of Persian with English as the official language of British India in 1837 as predicted by Professor Ibrahim.

7. "Mancunian:" the dialect in that area of England. Also referred to as Manc.

8. British explorers of Persia, Tartary and the approaches to India.

9. A derogatory name for Americans of that era.

10. The other college run by the East India Company, for training officers for their army. Haileybury being for the training of their commercial and civilian staff.

11. Men who pursued married women.

12. A list of perils from veterans of India, Pindaris, Marathan raiders, renegades, vagabonds or more charitably free companions who formed groups to plunder the countryside. So troublesome did they become that Lord Hasting lead an expedition against them, grandly called the Pindari War. He hunted them down and by 1819 the survivors were dispersed and resettled. The Thugee cult, that mysterious murdering religious sect, was then being hunted and dealt with in India. A number of sensational articles and publications had unsettled the populace over the extent and danger of the group. Dhobi, Indian washer men or women, who were noted for destroying clothes by their crude methods. Feral dogs were always a problem in India, not kept by Muhammadan's for they deemed them unclean. Hindu's wouldn't destroy them so they often grew bold and bothersome. India was infested with snakes, many of a very poisonous nature.

13. A traditional British Army salute but with a short 'jab' away from the head before returning to rest.

14. Driscol's siblings and their status as of September 1836.

Frederick Gideon (Gary): born 1785; businessman and farmer who managed the running of the estate; unmarried and living in Eccles, England; Captain in the Yeomanry.

John Hughes: born 1786; major in the East India Company's Madras European Regiment at Pondicherry, India; seconded for the last eight years to the Governor's staff; widower with a son, James, at a boarding school in Sussex.

Irish twins Stephen Hastings and Aaron Wesley: born 1792; the first a scholar, head master, and Militia officer; married with two daughters and a son. Aaron was the black sheep of the family; disowned; a defrocked Catholic priest who used the name 'O'Driscoll; location and status unknown in 1836 but not spoken of around his parents.

Mark Allen; born 1797. Covenanted pursuer and accounts clerk of the HEIC at the Straits Settlements, (Singapore) married, three children but none survived the harsh climate, Quincy, Samuel and Sully.

Joanna Grace; born 1798 died 1808

Zoe Nora: born 1808; Driscol's favorite sister and well educated for the times; unmarried.

Lauren Rose: born 1809; a talented artist she was very shy and uncommunicative; unmarried.

15. Karen K. Wainwright was a childhood friend whose exact relationship with Driscol has not been delineated in the few books so far translated. Yet in letters that survive from Driscol's mother to David, she refers to her both as her son's acquaintance, friend, god sister and conceivable marriage partner. She is described as being a small, lovely black-haired woman of round face, brown eyes and boyish figure. She had scholastic skills well above Driscol's; something that seemed to have annoyed him to no end. She was the daughter of Christopher and Hannah Wainwright nee Warden. He was a leading mechanic dealing with the steam engines of the textile mills and canal boats and helping to build some of the earliest maritime steam engines. She was an exception for that era as she acted as the leading clerk at the Manchester Bureau of Conveyances which had been a sinecure of her family for many generations. Miss Wainwright experimented with electricity and wrote papers on the subject under the name K. Wainwright.

16. "Muu:" was Driscol's family term for his mother, derived from the Danish term for mother.

17. This was the first of many recipes that Driscol would collect. After some experimentation and several tries, here is a modern version of this recipe highly recommended. It can also be made in a vegetarian style by substituting the chicken broth with vegetable. Two versions are shown; one good for two people and the other for a larger family or dinner party of 5.

<u>Small version</u>	<u>Large version</u>
$\frac{3}{4}$ cup of rice	$2\frac{1}{4}$
$\frac{1}{4}$ stick of butter	1
$2\frac{1}{4}$ cup of water or broth	$6\frac{3}{4}$
2 Chicken bouillon cubes	6
$\frac{1}{4}$ TPS Thyme	$\frac{3}{4}$
$\frac{1}{4}$ TPS Parsley	$\frac{3}{4}$

$\frac{1}{4}$ large yellow Onion $\frac{1}{2}$
$\frac{1}{2}$ TPS Pepper   1 $\frac{1}{2}$
$\frac{1}{4}$ TPS Garlic $\frac{3}{4}$

1. Melt butter over low heat in a fry pan. Layer on rice. Mix completely and brown.

2. Place water in a pan and add everything but the rice. Bring to a boil.

   a) Method one: Place browned rice in a casserole and add boiling water, cover and bake for 30 minutes at 375°.

   b) Method two: Place browned rice in an automatic rice cooker and add boiling water. Cover and turn on cooker.

3. Remove when finished, stir and add additional thyme to taste.

Additionally; Sod was a Danish sweet soup made with tapioca and dried fruit. Gule aerter was the favourite of Driscol's father, Angus, and was made of yellow peas, pork, onion, potatoes, carrots and thyme. Thyme it would seem was a popular spice in the Driscol household.

18. Although the family did not know it, the use of this medicine would ease Driscol's time in the east, for the patent medicine contained a number of ingredients and, from his journals, Driscol partook of the remedy religiously per his mother's instructions to do so. Warburg's Tincture was a secret, proprietary remedy and the formula was not published until 1875. It contained an array of ingredients, including a large portion of quinine, which may explain Driscol avoiding malaria fevers.

19. Royal escort duty consisted of providing men to accompany those members of nobility who so wished it. The 14th King's Regiment of Light Dragoons, later to be 14th King's Hussars, in my day the 14th/20th King's Hussars and presently the King's Royal Hussars. As a young Lieutenant FIST officer in the 1st Battalion 2nd Field Artillery, I had dinner with this fine unit in 1981. At that time my meeting Anne and obtaining the journals of Driscol were twenty-five plus years in the future. I reflect now that the regimental silver service would have been the same and the venerated chamber pot of King Joseph of Spain was there still. In retrospect it was another fortuitous crossing of my life with Driscol.

20. Gen. Sir Edward Kerrison; BT, KCB, GCH, (Baronet, The Most Honourable Order of the Bath Knight Commander, Royal Guelphic Order of the Knight Grand Cross)

21. This water source would later become part of France in 1859 and known to us now under the brand name of Evian.

22. This appears to be a distorted story of the actions of Major Brotherton which can be read in full in; *The Hawks a short history of the 14th/20th King's Hussars.* (p. 26). By Perrett.

23. Shipp, John. *Memoirs of the extraordinary career of John Shipp.* London: Hurst, Chance & Co, 1830.

24. Until 1833, in the East India Company one had to become covenanted prior to going east. You had to provide two sureties (persons of importance who backed your honesty), swear to obey the companies rules, take up an expensive bond to support your oath and if you violated it by trading for yourself and not the good of the company or otherwise did not do what one was told, it was forfeit. For doing so, you would receive the trust and support of the company and a rich pension at the end of your service. Driscol's brother Mark was so covenanted.

25. List of books bought by Driscol; those packed for shipping and those kept out for reading:

1-13. The Encyclopædia Americana: 1833 edition.13 volumes.
14. Washington Irving - Voyages and Discoveries of the Companions of Columbus
15. Sir John Barrow, 1st Baronet - The Eventful History of the Mutiny and Piratical Seizure of H.M.S. Bounty
16. Lord Mahon - History of the War of Succession in Spain
17. Edward Bulwer-Lytton, 1st Baron Lytton - Paul Clifford
18. Lord Mahon - Life of Belisarius
19. George Payne Rainsford James - Richelieu
20-24. Frederick Marryat - The Naval Officer, The Pirate, Mr Midshipman Easy, The Three Cutters, Peter Simple
25. John Franklin - Narrative of a Journey to the Shores of the Polar Sea
26. Edward George Bulwer-Lytton - The Last Days of Pompeii

Books sealed for shipment to India 20:

1. The Decameron of Boccaccio
2. Henry Summersett - The wizard and the sword
3-4. Godfrey Higgins - Anacalypsis (two volumes)
5. Washington Irving - Tales of the Alhambra
6. Victor Hugo - Written in French: Notre Dame de Paris (The Hunchback of Notre Dame)
7. John Stuart Mill - The Spirit of the Age
8. Barbara Hofland - Africa Described, in Its Ancient and Present State
9. James Fenimore Cooper - The Last of the Mohicans
10. Alicia Lefanu - Henry the Fourth of France
11. William Hazlitt - The Spirit of the Age
12. Sir Walter Scott - Redgauntlet
13. Hans Christian Andersen - (In Danish) Fodreise fra Holmens Canal til Østpynten af Amager i 14. 14. Aarene 1828 og 1829 (A Journey on Foot from Holmen's Canal to the East Point of Amager)
15. Robert Southey - Life of Cromwell
16. Charles Mills -History of the Crusades for the Recovery and Possession of the Holy Land
17. James Mill - The History of British India
18. Charles Mills - History of Mohammedanism
19. Collin de Plancy - (in French) Dictionnaire Infernal
The name of the last book is torn off from the bottom of the page but from other notes I believe it is 20. Washington Irving - A Chronicle of the Conquest of Granada

26. "The fishing fleet:" a term for unmarried women who in autumn of each year went out to India with the unprejudiced mission to gain suitable husbands. With the start of reliable steam navigation this would become a popular way to supply wives to the men in India to whom only native women had previously been available. This once acceptable situation was now changing and, with the coming of the Victorian age, only a white wife would be deemed acceptable within a generation.

27. Pablo Fanque was a rare item in 1830's England; an African who was a riding master and noted throughout the island for his skill at horsemanship.

28. "Trio:" a son to the orders of Church of England, one to the army and one for the navy. If they had had more sons, the next would have gone to the East India Company, the fifth to the City of London and a sixth son might have been allowed a scholastic life or to approach the bar.

29. "Maundy money:" Royal Maundy is a religious service in the Church of England held on Maundy Thursday, the day before Good Friday. At the service, the King or a royal official ritually distributes small silver coins known as "Maundy money". They are often kept as a token of the event and are not used as money.

30. "Mufti:" wearing the clothes of the local natives, used in the orient to mean an Englishman in disguise as a native but in this instance Driscol is making a witty comment about his acting the civilian.

31. "Sneeze Lurker:" a thief who throws pepper or tobacco snuff in a person's face then while they are discombobulated steals their wallet, watch and baggage.

32. "Lloyd's rules:" 19th century loading recommendations were introduced by Lloyd's Register of British and Foreign Shipping in 1835, the recommendation covered the amount of freeboard a ship must maintain to be safe from being overburdened.

33. "Tyke:" a person from Yorkshire. "Frogs," of course, refers to both Frenchmen and the Dutch. It was a term that first referred only to the Dutch due to their living in reclaimed swamps but in the 18 century had come to mean Frenchmen for their habit of eating frog legs. "Goans" were East Indians, often of mixed Portuguese blood and employed because they had no caste and could work at any trade.

34. Until 1856 when His Royal Highness the Duke of Cambridge became Commander-in-Chief, smoking was absolutely prohibited in barracks, mess-rooms and many public places. After the royal anointing smoking indoors became commonplace and people began to smoke inside buildings.

35. Howard Staunton was the best English player of his day and some now consider him to have been the first 'world champion' of chess.

36. It is from Mrs. Germann that we gain our first description of the appearance of Driscol who never described his own form. She wrote a letter to her own younger sister and that sister sent the news to her own relatives by marriage who were English. They spread it to the sister of the sister of the man she had married and who in turn had a daughter, who had married a cousin, who was in the same church as Angus Driscol's sisters' eldest daughter. Therefore, the description came, in time, to Mrs. Driscol who was delighted to hear of her son:

On our ship out, Millicent has made the acquaintance of an Ensign David Driscol who is a very tall slender young man; a full hand taller than my dear daughter, which is a relief to her, God bless her soul. His thinning hair is nearly the colour of hers. He is not poxed and had no mars to his character that I could see, and during the voyage proved himself to be a modest hero at a time of need.......description of the problems with the William Fawcett are deleted... and he has hazel eyes of green, brown and gold. He is a supporter of teetotalism, which brings such joy to my heart in consideration of my own troubles. He is of our church but not as observant as our own family, but he is very kind and respectful to her and friendly with Danae and even with Prudence who can be so trying at times. David is very well educated, if a quiet man, but sadly with no fortune. He is too young to marry and is out to India for four years but given how well the two are matched we may hear from him again as we, too will be in India for the foreseeable future.

37. "French admirals:" Jean-Baptiste Philibert Willaumez who commanded the French fleet at the Battle of Basque Roads in 1808 and Guy-Victor Duperré who won the Battle of Grand Port, destroying a British squadron and later led the 1830 invasion of Algeria.

Chapter II notes:

1. Russian frigate: Lazarev was the man who took her on a voyage around the world, 1822-1825.

2. Brand & Co's condiment for fish, meat and fowl. This would become known as A.1 Sauce many years later and labeled as 'steak sauce' when marketed in the US in 1895.

3. Cantrabarian: another name for the Biscay bay.

4. Sailor: this is mild insult by Driscol; only a landsman calls a seaman a sailor but perhaps he was quoting Perkins who was, of course, a landsman.

5. Rennell's current: named for Major James Rennell FRS, one of England's first oceanographers who charted the currents of the seas and in particular the one named for him that is found south of the Scilly Isles.

6. Orgeat Sirup is made from the following recipe that Driscol gathered from the Goan crewmen:

      1 pound of almonds, pounded into a paste
      10 bitter almonds, pounded into a paste
      These are mixed and then squeezed to remove the oil
      The mixture is left to itself for 24 hours in a cool place

Mix with $^1/_2$ quart of water (two cups) and the following:

$^1/_3$ ounce of tartaric acid (two teaspoons), a pound and a quarter of sugar (two and half cups) and one ounce of orange juice or orange flavouring

7. Pourtraicts: obsolete word for portrait used at that time to label those paintings done in an earlier style or not pleasing to today's (1836) tastes, i.e. obsolete.

8. In February of 1848 another Steam ship of the same line, the Great Liverpool, would strike this same reef. She, too, would make it to the Spanish coast, near Corcubion. Three lives were lost. The loss would again be blamed on the master trying to keep to his timetable and 'cutting' too close to the Spanish coast. This same reef had been claiming ships since Phoenician times and continued to do so until modern times.

9. The Carlist wars: began when the king Ferdinand VII died. His daughter Isabella II became Queen with his wife, Maria Cristina, acting as Regent. The country broke into two factions; the Cristinos, for the present Queen, and the Carlists who were the supporters of the deceased king's brother, Carlos V. The First Carlist War lasted more than seven years (1832-1839) and there would be 2 more civil wars, the last ending in 1876.

10. Careened or parliament-heeled: where a ship is inclined to one side to allow access to damage on her side.

11. Sack: a name for Spanish Sherry said to have come from the 'sacking' of Cadiz in late 16th century when the British got hold of a large quantity of vin de Jerez. Or more probably from the Spanish 'saca'; to extract or reduce, which referred to how the drink was produced.

12. In the tale of Hercules he has twelve labors to perform with the tenth being to bring the cattle of Geryon back to Eurystheus. This he did by slaying the monstrous Geryon whom he buried where the tower now stands.

13. Meaning it was built by the architect Gaius Sevius Lupus, from Aeminium (present-day Coimbra, Portugal)

14. Driscol's father had been in Paget's division, which had marched down to the port to embark for England. As the French attacked, the unit was recalled and moved to support the uncovered flank of the British army. They engaged and pushed back the French infantry and cavalry under general's Mermet and Lahoussaye, ending the battle at the foot of the French artilleries grand battery, which they were unfortunately not ordered to take.

15. Englishmen had lived for centuries in Portugal shipping the drink known as Port to England, which, of course, had come from the name of the city, Oporto.

16. Driscol was wrong on this point. The Port was transferred to land and decanted into bottles at Oporto and not in England. What Driscol saw was the movement of the large container by river to a nearby glass manufacturer where the final process would take place.

17. In this case, it was a false alarm but then even the casual Portuguese official took no chances when dealing with cholera.

18. The Lines of Torres Vedras were fortifications built by Lord Wellington to stop the advance of a French army under Massena's in 1810. It had been manned in part by the 52nd and Driscol's father had helped to defend it.

19. This is the narration of his cousin Hans Van Christensen. Driscol as a young man wrote up a 22-page history of this man, which makes interesting reading and will be related in a future Volume as an appendix when Driscol crosses the path of Uncle later on.

Chapter III notes:

1. He offered up his daughter as a burnt offering after making a rash vow to aid in his defeat of the Ammonites. (Judges 11:31).

2. Driscol and Perkins missed the bringing of the Spanish Civil War to Gibraltar for on the 21st of October, some days after they had departed. General Gomez a 'Carlist approached the fortress with seven thousand men and the local Spanish inhabitants fled to the walls of the British fortress for protection. The British aided Cristinos forces with cannon fire and the interloper left the area in late November after burning down Algeciras while the Carlist junta and supporters sought internment in Gibraltar for protection from the Cristinos. Protection was granted and they were later exiled to the Philippines.

3. His brother Mark and he played many types of games by post, from chess to those of their own construction, one of which called 'The Italian Wars' was quite involved and will be explored later. His being in Singapore had made turns somewhat long and difficult as the post often took 4-6 months to reach one or the other brother.

4. Battle of the Îles Saint-Marcouf: occurred on small islands off the coast of Normandy, France. These had been seized and fortified to allow the British to raid the coastal trade during the Napoleonic wars. In May 1798, the French moved to retake the island during a calm that allowed their barges to attack without interference from the Royal Navy but they were defeated in their attempt with heavy casualties.

5. No sign of this skull has ever been found and it may have been a Neanderthal skull for a similar such skull was found in the same place in 1848.

6. Phlogiston: a theory first put forward by Johann Becher in 1667 that postulated that there was an element called by this name, which was part of a burnable substance and was released during combustion. It was replaced in the 18th century by the concept of oxidation.

OTHER DAYS.

———

1.

How oft when by the cheerful blaze
   That shone around my fathe. s hall,
I've sat and sighed for other days!
   Oh, could I now those hours recall!
I left my home: my heart was light,
   And pleasure strewed my heedless way;
The world and all I saw were bright,
   Life seemed one joyous holiday.

2.

Years fleeted by: I gained the spot
   Where childhood's happy days had fled;
The sound of welcome reached me not,
   For those I loved were gone or dead.
My little brother's joyous tone
   No more will sing in infant glee;
The hearth is cold—I stand alone—
   Are these the days I pined to see?

7. Sacred Band of Thebes or the City Band: was an elite group of soldiers consisting of 150 gay couples in 4th century BC Thebes.

8. Words to the song Driscol heard in Gibraltar show to the right:

9. Scerri: actually, the name was a Sicilian moniker of a Semitic background but long since converted to Catholicism. Driscol appears to have been unaware of this.

10. A reference to the attack on that Sicilian city by the Athenians during the Sicilian Expedition of 415-413 BC.

11. Mudejares: a Muslim who converted to Christianity and remained in Spain after it had been reconquered by the Christians.

12. The convention of Cintra: allowed for the return of the defeated French army that had invaded Portugal to return to France and for the Russian fleet to go home to Russia. It was deemed a disgrace by the people of England. A dishonorable end to a victory over the French and her allies.

13. Driscol believed that saying Mon would have been a compliment for many in that period believed that this honorific had been dropped by order of Napoleon as a punishment. This myth held that French Navy officers were not to be addressed as "mon" since the lost Battle of Trafalgar. A French army captain is addressed as Mon Capitaine while a French naval captain is called Capitaine with no 'Mon'. This is what Driscol would have believed but it has no basis in fact. Calling a French Naval officer "mon capitaine" will attract the traditional answer "Dans la Marine il y a Mon Dieu et mon cul, pas mon capitaine!" "In my Navy there are 'My God' and 'my arse', but no 'my captain'!"

14. Polacre: a brig or ship found in the Mediterranean. Its masts are commonly formed of one spar from truck to heel so that they have neither tops nor cross-trees.

15. Greyfriars: a name given to the grey cattle of Tuscany often shipped live to other ports.

16. The French and Spanish fired when their ship lifted for they usually fired at the masts of a ship. The British and Dutch fired on the down sweep as they fired at the hull.

17. Raqib and Atid: the two recording angels said to sit on your shoulders, one writing down that which you say which is good and the other writing down your slanders and lies. Strangely, he used the Arabic names and not the Jewish angel Gabriel, who in that faith is the principal recording angel.

18. Isola San Ferdinando, San Ferdinandea or Julia Island: this mysterious volcanic island, being some 6 kilometers in circumference, would rise out of the sea and plunge back under many times in history. Its existence is doubted. Many people would claim to have seen the island but each time it would sink back into the sea. It rose in modern time in 1831 being claimed as their territory by the Kingdom of two Sicilies who called it Ferdinand, by the French 'Julia' and the British 'Graham' - it then sank again. It appeared once more in 1846 and 1863 garnering more names, Hotham, Sciacca, Giulia and Nerita but it soon sank again.

19. The Seven Sleepers of Ephesus: is a tale of Christians from 250 AD who hid near the city of Ephesus to escape the maltreatment of Christians during the reign of the Emperor Decius. They

went to sleep inside a cave and when they awoke it was nearly 180 years later and now during the reign of Theodosius II. They died soon afterwards.

Chapter IV notes:

1. Pratique: is the license given to a ship to enter port on assurance from the Captain to convince the authorities that she is free from contagious disease.

2. The unknown editors added that the lonely officer had married Frances Sarah on February 28, 1839 in Malta, despite objections from her father.

3. This is a mysterious reference by Driscol as nothing is known about this body of men who were thought to have faded away centuries before.

4. In 1837, the Hotel would be converted to the Caffe Gordina and would be there 175 years later and I can personally recommend the food, for what was good for Driscol and Perkins in 1836 I still found good 18 decades later.

5. When in Malta, I went in search of this graffiti and found them. These carvings exist still but are now only 3 ½ feet high, the road way having been raised during the 170 or so years since it was carved. Driscol put into the limestone DAVID A DRI--- --36; part of it having been damaged by shrapnel during the Second World War. To the right of his name and somewhat lower down, a sloppier carving shows the name 1836 DONALD PERKINS with the date having been covered by a faded Maltese political poster.

6. A regiment made up of Englishmen and other Europeans, mercenaries if you like, for the Honourable East India Company.

7. Miasma: This mysterious substance was at this time the excepted reason for disease and not the mosquito or germs. It was held that a gas like substance, which came from rotting vegetation and animal matter - the 'miasma', if breathed in, would cause one's illness. The rise of the medical bacteriology in the 1870-1880 finally overtook this theory.

8. The two pawns at the end of pawn row in chess. As they are limited to their movement by the edge of the board, they are considered less capable or limited.

9. On the back of a printed menu, the two Gentlemen from England had written the following down:

"A treble cabin cannot be appropriated to the accommodation of more than:

Four Ladies
Three Gentlemen
Six children
One Lady and four children
Two Ladies and three children
Three Ladies and two children
One Gentleman and three children

Two Gentlemen and two children
A Gentleman and his wife and two children"

Perkins was quite pleased that the French had worked this out and put it in the cabin for how else would some poor soul know how many people could fit in a cabin, especially some poor sod who was in a one bed room and wanted to know how many could fit into a larger one?

They added some additional possibilities:

Two pairs of Siamese twins and a small dog
A one-legged gentleman with a dwarf wife and three pin-headed children
Three Norwegian brothers with several large tins of reindeer meatballs
Napoleon and two Marshals of France
Ten and six foxhounds and one fox
Five drunken Ascot jockeys
The brains of twenty-two thousand and forty-six East India Company clerks
Once cavalryman and his horse and two grooms standing outside
A cannon - for an artillery man always sees to the care of his gun before himself and the walls - partitions - knocked down as field of fire are always prepared before an artilleryman rests even if this means the ship sinks

10. This book was the banned scandalous pornographic novel by the equally infamous Marquis de Sade.

11. A small fish with silvery scales used in the manufacture of artificial pearls.

12. This is the theory that was probability based on priori judgments of apparently equiprobable events could be illusory.

Chapter V notes:

1. Pharos: the fabled lighthouse of antiquity, which had stood on an island off Alexandria.

2. Navarino: this battle nine year earlier had an Ottoman armada which, in addition to its own warships, included squadrons from the eyalets (provinces) of Egypt, Tunis and Algiers, was destroyed by an Allied force of British, French and Russian vessels in a bay off the coast of the Peloponnese peninsula in Greece. It was the last major naval battle in history fought entirely with sailing ships, although most ships fought at anchor. The Allies' victory achieved through superior firepower and gunnery skills. Driscol's observation is puzzling, as others had noted several squadrons of the Egyptian navy in port during the year to include an additional 2 x 138, 4 100, 1 80 and 1 74 gun ships. Perhaps they were out at sea but that was something the Egyptian fleet rarely did.

3. Franks: a generic term for westerners in the east derived from the term used to describe the crusaders who were often Franks, or those from France.

4. This joke comes from swot meaning to 'study hard' or 'a person who studies hard', and the swatting of the Egyptian flies is more interesting than that endeavor. Another possibility is that he did mean swat which had a secondary meaning to squat, as in going to the bathroom.

5. Commander John Shortland of HMS Pandour had in the year 1803 flown a kite over the pillar. This enabled him to get ropes over it and a rope ladder. He then climbed up. When they got to the top he displayed the British flag, drank a toast to the King, gave three cheers and ate a beefsteak. As to the matter of it being called Pompey's, this mistake of identification came about because in the middle-ages the Crusaders mistakenly believed the remains of the great Roman general Pompey were buried in or under the column.

6. The one standing would be taken to London and the fallen one would end up in New York. Both would be called Cleopatra's needle.

7. The political question was over who should control the duchies of Schleswig and Holstein, a land of a mixed German and Danish population. The first war over this question was fought 12 years later followed by another war in 1864.

8. In this belief Driscol was mistaken for many other Egyptian cities rose on the east bank of the Nile

9. The Riograndense Republic, as it was also known, lasted nine years before the rebellion called the Farroupilha Revolution - as the Brazilians saw it - and was defeated. It was a custom of the times to hire a British officer for the armies of many smaller nations.

10. The era of guidebooks like those of our modern era would come about in just a few years with the arrival of steamships and trains transport then one could read all this information concentrated into one small source.

11. This Nilometer was actually built by the Arabs based on an ancient Egyptian model, for in the tenth century the Nile had shifted its bed and moved away from Cairo and the old Pharaonic Nilometer had to be replaced.

12. Johann Ludwig Burckhardt was a Swiss traveller and orientalist who wrote about the slave trade in the Middle East: Slavery, in the east, has little dreadful in it but the name, yet it was not harmless. Male slaves are everywhere treated much like children of the family and always better than the freed servants are. Female slaves were considered both children and chattels. Many Europeans looked upon their slaves as little better than domestic animals, while the oriental slave was an object of luxury, yet it was still slavery and crude slave masters were not rare and the concubinage of the females was not voluntary.

13. These Egyptian bulls were sacred. Well after Driscol's time, archaeologist found tens of thousands of mummified bulls, sacrificed to their gods. It is uncertain but unlikely that in Muslim Cairo of that era whether a man would have been put to death for accidentally killing a bull; Driscol may have misread the sign or not understood a local reference.

14. The first attempts to combat the slave trade were made by Dr. John Bowring' who traveled and studied the trade, and in 1837, he and the British counsel brought the matter to the attention of the ruler. Muhammed Ali was moved to make limited arrangement to halt the raids that supplied the slave markets of Egypt. These were only partially successful in suppression of the

trade. These acts would add to the unrest that would aid the rise of the Mahdi decades later in the Sudan.

15. This was the Royal Navy's gunnery training ship. The HMS Boyne had replaced the original ship of that name in 1835. She was berthed at Whale Island in Hampshire near Portsmouth. A great deal of scientific work with gunnery, cannon and other advancements were done there during Driscol's time.

16. In 1845, the Admiralty would resolve this question by a contest between two ships with similar engines, one equipped with a screw propeller and the other paddle wheels. The propeller-equipped HMS Rattler was able to tow the paddle wheeled HMS Alecto backwards with ease, thus ending the debate once and for all.

Appendix I-I: Genealogy of the Driscol siblings and the link between David Driscol and the present day Anne O'Driscoll.

Appendix I-I: Driscol's family lineage from his parents to Anne Lorraine O'Driscoll. From an original by Driscol, abridged to remove wives names

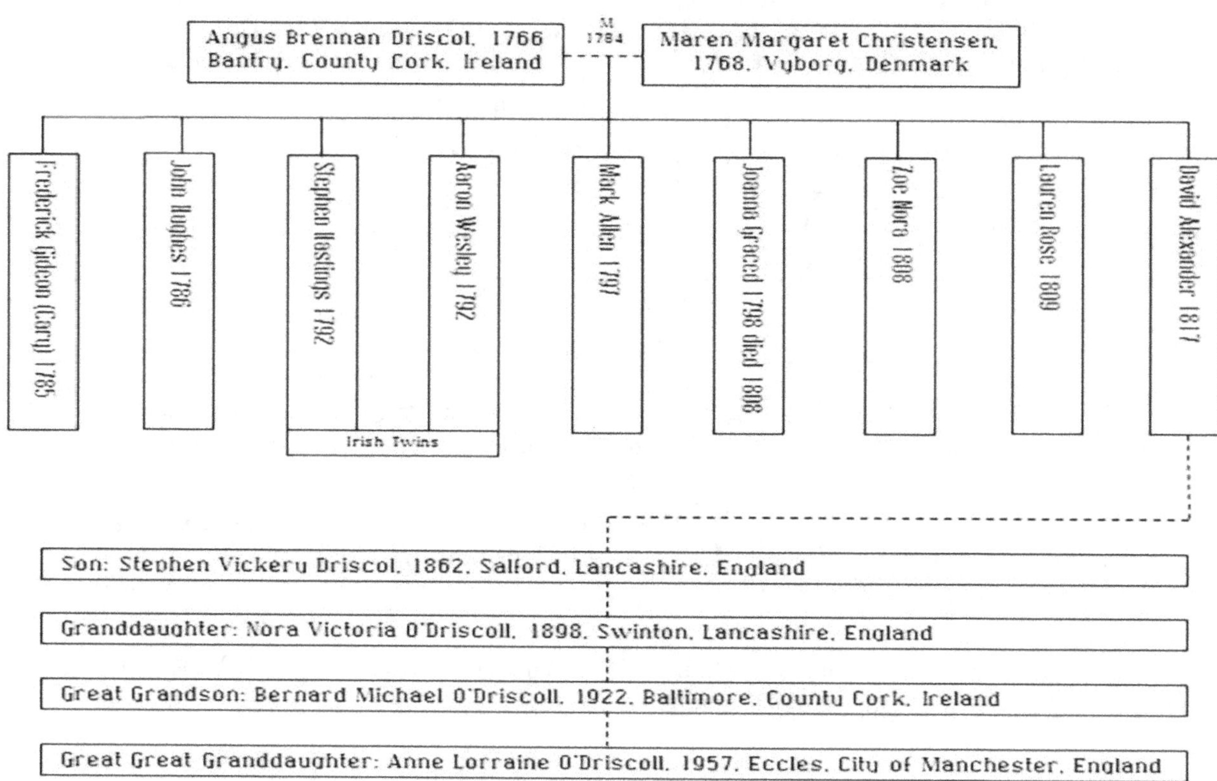

11. LATITUDE BY REDUCTION TO THE MERIDIAN.

1. *For the Apparent Time at Ship.*—Write down the month and day with the hours, minutes, and seconds by watch or chronometer; apply the given error, *adding* it if *slow, subtracting* it if *fast.* Also—
Turn the Diff. Long. into time and apply it, *adding* if *East, subtracting* if *West.* The result is the Apparent Time at Ship.

2. *For the Greenwich Date.*—Under the Ship Date, App. Time, write the Long. in time ; add if West ; subtract if East. The result is Green. Date, Apparent Time.

3. *For the Declination.*—Take the Declination from Naut. Alm. p. I. of given month, and correct it for the Green. Date.

4. *For the True Altitude,* correct the observed Altitude for Dip, Refraction, Semidiameter, and Parallax.

5. *For the Time from Noon at Ship.*—If question gives P.M. you have the time from noon in the Apparent Time at Ship ; if question gives A.M., then App. Time at Ship will be about 23h. &c., which take from 24 hours for the time from noon.

6. *For the Reduction.*—Write down in succession the Time from Noon, the Latitude by Acc., the corrected Declination, and the Zenith Distance by Acc. (*Note :* the Zen. Dist. is got by taking the *sum* of Lat. and Dec. when of *different names* ; by taking their *difference* when of *same name.*)
Add together Constant* Log. 0.30103, Log. of Hour-angle † for Time from Noon, Log. Cosine of Latitude, Log. Cosine of Declination, Log. Cosecant of Zenith Distance. The sum (rejecting *tens* in *index*) will be the Log. Sine of the Reduction, which take out in ..° ..′ ..″ or ..′ ..″ as the case may be.

			Constant Log.	0.30103
	m. s.			
Time from Noon	.. ..		Log Hor Ang	......
Lat	..° ..′		cos	......
Dec	.. ..		cos	......
Zen Dist	.. ..		cosec	......
Reduction	.. ..		sine	......

7. Add the Reduction to the true Altitude, for the true Meridian Altitude ; and subtract the latter from 90° for the Meridian Zenith Distance, naming it N. if sun bears S., but S. if sun bears N.

8. *For the Latitude.*—Under the Zenith Distance write the corrected Declination, and then, *Rule* " Latitude by Meridian Altitude of Sun " p. 5 sec. 5 applies to this Problem.

Incident of piracy off Algers

It has been reported that acts of piracy in the Mediterranean have not ceased and have instead increased since the French invasion of Algeria. In an incident in October, just off the port of Algers such an attack occurred. Two British officers and two civilian passengers along with a Maltese crew in a small native packet involving in the local trade and conveying the passengers to Malta from Gibraltar. The ship was assailed and fired upon by a piratic craft mounting four 4 pounders and a crew of thirty scoundrels. In a spirited action the crew and passengers used small arms to stop the enemy boarding attempt and the French naval guards, tardily showed up to drive the intruder away. One passenger and four crew were killed but the assault driven back at great loss. Its leaders two White men, were both killed and ten other native pirates slain. The report also spoke favourably about the use of repeating pistols by the officers and passengers and the reason for their success. This incident is another reason why the French attack on Algeria must be decried for it has not dampened piracy as claimed by their government but encourages it.

Appendix I-IV: Driscol's Pyramid Doodling

Driscol drew scores of these pyramids on his journals at various places, in ink and pencil, sometimes coloring them in and at other times leaving them as line drawings only. Usually they showed two different expressions on the pyramid's faces. Their variation went from tall to squat, from thin to fat, to humorous to sad. Two of his earliest are shown below taken directly from his pages.

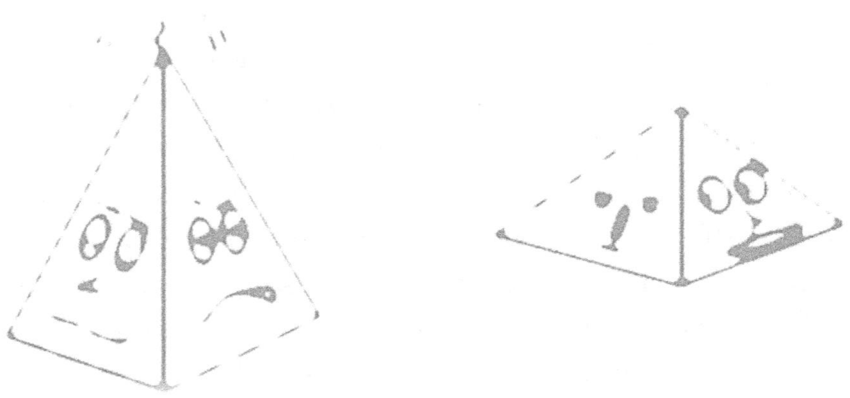

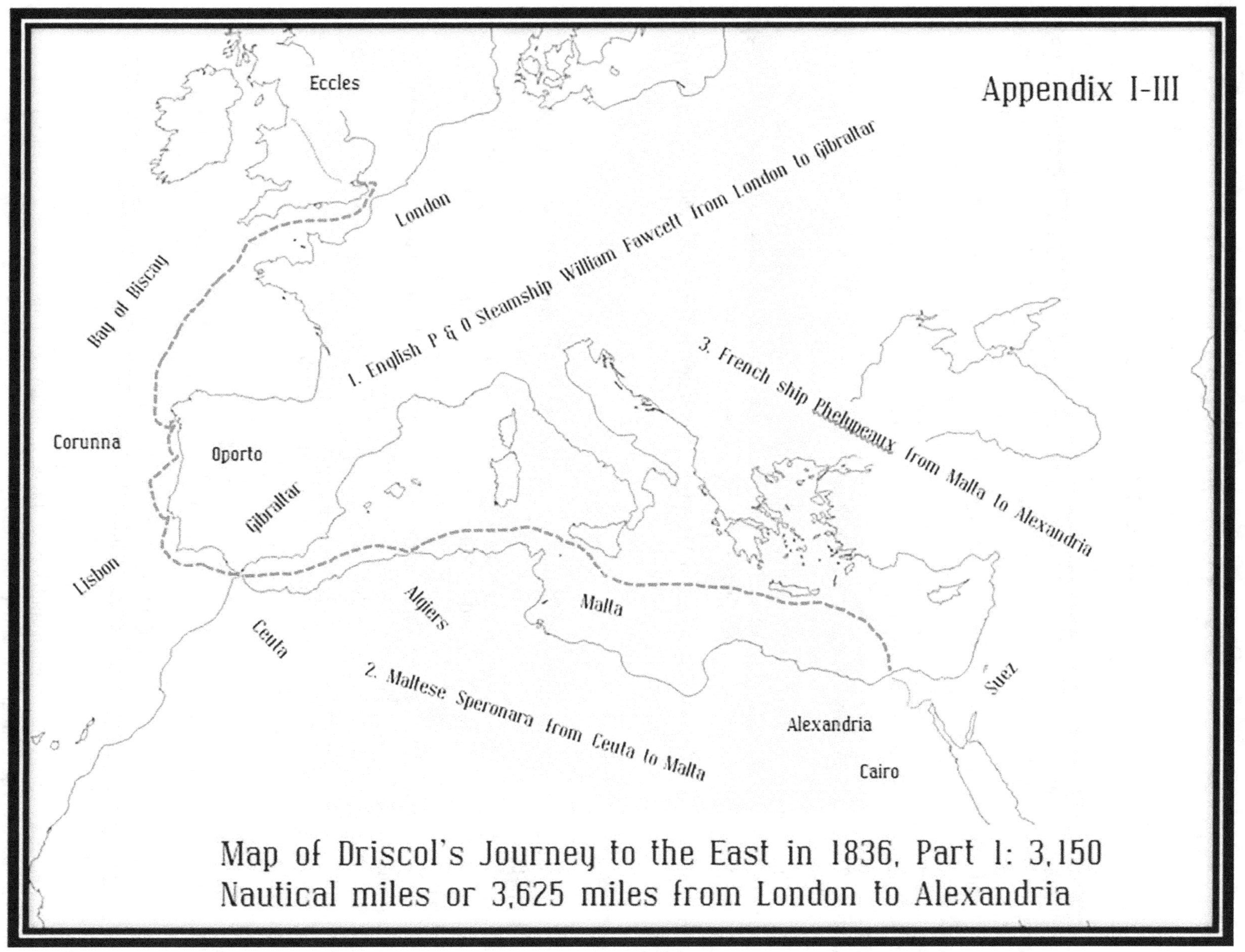

Appendix I-III
Eccles
London
Bay of Biscay
Corunna
Oporto
Gibraltar
Lisbon
Ceuta
Algiers
Malta
Alexandria
Cairo
Suez
1. English P & O Steamship William Fawcett from London to Gibraltar
2. Maltese Speronara from Ceuta to Malta
3. French ship Phelypeaux from Malta to Alexandria
Map of Driscol's Journey to the East in 1836, Part 1: 3,150 Nautical miles or 3,625 miles from London to Alexandria

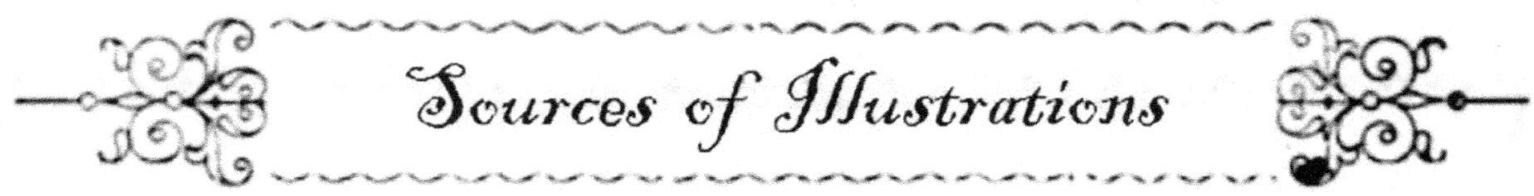

Preface of Driscol's journal

1-A: Bombay in the days of George IV: memoirs of Sir Edward West, chief justice of the King's court during its conflict with the East India Company, with hitherto unpublished documents, F. Dawtrey Drewitt, Longmans, Green, and Co, Calcutta, 1907, page 54.

1-B: Bombay in the days of George IV: memoirs of Sir Edward West, chief justice of the King's court during its conflict with the East India Company, with hitherto unpublished documents, F. Dawtrey Drewitt, Longmans, Green, and Co, Calcutta, 1907, page 45.

1-C: Bombay in the days of George IV: memoirs of Sir Edward West, chief justice of the King's court during its conflict with the East India Company, with hitherto unpublished documents, F. Dawtrey Drewitt, Longmans, Green, and Co, Calcutta, 1907, page 44.

The translation of the above sentence in Arabic; 'Not in vain the nation-strivings, nor by chance the currents flow, error-marred, yet truth directed, to their certain goal they go', written by Tey'yeeyat el Kobra', translated by Ebx-el-Farid.

Front piece: Richard Hussey Vivian, Claud Vivian, Isbister and Company, Limited, London 1897, Front piece

Chapter I

I-I-1: Memorial of old Haileybury College, Frederick Danvers, Archibald Constable and Company, London, 1894, page cl
I-I-2: Persia, Society for Promoting Christian Knowledge, London, R. Clay, 1846, page 144
I-I-3: An account of the manners and customs of the Modern Egyptians, by Edward Lane, John Murray, London, 1871, page 264
I-I-4: 1848 Ordnance Survey Map showing the Driscol house, Eccles & District History Society http://edhs.btck.co.uk/HistoryofEccles/Maps
I-I-5: The village homes of England, Charles Holme, The Studio, Ltd, London, 1912, page 42, Aldhampton, Somersetshire
I-I-6: Gray's new book of roads. George Carrington Gray, London, Sherwood, Jones and Co, 1824, page 172 map of Lancashire
I-I-7: Black's picturesque tourist and road-book of England and Wales - Black Adam and Charles, ltd, Edinburgh, Adam and Charles Black, 1853, page 22
I-I-8: Fox Hunting, a treatise by the Right Honourable, the Earl of Kilreynard, C.W. Bell, London Horace Cos, 1899, page xxvii
I-I-9: London, edited by Charles Knight, London, Charles Knight & Co, 1841, page xxx
I-I-10: London, edited by Charles Knight, London, Charles Knight & Co, 1841, frontpiece
I-I-11: The Oriental club and Hanover square, Alexander Baillie, Longmans, Green & Co. 1902, page 58
I-I-12: Sporting fire-arms for bush and jungle, forsyth Burgess, London, W. H Allen & Co. 1884, page 100 (modified by rearrangement and exclusion)
I-I-13: London, a complete guide to the places of amusement, Henry Herber & Co, 1876, no author, page 34 (modified by cropping out binoculars)

I-I-14: London, edited by Charles Knight, London, Charles Knight & Co, 1841, page 489
I-I-15: London, edited by Charles Knight, London, Charles Knight & Co, 1841, page 613
I-I-16: London, edited by Charles Knight, London, Charles Knight & Co, 1841, page 412
I-I-17: Firearms in American History: our rifles, Charles Winthrop Sawyer, The Cornhill Company, Boston, 1920, page 21 Plate 2
I-I-18: Editor's collection
I-I-19: Up and down the London streets, Mark Lemon page 96, London, Chapman and Hall, 1867
I-I-20: National History and Views of London and Its Environs, Allan, Bell & Co London, 1834, page 551
I-I-21: Drawing of the East India Docks from 1842, Tower Hamlets History on line, http://www.mernick.org.uk/thhol/ with permission
I-I-22: London, edited by Charles Knight, London, Charles Knight & Co, 1841, page 577
I-I-23: London, edited by Charles Knight, London, Charles Knight & Co, 1841, page 384
I-I-24: East India Docks, second image, Tower Hamlets History on line http://www.mernick.org.uk/thhol/ with permission
I-I-25: William Fawcett, The Times, 1839, March 7, page 2, Column 4

Chapter II

I-II-1: Modern Ships of War - Sir Edward James Reed, Edward Simpson, New York , Harper & Brothers, 1888, page 13 modifiedI-22: The Earth and its inhabitants, Europe, Elisee Reclus, New York, 1882 Volume 1, Europe, page 463
I-II-2: Stories from over the sea, Edinburgh, William P. Nimmo editor, 1873, page 65
I-II-3: Notices sur les pistolets tournants et roulants, dits revolvers - L. P. Anquetil, Bruxelles, Libraire de Deprez-parent, 1854, page 8
I-II-4: The Resting place of General Moore, J.P. Vincenti translated by Anthony Fuertes, Corunna Domingo Fuga, 1857, page 39
I-II-5: Oporto, The Earth and its inhabitants, Europe, Elisee Reclus, New York, 1882 Volume 1, Europe, page 479
I-II-6: Oporto, Old and New, Being a Historical Record of the Port Wine Trade, Charles Sellers, Herbert E. Harper, London, Crutched Friars, 1899, page 7
I-II-7: Oporto, Old and New, Being a Historical Record of the Port Wine Trade, Charles Sellers, Herbert E. Harper, London, Crutched Friars, 1899, page 124
I-II-8: Oporto, Old and New, Being a Historical Record of the Port Wine Trade, Charles Sellers, Herbert E. Harper, London, Crutched Friars, 1899, page 112
I-II-9: The Kedge-anchor; Or, Young Sailors' Assistant, William Brady, London, Sampson, Low Sons & Co, 1863, front piece
I-II-10: The Kedge-anchor; Or, Young Sailors' Assistant, William Brady, London, Sampson, Low Sons & Co, 1863, page xxx
I-II-11: The Earth and its Inhabitants, Europe, Elisee Reclus, New York, 1882 Volume 1, Europe, page 412

Chapter III

The adventures of Herbert Massey in Eastern Africa, Verney Lovett Cameron, George Routledge and Sons, London 1888, page 97
I-III-1: The Earth and its inhabitants, Europe, Elisee Reclus, New York, 1882 Volume 1, Europe, page 414
I-III-2: Gibraltar - Henry Martyn Field, New York, Charles Scribner's sons, 1888, page 35 the saluting battery

I-III-3: The Rock, Illustrated with Various Legends and Original Songs, and Music, Descriptive of Gibraltar - Hort (Lieutenant-Colonel), London, Saunders and Otley, 1839, page 190
I-III-4: The Rock, Illustrated with Various Legends and Original Songs, and Music, Descriptive of Gibraltar - Hort (Lieutenant-Colonel), London, Saunders and Otley, 1839, page 52
I-III-5: Wild Spain, records of sport with rifle, rod, and gun, natural history and exploration, Abel Chapman and Walter J. Buck London, Gurney and Jackson, 1893, page 14
I-III-6: The Gibraltar Gallery, Jacob Abbott, New York, Harper & Brothers, 1854, page 15
I-III-7: The Rock, Illustrated with Various Legends and Original Songs, and Music, Descriptive of Gibraltar - Hort (Lieutenant-Colonel), London, Saunders and Otley, 1839, page 65
I-III-8: Gibraltar - Henry Martyn Field, New York, Charles Scribner's sons, 1888, page 151
I-III-9: The Rock, Illustrated with Various Legends and Original Songs, and Music, Descriptive of Gibraltar - Hort (Lieutenant-Colonel), London, Saunders and Otley, 1839, page 170
I-III-10: From Driscol's journal
I-III-11: Recuerdos de Africa, historia de la plaza de Ceuta, D. Jose De Prado, Madrid, Impresa y Estereotripa, 1859, page xxii
I-III-12: Editor's collection
I-III-13: The Earth and its inhabitants, Africa, Elisee Reclus, New York, 1882 Volume 11, Europe, page 254
I-III-14: Select specimen of natural histroy, james bruce, page 296
I-III-15: A Compendium of Domestic Medicine and Companion to the Medicine Chest, John Savory, London, H.K. Lewis, 1886 page 352
I-III-16: Editor's collection
I-III-17: Editor's collection

Chapter IV

The three admirals and the adventures of their young followers, William Kingston, London, Grifith and Farran, 1878, page 354
I-IV-1: A History of Malta During the Period of the French and British Occupations, 1798-1815 - William Hardman (of Valetta.), London, Longmans, Green, and Co., 1909, page 1
I-IV-2: Historia de Malta y el Gozo, Frederic Lacroix, Barcelona, Imprenta de A. Frexas, 1850, page 34
I-IV-3: The Earth and its inhabitants, Europe, Elisee Reclus, New York, 1882 Volume 1, Europe, page 337
I-IV-4: John L. Stoddard's Lectures, Canada, Malta, Gibraltar, John Stoddard, Boston, Ralph Brothers, page 274
I-IV-5: Historia de Malta y el Gozo, Frederic Lacroix, Barcelona, Imprenta de A. Frexas, 1850, page 42
I-IV-6: Historia de Malta y el Gozo, Frederic Lacroix, Barcelona, Imprenta de A. Frexas, 1850, page 46 fountain in Malta
I-IV-7: The Historical Records of the Maltese Corps of the British Army, Major A. G. Chesney, London William Clowes and Sons, Limited 1897, page 184
I-IV-8: The Kedge-anchor; Or, Young Sailors' Assistant, Rigging, Knotting, William Brady, London, Sampson, Low Sons & Co, 1863, page 138
I-IV-9: Persia, Society for Promoting Christian Knowledge, London, R. Clay, 1846, page 96
I-IV-10: Ocean Steamships, A Popular Account of Their Construction, Development, Management and Appliance, Ensor Chadwick, New York, Charles Scribner's Sons, 1891, page 126
I-IV-11: The Earth and Its Inhabitants, North-east Africa, Elisée Reclus, New York, D. Appleton and Company, 1892, page 424

Chapter V

I-V-1: Voyages up the Mediterranean and in the Indian seas; with memoirs, compiled from the Logs and letters of a midshipman, James Abraham Heraud, London, James Fraser, 1837, page 75
I-V-2: Up and down the Nile, or, Young adventurers in Africa - Oliver Optic, boston, Lee and Shepard Publishers, 1894, front piece
I-V-3: Four Months in a Dahabëeh, Or, Narrative of a Winter's Cruise on the Nile - M. L. M. Carey, London, L. Booth, 1863, page x
I-V-4: Four Months in a Dahabëeh, Or, Narrative of a Winter's Cruise on the Nile - M. L. M. Carey, London, L. Booth, 1863, page 92
I-V-5: The Earth and Its Inhabitants, North-east Africa, Elisée Reclus, New York, D. Appleton and Company, 1892, page 427
I-V-6: Four Months in a Dahabëeh, Or, Narrative of a Winter's Cruise on the Nile - M. L. M. Carey, London, L. Booth, 1863, page 73
I-V-7: The Earth and Its Inhabitants, North-east Africa, Elisée Reclus, New York, D. Appleton and Company, 1892, page 493
I-V-8: An account of the manners and customs of the modern Egyptians, Edward Lane, London, M. A. Nattali, 1846 page 60
I-V-9: The Earth and Its Inhabitants, North-east Africa, Elisée Reclus, New York, D. Appleton and Company, 1892, page 486
I-V-10: An account of the manners and customs of the modern Egyptians, Edward Lane, London, M. A. Nattali, 1846, page 40
I-V-11: The Earth and Its Inhabitants, North-east Africa, Elisée Reclus, New York, D. Appleton and Company, 1892, page 489
I-V-12: The Earth and Its Inhabitants, North-east Africa, Elisée Reclus, New York, D. Appleton and Company, 1892, page 313
I-V-13: An account of the manners and customs of the modern Egyptians, Edward Lane, London, M. A. Nattali, 1846, page 14
I-V-14: An account of the manners and customs of the modern Egyptians, Edward Lane, London, M. A. Nattali, 1846, page 24
I-V-15: Illustrations from the art gallery, Charles Kurtz, George Barrie, Phiadelphia, 1893, page 24 book seller
I-V-16: Mentone, Cairo and Corfu - Constance Fenimore Woolson, New York, Harper & Brothers Publishers, 1896, page 192
I-V-17: The Earth and Its Inhabitants, North-east Africa, Elisée Reclus, New York, D. Appleton and Company, 1892, page 90
I-V-18: Steam Communication with India by the Red Sea, Dionysius Lardner, Calcutta, Baptist Mission press, 1837 page xlvi
I-V-19: Editor's collection
I-V-20: Oporto, Old and New, Being a Historical Record of the Port Wine Trade, Charles Sellers, Herbert E. Harper, London, Crutched Friars, 1899, page 211

End piece

Biographical sketches of the Queens of Great Britain, Mary Howitt, Henry G Bohn, London, 1856, page 119
Biographical sketches of the Queens of Great Britain, Mary Howitt, Henry G Bohn, London, 1856, page 591
Biographical sketches of the Queens of Great Britain, Mary Howitt, Henry G Bohn, London, 1856, page 421

By Chapter

Preface & Contents

Dalziels' illustrated Arabian nights' entertainments, H. W. Dulcken, London, Ward, Lock and Tyler, 1865, page 10
Handbook of Information for the Colonies and India, Watson, Ferguson & Co., Brisbane, Warwick & Sarsford, Printers, 1890, page xii
Stories from over the sea, William P. Nimmo, Edinburgh, 1873, page 93
Technique, published annually by the junior class, MIT technique board of ninety-eight, Boston, 1889, page 52
Scenes and Sites in Bible Lands - A. M. S. T. Nelson and Sons, London, 1869, page x
Illustrated India Its Princes and People, Upper, Central, and Farther India, Julia A. Stone, Hartford, Connecticut, American Publishing Company, 1877, page xx

Chapter I

Recuerdos de Africa, historia de la plaza de Ceuta, D. Jose De Prado, Madrid, Impresa y Estereotripa, 1859, page 10
General regulations and standing orders for the garrison of Gibraltar, John Pitt, Gibraltar, Printed at the Garrison library, 1825, page vi
Glimpses of old English homes, Elizabeth Balch, Macmillan and Co, London, 1890, page cxii
The Nabob's Cookery Book, a manual of East and West Indian Recipes, by P.O.P. Frederick Warne and Co, London, no date, page 54
The boy makes the man, T. Nelson and Sons, London, 1867, William Daveport Adamas, page lxi
Handbook of information, Nihon Yusen Kaisha, The Tokyo Tsukji Type foundry, Tokyo, 1904, page 296
Oporto, Old and New, Being a Historical Record of the Port Wine Trade, Charles Sellers, Herbert E. Harper, London, Crutched Friars, 1899, page 16
An illustrated dictionary of words used in art and archaeology, John William Mollett, Boston, Houghton, Mifflin and company 1883, page xiii
Recuerdos de Africa, historia de la plaza de Ceuta, D. Jose De Prado, Madrid, Impresa y Estereotripa, 1859, page xxi
The adventures of Herbert Massey in Eastern Africa, Verney Lovett Cameron, George Routledge and Sons, London, 1888, page 50
The boy makes the man, T. Nelson and Sons, London, 1867, William Daveport Adamas, page xv
The baked head and other tales, Putnam's library of choice stories, G. P. Putnam & Co., New York, 1856, page 50
The Englishwoman in Egypt: Letters from Cairo, Sophia Lane Poole, London, Charles Knight and Co, 1844, page 189

Gardening in India, Bombay, 1889 G Marshall Woodrow,Page xx
El Yèmen, tre anni nell'Arabia felice, Renzo Manzoni, Roma, Tipografi Eredi Botta, 1884, page 232
Tales of the sea - William Henry G. Kingston, London, Gall & Inlglis, no date. page 1

Chapter II

Oporto, Old and New, Being a Historical Record of the Port Wine Trade, Charles Sellers, Herbert E. Harper, London, Crutched Friars, 1899, page 252
The Earth and Its Inhabitants, India, Elisee Reclus, D. Appleton and Company, New York, 1881, page 113
Oporto, Old and New, Being a Historical Record of the Port Wine Trade, Charles Sellers, Herbert E. Harper, London, Crutched Friars, 1899, page 4 (Coat of arms of Oporto)
The Englishwoman in Egypt_Letters from Cairo, Sophia Lane Poole, London, Charles Knight and Co, 1844, page 175
Notices sur les pistolets tournants et roulants, dits revolvers - L. P. Anquetil, Bruxelles, Libraire de Deprez-parent, 1854, page vii
The History of Gibraltar, From the Earliest Period of Its Occupation by the Saracens, James Bell, London, William PIckering, 1845, page xvi
Showers cases in parliament resolved and adjudged, Whittinghan and Wilkins, London, 1876 Bartholomew shower, page xxix
The Earth and Its Inhabitants, India, Elisee Reclus, D. Appleton and Company, New York, 1881, India, page 41
Scenes and Sites in Bible Lands - A. M. S. T. Nelson and Sons, london, 1869, page 39

Chapter III

Die Sprache der Kossaer, Linguistisch, friedrich delitzsch, page 75
Glimpses of old english homes, Elizabeth Balch, Macmillan and Co, London, 1890, page cxliii
The boy makes the man, T. Nelson and Sons, London, 1867, William Daveport Adamas, page 95
The Moslem Noble, His Land and His People,Marianne Young, London Saunders and Otley, 1857, page xxviii
Recuerdos de Africa, historia de la plaza de Ceuta, D. Jose De Prado, Madrid, Impresa y Estereotripa, 1859, page 30
The Earth and Its Inhabitants, India, Elisee Reclus, D. Appleton and Company, New York, 1881, India page 40
Voyages of the slavers St. John and arms of Amsterdam, Edmund O'Callaghan, page 226, J. Munsell Albany NY, 1867
Glimpses of old English homes, Elizabeth Balch, Macmillan and Co, London, 1890, page 32
Celebrated women travellers, W. H. Davenport Adams, E.P. Dutton & Co., New York, 1903, page 51

Chapter IV

The regulations of the old hospital of the Knights W. K. Bedford, London, William Blackwood and Sons, 1882, page 35
Personal Reminiscences - Archibald Constable, Robert Pearse Gillies, New York, Charles Scribner's Sons, 1887 page xv

General regulations and standing orders for the garrison of Gibraltar, John Pitt, Gibraltar, Printed at the Garrison library, 1825, page 4

Portugal em Africa (Revista Scientifica, 1895, Volume 2, Typographia Da Casa Catholica, Lisboa, 1895, page v

The arts and artistic manufactures of Denmark, Charles Boutell, J. Mitchell, London 1874, page 62

Little journeys to the homes of English Authors, elbert hubbad, G.P. Putnam's & Sons, London 1903 page 77

Boat life in Egypt and Nubia - William Cowper Prime, New York, Harper & Brothers, 1857, page 152

Boat life in Egypt and Nubia - William Cowper Prime, New York, Harper & Brothers, 1857, page 346

Boat life in Egypt and Nubia - William Cowper Prime, New York, Harper & Brothers, 1857, page 114

Memoires d'artillerie, ouil est traite des mortiers, pierre de Saint-Remy, page 293

Memoires d'artillerie, ouil est traite des mortiers, pierre de Saint-Remy, page 287

Boat life in Egypt and Nubia - William Cowper Prime, New York, Harper & Brothers, 1857, page 258

Boat life in Egypt and Nubia - William Cowper Prime, New York, Harper & Brothers, 1857, page 105

Boat life in Egypt and Nubia - William Cowper Prime, New York, Harper & Brothers, 1857, page 372

Boat life in Egypt and Nubia - William Cowper Prime, New York, Harper & Brothers, 1857, page 280

Boat life in Egypt and Nubia - William Cowper Prime, New York, Harper & Brothers, 1857, page 470

Mentone, Cairo and Corfu - Constance Fenimore Woolson, New York, Harper & Brothers Publishers, 1896, page 210 skyline of Cairo

Scenes and Sites in Bible Lands - A. M. S. T. Nelson and Sons, london, 1869, page 19

The arts and artistic manufactures of Denmark, Charles Boutell, J. Mitchell, London 1874, page 62

The History of Gibraltar, From the Earliest Period of Its Occupation by the Saracens, James Bell, London, William Pickering, 1845, page viii

The adventures of Herbert Massey in Eastern Africa, Verney Lovett Cameron, George Routledge and Sons, London 1888, page 219

The Kedge-anchor; Or, Young Sailors' Assistant, Rigging, Knotting, William Brady, London, Sampson, Low Sons & Co, 1863, 262

Gardening in India, Bombay, 1889 G Marshall Woodrow, page xviii

End

Persia, Samuel Benjamin, G.P. Putnam's Sons, 1888 page 306, (modified with Chapter Notes)

Handbook of Information for the Colonies and India, Watson, Ferguson & Co., Brisbane, Warwick & Sarsford, Printers, Brisbane 1890, page 67 (Modified with Sources of Illustration)

Handbook of Information for the Colonies and India, Watson, Ferguson & Co., Brisbane, Warwick & Sarsford, Printers, Brisbane 1890, page 67 (Modified with Sources of Ornamentation)

The history of the Hawaiian mission press, Howard M. Ballou and George Carter, presented August 27, 1908, Honolulu, page 12

Cover and Back Cover

Typographia, John Johnson, London, 1824, front cover

Finis

November 2015, Ashland, Oregon

Hello reader

Thank you for reading this book. I would enjoy hearing from you about your experience in Driscol's world. I grew up in Hawaii, I now write books, and design games. My various career experiences have been working in Archaeology, Libraries, Artillery, Logistics, and Human Resources. I taught as a college instructor in IT, business, leadership, and military subjects. I graduated from the University of Hawaii (BA in Anthropology and MLS in Library Science), Long Island University (MBA), and the Command and General Staff College. I have worked in Europe and the Middle East for over twenty years. I have travelled extensively, some of my favorite places are Nepal, Rapa Nui, Switzerland, France, Egypt, India, Oman, and Eccles, in the United Kingdom. There are too many other exotic and exciting places I have visited to include. Oklahoma and Kansas however do not make the list. My hobbies are reading 19th century books, fishing, traveling, 1950's cult movies, exploring all history and archaeology (ancient to modern). I am fortunate to be married to my beloved Anne and I am the full time personal servant to a cantankerous Arab cat with definite ideas of what is proper and not proper to eat. Please contact me at: anofficerofthecrown@gmail.com

A picture of myself in the middle with my editors, bullyboys and assorted soft thinking lackeys, underlings and slob-jobbers. I had to use this image as the cat just ignored me (as is her wont).

Wayne

Mark Rutledge, immortal
Greg Hines, R.I.P.
Wayne Rutledge, questionable
David Notle, R.I.P.
Edward Joesting, one foot in the grave

The next book in the series is:

An Officer of the Crown

The Middlecombe Expedition to the Aral Sea in Turcomania and the
Khanates of Independent Tartary, 1837-1838
========
A Narration of the Actions Leading to the Formation of the
Middlecombe Expedition, 1836-1837

========
Volume II